DAUGHTER OF THE STOLEN PRINCE

To Christina—

Book Eleven in the Pantracia Chronicles

DAUGHTER OF THE STOLEN PRINCE

Be true to yourself.

Amanda Muratoff & Kayla Hansen

www.Pantracia.com

Cover design by Andrei Bat.

ISBN: 978-1-990781-00-1

Second Edition: February 2024

For Melissa & Audrey.

♥

The Pantracia Chronicles:

Visit www.Pantracia.com for our pronunciation
guide and to discover more.

Prologue

Spring, 2632 R.T. (recorded time)

DEYLAN STOMPED THROUGH THE WINDOWLESS hallway, fists clenched at his sides. Throwing the metal door to the dining hall open, he let it clang off the wall as he scowled.

Several faction members glanced up from their morning meals, but Deylan ignored their curiosity. He fixated through the dimness on a figure dining alone at the near end of one of the long tables.

Jelkin looked up, a half-empty coffee mug in his grip. "I know what you're gonna say, but it ain't my fault."

Rolling his eyes, Deylan approached. "How is this not your fault? You were supposed to watch her."

The low metal ceiling boasted several panels glowing from

behind to illuminate the hall. Matching panels covered the walls, emitting light in a similar fashion, though great shadows remained.

The clatter of silverware and dishes resumed.

Jelkin rubbed his jaw. "And I did. I watched her real good right up until she rode out of town. You've forgotten how stubborn that one is."

Deylan gritted his teeth. "You're a farrier. You could have said her horse needed shoeing or something."

"I did. She took a different horse and paid me ahead of time to look after Riot's hooves." Jelkin rolled his shoulders. "Coffee?" He held up a dented carafe.

"No, thanks. I can't stay. I just got here, and I need to figure out where she went."

Jelkin poured more coffee into his own mug. "Well, I can tell ya that much. She went lookin' for her father. He didn't reply to her letter about Lorin. Poor girl is worried about him. Can't say I blame her. She buried one father, likely terrified of losing the second." He glanced up, but averted his gaze under Deylan's glare. "She's headed to Treama. Ziona. That's where Talon was headed when he left last autumn." He set the carafe down and stood with his steaming mug. Shuffling towards Deylan, Jelkin ran a hand over his balding head. "She's an adult, my friend. But at least she ain't alone."

Deylan narrowed his eyes. "What do you mean she's not alone? Who's with her?"

"That boy she likes. Davros."

"I thought he was working the ships?"

"Was. Then he wasn't." Jelkin shrugged. "Nice boy. You should go easier on him."

"When it comes to Ahria, I can't afford to go easy on *anyone*. And you damn well know why." Deylan strode towards the door. "Let me know where they reassign you. I've got to clean up this mess now."

"Ain't you supposed to be taking leave? Head home for a change? What about the wife?" The farrier knew far more than other members of the faction about Deylan's personal life. One of the advantages he had after he was assigned to Deylan's home village to watch Ahria. Jelkin had attended Deylan's daughter's wedding three years ago. But his mention of Roslyn made Deylan cringe.

"Not really my wife anymore," Deylan muttered.

"Sorry to hear. Is, uh... Is that something you want to... you know, talk about?"

Deylan snorted. "Not much to talk about. I wasn't there. Hard to have a marriage while working here. Doing what we do. She's happier, now." He nodded and gripped the door handle. "See you later."

Leaving the dining hall, Deylan strode down the hallway towards the viewing rooms.

Despite the lack of natural sunlight, the hallways of the headquarters were perfectly lit without any obvious lanterns.

Copper panels hung on the dark metal walls like blank canvases, just like in the dining hall, imbued with the Art to illuminate from behind and provide light that wouldn't strain the eyes.

Any sense of claustrophobia the faction headquarters might have induced had long passed. Rather, the long, rectangular halls usually calmed his nerves. But his mind whirled with possibilities of where his niece may be.

A vaguely familiar faction member stepped from his path, nodding respectfully to him and his rank. And it happened again with the next, prompting memories of walking the same hallways with his father. Now the same rank Kalpheus had been when he died, Deylan felt the burden heavier than ever before. Where his father could no longer act to protect his sister, even from the faction themselves, Deylan would always protect Amarie. And her daughter.

Amarie may be in Slumber, but Ahria needs to stay safe.

Pushing the doors open to the viewing rooms, Deylan strode inside and unbuttoned his tunic. "I need to see the Scion. Anyone have eyes on her location?" He pulled his tunic off, tossing it over the back of a lonely chair.

A loud groan rumbled against the curved metallic wall, and Grallston's keys pinged on one of the numerous levers next to his post. His heavy boots thumped on the floor as he begrudgingly leaned forward to peer through the gloomy room at Deylan.

"Guess you finally heard the little vagabond is on the move, huh?" Grallston hacked a wet cough into his forearm.

Deylan glowered at the man. "Does anyone know where she is or not?"

"Course we know. She's the Scion. Vanguard ain't gonna let her out of their, you know..." He waved his hand in front of his own face.

"Set up a connection." Deylan ignored the attempt at humor, lifting the lid to the submersion chamber. The scent of rust and salt met his nose, the concave basin of the cylindrical mechanism full of water, the bottom impossible to see.

Grallston grunted as he lurched to his feet, wiping his hands at his sides. "You got papers?"

"I don't need *papers*," Deylan hissed. "Not anymore. And you know that, so unless you want me to bring *another* Locksmith in here to tell you, get that connection going."

"Whoa, hey." Grallston lifted his hands. "No offense meant, sir." He hacked again as he turned to the wall behind him and grabbed one of the main levers. It squeaked before it clanked down, and the man twisted the dial next to it. At the same time, he gently pushed a smaller lever forward until the mechanism made a humming noise. "Water's cold and ready for you."

Deylan huffed. "It's always cold." He stepped over the edge and dropped into the deep pool, closing his eyes.

Surfacing, he gasped at the abrupt temperature change to his body. Clutching the handle of the lid, he looked at Grallston. "Find me the closest eyes you can." With a tug, the lid clanked over him, engulfing the tank in impenetrable darkness.

Treading water for a few breaths, he flooded his lungs with deep inhales to prepare his body. Sucking in a final one, he plunged beneath the surface.

A low thrumming reverberated through the water, its rhythm quickening. Despite every attempt to remain relaxed, his body tensed as the beat morphed into a solid tone. The shock that ruptured through his body burned his skin, but he forced himself not to breathe as he opened his eyes.

"I know, believe me," Ahria's voice sounded distorted at first, clearing as his vision sharpened. "I couldn't find it, though. I tried." She made a kissing sound and offered him another bit of bread.

His vision twitched as the animal the eyes belonged to took the offering, nibbling at it with tiny little rodent hands. When his niece moved her boots, the animal skittered sideways a few steps.

"It's okay," she cooed. "I won't hurt you. Want more bread?"

Deylan's vision locked on her and then ventured to another outstretched speck of bread.

Wasting food on a rat. That's my niece.

"He's probably continued on to Treama without me." Ahria looked at her hands, rolling her lips together. Barrels surrounded her. Crates. A curved, wooden wall. The cargo nets secured to the ceiling gently swayed.

She's on a ship.

"If he's even noticed I'm missing. He's probably glad to be rid of me after all the trouble I caused him."

Davros won't just forget you, sweetheart.

Deylan watched her, wishing he could let her know she wasn't alone. The ache in his chest mirrored how he felt for Amarie, and it cracked his heart faster than an axe splitting kindling.

"Davros will come for me, though, even if the captain doesn't. I know it." His niece gave the creature a half-hearted smile. "But sometimes... I don't know. I wonder."

Captain? What? She wasn't talking about Davros before?

Deylan's sight jerked and blurred, suddenly racing away from her. It disappeared into darkness, and the connection waned. Then broke, his vision fragmenting like a glass window.

Stale salty air burned as it rushed into his lungs, his breaths echoing back to him from the roof of the submersion chamber. A faint red glow remained somewhere beneath the water, but it faded as the hum of the mechanism returned to a syncopated beat.

Gripping the side of the pool, Deylan banged his fist on

the lid. Only a few breaths passed before it opened, and he climbed out. "Stowed away on a ship, by the looks of it. Her mother would be so proud." Not a hint of sarcasm tainted his tone as he laughed dryly at the antics Amarie would have only encouraged.

"Exactly why the Vanguard ain't too pleased." Grallston waddled back to his chair, pausing at a large basket for a towel he threw at Deylan. "Wonder if she'll be a tempest like her mother."

Deylan rubbed the towel over his hair, grunting. His skin still tingled from the shock of the connection, and he rolled his shoulders. "It wouldn't surprise me in the slightest."

Easier to track a storm, anyway.

Grallston grunted as some unseen part of the mechanism released, and a clank sounded behind him. His ruddy complexion hardened as he stared at Deylan, something unspoken in the older man's look. But Deylan could guess its purpose all the same.

"Don't start."

"I'm just saying, your pa put himself right on the edge of the Vanguard's patience when he told your little sister about us. Hope you're not fixing to put yourself in the same precarious position."

"Who says I'm gonna tell Ahria about the Sixth Eye? Even if I think it's foolish to keep it from her." Deylan gritted his jaw. He'd already proven the familial connection could serve as a benefit in protecting the Berylian Key, but the Vanguard still clung to their secrets.

"I've known you long enough to know that look, boy."

Deylan held in his snarl. "*Locksmith*. I still outrank you, so watch your accusations. And don't talk about my father. He paid a steeper price than his actions deserved."

Grallston huffed, but his attention altered as a grinding sound overcame the chamber. He scowled and rammed his elbow into the metal panel beside him. The chaotic noise faded, returning to a faint clicking within the walls.

The man let out a slow breath, and his throat bobbed. "Your father was a good man. A good friend and a good Locksmith. I miss him. I don't wanna miss you, too."

Deylan held Grallston's gaze before his shoulders relaxed. "You won't. And I'm not going to tell Ahria. Even if she refuses to go home."

He wondered if he'd be able to convince his niece to return to Olsa, but doubted it.

If I can't bring her to safety, I can keep safety with her.

"I'll get a tail on her as soon as she hits dry land." Deylan made a face at his dripping breeches. "She'll have an ally near her, even if she doesn't know it."

Chapter 1

Two weeks earlier...
Winter, 2631 R.T.

IT WAS PERFECTLY DARK. SO dark, Ahria could hardly tell if her eyes were open or closed. The shadows embraced her, like a warm hug, but the comfort faded the longer it lasted.

Be still. Be quiet.

She let out another slow breath, scratching her thumbnail over the pad of her index finger.

Voices sounded like gnats outside her hiding place, a low buzz of excitement somewhere above her. They swayed with the roll of the waves below, an echoing creak reverberating into her bones.

Hours had passed since they'd loaded her crate onto the ship. At least, it felt like hours. Her stomach growled, and she cringed, silently telling her body to shut up.

Davros already thinks I never stop eating.

She shifted, trying to ease the pressure on her shoulder wedged against the side of the crate. Gritting her teeth, she braced the soles of her boots against the top, her back nearly flat on the bottom of her undersized container.

"Time your exit with other noise so no one will hear you," Davros had told her in a whisper while they stood on the dock the night before.

The moon cast silken streams of silver light over the ship she would stow away on, but their illicit plans failed to register on her moral compass.

"I know, I know. But why can't you just come get me out?" Ahria had eyed the crate, not even as tall as her hips. "This thing is too small."

"Any bigger and they'll search it. And you know why I can't just go get you out. I'll be on shift, and I can't leave my post or it'll look suspicious. You'll have to figure it out without me." Davros leaned into her, placing a kiss on her brow. "You've got this. Just pretend it's like the barrels we used to hide in in Viento's stable."

"What if I need to pee?" Ahria whined, but the glint in his eyes made her smile. "Fine. I'll figure it out. But don't leave me in the hold for long."

"Worried about where you'll find snacks?" Davros teased, poking her in the stomach.

"I can go a few hours without food." Ahria lifted her chin.

"Can you, now?"

The grumble of her stomach only confirmed his teasing accusations, and she glowered at the darkness of her crate. "Why didn't I stash food in here?" she whispered, willing her midsection to quiet.

Or at least water.

Ahria held in her chuckle.

But then I'd have to pee, right.

A wave struck the side of the ship, and it listed to the side with a groan. She held her breath, waiting for the next. As the water hit again, she kicked the lid of the crate. The nails squealed, and she stilled before the next crash.

It took three kicks to free the lid off the crate, and dim light poured over her. She cringed as the wood clattered to the floor. Peeking over the edge, she tapped the daggers attached to her hips before climbing out of the crate, quickly replacing the lid.

The cargo hold around her smelled. The reek of fish and briny water permeated through every inch of it. Warm light streamed down through the cracks of the loading hatch above her and from a partially open door on one far end. The light shifted as the ship teetered over another wave, the distant door swinging open and then closed with the movement.

Turning back to her hiding place, she frowned at the bent nails. The wood wouldn't lay flat, and she had no means of reattaching it, but it would raise alarms if found like that.

Grabbing another crate, she figured no one would notice with something on top of it.

Ahria grunted at the weight and shook her head. "Nope, that's not happening." She tried the one next to her hiding spot, and managed to slide it over onto the empty one.

As per their plan, she maneuvered through the storage hold to the back, hiding among the crates, and sat in the shadows. She'd have to wait for Davros to finish his shift before he could sneak away to bring her food and water.

The light in the hold grew bright again with another swell of waves, the distant door creaking in time with the ship. As the patterns of sound around Ahria became more discernible, she indulged in closing her eyes and tried to block out the stench of her surroundings.

She stretched her legs out in front of her, lifting her arms over her head to ease the tension in her muscles from being cramped in a small space for so long. Relaxing, she nuzzled further back to rest her head on several loose sacks of grain.

The rocking of the ship lulled her into a meditative state, but she didn't allow herself to fully slip into sleep.

Rhythmic clicks chimed in her ears, and she furrowed her brow but didn't open her eyes.

Something wet and cold touched the back of her hand.

Ahria squelched the instinct to shriek, jolting upright and opening her eyes.

A warm brown gaze greeted her, a pink tongue lolling out

of the side of the animal's mouth. The golden shine of fur made it easier to recognize in the darkness. With a broad doggy smile, the animal panted and sat, tail thumping against the wooden floor.

"Hey, pups," she whispered with a smile, turning her hand over for the dog to sniff. Her gaze lifted, ensuring no one had followed the animal, and she scratched between the dog's ears. "Aren't you a pretty one?"

The dog leaned into her scratches, its tail wagging faster. Its floppy ears quirked up after the third scratch, a playful wiggle jostling its collar.

Ahria touched the silver tag hanging from the leather, and read the pet's name.

Andi.

She resumed petting the dog. "Hi Andi, you're a good girl, aren't you? What are you—"

The dog barked, and she froze, withdrawing her hand.

"Please don't do that. Shh... You might—"

Another bark. And another.

"No no no, shhh. Go. Please go." Ahria scanned her surroundings, looking for anything that could quiet the creature. But her gaze fell only on her daggers, and she groaned. "I'm not killing a dog."

Andi scuttled back from Ahria, lowering the front of her body closer to the deck in play. Her butt in the air, her golden-feathered tail swished wildly. She yipped again, and footsteps echoed from the hold's entrance.

Shit.

Ahria scurried into the narrow space between a stack of barrels and the curve of the hull, wriggling her way into the shadows as Andi continued to bark.

Looking up, she searched for a porthole. A hatch. A way out. Anything. But found nothing as the footsteps grew closer and closer.

"Hey!" A gruff shout set her spine straight. "What are ye doin' down 'ere?"

Ahria cringed, pressing her back to the side of the hull as the man rounded the barrels and glared at her.

His eyes roamed to her daggers, her cloak pushed open just enough to reveal a few, and he reached for his sword. "Who are ye?"

She raised her hands, but held her tongue.

The man snarled through his grey-speckled stubble. "Don't matter none, anyhow." He grabbed her wrists, jerking her from the wall with more force than necessary, sparking pain along her bones. Twisting her arms behind her back with a growl, he hauled her the way he'd come. "We ain't about to tolerate rats on this ship. How'd ye get in here?"

Ahria's shoulders jolted, but she didn't fight back as he hauled her towards the steep stairs. She clenched her jaw. Any answer would give away that she had help, and she wouldn't give them Davros.

"We'll see if ye find yer tongue before the captain lets the sea have ye."

Chapter 2

"Remember to breathe..."

Talia ignored Talon, her dark complexion ashen. Her chest heaved as she tugged at the tiny buttons fastening the decorative collar. Her intricately painted nails caught on the fine fabric, and she growled as it tore.

"Now, that's not very suitable for a woman of your station." A smirk played on Talon's lips despite the glare it earned from her.

"I didn't bring you here for your sarcasm." She freed one of the buttons and took in a deep breath, leaning against the back of one of the study's chairs. "I can't breathe with all that fabric strangling me. That meeting was..."

"Necessary." Talon eyed the large oaken door behind him, ensuring it remained ajar.

Outside in the hall, boots shuffled nearer to the door, barely audible—even by his Aueric hearing. A guard or two intent on eavesdropping.

Good. They'll help to dissuade rumors of a romantic relationship.

She was already being scrutinized for employing an auer in her formal council.

Talia let out another long sigh. "Necessary," she repeated, walking to the front of the chair before she unceremoniously plopped into it. The elegant chandelier above cast a halo of golden light in her curls, like a crown perched on her head.

Talon clicked his tongue, and Talia frowned. Rolling her eyes, she straightened her back and settled both feet on the ground in a more proper position.

She held out her hands to him with an unimpressed look. "You've been gone for days. Please tell me you found him."

"Your son hasn't exactly made it easy to track him down." Talon crossed his arms, maintaining his protective position between the door and Talia. "But I found him."

Talia's gaze shot to him. "Where is he? Did you bring him here?" She braced a hand on the armrest, ready to stand with wide eyes, until he lifted a hand and shook his head.

"No, not yet. He's... not really in an accessible place at the moment."

Talia gaped. "He's not..." She glanced at the door before mouthing the question instead.

Talon laughed. "No, he's not in prison. He's in the middle of the Dul'Idur Sea. Seems your son took after his late father after all."

Talia's shoulders sagged, formality leaching from her again as she collapsed back into the chair. "Thank the gods. And you're going to bring him home?"

Pausing, Talon lifted his gaze to examine the ostentatious study Talia had been sequestered to while the Zionan parliament continued to meet. To discuss the future of their country and Talia's part in it.

"I'm not sure he'll think of this place as home. But I'll bring him here. In time." The auer gave her a reassuring smile. "I'll need to travel to his destination port and hope I make it there before he does. Otherwise, he'll set sail again, and I'll have another search on my hands. But at least I now know the name of the vessel he's on."

"How did you find him?" Talia began, but then shook her head. "It doesn't matter, as long as I can see him again. I've been without my son for so long…" She fished a dirty chain from beneath her shirt, twisting the rings on it.

Talon's heart tugged, and he looked down at the woven bracelet on his wrist given to him by Ahria nearly a decade ago. The leather had worn over time, and the braid wasn't perfect, but he still smiled.

Why hasn't she written me back?

He'd sent the messenger bird weeks ago, and it should

have reached Olsa and returned already. But he'd heard nothing, and with Winter's End approaching, she'd be wondering about him. They'd never missed spending the festival together.

Perhaps she didn't receive my letter.

He thumbed the leather, and a vision of Ahria running through the garden giggling made him suddenly homesick.

"I'm sorry," Talia whispered. "You must miss your daughter, too. How old is she now? Old enough to be married, isn't she?"

He snorted. "Gods help whatever poor fellow falls for my Ahria." Meeting Talia's eyes, he shook his head. "She's twenty." The thought of just how long it'd been since she was born brought memories of Amarie. And just how much her daughter looked like her.

Except she has Kin's eyes.

"I am sorry that I've kept you from home for so long. I hope all this madness ends soon so you can get back to her." Talia stood, crossing the intricate rug. Her steps faltered as her foot caught the inseam of her skirt. "Dammit. I swear, I'm going to make a law stating that I never have to wear a dress this long again."

Talon took her wrist as she stumbled again, righting her. "It's unfortunate I won't be here to hear the parliament's final decision regarding whether you'll have the opportunity.

I need to leave tomorrow for Treama if I'm going to beat Dawn Chaser there."

Chapter 3

A LOOSE STRAND OF HAIR fell from Ahria's ponytail into her face as she bowed her head. The man who found her shoved her forward again when her pace slowed, and she stumbled on the first step of the stairs to the mid level of the ship. Dropping to a knee, only his grip on her wrists prevented her from falling on her face. Pain sparked again in her shoulders, quickening her breath.

Withholding a snarl, she huffed and regained her footing, glaring up the steep stairs and wondering how her captor expected her to climb without hands. But she stubbornly took each stride, avoiding losing her balance again.

Behave. They have the upper hand.

She resisted the temptation to struggle, but fear touched her senses. Her father's advice rippled through her muscles, keeping them slack.

Stay calm. Clear headed.

The journey to the main deck gave her a rough layout of the ship, since they passed the armory and the galley. The eyes of the crew followed her as she passed, but she lifted her chin as she emerged above deck.

Fresh air greeted her lungs, and it nearly extinguished her regret for getting caught.

Smells so much better up here.

Scanning the deck, she defiantly met the gaze of the crew who paused in their duties to gawk at the stowaway.

Near the port rigging, Davros straightened, dark eyes widening as he watched her be escorted towards the captain's quarters. He looked ready to step forward and give himself away, but she subtly shook her head. His brawny shoulders remained tight as his shallow nod assured her he'd listen.

Looking forward again, she forced her feet to keep an even gait as they approached the double doors, ornate with sculpted iron handles and decorative hinges. The patchy windows on either side seemed out of place, their frosted glass cracked with other sections completely mismatched. Oddly charming, as if the ship endured its own identity crisis. Extravagant, yet weathered. In desperate need of restoration.

Maybe the captain is too cheap.

The man escorting her held her wrists with one hand to bang on the door with his other. The pause gave Ahria a moment to examine the locations of the crew, already trying to formulate a plan. Yet, the rolling blue waves surrounding the ship left her with no escape.

A thud echoed from inside the captain's quarters before footsteps grew closer, one door creaking open.

A set of wicked pale green eyes met hers, a salt and pepper beard framing yellowed teeth. One of the man's front incisors was made of dented iron, a gap behind it showing where another tooth had been lost. The gnarled scar across the entire right side of his head turned her stomach, but she refused to let it show.

"Caught a little rat aboard. Need to see the captain." The man holding her squeezed her wrists tighter, and she gritted her jaw.

Yipping, the dog that'd given her away pushed up against the back of Ahria's knees, wriggling through to the doorway. Her tail thumped as she paused in front of the grisly man who gave her a wary look. He reached to touch the animal's ears, but Andi shirked away, squeezing between his leg and the door frame to go inside the cabin.

Grunting at the dog, the man turned his attention back to Ahria. "Skinny little rat." The scarred man's voice came out raspy. "Hardly enough for Andi's dinner."

Ahria frowned, looking down at her corset which failed to flatten her breasts, and held her tongue.

Better than him wanting to put his hands all over me.

"Captain inside, Grinick? Or you just sneaking sips of his brandy again?" Her captor pushed her forward, forcing her to step closer to the scarred Grinick.

His breath reeked of ale and fish.

She closed her eyes briefly, keeping her chin up and her shoulders back.

"Will you two stop flirting and bring whatever you found in?" A woman's voice rang from behind Grinick, making him flinch. "And by the gods, if it's genuinely just another rat, I'm gonna kick both your asses overboard."

Andi barked from inside, as if in answer. And someone else, another man, chuckled.

Rough hands pushed Ahria again into Grinick, who clumsily grasped her shoulders before taking a step back into the captain's quarters. Making room, he passed Ahria towards the open space of the cabin.

Hands finally free, she rolled her wrists and shoulders. She stiffened as the door behind her closed, shutting the small cabin off from the rest of the ship. Sunlight struggled to enter the cabin through the frosted windows at the back of the ship, a few of them boarded over. Lanterns swayed from the ceiling, the brightest hanging like a beacon above a round table at the back corner.

Sitting at the table were the owners of the two other voices. A woman, her hair braided in a wreath around her head, sat with an unimpressed look on her face. She idly stroked the golden head of the dog who'd taken up a spot between her knees. Beside her, pushed further into the shadows of the corner, was the man who'd laughed. His eyes were two bright spots among his deep brown complexion, almost as dark as Davros's.

He may have lacked gruesome scars and a gruff voice, but Ahria knew better than to assume he wasn't a threat. She kept her stance, hands twitching within her fur-lined cloak. The man who found her hadn't tried to disarm her, and several daggers waited within reach like crouched wolves in a quiet forest. Her most trusted companions. Her blades. Her fangs.

Expressionless, Ahria kept silent, letting someone else speak first.

"Where was she?" The woman's free hand ran along the silver filigree of her sword's hilt.

"Cargo hold. That's what all the racket Andi was making was about."

The dog's tongue lolled out of the side of her mouth as the woman's scratches grew firmer.

"Good girl. Always knew you'd be a good investment."

The same chuckle as before came from the man in the corner as he leaned forward. "You didn't want the dog, Leiura. And if I recall, it was all my coin that got her." Light shimmered on a silver chain beneath the collar of his plain charcoal shirt.

Ahria's lips twitched before she corrected her expression.

"Is she armed?" Leiura narrowed her eyes. When her captor hesitated, the woman huffed. "You didn't *check*?"

Grinick scoffed. "She's just a wee bitty lass. Even if she does got a blade, ain't gonna be able to use it."

Leiura's eyes flashed, and her hand ceased its pets. "Just do it." Her voice shifted lower, a deadly tone that even Ahria wouldn't want to mess with.

As her captor grumbled and pulled her cloak aside, Ahria sucked in a slow breath, readying her body. "Don't," she whispered, and he paused, meeting her gaze with his hand near the hilt of the dagger at her hip.

Instead of recoiling as he should, he chuckled under his breath. "So the rat speaks." He continued his reach, fingertips touching the hilt.

Ahria released the hold she'd put on her muscles and slammed her arm down, striking his wrist away from her blade and twisting to grab his leathery skin. Her other hand snatched a different dagger from behind her back, and she wrenched him sideways, using his weight to her advantage as she danced behind him. Bracing his elbow, she trapped his bent wrist behind his back, forcing him to his knees.

Breathing even, Ahria held the blade to his throat, meeting the captain's eyes. Davros had said the captain seemed like a fair man, and she silently prayed he was right.

"There is no need for bloodshed," she murmured, refusing to ease the tension in her hold.

Leiura had risen at the table, her sword half drawn at her hip. But she paused, looking back at the man.

The captain leaned back in his chair again and laughed.

Chapter 4

MERRIL'S FACE CONTORTED IN SHOCK, color rising to his cheeks—more embarrassed than afraid for his life. Holding perfectly still, the ship's quartermaster seemed well aware that despite Grinick's insistence, the *wee bitty lass* could do plenty of damage.

Conrad hadn't been able to hold in the laughter that bubbled up, but his mind whirled to consider the threat they let slip onto his ship.

She's not an assassin, or she'd have just paid her way to get onboard. Besides, there isn't anyone worth killing on this ship.

Leiura's disapproving glance suggested he needed to handle the situation more seriously, and he waved a hand at her. If the woman didn't want to spill any blood, he wouldn't give her a reason.

"You're right, there's no need for violence." The laugh still lightened his tone. "Now if you would please release my quartermaster, we can discuss the most appropriate way to resolve this situation."

The woman didn't move a muscle. "No one will attempt to remove my daggers, and no one will harm me or my friend."

"Friend?" Grinick's shadowy glare made it clear he would love an excuse for the bloodshed, but the captain cut him off.

"No one will harm you. And we can discuss the daggers."

Leiura glared harder at him. He could practically hear her questioning his sanity.

The woman's jaw worked, fine hairs wisping around her face, free from the ponytail holding the rest of her dark hair. With a slow blink of her strange, ice-blue eyes, she removed the blade from Merril's throat and sidestepped. Spinning the short dagger, she tucked it between her sleeve and bracer.

"Thank you." Conrad pushed his chair from the table, standing while he kept his hands exposed for the stowaway.

Merril rolled further from her, stumbling back to his feet against the cabin door. Despite what promises his captain had made, the big man reached for the sword at his side.

All Conrad had to do was snap his head in his quartermaster's direction, and Merril froze with his fingers inches from his hilt. Like a bear, he growled and lowered his hand.

The woman's gaze darted sideways, her stance ready, but she didn't pull another weapon.

A knock came at the door, but no one moved.

Andi responded with a joyous bark, welcoming whoever it was inside.

The handle twisted, the door tentatively opening. "Captain?" A still relatively unfamiliar head poked in, black hair falling in thick curls against his dark forehead.

"Not a great time, new guy, come back later." He didn't remember the sailor's name. He'd only just signed on in Zola, and too many faces coming on and off his ship hadn't helped improve his memory.

"Actually..." The man peered into the room, drawing the stowaway's glare. "I should probably be here."

"Get out," the woman hissed, but the man shook his head.

"Ah." Conrad crossed his arms, thumbing his own chin as if in thought. "You're our little rat's friend, I take it?"

Even as he said it, the nickname hardly suited her. Too small to be a rat.

Maybe a mouse.

Merril straightened, glowering at the young man in the doorway. "Inside."

Obeying, the man shut the door. He shrugged at the woman, giving her an apologetic look. "I couldn't just..."

"Why make plans at all, then?" The mouse scowled, lifting her hands.

"Captain, this is my fault." Davros—that was his name—faced Conrad.

The captain lifted his eyebrows. "Actually, I'm rather certain it's my dog's fault. If Andi hadn't inspected the cargo hold, might have gotten away with keeping a stowaway on board. But I'm not one for freeloaders." He eyed the stowaway again. This time, he examined her fully. Evaluating the strength of her from the ground up. Lithe. Some decent curves at her hips. But the corset hid most else.

Kind of cute like a mouse, too.

"I offered to work," the woman grumbled. "No room on your crew for another woman, it seems."

The conversation came back to Conrad. How Davros had asked for his female companion to join him and work the decks. But she'd had no experience, so he'd only hired the man.

"Too small of a ship for inexperienced hands. Needed to keep a spot open to pick up more hands in Nolan." Conrad shrugged. It was all business. The day a stowaway understood the overhead and upkeep of a ship, he'd accept her criticism, perhaps. "But now that you're here anyway, might as well find a use for you. Not about to throw you overboard, despite what my bosun might recommend."

Grinick grunted, keeping his eyes on the girl.

The woman's shoulders relaxed, but only slightly. "You'll let me stay?" She exchanged a look with Davros, hesitant relief coloring her features.

"Only if you work, and efficiently. No slacking." Conrad's gaze shifted to Davros. "As for the mastermind here, I tolerate lying less than freeloading. So we'll be cutting that pay of yours we agreed on, seeing as I'm feeding two mouths on this boat now instead of one."

Davros looked at the woman before nodding. "Yes, Captain."

The mouse eyed the quartermaster before returning her attention to Conrad. "Thank you," she murmured, still wary despite his promise.

He couldn't blame her, since most captains he knew wouldn't be so lenient. But he didn't believe in condemning them to death for their actions, nor did he have time to stop and force their departure.

"Galley duty for you, miss...?" Conrad considered her again, this time focusing on her chilling eyes. It felt as if they could look right into the deepest parts of him, and the conflict it created in his gut made the room spin.

"Ahria." She lifted her chin. "My name is Ahria Xylata."

"A pleasure, I'm sure." Conrad gave the barest of bows with his chin. "But I'm certain the cook needs your help below deck. It's nearly lunchtime, and he's usually overly decadent after we've left a port. See to it." He gestured towards the door.

Ahria glanced at the others, stepping past them to Davros. She whispered something to him before opening the door.

"Ahria." Conrad's fingers brushed the back of Andi's head as she rubbed up against him.

The mouse halted, looking back at him, and Davros touched her arm.

Conrad gestured at his left sleeve. "Let's keep those daggers away. If you use them against any of my crew, I may have to reconsider my generosity."

Pausing, Ahria nodded. "They will not enter my palm unprovoked." She removed Davros's hand from her arm and walked outside. The sailor who'd snuck her onboard glanced back at the captain once more, giving him a grateful, nervous nod before scuttling out after her.

That boy doesn't know how lucky he is that I'm not a different captain. Making stupid decisions for a woman...

Grinick grumbled, exchanging a look with Merril.

Rolling his eyes, Conrad turned back to the table, studying the maps spread over it. He traced the planned route with his finger as the two officers behind him muttered and Leiura took a protective stance off his left hip.

"Stop muttering and say it, gentlemen." Conrad didn't bother to look at them, already able to sense the tension.

"Ain't a good idea letting her live, Cap. Sets a bad

example." Grinick, which was to be expected. It was Merril's grunt of agreement that was more surprising. Though, the mouse's actions against him probably provoked such a reaction.

"We're not murderers. She's a stowaway, not an assassin. So I see no harm in it." Conrad turned towards them, leaning against the table with his hands behind him. "Besides, my boat, my rules, gents. Which you both are well aware of. Don't like them, you're welcome to disembark. Either now or when we dock."

Grinick scowled. "Thought you weren't a murderer, sir."

"I'm not." Conrad shrugged. "But seeing as it's your choice, I don't really see it as murder. More of... a helping hand that you guide."

Merril straightened, but then shrugged. "Your boat, Cap." He bobbed his head and smacked Grinick in the side with the back of his hand. Then the pair left, and the only sound remaining in the room was the steady beat of the waves on the hull and Andi's oblivious panting.

Damn dog could be in the middle of a battle and still be wagging her tail.

Conrad paused to cradle Andi's head between his palms, scratching her jowls. "Good job, girl. Extra scraps tonight."

"Dumb mutt's lucky to be alive. Girl could have silenced her real quick with that hardware she's lugging around." Leiura plopped into her chair again.

He chuckled. "How many blades you count on her?"

Leiura sighed, putting one of her booted feet up on the chair across from her. "Seven. Maybe eight, but I didn't get a good look at her back."

Conrad rubbed Andi's face more vigorously, and the dog licked at his fingers. "We got to work on the *come and get me* rather than the *bark your head off*, you fool."

Andi groaned as Conrad stooped to roughly kiss the top of the dog's head.

Disgust echoed from Leiura as she plucked one of her little silver knives from her belt and used it to pick at the dirt beneath her fingernails. "Some days I wonder who you respect more. Your first mate or your dog."

"Always gonna be you, Leiura." Conrad moved to join her at the table. "Long as you have that cool head about you that keeps me sailing straight. Andi's got none of that sense."

Chapter 5

AHRIA HUMMED A TUNE AS she scrubbed the counters in the galley.

Orlin returned, carrying an empty, filthy pot. "What are you still doing here? You know we're crossing through the gate tonight." The cook put the pot down, eyeing Ahria's work. "The counters are clean enough."

She smiled, scrubbing over the rest of the counter. "I'm not quite done. You said clean. I'm making it clean."

"You sure work hard for someone who ain't gettin' paid." The cook chuckled, plucking an apple from the barrel of dwindling fruit storage and tossing it to her.

Ahria dropped the cloth and caught the bright red apple with a scowl. "You ever gonna stop throwing things at me?"

The first day she'd been put to work in the galley, she'd caught a knife that had slipped off the counter. Since then, Orlin enjoyed testing her reflexes whenever he thought she wasn't paying attention. He'd been reluctant to welcome her to his kitchen, at first, but she'd worn him down with her smiles and songs.

"Only if you stop catching them." Orlin grinned.

Ahria laughed. "But then my apple would have a big bruise on it." She bit it, enjoying the tartness on her tongue.

The cook crouched beside the uneven hanging doors of the cabinets beside the stove, pulling another massive pot from within. He waved a hand above the counter at her. "Go. I'll finish up. You'll miss it, otherwise."

Smiling, she dashed for the stairs, flinging her apron off on the way. Ever since she was a child, she'd heard tales of the great Dul'Idur Gate. When they'd boarded the ship, she'd assumed she would miss it while locked in the cargo hold, hiding. But now, with her freedom aboard...

Taking the steps two at a time, she reached the upper deck.

Stars speckled the sky, shining so much brighter at sea with only a few lanterns to diminish their glow. She stared up at them, spinning once before her gaze landed on a tall, dark shape ahead of them.

Grateful for the moon, her eyes adjusted to take in the faint details of the famous Dul'Idur Gate.

It spanned the entire channel from land to land, with enormous archways interrupting it at three locations along its impressive length.

Ahria gaped, wandering to the bow of the ship to get a closer look as they approached.

It stretched towards the sky, like a cliff risen from the depths of the sea. The gates stood ajar, like massive oak doors leading into a grand ballroom. All of them open and only half visible with their lower portion beneath the waves. Once, they'd controlled the flow of vessels, choosing who could pass and who couldn't. But those days were long gone, and the behemoth of a structure only served as a shadow of the past on the horizon.

Chains hung like garlands along the underside of the arches, connecting to great gears and mechanisms on the open doors. They vanished into the sea, as if somehow anchoring the giant gate blotting out the night's stars. Around them, a faint golden glow rippled with the waves as they lapped on the rusty supports. The Art infused the structure with motes like fireflies, enabling ships and their crews to steer clear of the hazards.

As Ahria's gaze rose to follow the gate while they sailed beneath, her mouth fell agape. "Wow," she whispered, wishing Davros was there to watch the sight with her. But he was on shift somewhere below deck.

Passing through the center archway, the tallest mast

cleared the bottom of the arch with hundreds of feet to spare. And four more ships could have sailed beside them. She imagined what wondrous creatures could have passed beneath these gates. If dragons had water-born cousins who could swim alongside the ship under the iron.

Chewing her lip, she looked straight up as they passed through to the other side. The water and stars reflected off the underside of the archways, casting eerie shapes on the dangling chains and iron beams. It reminded her of the fire artisans who lit up the air with sparks during Winter's End festivities.

Her heart twisted. The festivities at home were well underway by now.

Please be safe, Dad.

Her eyes burned, her throat tight as she squeezed them shut for a breath. When she looked back at the shrinking gate, she strode across the deck to remain closer to it. "I'll find you, I promise," she whispered, wondering where her Aueric father's travels had taken him.

He'd left months ago to help an old friend find her son. Shortly after his departure, Ahria's human father had fallen ill. Cerquel's plague had taken the life from him in a matter of weeks, and she'd buried one father without the other.

Did he even receive my letter?

Her childhood had been anything but ordinary. Not just because she had two fathers and no mother, but because she wasn't blood related to either of them. Nor were the men involved in a romantic relationship. Rather, they'd agreed to a partnership in raising her and her older adoptive brother, Lorin's child by blood.

Talon, her Aueric father, had loved her mother and told her stories of her.

Ahria swiped the tears for her late father from her cheek and put both hands on the railing of the ship. She breathed harder, emotion still burning her eyes as she watched the Dul'Idur Gate slowly fade behind them.

She sighed. Crossing her arms over the tall banister, she rested her chin on her forearms, touching her necklace with one hand. The pad of her thumb traced the silver etchings of the mystical flower, which she had never seen bloom before. More legends her father had filled her head with. Talon had often referred to her mother as araleinya. And the necklace was the only piece of her mother she had.

A murmur of voices penetrated the icy air. But they were difficult to discern. Curious, she tilted her head and brushed her hair aside. The chatter came from below, and she leaned against the aft banister to peer at the back of the ship.

The grand window within the captain's quarters just beneath her stood open. It was the captain's familiar, rumbling voice she heard. Barely audible over the churning white caps of the waves below, glowing with starlight. And for a moment, Ahria stepped back so she couldn't hear.

It's none of my business.

But then the memory of her empty coin purse returned. And the reality of how much they had planned to rely on what money Davros was supposed to make on this voyage. There was limited time for her to renegotiate with the captain on his behalf. And they needed that money.

Licking her lips, she returned to the railing, but it was too tall for her to lean over. She strained to listen, quirking her head over the banister.

"I don't think so." The captain's voice.

"Are you sure?" Leiura, the first mate.

"We have time to make port. They aren't that close."

"Maybe not, but Nolan is a main trade port for Delkest, Ziona, *and* Feyor. If they have posters up..."

Ahria furrowed her brow.

Posters?

"One night won't be a problem. And they didn't last time, so I doubt they will now. Aidensar won't honor Feyor's bounties."

Leiura snorted. "But Feyorian bounty hunters who are stopped in Nolan for the night will."

The captain's voice grew louder as he approached the window. "I refuse to be a prisoner on my own ship. One night won't hurt, then we can leave at first light. Sooner, if necessary. Just need supplies. Warrin won't catch us that fast, even with that fancy ship of his."

He's being pursued. There's a bounty on his head.

Ahria watched the gate fade into the dark horizon. She could use the new knowledge to her advantage, but the thought made her stomach turn.

I can't afford to care about his feelings, even if he was lenient with me.

Swallowing, she lost track of the conversation below as she debated.

He wouldn't kill me to keep me quiet, would he?

Ahria knew next to nothing about this captain, but he hadn't hurt her. It'd been five days since they caught her in the cargo hold and so far, he'd kept his word. But Davros still needed his pay, and if they came out of this with a few extra coins, it wouldn't hurt her search for her father.

"You still think I made a mistake?" The captain's voice echoed from within.

"Maybe. Only time will tell, right?" Leiura's words were barely audible. She said more, but Ahria couldn't make it out.

The door to the captain's quarters creaked open, and she skirted sideways, pressing her back to the upper deck's wall. Footsteps, then they diminished and disappeared.

He's alone.

Ahria steeled her nerves and strode around the edge of the deck towards the captain's quarters, pausing at the doors. Taking a deep breath, she knocked twice.

"Enter."

Not letting herself reconsider, she turned the handle and swung the door open. Walking inside, she shut the door behind her.

It was darker in the cabin than before. Only the lantern above the table was lit, but the captain wasn't sitting there. Instead, his vague shadow hovered near the far left wall, where several glass-doored shelves were burdened with books. One of the panes squeaked as he closed and latched it back into place, a thin book in his hand.

A thumping started somewhere in the direction of the bed, and Andi let out a low whine.

"Speak." The captain hadn't fully looked at her, flipping the book open and squinting down at it in the dimness.

Ahria stared at him, her pulse picking up its pace. Her tongue dried as she tried to find words, but she waited for him to look at her.

He snapped the book shut as he turned and lifted his head. When he spied her, a tension rose in his shoulders, and his eyes widened ever so slightly.

Find their weakness. Always be ready to use it.

Talon had coached her diligently as soon as she was old enough to hold a blade, despite Lorin's protests.

The tension faded almost as abruptly as it had come. But she couldn't tell if it was the captain being a fool, or trying to cast a certain appearance. Regardless of his intention, he turned towards his table and stepped into the light without letting her leave his peripheral vision.

"This is a surprise visit, Ahria. Come to kill me in the dead of night? Or have you been behaving with those daggers of yours?" The captain casually leaned against one of the chairs, but she could see the strategy in it. A sword lay across the table in front of him, and the position allowed him to be closer to the weapon while appearing relaxed.

Smart man. I'd still win, though.

But killing the captain would gain little. She just needed to make sure Davros was fairly compensated.

"You think you can reach your sword before I put a dagger between your eyes?" She smiled sweetly, lifting an eyebrow.

He mirrored the expression. "I'm not sure. Are we about to find out?"

Ahria took a step towards him. "Not unless you'd like to."

"As amusing as I'm sure that would be, it'd probably be better to avoid bloodstains." He didn't move from his position, but pushed his sleeves up to his elbows. Despite the cold outside, his cabin seemed to need the back window open to even be a tolerable temperature.

The warmth relaxed her body, though, and she let out a breath. "I've actually come to see you because I thought I might ask if you'd reconsider Davros's pay."

His jaw twitched as if he was restraining a smile. "Oh?

And I suppose you have a reason why I should. Despite him assisting in smuggling a—"

"A diligent galley worker aboard?" Ahria finished for him. "I do believe I've been performing well in my... albeit unintentional post, and I'm rather sick of being called a rat."

His eyes narrowed a fraction. "I was going to say mouse. But your performance has been acceptable. Which is good, considering worthless lumps go overboard."

Ahria's blood heated, and she clenched her jaw, losing her sense of humor. "But you see, Captain, Davros's post would generate enough coin for us to—"

"Stop." The captain held up his hand. "The sob story you're about to paint me is not my problem, and still doesn't excuse the *crime* you have committed. Would you rather I throw you in the brig and turn you over to the authorities in Nolan?"

"Oh, but couldn't I threaten the same?" she whispered. "It would be a shame if any bounty hunters in Nolan learned who was docked in their port."

The air between them suddenly grew icy as the captain straightened. His handsome face turned to stone, and she held her breath, bracing herself for his anger.

I have no choice.

"Careful, Ahria." His voice grew dangerously low. "This is treacherous ground."

Daring her legs to be steady, she walked closer, boots

barely making a sound. She pinned his gaze with hers, entranced by the hazel of his irises.

Storm clouds brewing with thunder.

Swallowing, she exhaled the tension building in her chest. "Treacherous... or lucrative?" She approached until she was within arm's reach, lifting her chin to look up at him.

"Too frequently those are the same." The captain eyed her, as he had when they'd first met. Assessing what exactly she was capable of. It made her insides squirm.

"But I have no desire to see you taken by Feyorian thugs. I just need enough coin so my *sob story* doesn't end in Treama." She tilted her head, batting her eyelashes. "What if I say please?"

The twitch of a smile touched his mouth again, but it didn't appear. "Half." The captain crossed his arms and took a step away from the table and his sword. "I have to maintain some appearances with my crew and my tolerances. I'll agree to half of *your boy's* pay, but no more."

Relief flooded through her, and before she could steel her face, she smiled. Rolling her lips together, she huffed. "Fine. But why do you insist on calling Davros a boy? Pretty sure I've never seen such a baby-faced captain before." She eyed the thin stubble over his jaw, unable to tell exactly how old he was.

"Age rarely determines if someone is a man or not." He narrowed his eyes. "Or a woman."

Ahria flicked her gaze down his body and back to his face. "Oh, I'm well aware."

A new tightness overcame his posture.

She turned, breathing through her discomfort at having her back to him, and walked towards the door. "Thank you. For the compromise." She looked at him over her shoulder. "I feel like now is a poor time to ask your name."

Finally, a smile broke on his lips, and he shook his head. "A very poor time. Good night, little mouse. Thank you for the enlightening chat."

She paused, hand on the door handle. "Goodnight Captain. Sleep well." Exiting onto the deck, she breathed in the crisp night air and shut the door behind her. Sagging, she leaned against the perpendicular wall.

Ahria ran her hands over her face, realizing they shook. Blowing out a slow breath, she closed her hands into fists and shook her head.

Why was that so hard?

She looked at the doors before walking away, boots tapping over the wood. "Well, now he hates me. Hopefully that doesn't come back to bite me in the ass."

Chapter 6

STANDING NEAR THE HELM, CONRAD could feel Leiura staring daggers into his back. He ignored it as he watched Ahria walk down the gangplank onto Nolan's dock. Alone. He'd been certain to schedule Davros the double shift for the day, so he was stuck on board, ensuring neither of them would slip away into Nolan's busy fishing markets.

She'll come back for him.

The docks grew into a sprawling maze the further they stretched from the shore. Nolan's beach had never been big enough to support the thriving city the port town had grown into as a major trade hub between all of Pantracia. Entire sections of the city were now built on the water itself, floating taverns and inns wedged between fishing and trade vessels. The thick forest of Aidensar hung like the foreboding entrance to another world beyond the few city blocks built on land.

"Ahria!" Orlin hurried after the woman, and she paused at the bottom of the gangplank.

They engaged in a lively conversation, with Orlin showing her something Conrad couldn't make out.

Ahria nodded, sniffing something he'd given her, and then nodded again. She resumed her walk away while the cook reboarded the ship with a content smile.

Orlin looked up at Conrad and lifted a hand. "Splendid day, Captain."

"Indeed." He gave a brief, suspicious nod to his cook. He pursed his lips, debating asking straight out what he'd given her.

Why the hells do I care?

Leiura cleared her throat obnoxiously, and he cringed.

"For gods' sake. She's got you wrapped around that little finger of hers." Leiura huffed.

"Don't be ridiculous. I'm merely playing the part she expects of me." Conrad fidgeted with the laces of his bracers, tucking them beneath the leather. "Need her to think she does."

Leiura snorted. "Right." Her tone reeked of sarcasm. "I still can't believe you went straight to half. Did a quarter pay ever cross your mind?"

"She wasn't going to take it." Instead of looking at his

first mate, Conrad watched his crew as they mulled about the ship.

My ship.

Dawn Chaser had fallen into his possession out of dumb luck rather than his own worthiness, but he wasn't about to take any of it for granted. Regardless of his age, he'd earned the respect of his peers and kept it through careful management of his rotating officers and crew. Leiura was his single constant. Because he trusted her more than himself in so many ways.

"So we sticking with the plan of no new hands? Seeing as she took up our only open position?" Leiura clicked her tongue. "And with your refusal to listen to Grinick's good sense..."

"I'm not throwing a stowaway overboard, and you know exactly why." He glanced at her out of the corner of his vision, spying the dry smile on her face. "And you hate the idea, too. You hated Grinick the moment I hired him."

Leiura shrugged. "He'll serve his purpose. And when we return to Zola in six months' time, his contract will be over, and I won't ever have to see his ugly ass face again."

Conrad grunted, watching Davros appear above deck to start his second shift. The man worked hard, he'd give him that, and hadn't complained once about his reduced pay. He wondered if the destination of Treama was for Davros's sake, or for Ahria's.

I'm betting it's hers. And tonight, I'm a betting man.

"Try not to sink my boat while I'm gone." He clapped a hand on Leiura's shoulder before he started towards the stairs from the quarter deck.

"Aye, Captain." Leiura's annoyance with him carried through her tone as he descended. "You'll find her better than you left her."

"Of that, I have no doubt, Lei Lei." Conrad turned enough to give her a devilish grin as he ran his hand over the banister, fingers catching on the familiar cracks.

Fortunately, Leiura wasn't in range of anything she could throw at his head.

His boots thunked onto the hollow dock, and the comforting bob of its wood on the sea made him feel completely at home. Of all places to get off the ship, Nolan was the least offensive to his center of balance. The floating taverns would at least all keep the same sway as his ship did while at dock. A destination wasn't difficult to decide on, either, as Conrad had his usual haunt. He'd been through Nolan so many times he'd stopped counting. And all the years at sea began to blend together. Home had never felt quite right, and when he was fifteen, the waves had finally won in their beckoning to him.

A flock of gulls shrieked as they wove through the labyrinth of naked masts. Packed in every available space, the docks of Nolan were flooded with ships still moored for the season. At the tail end of winter, Conrad would be considered one of the foolish captains to be braving the Trytonia Strait.

Raucous laughter poured through the air from the massive body of a ship he might have assumed was docked if the back end of it hadn't been built into floating wings to house more gambling dens. The nose of Siren's Song butted up against the dock, now permanently constructed to lead into the door cut straight through the old ship's bow. A finely carved figurehead guarded the way above the door, a harp clenched in one hand, and a dagger in the other.

As he always did, Conrad slowed to stare at the crescent pupils carved for the woman. Not a siren, but an alcan, which only fed into the human stereotype of the elusive people of the sea.

His gut churned. No matter how many times he passed under the figurehead, the feeling never went away.

A pair of sailors stumbled from the doorway, their arms wrapped around each other, so entranced they nearly ran into Conrad. He stepped out of the way, breaking his eye contact with the carving.

The hearth's warmth greeted him as he stepped inside, the aroma of lemon fish and fresh bread making his stomach rumble in a more pleasant way. Patrons filled the tables, mostly men, some playing dice or cards, with a few linen-lined tables on the far side. The right side of Siren's Song boasted three pentagonal tables, all occupied by players of the game Conrad had never fully grasped. Long smooth sticks with metal tips stood in racks, with sets of balls meant to be tapped into the pockets at the tables' five corners. A hole in the center would gulp a poorly aimed ball, ending a player's hope of victory.

His eyes wandered back to the card tables, his preferred method of losing coin. And the silver florins he carried were growing heavier, begging to be wagered.

A tavern master strode past him, carrying a tray of empty steins. He gave Conrad a sideways look as he passed. "Something to eat or drink for you tonight, sir?"

Conrad stripped his coat off, the heat of the room causing sweat to form on his back already. "Brandy. Neat."

Scanning the room for a table to join, his gaze snagged on a pair of painfully familiar ice-blue eyes.

Just my luck.

Even as he thought it, he couldn't decipher if the luck was good or bad.

Ahria stood at the middle pocket ball table, talking to a man who had his back to Conrad. She grinned, touching the man's shoulder as she spoke.

Conrad had never seen her dressed in anything but the traveling clothes she wore, usually a white tunic with leather breeches and corset. But now she donned a blouse, unbuttoned to her cleavage, and high-waisted leather pants with buckles across the abdomen. Not a single blade was visible, but he knew better.

No way she'd leave them unattended on my ship.

Not after her reaction when Merril had tried to take one. She'd dropped him to his knees before Leiura had even stood.

Ahria lifted a mug of ale to her lips as the man's shoulders shook with laughter.

"Sir?" The tavern master had returned, holding a square crystal glass towards him. Not tin or metal like all the other taverns in Nolan. Real crystal. Only one of the reasons Siren's Song was a far more refined location to lose all your money than the rowdy taverns closer to land.

While the sailors and general public in the gambling hall certainly had a good time, they abided by a strict code of conduct set forth by the ownership. Codes like the silver florin Conrad passed to the tavern master in exchange for his drink, which only cost two iron marks. The larger coin proved his intention to spend at least that on drinks and food, as well as pay the traditional charge for simply walking through the doors.

So how did Ahria get in here?

She'd claimed to have no coin.

The tavern master palmed the silver. "Name for the tab?"

"Conrad." He didn't bother with a last name, especially when such information so close to Feyor could get him in trouble with the very things Ahria blackmailed him with. Blackmailed him in a way that left him wondering if she'd ever done it before. Likely not, given how her hands had shaken. Whatever she needed the coin for, she'd abandoned her own comfort to get it.

The stocky master nodded his balding head. "Enjoy, sir."

With a distracted nod, Conrad lifted his drink to his lips. The sweet burn of the liquor urged him to forget Ahria's presence, and he moved towards the open archways to the card tables. They were positioned on one of the floating additions to the structure of the ship, and he stepped down into the quiet, focused space. His coat draped over his arm, he silently observed the various games as he made his way along the outside wall.

He settled on a simple game of nines, which didn't require much thought beyond staying below the face count of the others' cards.

Time blurred between a nursed glass of brandy, small plates of expensive cured meats and cheeses, and each round of cards. He won a few games, lost a few more, but when he'd finally finished his drink, he'd nearly broken even on his coin. Popping a piece of soft, herbed bread into his mouth, he pocketed his coin. The meager loss of the cost of his meal was well worth the evening away from the pressures of captaining. In Siren's Song, no one cared about his rank or responsibilities. They only cared about the next hand. It was a beautiful way to enjoy an evening to himself.

As he crossed towards the exit, beginning to pull on his coat, a voice murmured beside him from the bar.

"Leaving already, Captain?" The stowaway mouse quirked an eyebrow at him, sitting on a stool that she swiveled around to face him. Her mug of frothy ale was half-empty, but her eyes were sharp.

A now familiar tension passed through his muscles, encouraging a falter in his step as he faced the bar. He tried to look surprised, but the comfort of the evening made acting harder. The only part of it he hadn't expected was her speaking to him. "Afraid I am. Have a good evening."

"Won't you stay? Drinking alone is rather... lonely. Though, I suppose a man who nurses one glass of brandy all night likely isn't much of a drinking partner." Ahria tilted her head, posture relaxed, despite the subtle challenge.

Has she been watching me?

Conrad hesitated, curiosity burning in his gut. Shrugging back out of his coat, he tossed it over the vacant stool beside Ahria. He didn't know what game she was playing at, but damned if he wasn't going to try to figure it out.

Her smile looked more genuine than the ones he'd seen before. "Were the cards kind to you this evening?"

"Not particularly. But they weren't cruel, either, which I take as a positive conclusion for the evening." It took a brief glance to make eye contact with the tavern master, and a quick lift of his hand for the balding man to pour him another brandy. The crystal clinked onto the bar top before he took it in his hand. "How was the pocket ball?"

Ahria narrowed her eyes at him, but the expression was playful. "So you did see me here. And you didn't leave. I'm shocked." She said the last word slowly, then sipped her drink.

"Why would I leave?"

"Well, of all the people I imagine you wanting to be near, I cannot possibly be one of them." She cleared her throat and opened her mouth to say more, but he interrupted.

"I'm sitting here, at this bar, right now, aren't I?" He smirked as he lifted his drink to his lips. For her benefit, he took a larger gulp than any he'd taken before. The burn tingled across his tongue and into his throat, but he savored the flavor of it.

Another hesitant, genuine smile from her. "Fair point." She paused. "Pocket ball was fine. Lucrative enough for me to enjoy another drink or... four. If I so choose."

"Very lucrative then, considering I was under the impression that you were a little hard pressed for coin just a few days ago. When you *blackmailed* me into paying your boyfriend again."

Color touched her cheeks, and she looked away. "Every iron mark helps."

"You must have an important reason for traveling to

Treama." Conrad tapped the glass with the soft part of his index finger.

Ahria stared at her ale long enough that he wondered if she would answer him at all. "I'm trying to find my father." She met his gaze, then motioned to his brandy with her eyes. "I pictured you more of a whisky drinker."

Conrad shrugged. "I like the sweetness." He drained the last of the second glass.

She chuckled. "Trying to prove something, Captain?"

"Perhaps. Or indulging, since you're clearly picking up the tab for this one." He tapped the glass again. "I was going to have another anyway, just back in my cabin where the booze is free."

Ahria let out a laugh, grinning in a way much different than she had at the stranger during pocket ball, and it sent lightning down his spine. "I suppose I deserve that."

Again, curiosity got the better of him. "Who was that man you were playing with? It looked like he was teaching you the game."

Huffing, she shook her head. "I'm sure it did. And I don't know, honestly. I never got his name."

"But how much coin did you swindle him out of?"

She shrugged. "Enough to ease my stress, but not enough to draw suspicion." Her eyes glittered. "With Davros only earning half, I needed to make up the difference somehow."

"And your boyfriend approves of this tactic?" It wasn't

any of Conrad's business, yet he'd noticed how fiercely protective the man was of Ahria. He'd been reprimanded by Leiura after growling at one of his crewmates, actually *growling*, when the man had made an offhand comment about Ahria's backside.

It is a good one, though.

Ahria scowled as she drank her ale. "Davros doesn't *own* me. I will do what I must to get by, even if it displeases him." Tapping the bar top, she gestured for the tavern master to refill her mug.

Her exposed skin showcased the raw muscle in her arms, honed through some sort of training, he was sure. Her ability with daggers certainly suggested she didn't need anyone else looking after her. If anything, Davros seemed an accessory to her. Something convenient.

Her way to get to Treama, perhaps?

Conrad leaned forward, putting his hand over Ahria's mug before the master could refill it. "Have you ever had Xaxos fire wine?"

Ahria's brow rose. "No. Trying to spend my coin faster?"

"This one will be on me. The second glass, however, is on you. You'll want another."

"All right, Captain," she murmured, the corner of her lips twitching.

The tavern master must have eavesdropped because the twisted glass bottle appeared on the bar top beside them. The cork gave a satisfying pop before the master placed two smaller glasses on either side. Before pouring, he swirled the bottle around, the liquid inside splashing up into the small crevices and curves.

Ahria leaned an elbow on the bar top, touching the pendant that hung from a fine silver chain around her neck. She turned it over, pressing her thumb to the front before letting it go. It fell back against her skin, and he stared at the jewelry. He'd never seen anything like it before, the type of flower it depicted or the craftsmanship. An opal-carved bloom with inlaid sapphires along the stamen.

The tavern master filled their glasses nearly to the brim, carefully sliding them across the bar towards each of them.

Ahria reached towards her glass, but Conrad caught her wrist gently.

"Let it sit. It'll taste better."

She looked at his hand on her wrist, then at him. "What's this from?" She turned her wrist in his grip and slid her touch to his palm, where a faint, inch-wide scar ran across it.

"Nothing glorious or impressive." He flexed his hand on impulse, but opened it again for her. The touch of her fingertips along the old scar felt distant. "Tried to grab some rigging that'd come loose up in the mast. Was too heavy and falling too fast, the hemp tore right through my skin."

Ahria ran her thumb over it. "Must have hurt."

"Hells yeah it did. I bawled like a baby for a good two

hours, though the second hour was me pretending to sleep in my bunk so I didn't completely lose face in front of the crew. I was fifteen."

She laughed, then gave him a playful pout. "You poor thing. Why weren't you wearing gloves?"

"Older sailors didn't. But I didn't realize at the time it's because they have calluses as thick as the rope itself."

Ahria made a face and shuddered. "Sounds lovely."

"Comes with a life at sea."

"Why aren't your hands so callused, then?" She eyed his hand again, turning it over like she was looking for evidence of the life he spoke of.

"Ah, well that comes with the luxury of a high rank during said life at sea." He'd almost forgotten she still held his hand until she'd begun turning it over. The casual touch suddenly felt foreign, though not uncomfortably so. He contemplated pulling away, or clearing his throat, but neither came.

"Ah, yes, the nameless captain." She rolled her lips together and let go of him as if coming to a similar conclusion. She flexed her hands, then slid one playfully towards the untouched fire wine. "Has it breathed long enough?"

As if the physical action was finally catching up to his brain, he coughed and cleared his throat. "Yes, I think so." He reached for the short glass, lifting it between them. "To prolonged mysteries." He proposed. "Like names and combat-trained stowaway mice."

Ahria chuckled, rolling her eyes as she clinked her glass against his. "I'm not a mystery, but thank you for not calling me a rat again." She sniffed her drink before sipping. Her expression distorted, and she coughed, breathing deeper before staring at the drink. "Are you sure this is safe to consume?"

He smiled, not hiding it like he had in his cabin while she blackmailed him. Her audacity in the moment had been remarkably amusing, despite how much he suffered for it. Though, she hardly had enough information to truly condemn him. In a place like Nolan, he'd be back on his ship and halfway out to sea before anyone could pin him down.

Instead of answering, he allowed the sweet, tangy scent of the spiced drink into his nostrils. It stung even there before he tipped his head back, emptying the entire glass into his mouth. The burn was twice that of his brandy, but the sharp sweetness hovered on his tongue even after he'd swallowed. After a moment, the cleaner aftertaste settled in.

Ahria's brow lifted as she watched him, subtly shaking her head before a determined look overcame her face. She followed his example, emptying her small glass in one swig.

"That first flavor there," Conrad tried not to laugh at her cringe. "That's the famous desert berry that grows only outside Xaxos. Then the second which should be hitting you now... That's rose sugar. Then the final note." He lifted the empty glass back to his nose, taking a deep inhale of the remaining alcohol still clinging to the crystal. "That's—"

"Pepper oak?" Ahria licked her lower lip, putting the glass down.

His brow lifted. "Impressive." He slid his glass onto the bar beside hers. The tavern master had stepped away, leaving the bottle of fire wine on the counter beside them. Though Conrad had no delusions that he'd be able to sneak a refill without the man noticing.

"In the village where I grew up, Mr. Bennis used pepper oak to make barrels for whisky makers. Nothing quite like that taste, though." Ahria reached for the bottle, and the tavern master looked at her as soon as her fingers touched the glass. She offered him a broad smile, pouring their glasses full without breaking eye contact with the man. He nodded once at her, and she returned the gesture.

"No, I suppose it is rather distinct." Conrad eyed the full glasses, realistically considering how much more he could take and still make it back to the ship without stumbling into the water.

One more.

"So, your father. He's in Treama? Pretty crazy time to be visiting Ziona on holiday right now." The news of Ziona's political strife had made its way across the sea, even to their always-moving vessel. Of course, hailing from Ziona himself and flying the country's flag made the topic of the military coup one that complete strangers loved to bring up in casual conversation at any tavern. But he'd never known anything different for his homeland. The coup had started before he was even born. It was the sudden shift in power, a new parliament rumored to be reinstating the monarchy, that was strange.

It doesn't affect me and my boat, so there's no point in caring.

"Yes. Well, no. I don't actually know where he is, other than in Ziona. I'm hoping to track him down, since he's bound to draw attention." Her voice lowered as she spoke, and she stared at the fire wine with a thoughtful expression.

"Again, seems like a bad time to be drawing any kind of attention there. Everyone is on edge during transitions of power. I'd almost rather not go to Treama, but I go where the trade is." Conrad considered the bit of information Ahria had almost offered, suggesting her father would be of interest to the common person, but opted not to pursue it.

No need to give her reason to stop talking.

Ahria shrugged, then met his gaze. "I've already buried one father this month. I'd like to see that he's safe, so I don't need to bury another." Her throat bobbed. "Sorry. I don't mean to..." Reaching for the glass of fire wine, she downed it in a gulp, wincing less than the previous time.

"Don't mean to what?" Conrad retrieved his glass, but

held it where the scent could overpower his senses and make his sinuses tingle.

"Put a damper on things. My *sob story* isn't your problem." A smile spread over her face, but it didn't reach her eyes.

"Maybe not, but I am sorry for what you're enduring. I never knew my father enough to mourn losing him, so I can't imagine what you must feel." The words slipped out before he realized what he said. The fire wine stung as it hit the back of his throat in his hasty gulp. He rarely thought about his long-deceased father, let alone bring him up in conversation. With a stranger.

A stranger who'd *blackmailed* him.

Maybe one more was the wrong choice.

Then again, he'd blurted it prior to taking that drink.

Ahria paused, looking at him in the now familiar way that felt like she stared into his soul. "You seem to have done pretty well for yourself, regardless."

"Had my mum. That's all I needed." He shrugged as he returned the glass to the bar again. His mind had begun to haze, the comfortable lull of drunkenness following the sweet taste of the fire wine still on his tongue. "She worked her ass off to raise me right on her own." Imagining his mother's smile sent a crack through his chest. Guilt and anger. Then he just simply missed her.

"She sounds like a remarkable woman." Ahria touched

her necklace again. "She must be proud of you."

Why am I telling her all this?

"Gods can only hope." He considered the twisted bottle on the counter again, licking his lower lip. His hand itched to reach for it again, but he tucked it into his pocket instead and looked to Ahria. He made no effort to conceal his look at the necklace, gesturing with his chin. "That's a fancy piece you've got there... That could probably buy out half of Dawn Chaser right here and now if you wanted to. For a girl without coin, you've got a quick way to fortune if you sold that trinket."

Ahria smiled. "Are you offering me a partnership on your ship?" She lifted her chin and mock-saluted him. "Captain nameless, the second, at your service."

He laughed, shaking his head. It caused a dizzying wave to crash over him. "Hells no, Leiura's all the partner I can handle. And it's Conrad. Though, I've gotten rather attached to you calling me Captain."

A little voice in the back of his head repeated his phrase back to him in a nattering tone, *I've gotten rather attached to you calling me Captain*, and he could have slammed his forehead into the bar top.

Her mouth fell agape briefly, and she gave a wider smile. "It's a pleasure to meet you, Captain Conrad."

"You met me a week ago. Name isn't gonna change that."

"But did I?" Ahria tilted her head. "Because I don't think

you met *me*, so I dare say it wouldn't be a far reach to say I hadn't truly met *you*, either."

"Didn't I?" Genuine confusion tangled up with his suffering sobriety.

"I met a mysterious ship captain, and you met a stowaway. Neither of these things makes up who we are, do they?"

"Ah." Conrad tapped the side of his nose in understanding. "I see now. And I suppose not. I suspect you are a great many more things than a stowaway mouse."

Ahria pulled the necklace away from her sternum and looked down at it. "It was a gift. One I will never part with." She closed her fist around it. "Not for all the money in Pantracia." She smirked. "Not even for *half your ship*."

Smiling, Conrad eyed the bottle on the counter again with a brief flicker of temptation. After a moment, he shook his head and slid one of his florins onto the bar top. He'd meant to go home only shy the one he'd paid upon entry, but somehow the price of the evening still felt worth it.

Ahria reached for her coin purse, but Conrad waved his hand.

"I got it. Keep the coin for finding that father of yours." He caught the tavern master's eye and pushed the florin further onto the counter. The master nodded his thanks as he crossed over, tipping the coin off the back of the counter into his palm. It jangled with the rest of the coins as it landed in his pocket.

She smiled and stood, walking a few feet away while he pocketed the change from the tavern master. Retrieving her cloak from the rack, she pulled it over her shoulders with a slight sway. "I should... turn in." He could tell she almost said more, perhaps something about Davros, but the words didn't come.

He tugged on his own coat, forcing his steps to be steady as he crossed towards her. "I'll accompany you for the walk. Together, we can make sure neither of us end up in the water." Before he could fully comprehend his own intention, he offered his arm to her.

Ahria hesitated before taking it, resting her hand on his forearm. "Spoiling the fun, already? And on such a lovely night for a swim."

Chapter 7

A BOOM CRASHED THROUGH AHRIA'S awareness, jolting her from sleep.

She groaned, pulling the thin pillow over her ears and rolling onto her stomach. She'd worked late the night before with Orlin, and her shift that day didn't start until noon.

The obnoxious bell tolled with renewed fury, and she growled.

Fast footsteps through the halls made her pause, though, and she lifted her head. "Hey, you," she called to a young man running past. "What's going on?"

"We're about to be intercepted." He hurried off, leaving her gaping at nothing.

"Shit." Ahria yanked her boots on, not bothering with the laces before wrapping her cloak over her shoulder. Racing towards the deck, she squinted at the sun as her eyes adjusted.

Crew hurried everywhere, arming themselves, though no arrows flew.

Where is Davros?

Ahria scanned the crew for him, failing to recall what shift Conrad had given him that day.

Davros stood, sword in hand, with more of the crew near where the other ship angled to broadside them.

It was a bigger ship, but thinner with a lower bow. And it was gaining fast.

Too fast.

In an instant, Davros was at her side. "Get below deck," he whispered. "We've got trouble."

"I can see that." Ahria refused to budge when he tried to guide her. "I'm not going anywhere." Before he could complain, and he *would* complain, she took off across the deck towards the helm where Conrad stood.

Ever since their evening at the tavern, she'd struggled with how to talk to him with others present. It resulted in her usually avoiding him, unsure how friendly to be.

She took the stairs to the upper deck two at a time, finding him standing with Leiura at the helm. The first mate looked particularly grumpy, her cropped red hair messy as if she, too, had been woken up by the alarms. Conrad's traditional cup of coffee sat on the top of the helm's pedestal, still steaming.

Ahria's instinct was to retreat since he wasn't alone, but he spotted her before she could.

"Ahria, you shouldn't be here." The captain shook his head and looked at Leiura. "It's in my quarters, under the glass shelves. Do a better job hiding it, will you?"

Leiura nodded and took off down the opposite stairs.

"What's going on?" Ahria glanced at the oncoming ship, then back at him.

Conrad ignored her, lifting a spy glass to peer at the ship behind them. "Bastards. How'd they know our course?" he muttered, snapping the spyglass shut before he went to the helm. The crew there moved aside without question as Conrad took hold of the wheel and threw it hard to the right.

The ship gradually tilted starboard. The wheel thunked as it hit its full rotation.

"Who?" Ahria stepped fully onto the upper deck, but kept her distance.

"Gelsen, get Yelder. And tell her to bring the red fletched ones this time." Conrad lurched forward as his mug began to slide off the pedestal, catching it before it could tumble to the deck.

When Gelsen ran off and the captain still didn't acknowledge her, Ahria sighed and turned to descend the stairs.

"Old rival." Conrad's words seemed pointed at her. "Though I thought we'd make it to Treama before he even knew we were in the Dul'Idur. He... enjoys relieving us of certain commodities on board."

Ahria abandoned her retreat and approached, touching the hilt of the dagger tucked into her bracer. "Not a friend, then," she murmured. "Are you expecting a fight?"

"Usually is one." His eyes flicked to her wrist as if he knew what she touched. "And while not a friend, not an enemy, either. Let's avoid the maiming and killing, please and thank you. Since I know there's no way you're going to stay below deck."

She let go of the weapon with a nod. "No killing or maiming, got it." Looking over the sea, she eyed the ship that kept gaining on them.

Conrad let go of the wheel and started spinning it the opposite direction until it thunked again. The ship turned hard once more, causing them to zigzag through the water.

Something whizzed through the air, and a ripping sound echoed from the sail above their heads. A small tear appeared in the canvas.

"Shit, was that a red one?" Conrad only let the ship remain at full port for a couple seconds before twisting back to the starboard.

"I couldn't tell." Ahria gripped the banister, furrowing her brow. "Do you know the captain?"

"Captain Warrin. A real son of a bitch with a hell of a temper." Conrad looked back at the ship again. He looked down towards the main deck, his face tight. "Where the hells is Yelder!"

"What does he want?"

"Little busy here." Conrad spun the wheel again.

Ahria pursed her lips, snatching the spyglass from the holster on the side of the helm. Striding away from Conrad as she extended it, she aimed at the oncoming ship and lifted it to her eye. At first, she focused on a crew member on the rigging, then altered to the helm where the captain stood. She studied his tricorn hat and clean cut white beard, and spied another man behind him.

They don't look like criminals.

The man behind the captain sidestepped, his face becoming visible, and she froze.

"Oh, shit." Ahria lowered the spyglass and chewed her lip before raising it again with a soft whimper. "No, no, no. Please don't let it be..." She focused on him again, and her heart skipped a beat.

The stranger from the tavern.

She stared at the man she'd hustled at pocket ball. The man she'd laughed with. She never got his name...

"Nymaera's breath," she whispered, gripping the banister as she tried to compose herself.

"That's a fair bit of cursing over there." Conrad only half turned to her as he held the wheel in one of the hard turn positions. "Everything all right?"

Ahria cringed, facing the captain. "This is my fault."

"Your fault?" He straightened, looking at the spyglass in her hand and then towards the ship pursuing them. Eyes narrowing, he focused back on her. "What'd you do?" A vein of anger flowed through his question.

Gulping, she shook her head. "I didn't know, I swear. That man on the ship, he's the one I played pocket ball with in Nolan. He asked what ship I was on, and where we were going and when... I didn't think..."

Conrad's expression changed to one of perturbed understanding. "Which man?"

Ahria offered him the spyglass. "The one beside that captain at the helm, with the short black beard."

He smacked the side of the wheel, and a piece of metal popped into place. As he let go of it, it started to rotate back before getting caught and holding its rotation. Moving towards the back of the ship, he snatched the spyglass from her hands and lifted it.

"Shit. Zelinger. You told Zelinger you were on the Dawn Chaser and headed to Treama. Providing the *exact* information needed to know the *exact* passage we'd be sailing at this *exact* time to my rival's first mate."

Ahria cringed again, dread churning her stomach. "I'm sorry. What can I do?"

"I think you've done quite enough." Conrad stomped back to the wheel, the metal hold snapping back as he took up the wheel again. "Just—"

Without waiting for the rest of his reprimand, Ahria descended the stairs to the main deck, pausing only briefly to look at the ship that had nearly overtaken them. Rushing to the stairs, she ignored a shout from Davros before returning below deck. The last thing she needed was Zelinger seeing her, so she'd spy from below the grate.

Maybe I can fix this.

Indistinct shouting continued on deck as Yelder finally emerged from the crew's sleeping quarters, still pulling her hair into a messy bun. She begrudgingly snatched her bow and a colorful quiver of arrows from a weapon rack across from Ahria. She didn't even acknowledge her before she stomped up the stairs, hardly looking like she was in enough of a hurry for whatever was going on.

The ship eventually slowed and stopped dead in the water. Wood groaned, and Ahria hurried to one of the small side hatches. Flinging it open, she peered out at the other ship, too close for anyone to see her. Above her head, a makeshift gangplank had been drawn from the attacking ship onto Dawn Chaser, and Ahria returned to look through the grate.

Both crews had assembled on Dawn Chaser's deck, one on either side of the mast. Conrad and Leiura stood beside the mast, almost directly above where Ahria peered up. The only steel she could see were two boarding axes, held by members of Warrin's crew.

Whatever Warrin aimed to steal from Conrad, she wanted to see it.

Then maybe I can get it back.

It hadn't been her intention to give away their location, since the first mate's questions were woven delicately into their flirtatious conversation. She thought she'd been swindling him out of some coin, but he'd stolen information from her. Her own daftness heated her blood, desperate for redemption.

She couldn't hear what Conrad was saying to the opposing captain, but the tones weren't friendly. The other ship's crew rushed up and down the stairs, holding Dawn Chaser hostage as they searched for whatever it was they wanted. As soon as someone approached the armory, where she stood, she hid behind a weapon rack, hood over her face.

Leiura's hiding job didn't hold up, and Warrin laughed. A rough, throaty sound full of gloating.

Exiting her hiding place, she peered up through the grate as one of his crew handed him a large black velvet box, at least two feet wide.

The captain's voice carried below. "Looks like I win this

one, Connie. Let's see you catch me without your sails."

Ahria cursed, listening to all the boot steps returning to the enemy ship.

Think, think.

She crossed to the open hatch, looking down at the water sloshing between the two large vessels. They nearly bumped together, leaving a gap of only six or so feet. Directly across from her, a port window hinted at her only option.

The boarding axes thunked against some part of Dawn Chaser, and the main mast beside her let out a protesting groan as weight shifted thanks to whatever Warrin's crew did.

The makeshift gangplank, made from old doors nailed together, bore two handles on the underside. She eyed them, then looked down again. "Gods, I must be insane."

Ahria climbed onto the narrow hatch ledge, took a deep breath, and leapt. She grabbed the handles just as someone stepped onto the gangplank again, and she hung still as they crossed. Swinging her legs, she built enough momentum so her boots could strike the port window.

It didn't budge, and she growled and tried again. On the fourth hit, it snapped open inward, barely wide enough for her to climb through. Another swing, and she let go, colliding with the enemy ship and grabbing onto the porthole. She pulled herself inside, landing in a cargo hold similar to Conrad's. Breathing hard, she forced the broken window shut.

Chapter 8

As Warrin sailed away, Conrad stalked back to his quarters. "I want that rigging fixed by nightfall."

Leiura rolled her eyes, but nodded. "I assume you're wanting to go after it."

"Hells yes I do, but you and I both know we have cargo due in Treama. And a certain pair we're looking to offload there, too." Conrad paused at his door, looking back to his first mate who'd followed him there.

"They can wait," Leiura mumbled. "Warrin looks like he's headed for Haven Port."

"Of course he is. Knows damn well about the bounties on me and is taunting me closer to Feyor." Conrad waved his hand, trying to persuade himself to let go of the desire to get his property back. "It can wait. Let Warrin think he's won for a while."

Treama first. That can't wait.

Ever since Ahria had told him about her search for her father, Conrad hadn't been able to stop thinking about it. With the political turmoil and her suggestion that her father would be of interest, he didn't want to risk her genuinely losing another parent. There hadn't been a chance to ask her any more about her father since their night drinking together. She might have been avoiding him, but he hadn't pursued talking to her, either. As he thought of her, he remembered the horror on her face when she realized her part in them being found.

I better go explain to her what's going on...

"Captain!" Davros rushed onto the main deck from below, his dark skin pallid. The crew gave him wary glances, but the young man paid them no heed as he hurried closer. "Captain, I think we have a problem."

Looking at the man, Conrad tried to wrestle with his general distaste for Davros. He hadn't quite been able to pin down what it was about the man that agitated him. "What?" While he managed to steel his expression, he failed at hiding the annoyance from his voice.

"It's Ahria. She's not on the ship." Davros's tone was hollow.

Conrad's blood ran as cold as the icy waters below. "What?" The question lost its previous annoyance.

Davros shook his head. "I can't find her, and there's a hatch in the starboard side of the armory that's been left open."

"She fall in or something? We ain't moving, you should..."

Before Leiura finished, Conrad spun and ran up the stairs to the helm two at a time. Snatching the spyglass, he hurriedly aimed it at Warrin's ship as it grew more distant. The angle still allowed him to see the port side, and he scanned each and every inch of it for her. He almost missed the uneven cracked hatch towards the aft of the ship.

"Son of a bitch..." He lowered the spyglass and shoved it towards Leiura. "Change of plans. Rigging needs to be done in two hours, and chart our course to Haven Port."

"What's going on? Where is she?" Davros joined them at the helm, worry on his expression.

"Your girlfriend seems to think she's a professional stowaway now." Conrad glared at Davros, wishing he could blame him instead of himself.

If I hadn't gotten so angry with her...

"Are you saying she's on that other ship? Why would she do that?" Davros's tone took on a frustrated air. "Damn it. Why would she..."

"Damn good question. I intend to ask her. And assuming they don't throw her overboard first, might just do so myself this time," Conrad grumbled as he stomped back down the stairs. He considered his cabin door before turning towards the mast and pushing up his sleeves.

Davros scowled, his jaw flexing at the threat. "With all due respect, Captain, you'd have to throw me over, too." He huffed. "And possibly Orlin."

"If you don't start making yourself useful, that might happen sooner rather than later." Conrad turned from Davros, untangling a rope from its bollard at the base of the mast. He didn't hesitate before moving on to the next, the slackened sails rustling as they lowered to the deck.

Davros's footsteps sounded a moment later, finally taking him back to his duties. His movements were abrupt and his jaw set tight as he helped loosen the rigging.

The captain caught himself glowering in Davros's direction, where his tall shape was shrouded behind the lowering sail. More of the crew had joined on the mainsail, rapidly untying the damaged ropes to replace with new.

The fresh hemp brought back memories, reminding Conrad of when he'd first been taught how to tie knots and rig sails. Tiny splinters broke through his skin, and he suddenly missed the calluses Ahria had pointed out that he no longer had.

The thought of her, in the dim light of Siren's Song's bar, brought warmth to his limbs like the fire wine. And his distaste for Davros's close proximity to him increased.

A man like him is never going to keep hold of a woman like her.

The thought deepened his frown, but for a different reason.

And I have no business thinking about such things.

After a shout from one of the crew on the mast above, he caught the dropped rope and looped it around a bollard before pulling. The strain in his muscles quickly banished his thoughts of Ahria and Xaxos fire wine.

The repairs to the sails took the better part of two hours. Davros didn't say a word to Conrad the entire time, despite their close working proximity, though his lips were often pursed into a hard line.

By the end of it, Conrad and most of the crew had stripped layers of clothing, despite the lingering winter chill. Sweat beaded on his chest, turning to a cool trail as the work subsided. The sails billowed with a satisfying ripple of canvas and wind.

Running his dirty shirt over his bare shoulders, Conrad met Leiura's eyes from where she stood at the helm. He knew the look almost immediately and only scowled back at her and nodded. Even if it'd been her suggestion first to proceed to Haven Port, he could tell she questioned his reasoning for his change of order.

"We should drop more sail." Davros failed to control the irritation in his tone as he looked back and forth between

Conrad and Leiura. "It's bad enough she'll have to spend a night on that ship." Something else hid beneath his anger. Worry. Perhaps even a touch of fear.

What will Warrin do if he finds her?

"She's smart, she'll be fine. And even if she's caught, that girl could talk her way out of a Helgathian prison." Conrad rubbed at the blisters forming on his palms.

Davros straightened, his brow furrowing. He hesitated in speaking, looking confused. "How could you possibly know that?"

"Call it a hunch." Conrad didn't look at Davros as he wove around the man, starting towards the doors of his cabin. "Person doesn't get where I am without being able to read people." He lifted his chin at his first mate as she stepped down from the helm. "Take her to full sail, Leiura. It will take a while to catch up to Warrin."

"Aye, Captain." Leiura kept her opinions from her voice this time. "But we won't reach Haven Port until tomorrow evening, even if the wind stays with us. We'll get turned away from the dock if it's after sundown. You know Delkest."

"Then we'll anchor just outside the sea wall until morning. Start putting together a crew for the longboat. We'll sneak up on Prosperity like they did us in Lazuli."

"Water's a might bit colder here than Lazuli, Cap." Merril's voice came from behind Conrad, forcing him to hold in a surprised flinch.

The captain hadn't even noticed him approaching, and suddenly the deck in front of his cabin felt far too crowded. "Doesn't make a difference. I gave my orders, or do I need to make them more direct for you, Quartermaster?" An edge crept into his voice, his chest tightening.

"What else can I do to help, Captain?" Davros's tone softened, his hands in his pockets.

Leiura waved a hand. "Your shift ended a half hour ago."

"I know, but..." Davros shifted his stance, eyes pleading with the first mate. "I don't rightly feel like relaxing right now. Perhaps I can relieve Vesti in the crows' nest?"

The worry on his face crippled the anger in Conrad, renewing his own anxiety for the same thing Davros worried about. Digging his nails into the blister on his palm, Conrad urged the sensation back towards frustration. He wouldn't let himself be consumed with worry. It wouldn't do anyone any good.

Besides, not my place. Davros has the right.

Conrad lifted a hand as Leiura opened her mouth to answer, the knitting of her eyebrows proof of the reprimand she was preparing for Davros. They both knew an overworked sailor led to injuries, and frequently, more than his own.

"Go. But keep Vesti up there in case you start dozing."

"Thank you, Captain." Davros nodded, something fiery still in the back of his gaze as he turned and climbed the rigging.

Leiura clicked her tongue. "Stupid." She muttered it low enough that Merril didn't hear as he started up the stairs to the helm.

Conrad shook his head as he stormed over to the decorative double doors of his cabin. "I don't need it from you, too." He pushed through, and before he could latch the door behind him, Leiura's boot wedged into the doorframe.

Andi's tail whacked the floor in a happy rhythm as she lifted her head.

"Now's the time to be smart, Cap." Leiura met his gaze. "What's gotten into you? I can't be a good first mate if I don't understand where your head's at."

"I'll get it sorted." Conrad kicked at her boot.

Leiura stepped back, and Conrad closed the door quickly before she could get another word in. His lock clicked into place, the sound foreign with how rarely he secured it. There was little reason to on his ship, and his crew was always welcome. But right now...

Conrad whipped his loose shirt from where it rested over his shoulder, having completely forgotten his chest was bare. But in the humid, warm air of his cabin, the pressure felt good on his skin. With the galley directly below, his cabin never fell victim to the cold temperatures outside. Instead, it caused fog to constantly cloud the diamond shaped panes of his back windows.

Andi rushed past him, weaving around his legs to jump up onto the bed as if she sensed he was heading there. Plopping her head on top of her paws, she whined as he stopped beside it rather than joining her.

"Just a second." Conrad chuckled and hefted the side of his mattress up with one hand while fishing out the small leather-bound journal hidden beneath it.

Andi groaned as she pawed to keep on top of the mattress before he dropped it back into place.

Thumping the binding against his leg as if it would somehow organize his rampant thoughts, he chewed the inside of his lip. "What's gotten into me?" He eyed Andi as she wagged her tail, still happily settled on top of his bed.

The dog crawled closer to him, nudging his hand with her nose until he started to pet her.

Flipping the journal open with one hand, he stared at his last entry. He'd written it the night he'd returned from Siren's Song, his handwriting loose with his lingering drunkenness, yet lacking the usual hesitation of his pen. Writing didn't come easy to him, but it provided an outlet when he needed it. Looking at Andi, he sighed. "Well, pup, I might be in a bit of trouble."

Chapter 9

AHRIA STARED AT THE DRINK in front of her, still untouched. The amber liquid sloshed as she slid the glass closer, holding it but not drinking. Her mind felt foggy, retracing her steps over Warrin's ship. Her useless, fruitless steps.

No matter where she looked, she couldn't find the black box. Or whatever had been inside. Not that it made a difference.

The captain won't come for me. He probably has no idea where I am, anyway.

She only knew where she was because she'd overheard the dockmaster say it after she had the good sense to sneak off Prosperity. There was no telling what Warrin would have done if she'd been found, and retreating to the city as soon as the evening dark settled in had made the most sense. She'd have to find her way to Treama on her own to meet Davros. The slight bulge in her cloak pocket now felt silly, but it'd been an absent thought to purchase the gift from a vendor.

Chewing her lower lip, she finally sipped the rum. It slouched her shoulders, and a lump formed in her throat.

What was I thinking?

She wasn't a traveler. She wasn't a warrior or assassin or even a petty thief. She belonged in her small town, and nothing more. Talon may have taught her how to fight, how to use leverage, and how to get what she needed, but... She'd failed. In almost every aspect. And the only reason she still breathed was because of Conrad's leniency and Warrin's inability to notice the mouse that she was, scurrying around his ship.

Her chest weighed with the death of her father, though it had hit her adoptive brother harder. He'd actually returned to town days before his father's passing, but their relationship was tenuous at best. From a young age, he'd resented her, pushing her to have a closer relationship with Talon rather than Lorin. Not that it mattered anymore.

He hadn't even stuck around a day longer than Lorin's funeral, leaving her alone in Gallisville.

Now she'd lost Davros, too, stranded in a foreign country without another soul in the world to keep her company.

The tangy scent of the trade port permeated through the

open dining hall, the air hanging with a haze of smoke from the stove. There was no division between the packed tables and the kitchen, where a portly woman bustled from counter to counter, smacking the squirrelly looking barkeep with a towel whenever he stepped in her path. Thin timbers of natural birch, still with bits of unworn bark on it, stood as columns to support exposed beams of the roof.

Every table was filled, mismatched chairs shoved close together to fill the tavern well past its usual capacity. And the cook's growing irritation with the barkeep further proved there were more patrons than the single room tavern was accustomed to.

Swallowing hard, Ahria clenched her jaw to keep the glassiness from her eyes. She needed to be on her game without any allies, and that took focus. Not tears.

But what was she thinking when she'd decided to cross the continent and sea to find Talon? She didn't have the skills necessary. The connections. The experience.

Definitely not the experience.

Pots banged against each other in a raucous as people passed by the tavern, shouting gleeful verses of some ballad into the night.

The last night of winter. The dawn of the next year. The first ever she would begin alone.

Utterly and pathetically alone.

Ahria took another sip, shivering as a cold wind gusted

through the place with the brief opening of the tavern's front door. Pulling her cloak tighter, she swiveled on her stool to put her back to the door. Even though she couldn't stomach drinking her rum with any semblance of speed, she'd devoured an entire plate of roasted pheasant and vegetables. Plus a side of baked butter biscuits and cinnamon twisted bread. Her stomach finally stopped begging for more food, and Davros's teasing tone floated through her mind. "You eat more than you weigh."

She smirked, but the expression promptly faded.

At least I had my coin on me.

Someone bumped into her back, jostling her forward enough to spill rum from her glass onto the bar top.

She closed her eyes, willing patience.

"Let me get that." The barmaid's rushed voice made her open her eyes.

Ahria lifted her glass. "Thank you."

The woman wiped beneath it, then the bottom of the glass, and took the empty plates that'd donned her meal. She hesitated before asking. "Anything else to eat?"

Ahria shook her head. "No, but thank you."

The woman carried on, overwhelmed with patrons, and Ahria felt grateful for the lack of forced conversation.

She'd need to move on, soon, too. The inn upstairs was fully booked for the night with the festivities, and she wondered if she'd be able to find a room anywhere in the city.

Won't be my first time sleeping under the stars.

Sliding enough iron marks over the counter for the food, she left her half-full glass of rum on the counter and made her way outside.

The evening air felt crisp in her lungs, waking her drowsy mind.

She pulled her hood over her head, striding through the busy streets as endless streams of people walked in every direction. Colorful streamers trailed behind children on their parent's shoulders, candy floss adding an odd sweetness to the seaside air.

In all the movement, the slow shift of a black shadow beneath the hanging sign of one of the shops caught her attention. Trying to watch the hooded figure in the corner of her eye, she dared a more direct glance as the person stepped down from the elevated doorway and stalked in her direction.

Ahria sucked in a deeper breath and shoved her coin purse deeper into the inner pocket of her cloak. She pushed past people, but with the crowds so dense, she struggled to move any faster than the rest of them. Breath felt harder to draw with so many so close. There were more people in this single block than her entire home village.

She just needed to find an inn, get off the streets, and wait out the crowds until morning. Then she could find a ship... get to Treama... reunite with Davros.

Conrad would be long gone, and the thought made a surprisingly heavy rock sink to the bottom of her stomach.

She contemplated checking behind her to see if the sensation of being watched was pure instinct telling her that hooded figure followed her, but she shook the feeling away.

I'm paranoid because of the crowds. It's nothing.

A vice suddenly closed on her arm just above her elbow and her heart leapt into her throat. Without conscious thought, her training flooded back to her, just like it had when the quartermaster had tried to take her dagger. Talon's instructions rang through her mind as her elbow shot back, catching her captor in the sternum.

The tightness on her arm slacked, his grip broken with a burst of surprised breath. He stumbled back, face lost in the shadows of his hood.

Before he could attack again, she ran.

Ahria ducked low, weaving through the throngs of people by avoiding the width of shoulders in her way. She spied an alley to her left and aimed for it, racing past oblivious partiers to escape into the darkness. No one else occupied the narrow alley, giving her plenty of space to lengthen her stride and sprint for the fence at the dead end. Jumping, she grabbed the top and pulled herself up.

"Whoa, hold up, Mouse." A wheeze accompanied the

familiar deep voice, and she looked back. "It's just me."

Ahria stilled, crouched on top of the wooden fence, and stared at the man. Her eyebrows knitted, and she let her boots slip off the side to land back within the alley. "Conrad?" she whispered, disbelief dulling her senses.

The captain tilted his chin back, opening his face to the dim light of the alley way, but didn't push back his hood. He pulled down a thick scarf he'd wrapped around his throat and shoulders beneath the cloak. "Who else would be crazy enough to chase you into a dark alley like this? This is where people get murdered."

Relief crashed through her without mercy, and Ahria nearly let out a sob as she propelled herself at him. She collided into him, flinging her arms around his shoulders as she breathed, "You came for me."

Conrad's entire body went rigid beneath her, his stiff shoulders shrugging off her hug. He shifted his hands to her biceps, gripping her hard like he had in the crowd. "What were you thinking?"

She blanched, recoiling from his rough touch. "What?" Her memory graced her with the image of her boarding the enemy's ship. "I was..." The anger in his expression made her step back. "I was trying to get it back."

He's still pissed at me.

"You could have gotten yourself killed. Warrin isn't nearly as kind to stowaways. If he or Zelinger had found you..."

There was something else in the anger, but she couldn't recognize it. "You didn't even know what you were looking for."

Ahria frowned. "But they didn't find me." She gritted her teeth. "I was looking for a black box. *That's* why you're here, isn't it?" Her body chilled as she backed up further. "You're not here looking for me, you're here for your cargo."

"What?" He tensed again, dropping his hands to his side, the tattered scarf still in his grip. "Are you kidding? We were about to continue on to Treama until your fool of a boyfriend came running up in a panic and we realized where you were. I wouldn't have come to Haven Port for that *thing*. Not with the bounties." There was still fervor in his tone, but he didn't move.

She stared at him, crossing her arms. "Then where is Davros? Why isn't he with you?"

"We split up to search this gods forsaken city for you. Ain't no way we'd find you if we stuck together with it being Winter's End."

Her shoulders slowly relaxed again, and she muttered, "I didn't find it. So go ahead and yell at me some more."

"I'm not..." His tone remained loud but he trailed off. He rolled his shoulders as if actively working to control whatever anger still reigned in him. "I'm sorry. Yelling at you is what got us into this in the first place." His stormy eyes met hers in the dimness. "I... didn't mean for you to blame yourself. Or to make you think that you had to *stow away* on another ship."

Ahria looked at her feet. "I just wanted to fix my mistake. I didn't think you'd be angry if I put myself in jeopardy. You have no reason to care what happens to me."

"Ahria." He stepped forward, but paused after only one. His jaw tensed in the shadow of his hood and he shook his head. "I appreciate that you wanted to help, I do... but your safety is not worth a hat."

"But I—" Ahria's gaze shot back to him, her mouth agape. "I'm sorry. Did you say... a hat?"

He held out his hands in a placating gesture. "I told you it wasn't worth your safety. It's a... game of sorts me and Warrin have been playing for the better part of two years. Nothing of worth was ever in danger."

Her jaw worked as she held her tongue, unexpected fury scorching through her. Taking three strides towards him, she used both hands to shove his chest. "You yelled at me over a hat!" She gaped at him, unsure whether to cry or laugh. "That's not funny. I could have died!"

He rocked with her push, but didn't lose a step. "I didn't *really* yell. And it's a very heated game. I told you your safety wasn't worth it. You should have told me what you were thinking before just jumping onto a stranger's ship."

Ahria sighed, shaking her head with a frustrated growl. She glanced at the arms that had refused to return her embrace and yearned for the denied comfort. Her chin trembled, and she rolled her lips together as she turned away.

I will not cry in front of him.

A gentle pressure settled on top of her shoulders. "Hey. Are you all right?" Conrad's presence behind her grew more palpable as he took a step closer.

"No," she whispered, vision blurring as she faced him again and stared at the clasp of his cloak.

Conrad squeezed her right shoulder, and dipped his head lower to try to catch her eyes. "Are you hurt?" He examined her in the same fashion as when they'd first met. "If any of Warrin's crew laid a finger on you..."

Ahria let out a mirthless laugh. "Nothing like that..." She swiped a hand under her eyes to catch the tears before they could roll down her cheeks. "I'm halfway across Pantracia, with a single ally. Weeks ago, I buried one father, and the other might be dead, for all I know. And up until five minutes ago, I thought I was stranded in this place and that I'd never see... any of you again, and..." She blinked back more tears, but they kept falling. Using her cloak, she wiped them again. "I just want to go home. But it's not home anymore."

His stony expression softened, his thumb gliding over the seam of her cloak. He was silent for a moment, then opened his mouth before closing it again without speaking.

Clearing her throat, Ahria shook her head and took a deep breath. "Can we go back to the ship?" She met his gaze, forcing herself not to waiver. "Then we can just forget all this."

"I'm not much of a forgetter."

Ahria huffed. "Maybe you can try, for the sake of my pride. I doubt it will take long, anyway, after you drop me off in Treama."

"I don't think you give yourself enough credit, little Mouse." Conrad's hand lifted from her shoulder for a brief moment before it settled back into the same spot again. "I don't think I'm going to forget a woman who stowed away on my ship, only to stow away on another trying to get my hat back from my old crewmate."

She narrowed her eyes at him. "And failed at both."

He clicked his tongue. "Considering I didn't fish you out of the waters of the Dul'Idur, I'd say you succeeded at least in part. I don't doubt you'd master just about anything you put your mind to."

Ahria contemplated his words before tilting her head. "Did you and Davros come into town without any of your crew?"

Pursing his lips, Conrad's hand slipped from her shoulder before he tucked it into the pocket of his cloak. "Dawn Chaser didn't make it in time to get a slip in port. She's anchored off the southeast point. Crew gets to watch the Winter's End celebration from there."

"But why didn't you bring more people? It would have

been safer to send someone else."

Conrad frowned. "Is it normal for you to question everything about a person who comes looking for you worrying you're dead? If so, then it's a wonder Davros puts up with all of it. Man seems a bit more simple minded than willing to play such games."

Ahria scowled. "It's not a game, and Davros has nothing to do with it."

"Well, he was in quite the tizzy after realizing where you'd gone. Lucky he didn't pull apart my ship from sheer anxiety."

"Unlike you, right?" Ahria swallowed, keeping her frustration from her tone as best as she could. "Nothing fazes you."

"Keeping calm is part of my job. Wouldn't be able to be a captain if I couldn't."

"Of course. Calm. Collected... Cold." Ahria shivered and wrapped her arms around herself.

"Look." Conrad stepped back, lifting his hands again. "I'm not criticizing your personality beyond the slight insanity of jumping onto another ship at mid sea. I haven't even asked more questions about how in the hells you're able to pull a stunt *like that* when you've apparently never even left home."

Ahria straightened. "Just because I never left home, doesn't mean I wasn't subjected to *ruthless* training."

"Ruthless training, huh? What for, if you're not enlisting

to be a Zionan assassin or something?"

She shrugged, exaggerating the gesture to mimic how he always did it. "My father wanted me to be prepared."

"Prepared for what?"

"I don't know. Maybe for a time when a stranger grabs my arm in the middle of a crowd?" She made a face at him, shivering again. "I'm cold. Can we go back to the ship now? Or now that I'm off, I need to pay for the travel?"

He sighed, shaking his head. "Ship's a long ways off, and it's a cold trip by longboat. Davros and I weren't going to return there for at least another two hours. Better to warm up in a tavern until then." He turned sideways, lifting his arm to gesture down the alley. "Maybe you should buy me another drink of fire wine. After all, I *was* worried. Wouldn't be so angry if I wasn't."

Ahria rubbed her arms beneath her cloak, clutching the material tighter as she watched him with a raised brow. "So you get angry at those you care about?" She strode next to him, following his gesture. Her voice softened to something more genuine. "I'll buy you a drink of fire wine. Maybe I'll even buy you a bottle. Gods know you deserve it for putting up with my shit." She tried to smile at him.

"I've put up with worse." He smirked, tugging his cloak's hood down further over his face.

As they reached the end of the alley, Ahria started walking back towards the tavern she'd eaten at.

Conrad's hand brushed her lower back as he stepped up beside her. The touch was subtle, almost as if he hadn't meant to do it at first, but he didn't pull away. "So, you've never been to Haven Port before?"

Ahria huffed. "I've never been anywhere before." She eyed the many faces in the streets and wondered if Davros was among them still searching for her.

But Conrad said they would rendezvous at the longboat later.

The pressure of his touch grew stronger as he encouraged her to turn down a different path, where the crowds grew thicker. "This way. Since you're here, might as well enjoy what the city has to offer."

"And what *does* the city have to offer?" Ahria rested a hand on a hidden dagger's hilt, finding comfort in the small weapon. A stranger bumped into her, making her stumble sideways into Conrad.

He caught her waist as she fell against his chest, keeping a steady pressure on her as he stabilized them both. A moment later, he stepped back and held her with a hand on both shoulders.

"Sorry," Ahria muttered, resuming her pace with her left hand still on the small hilt. "I've walked before, I promise."

"Probably not in a crowd like this." His hand pressed into hers before she realized he was even reaching for her. Entwining their fingers, he lifted their hands between them with a pointed nod of his head. "So we don't get separated."

Ahria's gaze flickered to their hands and back to his face. "Of course."

His hand warmed hers. Enough that she hoped Davros wasn't near. Wouldn't see. The conflicting feelings warred in her gut, sprouting guilt within her chest.

It's only to get through these crowds.

As much as she reassured herself, she knew that wasn't all it was. At least for her. And she couldn't understand why her chest felt so tight.

Conrad wove through the crowds with ease, slowing when necessary for her to catch up without their grip breaking.

She hadn't realized they were walking up an incline in the road until she felt the burn in her calves.

The crowds had thinned, yet, he still held her hand as he led her towards a stairwell cut into a retaining wall on the left side of the street.

The smell of the port had begun to fade, and Ahria paused to look back the way they had come. "Where are we go—"

The sight nearly took the breath from her lungs, and she froze, hand dropping from Conrad's. The street behind them sloped down towards the port, where ships' lanterns glowed like fireflies around a shallow pond rather than ships on an ocean. The colors of the Winter's End revelers wove through the streets, streamers of bustling movement and celebration. The sound of tin drums and music had faded to a low hum, mingling with the laughter of the people.

"Conrad..." Ahria breathed his name, staring at the incredible view. She no longer shivered, warmed by the trek uphill, and she blindly reached behind her for him. Her fingers brushed the hem of his cloak, before her second blind reach caressed the cold metal of his belt buckle.

But then his hand closed around hers. A low rumble of the beginning of a laugh came before he stepped beside her. "Bet you've never seen a view quite like that before."

She glanced at him, heat rising to her cheeks. "Can't say I have."

He brushed his thumb against hers, but then abruptly the warmth of him dropped away again. "Come on." He gestured to the stairwell, lanterns glowing in their recesses on the wall. "You can enjoy the view *and* some fire wine inside."

Ahria hesitated, staring at him. In all the moments of her sheltered life, she'd never encountered one with so much tension. So much... potential. Walking with him felt like crossing some kind of line, yet, walking the other way felt like it could break her. Her mind flitted to Davros again, reminding her she had a man waiting for her. Looking for her. But...

Conrad paused, one foot already on the first step when he noticed she wasn't following. His hood had shifted back from his face, showing the rough stubble on his chin. His light eyes did a quick assessment of her, as they always did, as if looking for something he couldn't see. "What's with that look on your face? You coming?"

Sucking in a quick breath, Ahria looked back at the view before jogging after him. "Nothing. It's nothing," she murmured, shaking her head and climbing the stairs.

Another hint of a smile touched his features before he led the way up. At the top, an inclined cobblestone path led through a hedge before another set of stairs.

"Is there a hearth to warm me, soon, or is that the purpose of hiking a mountain?" Ahria smiled, resisting the urge to poke the back of his leg.

"Are you complaining?" He slowed to look back at her for just a moment before resuming the climb.

"No. This isn't a terrible view, either," she blurted, heat rushing to her face. Cringing, she shut her eyes, silently cursing herself before daring to look at him again.

Stop talking.

There was a hint of pause in his step, but he didn't turn back, perhaps pretending he didn't hear. Because that would be preferable than acknowledging her stupid comment.

The stairs emerged onto another street which curved along the edge of a towering retaining wall that looked out over the city. The tops of the roofs created the perfect bottom frame for the glittering picture of the harbor.

Eager to fill the silence, Ahria coughed. "Well, if you ever need to find me in Haven Port again, you'll know where to look first." She admired the view, wind whipping her hair sideways.

"Shall I leave you here, or did you want to join me at the tavern?" He pointed back up the hill slightly, drawing her attention to the building for the first time. A two-story behemoth dominated the inside of the curve of the road, large windows glowing from within. As the front door swung open with the departure of some patrons, the soft sound of a lute drifted to her ears.

"As long as the view is just as good inside." Ahria started up the last hill to the tavern. "I think my legs would appreciate sitting for a bit after all those stairs."

"Downhill is easier." Conrad waited, gesturing again to the tavern door. "After you."

Narrowing her eyes at him as she passed, she reached the door and opened it. The scent of ale greeted her, warmed by burning wood and the aroma of cooking herbs. The tavern was decently populated, but not nearly as packed as the taverns in the city center.

"Captain Conrad." A sultry voice spoke as Conrad pushed his hood from his head and met the eyes of a red headed woman dressed in Zionan style. The long front and back of her tunic might have seemed like a dress without the linen pants beneath. The light caught strands of grey in her hair, and she crossed her arms as if about to reprimand him. "It's been what, a full year since you graced us with your presence?"

"Evening, Keika. I'm sorry, but I promise it's for good reasons. Hoping I'm lucky and no one else has taken up residence at my usual table." Conrad unhooked the clasp at the front of his cloak, slinging it from his shoulders as he stuffed the scarf in one of its pockets. Beneath, he wore his traditional cream shirt and tight fitting grey vest.

Keika took his cloak. "You're in luck, couple just vacated, so it's open." She twitched her head towards a set of stairs to the left of the doorway before holding out her hand to Ahria in a silent offer.

Ahria looked at the woman's hand and reluctantly removed her cloak. One of her pockets was fatter than the others, reminding her of what she'd purchased earlier that afternoon, but instead of awkwardly retrieving it right then, she handed the cloak to the woman. "Thank you."

I can deal with that later.

Goosebumps rose over her arms beneath the thin shirt she wore, covered by a laced leather vest.

Conrad walked towards the stairs as Keika departed towards a closed doorway. He stopped at the door frame, leaning on it as he looked back at Ahria. "Shall I go first to provide a view again, or...?"

Ahria stared at him, her face as hot as the Xaxos sun. She forced herself to smile through her embarrassment. "I mean, I wouldn't complain..." Rolling her eyes, she walked sideways past him through the doorway. "But it would seem rather selfish of me, no?" She inwardly cheered at her own bravado as she climbed the stairs, making sure her hips moved a little extra for effect.

Chapter 10

FIRE WINE COULDN'T POSSIBLY COMPETE with the buzz in Conrad's mind as he looked up the stairs after Ahria. The sway of her hips made his tongue swell to fill his mouth and he tried to remember how to swallow.

What the hells is wrong with me...

The thunk of his own boot on the first step made him jump as he finally brought himself to follow, still enjoying the view. He watched his step, hyperaware that now would be a terrible time to trip on the familiar stairs of the Crow's Nest.

Ahria glanced back at him. "What's with that look on your face?"

A muscle in Conrad's jaw twitched, but he didn't allow it to show as he urged his face back to neutral. "What look?"

Her only response came in a quirked eyebrow before she disappeared around the corner.

He took the final steps two at a time to catch up, finally able to focus on his own movement without her distracting him. The glow of the city beyond the tall windows shone through the dim light of the upper floor, and sparse lanterns lit the hall leading to the varied dining rooms.

Ahria stood at the glass, her back to him. Without her cloak, many of her blades were visible. One at her lower back explained the bump he'd felt when he touched her. A little pommel glinted within each boot, but those three wouldn't be the only ones she had. Her long, dark hair was windswept, and he caught himself imagining untangling the knots.

I'm torturing myself.

With effort, he walked down the hallway past her and welcomed the familiar smells and sounds of the upper dining hall. There was a rather loud crowd of sailors towards the back of the room, but even with their celebration, the tavern remained far quieter than most.

Walking past the doorway to the room with the group, Conrad focused on a single table wedged into the corner of the hallway itself. The massive windows stretched from floor to ceiling, and a single candle guttered on the narrow table top. As his fingers brushed the familiar wood of one of the chairs, a tickle entered the pit of his stomach.

Well this is... unintentionally intimate.

Ahria followed him, her boots silent on the hard floor. She slowed at approaching the table, watching him with that same, soul-seeing gaze. "This is…"

"Best table in the house. Gets a little extra traffic as it's in the hallway, but makes it easier to wave down a barkeep. And…" He gestured to the city. At this end of the hall, the road that curved back down into Haven Port's markets was visible, twinkling lights draped between buildings. The glow of the Winter's End celebration in the market streets hung with prismatic color like a field of wildflowers. "There's really no beating the view."

Tentatively approaching closer, Ahria finally looked away from him and admired the glowing city. "Was this your intention all along? To come here after you found me?"

He disguised his smile while sitting down, twisting the chair towards the table more than he typically would when alone. "I try to come here every time I visit Haven Port. Usually without company, but I'm certainly not opposed to it. I'm happy to be able to fit in a drink at this table during my time here, no matter how much of a surprise the reroute was."

Ahria slid the other chair from under the table and sat, her gaze flickering from him to the approaching barkeep.

Keika smiled warmly. "What can I get the two of you?"

"Can we get a bottle of Xaxos fire wine?" Ahria held out a half florin for the woman and side-eyed Conrad. "So you can't pay for it before me again."

He lifted his hands in a placating gesture. "I wouldn't dare." He gave Keika a subtle smile. "Do you have those little pastry wheels tonight?"

"Sure do. Half dozen?" Keika took the silver coin from Ahria, pocketing it.

"Better make it a dozen." Conrad looked at Ahria, already imagining how many her tiny frame would be able to pack away. He'd caught glimpses of her during meals in the galley on the ship, and her ability to eat rivaled a man twice her size.

Keika nodded again before returning the way she'd come, from the back stairwell to the kitchens. Leaving Conrad able to focus on Ahria and her lightly illuminated silhouette against the star-riddled sky.

"A whole bottle, huh?"

"Then you can take what we don't drink with you." Ahria gave him a sly look. "I told you. You deserve it after dealing with my mess of a life for as long as you have. You must be eager for Treama."

He shrugged, silently cursing himself for the habitual gesture. "What's life without a little adventure here and there? But if that is the cost for evenings like this..." He caught himself imagining his hand in her hair again, and swallowed.

Her brow twitched, and she fell silent as Keika brought their bottle with two crystal glasses. The server set down a plate of round pastries, nodding at Conrad and looking towards Ahria. "Let me know if either of you would like anything else."

He nodded, not fully looking away from Ahria. Keika waited for Ahria to nod as well before she walked away.

Ahria poured them each a glass, but didn't touch hers right away. "Are you saying that cold... *calm* Captain Conrad is pleased that I stowed away on his ship?"

"I have a certain soft spot for stowaways." Conrad slid his glass closer but resisted the temptation to down it.

"Why?" Ahria swirled her drink.

Conrad considered his own story, wondering if he really wanted to open that door with Ahria. So few knew his past, and he liked it that way. But the way her steely eyes looked at him made him want to tell her every intricate detail.

He touched the glass again, swirling the liquid without picking it up. "I may have been one myself, once upon a time. And it was a generous captain who didn't throw me overboard and saw a boy with potential desperate to escape. She took me in, made me a member of the crew. Taught me everything... made me the man I am today."

A soft smile touched Ahria's lips. "What's her name?"

"Captain Andirindia Trace. Pretty sure she's still captaining her own ship too. Would be hard to imagine Andi in any life but the one on the Herald."

"Andi." Ahria scoffed. "You named your *dog* after her?"

He couldn't help the smirk, even as he picked up his shot of fire wine. "It's a form of flattery, and I knew she'd hate it. It's the type of relationship we formed in the end before I left to forge my own path on a different ship."

Ahria lifted her glass, holding it under her nose. "How come you ran away from home?" She spoke slowly, as if unsure if he'd answer, and then downed her shot in a single gulp. Cringing, she shuddered and put the empty glass down.

He considered the gentle waves on the top of his drink with her question. He pursed his lips before he downed it, savoring the hot flavors on the back of his tongue before the burn coated his throat. Then the second wave as he settled the empty glass onto the table. "Just didn't feel I belonged there anymore."

"What of your mother?" Ahria filled their glasses again.

A small tear opened in his chest, thinking about his mother. He knew how much she had sacrificed for him to have a normal childhood, and leaving her had been the most difficult part of his decision. But he'd assured himself he'd keep in touch without having to deal with the constant nagging of his grandmother.

"I left her a note saying I'd secured a job on a ship so she wouldn't worry. Wrote her pretty regularly, at first. She wasn't the reason I wanted to get away, it was my gran who pushed a lot of old traditions on me that I didn't much care for. So I left." The words felt odd to be speaking. He'd only truly told the story to Leiura, and that was after they'd been friends for years.

But some fire wine and an attractive woman...

A shadow of something passed behind Ahria's eyes, but she picked up her glass. "I'm sorry you had to go through all that. You *still* write her, I hope?"

He flinched. "Not in a while. Kind of got wrapped up in all my own bullshit with running a ship and all. But I'm sure she's fine and living a happy life in Treama." The last few bits of correspondence he'd sent her contained only short notes, and a modest amount of coin in case she needed it. He always sent whatever he could spare, as if it could assuage the guilt he still felt for leaving her.

Ahria's throat bobbed. "Must be hard without her son, though. Must feel like a piece of her is missing."

Conrad cleared his throat, the burn of the fire wine coming back momentarily. Picking up his refilled glass, he considered the damage drinking so quickly could cause. But the urge to forget the memories spurred him to lift the drink to his lips and gulp it down.

The crystal thunked back to the table before he reached for one of the pastries. A buzz already started to take over his mind.

"You should try one of these. I'm sure you'll be devouring the whole plate after one bite."

She drank her fire wine, setting the empty glass down again. "Don't tempt me. You have no idea." Smiling, she chose a pastry and took a delicate bite. Bits of sugar crumbled from the edges, sticking to her lips. Her expression broadened and she took another bite, making more of a mess. "I feel like you're purposely sabotaging my ability to be neat."

A chuckle bubbled past his lips as he pushed the plate closer to her. "I'm happy to be a temptation." He plucked the fire wine bottle from in front of her, their glasses clinking together as he pulled them beside each other on the table. He carefully poured each glass full without spilling a drop of the delicious liquor. Setting down the bottle, he leaned back in his chair and carefully nibbled on a corner of his pastry. The sweet flavor complimented that of the wine still lingering in his mouth, and he knew the next shot would be even richer.

Ahria smirked, color touching her cheeks again. "Temptation, indeed." She reached for another pastry, gaze drifting out the window as she ate it. "Is there anywhere you *haven't* been?"

He considered while he chewed. "Sure there is. Where are you from?"

"A little town on the east side of Dowgess Lake, in Olsa, called Gallisville. It's south of Drych."

"Haven't been there." Conrad offered her a smile as he slid her glass towards her and took up his own. Memories of Davros's resume while looking for work resurfaced. He controlled a frown as his thumb tapped the side of his full glass.

Ahria downed her third glass of fire wine.

"I remember now that Davros learned to sail on that lake, so you two must have known each other for a long time?"

She coughed, clearing her throat and nodding. "Since we were kids."

"Got that impression a little. He's mighty protective of you." He thumbed his glass again, but resisted taking the drink. He didn't want to entirely forget their conversation, and if he continued at the rate they were going, he would. "You must love each other quite a bit."

Ahria rolled her lips together, looking down at her empty glass. Her voice quieted to barely more than a whisper. "I don't know, really."

A boil of some unknown emotion emerged within Conrad, and he considered Ahria in a silence that fell between them. "Having doubts?" His voice came out no louder than hers had.

She shrugged. "Maybe. I... I don't know, everyone kind of just expected us to become a thing, so when he asked, I saw no reason not to, but..." She huffed and shrugged again. "But I don't know, and I..." Meeting his gaze, she took a deeper breath. "I care about him a lot. I don't want to hurt him."

He pursed his lips before finally lifting his drink and downing it.

Might be a bit too late for that.

He reached for the bottle, seeing that Ahria was already doing the same. The instinct to politely recoil came, but then he shoved it away. His fingers brushed the back of Ahria's hand atop the bottle. "It's alright to question it. You don't have to love someone in that way to care about them." He slid his hand gently beneath hers, slipping her hand away to take up the bottle himself and refill their drinks again. "But you might want to be honest with him."

Ahria sighed. "I always thought I would just grow to love him, too." She looked out the window, chewing her lower lip. "Conrad... Can I ask you something?"

His body tensed, an internal alarm warning him of the danger should he answer. But he nodded, anyway. Even he had hated the way he recoiled when she'd launched herself at him in the alley. She'd needed comfort, and had obviously been going through a dark place in her mind. And he'd shoved her off, incapable of returning the embrace. Like a damned fool. Perhaps if he could answer her question... If he could be honest with her, it would start to repair whatever damage he'd surely caused.

She leaned forward in her chair, closer to the view. "This hat Warrin took. Was it black, with gold stitching... Tricorn, with a crazy huge feather along one side?"

His brow furrowed, his body relaxing in the confusion. Not the question he'd expected. "Yes, why?"

Ahria's chair ground out from under her as she stood. "Because he's here. Warrin's here, and he's wearing it." She pointed out the window.

With a shock, Conrad leaned forward to peer outside in the direction Ahria looked.

Sure enough, Warrin walked, alone, up the steep incline of the road towards the Crow's Nest. It certainly wasn't a surprise for him to frequent the same tavern, considering it was Warrin who had introduced Conrad to it in the first place during one of their stops when they both worked on the Herald. The long feather, which curled at the end, bounced with each gloating step.

"Bastard was always one to flaunt when he's got it. I stole it the first time as a joke because I thought it was so obscene." Conrad settled back into the chair, lifting his shot of wine before downing it.

Ahria remained standing, looking at him with a wild, playful expression. "What are you doing? This is our chance to get it back."

He lifted his brow as the burn elicited a sharp cough. "Nah, as soon as he walks over the threshold, he's in neutral territory according to the laws of the game. Taverns are off limits. Didn't want to accidentally start any brawls with drunks not aware of the game."

"So you're not allowed to steal it from him while he's in here?"

"Nope."

"But I can, can't I?" Ahria picked up her glass of fire wine and drank it. "I'm not a member of your crew. Rules don't apply to me."

"Do they *ever* apply to you?" Conrad thought about what she said. "But... you're not wrong. He'll probably be here in a few moments though. He won't be able to resist bragging to my face as soon as Keika tells him I'm here."

A bell jangled on the door downstairs as it opened.

"Stay here." Ahria grabbed a pastry, hesitated, then grabbed another and put it in her mouth. She rattled something off while holding it in her teeth that he couldn't understand, then she frowned and bit it, dropping the remainder into her palm. "Just gotta get him to take it off. Can you do that?" Without waiting for his response, she shirked backwards and ducked around a corner into an unoccupied room.

Conrad struggled to erase the surprise on his face as he stared at the vacant chair beside him. The task at hand rushed through his dazed brain as he looked at the hallway walls beside the table. There was a line of hooks along the wall behind him, places for patrons who didn't leave their cloaks and hats downstairs to hang them if they wanted. There was no way in hells Warrin was going to come up without the hat, but he'd need his back to the only location he'd possibly put it.

Standing quickly, Conrad spun to switch seats and the world around him blurred as more alcohol rushed into his system. He'd only eaten one pastry with four glasses of liquor. He fell, more than sat, into Ahria's chair, blearily blinking at the table. He spied the second glass just as boot steps sounded on the stairs, and he slid it off the table into his lap, wedging it uncomfortably between his legs before grabbing another pastry. He prayed it would help soak up some of the liquor in his gut as he downed it in two quick bites.

"Connie!" Warrin's boisterous call caused Conrad's shoulders to bunch, and the smack on his back lodged a bit of pastry into his throat.

He coughed, chewing it faster to swallow while regretting the only liquid he had to wash it down with was fire wine.

Warrin stepped around the table, the tricorn hat atop his head. The cream feather off the back was preposterously large, nearly brushing the walls of the hall as Warrin turned, inviting himself into the seat Conrad had occupied moments before. "Didn't think I'd see you here in Haven Port. You caught up fast, Connie-boy."

Conrad pursed his lips, genuinely irritated with Warrin's continued use of a childish name. "Funny what a competent crew makes possible."

"Competent?" Warrin barked a laugh. "*Your* crew member is the one who gave you away. Blabbing like a loose-lipped harlot after only one drink."

He frowned, making no attempt to hide his anger, and snatched the fire wine bottle as Warrin reached for it. "Watch your tongue. Friendly rivalry or not, I'll punch that ugly ass hat off your head if you say crude things like that about a woman."

Warrin chuckled, leaning back in the chair enough to lift its front legs from the floor. His beard had greyed more since Conrad had last snatched the hat from him. "Right, forgot you were Zionan for a moment there. Harlot would be a word used for the men where you grew up." His eyes darted to the bottle. "Drowning your sorrows? Hope you ain't had enough to forget the rules."

Conrad lifted his hands. "I know 'em as well as you do. I won't touch the thing within these walls."

The captain of Prosperity nodded in approval, tipping the hat to Conrad before he removed it. Leaning back further in his chair, he reached up to dangle the hat from the closest hook behind him before dropping his chair back down. The hair on the top of his head was thinning, and Conrad contemplated teasing him about it.

Don't want to give him a reason to put that thing back on.

"Gonna share in your wealth there?" Warrin eyed the bottle again.

Conrad considered his empty glass before he poured a minuscule amount into it and slid it toward Warrin. "Don't want to have to carry you out of here, old man. Even if it would make snatching that hat easier."

Ahria peeked out of the doorway behind the old captain, but Conrad didn't look at her. She slid along the wall, not making a sound as she crept towards the hooks.

Without letting the liquor breathe, Warrin downed it. "Gods. This stuff is terrible."

Reaching, Ahria lifted the hat from the hook, slowly withdrawing it to herself.

Conrad did everything in his power not to react, locking his jaw as he poured another small amount into the cup in front of Warrin. "Let it breathe this time, you heathen."

To his horror, Ahria put the hat on. She slid further down the hall, grinning as she twirled in a dance with her retreat. She spun and bowed, dipping her head so the hat rolled onto her arm, then lifted it back to her head as if she belonged in some traveling troupe.

He bit down on the inside of his lower lip, trying to control the instant reaction to burst into laughter. Body tensing to hold it in, he set the bottle back onto the table with more force than he meant to. He hastily pushed a pastry into his mouth to hide the smile.

Warrin gave a questioning look, picking up the glass in front of him. "What's wrong with your face? You look like you're about to shit yourself, son."

Nearly at the end of the hallway, Ahria twirled again, landing with her arms outstretched like she'd finished a performance. She still held a pastry in her mouth, and bent at the waist in a low bow.

A snort caused a bit of sugar to go up Conrad's nose, and he flinched and fought the urge to sneeze.

Warrin recoiled from the table with a disgusted look on his face. "You've had too much of this already, haven't you?" He waved his glass in Conrad's direction before he downed it. But the man's eyes narrowed, and with dread, Conrad realized he'd glanced at Ahria.

The older captain spun in his chair, looking first at the empty hooks and then down the hallway where Ahria still danced near the back stairs. "Son of a bitch!"

Ahria straightened, eyes wide as she looked at Warrin. Pausing, she bit her pastry. "Finders, keepers," she mumbled through her mouthful.

Warrin turned back to Conrad and slammed his glass down on the table. "The rules, boy!"

"I'm following them." Conrad lifted his hands, still trying to clear sugar from the back of his throat. "She isn't part of my crew. And I haven't laid a finger on the hat." He pushed back his chair and stood, trying not to wobble. "Happy Winter's End, Warrin." Conrad snatched the quarter-full bottle of fire wine. "Here's to a new year without that gods' awful hat on your bald head."

Letting out a roar, Warrin turned and charged after Ahria, who quickly disappeared down the stairs.

Conrad bolted the other way, descending the stairs in a flurry to retrieve their cloaks from Keika before Warrin could catch Ahria. The woman didn't question as he raced past, thanking her as he burst out the front door with their cloaks over his arm. He hopped down the stairs, looking up and down the street for any sign of Ahria and the hat. He could hear Warrin cursing near the back door then take off running back the way they'd come.

Silence settled, and he debated rushing after Warrin.

"Psst."

Looking behind him for the source of the voice, he met Ahria's bright eyes under the wide brim of the gaudy hat, shrouded where she hid between hedges.

"Is he gone?" she whispered, grinning.

Conrad laughed, remembering the look on his old friend's face as he spied Ahria. He threw her cloak at her as he laughed again, a sound he so rarely heard that now it seemed bizarre. "I think you're in the clear." He shook the fire wine bottle in her direction. "A brilliant performance."

Ahria stepped out, wrapping her cloak over her shoulders and took the bottle with another bow. "I aim to please." She sipped from the bottle before handing it back. "We should get back to the ship before he comes looking."

They hurried through the streets, laughing each time

Ahria dipped her extravagant hat at strangers. She'd curtsy and say, "G'day, sir!" to each one, trading out the 'sir' depending on whether she addressed a man, woman, or stray cat.

"Where is the—ow!" Ahria grabbed her own elbow, cringing after smacking it into a brick wall by accident. "Ow. Ow. The longboat. Ow. Where is the longboat?"

Chuckling, Conrad looped an arm around her waist without thinking, pulling her close to his side. "Better stay close so I can protect you from those walls. I totally saw it jump out at you."

Ahria stuck out her bottom lip. "They're mean walls."

He laughed, the haze of the fire wine still ripe in his consciousness. It encouraged his head close to hers, catching the sweet scent of her hair, which only made his drunkenness worse. He turned them out of the alley they walked, towards the stairs that led to the beaches below the docks, where they'd stashed the longboat.

Loose rocks slipped beneath their boots, and Ahria shrieked as they slid a few feet down the embankment.

"Shh," Conrad managed, chuckling as she held tighter to him. "Warrin's ship is right over there. Might hear you."

"I'll be quiet when the ground stops moving." Ahria stepped onto the firmer sand, facing him. She grinned, face shadowed by the planks above before her expression dimmed. "Thank you. I mean it. Thank you for coming for me."

Looser than he'd felt in years, Conrad turned to her, the bottle of fire wine still in his hand. "I'd do it again." He lifted the drink between them and tipped the mouth of the bottle towards her. "Thank you for helping to get that terrible hat back. Though, I will say, it has a certain charm on you."

Ahria took the bottle, but lowered it. She breathed hard from their rush through the city, her lips twitching in the hint of a smile. "You make me question everything."

"Everything, hmm?" Conrad allowed the chill in the air to bolden his touch, the fire wine encouraging him to take advantage of his arm still around her waist, beckoning him closer. "What kind of everything?"

The excitement of the evening multiplied the heat she stirred in his blood. The adrenaline still rushed through his system from the run down the hill fleeing the Crow's Nest and Warrin. From his failed attempts to hold in laughter. The sweetness of the pastries still hung in his nose, now mingled with scents of Ahria. A fleck of sugar clung to her lower lip, and he suddenly wanted to taste it, too.

Ahria tilted her chin up, eyes flickering around his face but giving nothing away. Nothing but a sense of vulnerability. "You're just..." She touched his face, thumb moving over his jaw as her breath touched his lips. "I want..."

Lightning passed through him at her touch, and his throat clenched as he took in the look on her face. Embraced how different her mere presence felt compared to everyone else he'd encountered. The temptation and desire won out as he leaned into her, his lips moving against hers in a slow, lingering kiss.

A soft sound escaped her, and her mouth responded to his. She tasted like fire. The sweetest fire he'd ever experienced, and her arms slid around him.

He wanted more, and his arm wrapped further around her waist to draw her lithe body into his. His tongue traced the line of her lip where he'd seen the sugar, and she opened for him. His fingers glided through the knots in the length of her hair as the kiss grew hungry and his heart felt ready to pound out of his chest. The bottle of fire wine thunked into the sand at their feet as Ahria dropped it, running her hand up through his short curly hair.

Gasping, she withdrew, lips swollen and wet. She looked at him, shaking her head. "Conrad, I—"

Rocks clacked as someone else descended the embankment, and Ahria pulled from Conrad in a rush. She closed a hand over her mouth, turning in time for Davros to see her as he met the sand.

The air felt so much colder as Conrad tightened his cloak around his shoulders and stooped to pluck the bottle from the sand. Only a splash had been sacrificed, but he'd have willingly given up a lifetime of the wine to experience the sensation of her again.

Davros sighed and rushed for her, scooping her into a

tight embrace that lifted her boots from the ground. "Gods, I was so worried about you." He set her down, placing a hard kiss on her mouth that she quickly broke. "What's wrong? Have you been drinking?"

Ahria shook her head. "Nothing. But I did drink. I was... feeling a little low."

"Found her in the tavern off in the north market," Conrad supplied, looking at the longboat instead of at how Davros still held onto her. The sensation in his stomach was becoming far too familiar, even if he didn't understand it.

"Are you all right?" Davros inspected her, touching her chin. "What's with the hat?"

She shirked out of that touch, too, stepping away from him. "It's nothing." Removing the hat, she offered it to Conrad. "One less thing to find, I suppose."

Davros looked between them as the captain took the hat. "Let's get you back to the ship. You look exhausted."

Ahria bowed her head, shutting her eyes while she nodded.

Conrad tucked the hat beneath his arm and dared another look at her, only to find her watching him as Davros walked to the longboat.

She tilted her head, eyebrows pinching in the center as she bit her lower lip.

I'm insane. And a masochist.

He broke the look first, climbing into the longboat, and

wedged the bottle of fire wine against the bench. He arranged the oars while Davros prepared to push the boat out into the water.

No one spoke as they rowed back to Dawn Chaser and boarded. On the main deck, Davros put an arm around Ahria's waist to lead her below to the crew's sleeping quarters.

Conrad strode for his cabin, hearing Ahria whisper something to Davros before her footsteps carried her closer to him.

"Captain," she murmured behind him, and he faced her. "Tonight was incredible." Her voice barely reached his ears as she ensured Davros wouldn't hear from where he waited by the stairs.

His throat tightened as he looked at her, wanting desperately to take her into his cabin with him so they could finish the bottle and he could explore more of her. Instead, he gave a tight nod. "I enjoyed it thoroughly, as well."

Her jaw flexed, a pained expression on her face. "I have something for you." She reached into her cloak, retrieving a wrapped parchment the size of her hands.

He looked down at it, trying to recall when she might have had a moment to purchase something. She had to have done it before he found her initially, which led to more questions, especially if she genuinely didn't believe he'd come to Haven Port for her. He met her eyes, feeling his own expression weaken. "Ahria..." He couldn't find anything but her name.

She shook her head, silver glimmering on her lower lids. "It's nothing. I just... I saw them, and I thought of you, so..." She held the package out to him.

Tucking the wine under one arm, and the hat under the other, he tentatively took the parcel from her. He considered waiting to open it until he was alone in his cabin, but just as he began to undo the twine on it, she withdrew her hand and stepped back.

"I'm sorry my life is such a mess, but I am ever grateful that I chose your ship. I..." Ahria's voice cracked and she drew a slow breath. "Goodnight, Captain."

"Goodnight." Conrad paused, holding the package as he watched Ahria rejoin Davros and disappear below deck.

He urged all jealousy for the man to leave him. It was not his place to feel such things, nor did he have a reason. She'd told him she didn't know if she loved Davros or not.

Lost in his thoughts, Conrad turned to his cabin and awkwardly balanced the package so he could twist the door knob. Using his boot to close the door behind him, he set the bottle and hat down on his desk. He examined the package, turning it over before untying the twine. Unwrapping the contents, he held his breath when his eyes landed on the beautifully crafted pair of black leather gloves.

Conrad eyed the still healing blisters on the palms of his hands and smiled to himself as he recalled their conversation. Now there would be little reason not to join his crew in working the rigging again, until his hands grew tough once more. He ran a finger over the leather before picking them up and trying them on. The supple leather gave just enough for them to fit perfectly.

There was a light knock at his door as he slid them off, and Andi's nails clicked on the deck as the door swung open and Leiura popped her head in. "Andi says next time you're taking her with you."

Conrad smirked. "Speak dog, now?"

"Just well enough to be able to interpret her whines from your cabin while you're gone. She's an ironic companion for someone like you who thrives on being alone." Leiura didn't fully enter, hanging in the door frame. "You find her?"

"Yup. She's back on board." His fingers idly scratched Andi's ear as she rubbed up beside him. "We'll depart for Treama in the morning."

Where I'll have to say goodbye.

Chapter 11

AHRIA'S HEART POUNDED IN HER ears with each step back to the sleeping quarters they shared with the rest of the crew. Faint snores already drifted through the air, and the dim light of a lantern hung in the far corner where some of the crew were still awake playing cards. As they walked towards the doorway, it suddenly felt far too crowded.

"Wait."

Davros paused, looking back at her. "What is it?"

"I want to talk to you, but..." Ahria sucked in a deep breath, her insides trembling. "I'd like somewhere more private. Can we return to the deck for a few minutes?"

A shadow crossed Davros's expression, but he nodded and followed her back the way they'd come.

The cold night air greeted her, waking her senses a little more from the mind-numbing effects of the fire wine. With a glance at Conrad's door, she eyed the first mate standing within it.

Leiura didn't look at her, head poked within Conrad's cabin.

The city still didn't sleep, the distant echoes of the celebration murmuring over the salty breeze to where Dawn Chaser anchored just beyond the harbor's break wall. The city was hidden behind the human built stone landmass, but the moon shone on the colorful banners adorning the top.

It all returned to her in a crashing wave. The excitement. The thrill. Running and stumbling through the city with Conrad after stealing back the hat. Only to end with his mouth against hers beneath the docks. It rocked her harder than she ever thought possible, and it made her feelings painfully clear.

Ahria led Davros to the bow, her boots heavy as she climbed the few steps necessary. The gentle slosh of waves against the hull calmed her, and she took comfort that they'd yet to leave port.

If he can't stand to be near me, at least he has an exit.

Davros came to stand next to her at the banister, his face devoid of emotion. "Did something happen in Haven Port?"

Something. Everything.

Ahria shook her head, wrapping her guilt up in a dense

cloth and hiding it in the deepest part of herself. "I... realized something and I think it's only fair that I share it with you."

Moonlight glimmered off his dark complexion as he nodded again. "Tell me. We've never kept secrets before."

Ahria hesitated.

Just say it.

"I think you should stay on with Dawn Chaser." She gulped. "The captain seems amicable with you, and you keep saying how much you love this adventure. Maybe it's best if it doesn't end for you in Treama."

Davros fell silent, looking out at the water for so long she wondered if he'd say anything at all. "You don't want me with you anymore?"

Ahria clenched her jaw, heat rising in her eyes. "Dav, you're amazing. You've been my friend for as long as I can remember, and I so desperately want you to be happy. I just can't be that person for you."

Meeting her gaze, he tilted his head. "Why? When did that change?" Only a hint of frustration tinged his tone.

"It doesn't matter. But I can't love you the way you deserve. And dragging you all around Pantracia doesn't make sense when you've found the life you want, and it's right here."

He frowned in a familiar way, a way she'd sometimes tease out of him. But it felt so much more grave now. "I always imagined you'd be part of that life." He sighed, rubbing the back of his head. "But I know you need to find Talon, even though we both know he's probably fine." Davros turned to lean heavily against the banister, staring at the waves lapping against the side of the ship below. "You know I love you, Ree." He used the affectionate nickname everyone in their town used with her since she'd been little. Talon used it, too. According to her uncle, it'd been a nickname for her mother as a child, as well.

His words made her heart squeeze with the guilt of how Conrad's lips had felt against hers. "I know, and I'll always love you as a friend. But... right now our paths are taking us different ways and it's better if we accept that." She crossed her arms tightly, trying to banish the lingering pain from the look on his face. She needed to remain strong or she'd be consumed by a different kind of guilt.

"Our paths are taking us different ways? Seems to me like *you're* taking us in different ways. One night you're happy with me and the next?" Davros bit the words out, and she flinched, swallowing hard, but said nothing. He nodded without looking at her, sucking in a deep breath through his nose. "You think the captain would let me stay aboard after the turmoil we've put him through?"

You mean all of the turmoil I've put him through.

She wanted to believe Conrad wouldn't hold her mistakes against Davros. The delays, the slip of the tongue... it'd been all her fault. Not his. And the captain seemed like a fair man, even without her bias.

"I think so. You should ask him tomorrow if you can stay on." Ahria caught his wrist when he started to walk away. "I'm sorry, Dav. Really. The last thing I wanted to do was hurt you." Wetness threatened her eyes, but it didn't feel fair to force him to console her. Not when she was the one doing the hurting.

Davros paused only long enough to remove her hand from his arm. His tone darkened. "Little late for that. I hope you find everything you're looking for." Turning, he walked away, descending the stairs to the main deck before disappearing towards the sleeping quarters.

Ahria bowed her head, a wave of isolation washing over her like a frozen blanket. She faced the bow, a betraying sob shaking her shoulders as she squeezed her eyes closed.

I'll be truly alone in Treama, now.

How could the evening develop like this? She'd seen none of it coming. Not the defeat, feeling lost in Haven Port, not the captain coming for her. And certainly not the Crow's Nest or what had transpired after. But she wasn't naive. Conrad's place was with his ship, and she needed to find her father. Their parting ways was inevitable, but at least this way, Davros would have a life he wanted. And she...

Ahria would find Talon, whatever it took.

And Conrad would forget her, regardless of what he'd said.

But the way he'd kissed her…

Ahria slid to the deck, sitting with her back against the banister and her knees to her chest. Burying her face in her arms, she shivered.

I can't sleep near Davros now.

At least not until he'd be asleep.

She sighed, looking up at the sound of clicking on the wooden planks.

A furry golden face peeked over the stairs, and Andi yipped and raced for her. Tail wagging wildly back and forth, the dog collided with her, climbing over her lap to lick her face.

"Andi! By the gods—" Ahria cringed, wiping the slobber from her cheeks as the dog hopped around her, whimpering and nudging her with her cold nose. Trying to calm the dog down with slow pets, she laughed, squealing at her inability to get the animal off her.

"Now, are those sounds of distress or enjoyment?" Conrad's warm voice drew her attention as he climbed the final stair. His hands were tucked into his pockets, a leather coat he hadn't been wearing before tight across his chest.

Her heart thudded harder, and she hurriedly wiped any remnants of tears from her face. "Bit of both, perhaps." She held Andi at bay, scratching under her chin.

A hint of a smile touched his lips as he walked towards her. "Need me to call the vicious beast off?"

As if in response, Andi collapsed onto Ahria's lap, whining as she rested her chin on her forepaws.

"I think she says no." Ahria stroked the dog's head, grateful for the creature's warmth, if nothing else. Bending over, she kissed her soft fur.

"Want some company? Other than my dog, I mean." Conrad stepped closer, but kept a respectful distance. Something in his eyes told her that he already knew what had happened.

Ahria nodded. "Company sounds nice. How did you know I was here?"

Quietly, he lowered himself to the desk beside her, leaning his back against the banister as well. He stretched his legs out in front of him, crossing his boots over each other. "Leiura." He'd kept his hands in his pockets the entire time, his elbows wedged between the banister posts.

"She overheard everything?" Ahria studied his face.

"Enough of it." Conrad leaned his head back, as if trying to grant her some privacy by not looking directly at her. "Hard to keep secrets on a vessel this size. And sailors are gossips."

"It needed to happen. Will you keep him on?" Ahria rolled her lips together, feeling the growing ache that it'd only be a few days before she'd be saying goodbye to Conrad, too. "Please? He never caused any trouble himself."

With a shrug, he turned his head towards her. "If he wants to, we'll keep him on. He's competent enough." His face hardened as he met her eyes. "Wish there was a way you could stay, too."

Ahria's chest tightened and she gulped, still stroking Andi's head. "Me, too," she whispered. "I don't want to depart in Treama, but..."

"I know." He tilted his head back again. "I'd never ask you to abandon your search. I just..." He paused as he took a steady breath in. His hand withdrew slowly from his pocket before he moved it to hers. He encouraged her hand from Andi's fur, his rough skin rubbing against hers as he entwined their fingers. "Thank you. For the gift."

Squeezing his hand, she smiled. "It was silly, but you're welcome." Running her thumb over his, she took a deeper breath. "And thank you, too."

He squeezed her hand back, offering her a regretful look. "For what? Somehow making it so you'll be alone in this search? At least with Davros you had someone at your side."

Trying to maintain her smile, she shook her head at him. "For showing me what this is supposed to feel like. Even if it means going on alone. I needed that."

Andi whined as she lifted her head, bopping their held hands with her nose, but Conrad's grip tightened. He withdrew his other hand to reach across him to scratch his dog's ears. "I wish things were different."

Ahria used her free hand to pet the dog, too. "You belong with your ship." She sighed. "But my search won't last forever. Maybe... Maybe I can find you again... if that is something you'd want?" Her tone held her uncertainty as she looked at the animal.

He turned to her again, his answer drawing out in silence before he lifted her hand, drawing it closer to his chest. "If you're asking if I want to do more of this..." He brought her knuckle to his lips, placing a tender kiss on her fingers before kissing onto the back of her hand. "I couldn't ask that of you, either. A life at sea is not for everyone, even if it's the one I've chosen."

Tilting her head, Ahria admired his light eyes. "I would choose it, too, if it meant..." She swallowed, feeling her boldness wane. "I would be perfectly happy on a ship, stealing hats and seeing all the places you have."

"I'd happily show them all to you." He shifted as he turned, resting more on his hip.

Andi groaned as his movement displaced her and she rolled onto the deck, shaking as she stood, seemingly happy to wander now that the humans were more distracted by each other.

"But is that what you want?" Ahria mirrored his turn, facing him.

"I want to know you, Ahria. To learn more about you. And more of this." He drew her hand back towards his chest again, holding it where she could feel his heart beating beneath the soft leather jacket. "I only worry because I know I can seem hard at times. But I don't want to be that way with you."

A bittersweet warmth spread through her. "I want to know you, too. And if it takes a week, a month, even a year... I'll wait for that chance. Because I think there's something between us that could be amazing. Just tell me how to find you after, and I will."

A smile crossed his face as he kissed her hand again. "Come with me." He stood, never letting go of her as he helped her to her feet.

Ahria furrowed her brow, but obliged, walking with him as he led her down the stairs towards his cabin.

With a short whistle from Conrad, Andi bounded after them and pushed through the ajar door first. She launched herself at the bed, spinning in circles as if looking for the perfect spot as the captain led Ahria inside.

The chill faded from her skin as the cabin's heat permeated her cloak. Her shoulders relaxed finally, and she shut the door behind her. "What are you thinking?"

Conrad released her as he crossed towards his desk, the hat they'd stolen together perched on top of it. He unbuttoned his jacket, slipping it from his shoulders as he reached the desk, and draped it over a chair.

Her pulse hammered faster, but she kept her expression neutral.

"Dawn Chaser has certain berths we always match throughout the trade year." He pushed the hat to the side as he reached for parchment and an inkwell. "After you find your father, you'll be able to meet me at whichever port is closest when you're ready."

Hope blossomed in her heart as she approached him. "And you're... willing to just give me that information?"

He tilted his head towards her as he popped open the inkwell and dipped a pen into it. "I trust you. Even if you did try to blackmail me."

A sheepish smile touched her face. "Sorry about that."

A low chuckle made her spine tingle as he started slowly writing dates next to seaside cities from all over Pantracia. His quill moved unsteadily, like he thought about each and every letter. His brow knitted, and she wondered if he regretted the offer. "I can hardly blame your tactics, considering what I know now." He left the paper to dry, reviewing the list silently, his mouth moving in the names of the cities. "Just... try not to let this information fall into the hands of any Feyorian bounty hunters."

He lifted the paper, holding it out to her.

"I'll guard it with my life." Ahria took it, looking it over.

"End? That's a ways north."

"And a lucrative trade route in late autumn when most sane captains don't brave the early frosts." Conrad jerked his chin at the list. "That make you reconsider the life at all?"

He hadn't left any cities on his route out, it seemed. No matter how distant.

Ahria lifted her gaze to his, seeing the vulnerability hidden beneath the offhanded question. She shook her head. "Not even a little. Though I'm kind of a wimp with the cold, so I'd need lots of blankets."

He laughed again, and she realized it was the most she'd seen him do so since they'd met. The sound led into his movement forward to her. "I can be sure to provide that. And will try to find other ways to keep you warm." His hand slipped to her waist, a move far more intimate than any of his touches before, and her heart lurched faster.

After laying the list of dates and locations down on his desk to let it fully dry, Ahria wrapped her arms around his shoulders, her stomach flip flopping. "I wouldn't blame you if you didn't wait for me, but I must admit, I'd be so wonderfully happy if you did. So selfishly, selfishly happy."

"I doubt you'll find it surprising to know that the life of a ship's captain doesn't typically lend itself to pursuing any kind of romantic relationship." His face hardened slightly, but he didn't withdraw. "And I don't mean to presume anything between us, either. But I do hope that maybe, this time, things will be different with you, Mouse."

She smiled, both at her lingering surprise, despite his suggestion, and at the nickname that cemented his affections. "There is no need to presume. I'd like to pursue this as soon as we can." Touching his hair at his neckline, she ignored the internal war within her at the limited time they had now. "And eventually, at one of those stops, you'll end up with a stowaway."

"A very welcome one." His fingers tangled with a strand of her hair, trailing it over her jaw. "I'm... grateful you didn't pull away back there, on the beach. I surprised myself, so I can't imagine what it was like for you."

"Probably something like this," she murmured, and rose onto her tiptoes to kiss him.

His grip around her tightened, encouraging her closer as their mouths met. The tightness of his face hovered within the kiss, but only for a moment before his lips followed the movement with hers. Then it was like everything in his body relaxed at once, and she kissed him again.

The room blurred and Ahria shut her eyes, losing herself again in the way he tasted, felt, and the scent of his skin. Sea water and cedar, touched with a hint of the fire wine from earlier. Tilting her head, she parted her lips, and their tongues greeted each other with a pulse-pounding wave of heat.

The pressure of Conrad's hands on her hips grew, and she pressed her body against his as his touch trailed up her back and into her hair. It played in the roots at the back of her head, slowly brushing through as he deepened the kiss, like he wanted more of her. Yet, there was a restraint in it all, as if he still struggled to keep control as their tongues moved in tandem.

The back of her thighs bumped against the edge of the map table, sending one of the chairs grinding across the floor before she even realized they'd begun moving.

Ahria worked the buttons on his vest, wanting nothing more than to touch his skin. With his cooperation, she dropped it to the floor and pulled his shirt from where it was tucked into his pants.

His hands roved down her body as he leaned her against the table. They slipped beneath her cloak, toying with the edge of her belt and breeches as their mouths parted and he sucked in a steadying breath. Eyes fluttering open, he met her gaze with his lips still parted before glancing down to her mouth.

Tugging at his shirt, Ahria smiled. "This needs to go."

Conrad caught her hand, but entwined his fingers with hers before pulling it to his lips. He kissed her skin hard, his eyes closing again as he shook his head subtly. "Not yet. Not when this could still be a goodbye."

Ahria pulled his lips to hers, kissing him hard before withdrawing. "It's not."

"Then we have nothing to worry about." Conrad stroked

his hand through her hair, still pressed against her. "We can wait."

"We can. But until then, can't I keep kissing you?"

His answer came with a tilt of his head as he caught her mouth again, lowering their hands together onto the table top as he whispered, "Yes, please."

Chapter 12

THE SCENT OF EARLY SPRING blew from the rolling hills behind Treama, dancing along the secured sails of Dawn Chaser. Most of the crew had vacated the ship around midday, after they'd docked that late morning. Likely to go spend their recent pay at the taverns and gambling halls.

A strange feeling of nostalgia drifted in the sea breeze, like it always did for Conrad when he visited his old home. Looking out from the banister beside the helm, he could just spy the worn purple roof tiles of Thorn's Edge, the tavern he'd basically been raised in. His cheeks burned as if Yedra had just pinched them.

He debated if he should disembark and pay a visit to the old bar matron, but she'd most definitely tell his mother, and that would lead to more awkward reunions.

Better to just stay on the ship while we're here. Like always.

He drummed his thumbs on the banister, making Andi's ears perk up from where she lay on top of his boots. A knot had formed within him that he couldn't untangle. It only worsened as he saw Ahria emerge from below deck, a bag slung over her shoulder.

She wore her usual black leather breeches, white shirt and black vest. Her cloak covered her shoulders, but hung open, revealing the hilts of various blades only visible to the trained eye. Her steps were sluggish, half-hearted, and she dropped her pack near the gangplank.

Davros had departed earlier with the crew to seek entertainment, but Conrad hadn't witnessed their farewell.

If they even had one.

Pulling his feet from under his dog, the captain stepped down from the helm, his own gait heavy. "Got everything?" He absently touched the fine pair of leather gloves he'd tucked into his belt, but felt for the lump in his pocket beneath them.

Ahria's steel blue gaze met his, and she huffed. "Doesn't feel like it." She took a deeper breath, running a hand over her braided hair. "Feels like I'm forgetting something, but it's just my mind playing tricks on me."

He wanted to smile. To reassure her, but the truth wouldn't allow it. "Tell me your plan, again." They'd gone over the steps together in his cabin. If he couldn't go with her, he'd do what he could to make her search more efficient.

"Buy a horse. Talk to the innkeeps in town and ask after anyone resembling my father. If nothing turns up, I will ride east towards Daygon's Pass and make camp along the way to Dragon's Gate. And repeat, until I find some information that will help me. I will keep to myself and not draw attention. With the civil unrest, I will never assume safety and I'll extinguish all fires before nightfall. Don't worry, I know how to be careful. Invisible. I'll be fine." Ahria sighed. "And when it's all done, I'll meet you." She patted her cloak, where she'd stashed the list of dates and locations he'd given her.

"And you can always send letters to the ports ahead of my arrival if you need anything. Even if I'd have to wait for you." He pulled the small leather pouch from his pocket and, before she could protest, he pushed it into her hand. "Keep that in one of your boots. It's the obvious place, so no one will look for it there."

Ahria looked down at the coin purse and shook her head, shoving it back towards him. "I don't need a handout. I can figure it out."

"It's not a handout. It's the fair wage you would have made if I'd been paying you as a member of the crew. And maybe a little bonus." He took her hand in his, gripping her fingers to close it back around the coins. "You'll need it. If you don't have to worry about money, then you'll be able to keep up the search and find your father sooner. Which means you'll come back to me sooner. It's selfish, really."

Her throat bobbed as she nodded, trying to smile while stuffing the small leather pouch into her cloak. With a half-hearted roll of her glassy eyes, she muttered, "There's no extra room in my boots with all the metal there already."

"Fair, I suppose the knives should take priority." He reached for her hand as she pulled it out of her cloak again. He closed both hands around her one, lifting the back of it to his lips. "Be safe." The twist in his stomach only grew worse, urging him that letting her go was a mistake. But he couldn't ask her to stay.

Ahria squeezed his hand. "This isn't goodbye. I'll see you again before you know it."

"That's what I'm counting on." He touched her hair, gently running his fingers along her braid. With a slow step, he moved into her, lifting her chin so he could kiss her, no longer caring who might see.

Her lips moved against his as she touched his face before reluctantly pulling away. "You be safe, too. Promise me."

"I promise." He forced a step back from her. He schooled his face to hide the screaming in his chest. He'd only known her for a few weeks, yet she'd burrowed so deeply into his soul that the very concept of not seeing her made everything ache.

Turning from him, Ahria picked up her pack and walked to the top of the gangplank. She paused there, then looked back at him. Her jaw worked for a breath before she dropped her pack and launched herself at him, colliding with his chest and throwing her arms around his shoulders the same way she had on seeing it was him chasing her in Haven Port.

He half expected his body to react as it always would, suddenly claustrophobic at being assaulted, even if affectionately. But with Ahria, he suddenly wished he could take her further into him. He wrapped his arms around her, holding her tightly to his chest as he felt her heart beat against his own.

"I'll miss you, Captain," she whispered near his ear, burying her face into the side of his neck. "If I can manage it, you'll have a letter from me at every port, regardless of where I am."

He smiled as he leaned his face into her hair, a kiss forming there. "I hope they will help me overcome how much I miss you."

She kissed his neck, pulling away and looking at his face. "I... am grateful you didn't throw me overboard."

"Best decision I made that week, for sure." Conrad smirked as he pinched her chin.

Huffing a breath, Ahria cringed and pulled away. "If I don't go now, I doubt I will, so..."

He nodded, pursing his lips to hide the frown. "I know. You're losing daylight." He stepped back again, tucking his hands into his pockets. "You'll find your father, and I'll see you soon."

Ahria nodded, picking up her pack and slinging it over her shoulder. She opened her mouth to speak, but closed it and only nodded again. Turning, she hurried down the gangplank to the dock, looking back only once she reached solid ground, and then disappeared into the crowded street.

He remained on deck and stared at the unfamiliar heads moving around the fish market, finding himself hoping her face would re-emerge and she would make her way back up the gangplank.

Andi pushed into his calf, her angle making his knee buckle slightly as he turned to her brute force attempt to get his attention. She sat on top of his foot and looked up at him, her tongue lolling out the side of her mouth.

"Oblivious, as always." Urging himself to relax, he idly scratched Andi's head. With little else to do until the ship was ready to depart the following morning, he returned to his cabin.

The sounds of the busy Treama dock carried through his open door, including the bartering of the dockmaster with newly arriving ships. Small groups of the crew returned, disappearing below deck, likely for a nap so they'd be able to spend their money later into the night.

A knock at his door lifted his gaze, and Davros stood in the frame. The man looked better than he had immediately after Ahria ended things with him, and he even smiled at the captain. "Evening, Captain. Leiura gave me my new contract this afternoon, and I wanted to thank you for the continued opportunity of working aboard your ship. Mighty gracious of you after all the trouble we caused."

Conrad glanced up from the map, where he'd found himself trying to chart Ahria's possible path. "Sure. You proved yourself experienced enough over the last couple weeks." He pursed his lips, glancing over the tall man's shoulder to the rest of the deck as Leiura's familiar shape returned to the ship. "Glad you're staying on. But hey, look. I'm sorry about things not working out with Ahria."

Davros nodded once. "Appreciate it. Shoulda known she'd find her way to someone far grander than me." He smirked at himself, shaking his head, his tone lacking the hostility it had days ago when referencing her. "I just hope whoever it is has the mind to treat her right. She deserves that much, even if she can be a pain in the ass."

Conrad huffed, but nodded. "That she is, and does." He lifted his chin as Leiura walked up behind Davros, patting him on the shoulder.

The young man dipped his chin and exited, leaving Conrad alone with his first mate.

"You're still here?" Leiura leaned on the door frame, an amused look on her face.

Conrad only frowned. "Of course I'm still here. You know I don't get off the ship in Treama."

"Nah, I mean you're still *here*. I half expected to come

back to a note tied to Andi's collar saying 'don't sink my ship or kill my dog.'" She stepped into the cabin, pausing to scratch Andi's head where she lay on his bed.

"What are you talking about? I can't just abandon the ship to go off with her."

"Sure you could. Not like I wouldn't have taken care of Dawn Chaser. I'd give her back..." She leaned on the his bed. "Probably..." She wiggled her hand back and forth. "Maybe."

Conrad's gut twisted. "You're serious?" He stood. "Why didn't you say something sooner?" He'd only briefly considered the possibility of going with Ahria. The idea felt insane after all he'd worked for with Dawn Chaser, and it'd feel like he was abandoning everything he'd sweated and bled for. He'd never ask Leiura to take on the burden of managing the ship as captain, then return and force her back into a first mate position. But if she was offering...

Leiura straightened. "You never asked, and I thought you would have if you loved the girl. And by the way you two were gawking the last two days, thinking you were being sneaky..." She shook her head. "Like I said, figured you'd be gone when I got back."

Conrad sighed, running both hands back over his head. "You can be so..." He looked to the open doorway where the horizon darkened with the encroaching night. As he considered his first mate, the anxiety in his stomach turned towards excitement for the first time. "You're serious? You'd take Dawn Chaser, stick to the planned course, and be all right being my first mate again when I'm able to come back?"

Leiura smirked. "I said maybe, but I'm willing to go back to *probably* with that look in your eye." She lifted her hand towards Andi. "I ain't keeping the dog, though. She'll just complain every moment you're gone, and I warned you that getting her was going to be a commitment."

Conrad scoffed. "I'm not leaving Andi."

The dog's head lifted from the bed at her name, tail thumping for a breath before she stiffened and growled.

Leiura whirled around, and suddenly jogged from his room without another word as the sound of heavy boots on their gangplank overtook everything else.

Conrad held his hand out to Andi, commanding her to stay before following his first mate out onto the main deck to see a formation of formidable soldiers, half on his ship and the other half still on the docks.

Onlookers gaped, giving them a wide berth as they whispered to each other.

"What is this?" Conrad approached the woman who looked like their leader. "You don't have permission to board my ship."

"We don't need your permission." The armored soldier held out a scroll, sealed with a dark purple wax insignia stamped with the royal crest. "Are you Conrad Pendaverin, living under the alias of Conrad Penderbroke?"

"Alias?" Conrad stiffened, snatching the scroll from the soldier. "I'm Captain Conrad Penderbroke, and who the hells are you?" He snapped the seal, starting to unravel the rather official-looking document.

"Then you are under order by the queen of Ziona to come with us." The commander stood her ground, waiting. "You have twenty minutes to pack your things and attend to any business. Any attempt to flee will be taken as an act of treason against the crown."

"Excuse me?" Conrad's hands tightened on the scroll, crumpling the fine paper before he even attempted to read it. "Orders from the queen? Ziona's got a queen now?"

Leiura stood next to him, holding out her hand. "Let me see it."

Conrad handed it over without protest, looking past the commander at the front of the battalion to the line of soldiers still standing on his gangplank.

His first mate unraveled it, reading over it with darting eyes. "It even names you as the captain of Dawn Chaser," she murmured. "It's not a mistake. This is a royal decree for you to attend a formal conference at the capital with the queen and the newly reformed parliament. You can't ignore this."

"When did we get a queen?" Conrad knew he focused on the most mundane of the details presented to him.

The commander of the battalion gave a dry smile, glancing around the ship. "Been a while since you've visited your home berth, hasn't it? Missed all the big news." She crossed her arms. "You have fifteen minutes remaining."

"Shit." Conrad looked back at his cabin, already trying to inventory what he might need for a visit to the capital. "When will I be able to return?"

The commander blinked. "Your return is unlikely."

Disbelief rippled through him, everything numbing. "Some new queen...What the hells does she want with me?" He spun back into his cabin, rushing towards his bookshelves, trying to remember his plan if he ever found himself in a position of needing to abandon ship. He needed to prioritize the most important of his belongings.

Leiura followed him into his cabin, but the soldiers didn't. Thankfully. "Fucking monarchy already messing up things they don't have the right to put their nose in. What could they possibly want with a ship's captain?"

His eyes roamed over the maps on the table, to where the ostentatious hat sat on the top of his desk. He heard Leiura, but he didn't have time to consider what it all meant. The royal guards meant to take him, willingly or otherwise. And he had greater concerns than Leiura's care of his ship.

He couldn't go after her now. And he wouldn't be able to meet her. Not if this trip to the capital was as permanent as the guards made it sound.

He rushed to his desk, whipping out a piece of parchment and hastily wrote a note. The letters came out jumbled.

"Shit." Squinting to urge the lines on the page to align correctly in his brain, he crossed out words and rewrote them more times than he was proud of. The task took ten of his remaining fifteen minutes and every ounce of his concentration.

Dearest Ahria,

I'm sorry I'm not here. I know I promised I would be, but this was something I never could have predicted. I've been summoned to New Kingston by Ziona's new queen, and given little choice in the matter. If you're here, and reading this, it means I haven't been able to return yet. But I'll find a way back to you.

Conrad

He left it drying on the desk as he rushed to his bed, Andi jumping off in surprise. She barked, growling in the direction of the commander waiting outside until Conrad hissed at her. He fished his journal out from under his bed, ignoring Leiura's amused look. From there, he rushed about the cabin, stuffing odds and ends into the bag. Things that he knew were irreplaceable, but anyone else would likely scoff at.

Brass bookends Captain Andi had gifted him. A small carved dolphin made from driftwood, Leiura's first and only attempt at the craft. A necklace, featuring a marble size glass bead, that once belonged to his father was among them, along with the letters his mother had sent him.

Andi's tail wagged as she chased Conrad around the cabin, but the excitement dwindled as she caught onto the tension permeating every muscle.

"So, does this mean I get to *keep* Dawn Chaser now?" Leiura's tone was teasing, but the look on her face was far more serious.

"Not if I have something to say about it." He flinched with how harsh his words sounded. "Sorry, Leiura, but I'm hoping I can sort this out and be back before Ahria even thinks about meeting up with the ship."

"Is that for her?" Leiura gestured to the letter.

"Just in case I don't make it back in time, yes."

"You think this new queen is an acquaintance of yours or something?"

"I have no idea. Didn't think I knew any of the old royals. But I guess with the coup, whoever they were probably kept it real secret." Conrad rubbed the back of his head as he stared at the bag on his bed, trying to sort through his list of treasures again.

"I don't know the old lineages, considering it all got buried by the military when they took over." She made a face. "But they called you Pendaverin. Maybe your mum—"

"Time's up." The commander stepped into the doorway, a hand on her hip near her sword.

Conrad scowled. "Are you arresting me or escorting me?"

The commander shifted, her steel armor rubbing against the leather beneath it. "You're not under arrest."

"Then calm down. I'm not going to run off, and I'll go with you in a minute. Have some decency to let me say goodbye." Conrad tried to control his anger, but could tell he hadn't succeeded by the way the commander narrowed her eyes.

Leiura stepped between them, putting both hands on Conrad's shoulders. "Just don't be a pain in the ass, and I'm sure I'll see you before the season's end." She squeezed him through his leather coat harder than he deserved, but he smiled with his wince.

"Take care of her." As he said it, he realized he was talking about Ahria more than his ship, but didn't know which way Leiura would interpret it.

His first mate just nodded, stepping around him towards his desk where the letter still sat open.

Conrad didn't look back as he stepped towards the commander and whistled. Andi bounded forward, looking suspiciously up at the commander before she sat next to Conrad, leaning against his leg.

The commander lifted an eyebrow.

"Dog goes with me. Non-negotiable."

"Very well," she ground out. "Carriage is close. Your palace liaison awaits within."

With a schooled expression, Conrad hid his confusion. A liaison suggested that they expected him to potentially visit or interact with people that would require him to behave in a specific way. One of the old traditions he'd heard about that he had no taste for. Whoever was the one to school him on his behavior would probably think him a mannerless ruffian from the seas.

Yet, as Conrad made his way down the gangplank, his small bag of worldly possessions clutched at one side, his dog on the other, he already felt the weight of formality settling back into his gait. His grandmother never would have let him see his tenth birthday without at least a basic understanding of how one was to act in public.

Another small regiment of decorated guards stood beside the carriage, which was embossed with gold and purple filigree. He'd never seen something so horrendously fancy in his life.

A man moved to the curved door and opened it, a hanging lantern illuminating the interior where only one other person sat. As Conrad grew closer, he realized it wasn't a lantern at all, but a sphere of light, crafted by the Art.

The captain carefully stepped into the carriage, ducking through the doorway. He didn't get a chance to sit before Andi leapt in behind him, forcing him to catch himself on the carriage frame.

Thanks, girl. Help me prove my ineptitude.

The man inside chuckled at the dog and offered a hand as Conrad took a seat, his skin almost as dark as the captain's. As he shook it, Conrad met the man's emerald green eyes, his pupils no larger than pin pricks even in the dim light of the carriage.

"A pleasure to see you again, young man." Auer. This was no human at all, but an auer. "Though, I suppose you don't remember me."

The carriage door shut, and the auer released Conrad's hand to gesture at the sphere of light, making it brighter as they lurched into motion.

Andi groaned before she awkwardly stumbled up onto the cushioned bench Conrad sat on, throwing herself across his lap.

"Can't say I do..." Conrad ignored his dog and racked his brain to recall his various visits to Eralas. But it was possible if he had met the auer there, he'd have promptly forgotten.

"I'm Talon Di'Terian. A friend of Talia, your mother. We met at Thorn's Edge many years ago." Talon leaned back in his seat, a content look on his face.

The names he uttered linked together in Conrad's memories, and he sucked in a steadying breath as he leaned back. "Talon." He repeated the name, wishing he could somehow conjure the memories from his childhood to help confirm the auer was who he claimed. Conrad's mother had told him stories about an auer who used to help care for him in the inn she used to work. "Why are you here?"

"I've been looking for you for a few months. You're needed in the capital."

"What in Nymaera's name for? Could have been a bit more civil about the summons." He crossed his arms, leaning back against the jostling wall of the intricate carriage.

"Apologies for that, but we are short on time. We'll need to reach our destination within the next three weeks. And as a ship's captain, you should know, the tide waits for no person."

Conrad frowned as the carriage lurched to a stop, causing him to bump his head on the wall behind him. He winced, a growl entering his tone. "You still haven't told me what I'm needed in New Kingston *for*."

Talon smiled, offering him a gold leaf-rimmed invitation. "For your mother's coronation."

Chapter 13

AHRIA SQUINTED, GROANING AS EARLY morning daylight pierced her curtains and ruined her deep sleep. Rolling over, she blinked a few times before her gaze settled on her pack, slumped against the wall next to her bed.

Her bed. At the inn. The inn in Treama.

"Shit." Ahria whipped the blankets off, dressing and lacing her boots with unprecedented speed. All while making sure her hidden blades were still in their proper places. She'd gotten distracted the night before, talking with a barkeep in the city who'd known her father once. It'd grown too dark to leave, so she'd stayed, but a new purpose had filled her as she fell asleep.

It had occurred to her that if she could write to Conrad through port cities, she could also write to Talon in the same manner. Her father would be fine. She would find him eventually, and until then, she could stay aboard Dawn Chaser with Conrad.   Hells, it'd probably be even more efficient than her wandering blindly through Ziona. Sure, Davros would be there making things awkward, but she wouldn't let that stop her.

As long as Conrad hasn't set sail yet.

As she raced into the street, she looked towards the docks, praying his ship was still there. Flinging her pack over her shoulder, she jogged to the pier, everyone around her still sluggish in the early hour.

Once she set eyes on Dawn Chaser, she slowed, sighing a breath of relief. Excitement at seeing him again so soon built in her gut. Her heart thundered as she strode up the gangplank, and she spotted Leiura standing near the helm.

Biting her lower lip, she headed straight for the open door of Conrad's cabin, but the first mate stopped her.

"He's not here." Leiura turned and addressed the crew member next to her before descending the stairs to greet Ahria. "What are you doing back?"

"I thought maybe I could continue my search while on the ship... What do you mean he's not here?" Ahria's chest tightened, unease swirling within her at what could have possibly taken Conrad from his ship.

Leiura sighed, shaking her head. "Your timing is about as spot on as that of those soldiers who came looking for him."

"Soldiers?" Ahria bristled, her pulse picking up speed. "He got arrested?"

"Nah, nothing that dramatic." Leiura waved her hand as she strode through the open doorway into the captain's cabin. "Summoned. Apparently our boy has some unknown connections with whoever they've saddled with the crown. The queen summoned him by name."

Ahria's mind spun as she tried to keep up. "Where is he going, then? The capital?"

How had she just missed him like this? The irony made her insides churn. If she'd only stuck to her plan and left the day before, maybe...

"That's what the tin-can said." Leiura reached the desk and picked a scrap of paper scrawled with Conrad's messy handwriting. The woman gave it to her. "He wrote this for you."

Ahria took the paper and read over it. "The capital indeed," she muttered. "They're taking him by land?"

A wide river ran from the sea to New Kingston, large enough for a full size galleon to maneuver within. Conrad had warned her about crossing that river, and to plan her journey accordingly. They could have traveled by sea if they were in a hurry to get him there, but it would be impossible for her to follow unless they went by land.

Leiura shrugged. "Saw him climb into a fancy carriage and start south through the markets. Can't say for sure. There are plenty of docks still further south, but they're all privately owned and not for trade vessels."

"Privately owned. Meaning one of them is owned by the government." Ahria frowned, her excitement extinguished in a breath.

"Nymaera only knows. Ziona hasn't exactly had a sound government structure for a few decades."

"I need to find him," Ahria murmured, folding the letter and slipping it into her pocket. She crossed to the door and looked back at Leiura. "Thank you."

"For what?" Leiura crossed her arms as she leaned against the desk. "I didn't give you much to go off of."

Ahria shrugged. "What you gave me is much better than nothing." She dipped her chin, exiting the captain's quarters as she called back, "I hope we meet again!"

Travel to New Kingston took Ahria longer than she had predicted. Her new mount, Tyn, carried her swiftly through the flat lands, but Daygon's Pass hadn't fully thawed. It slowed her travel, forcing the sturdy bay horse to trudge through knee-deep snow near the top.

In the quiet nights, alone with Tyn, she found herself missing Riot. The Friesian horse remained at home in Gallisville after the farrier had insisted he couldn't travel with the condition of his hooves. It'd hurt to leave him, considering the legacy the young stallion represented. He'd grown to look just like his sire, Viento, and was another piece of her mother she would have preferred to keep with her. But Lorin's death and Talon's lack of reply spurred her to take the first exit from the small town she could. She and Davros had ridden a paint mare that she'd ultimately sold in Zola before stowing away.

Having Riot with her would have only ended up complicating matters.

Snow faded and spring emerged with greater intensity as she descended the other side of Daygon's Pass. Dappled fields of wildflowers and trees with fresh leaves framed the worn trade road, still mostly untraveled in the early season.

Sticking to the plan she'd concocted with Conrad, Ahria kept to herself, and usually opted to sleep in the forest rather than small villages. Only on the coldest of nights had she ventured into an inn, seeking the comfort of a hearth and hot meal. No one paid her any heed, and she often noted she wasn't the only woman traveling alone. And they weren't bothered, either. Not like at home in Olsa. Usually women were respected there, too, but here... it was just different.

And she had to admit... She liked it.

Finally arriving at the outskirts of New Kingston, Ahria marveled at the city's great walls and architecture. She'd seen some incredible infrastructure on her journey so far, but this would be her first visit to a capital city. Any capital.

Trade merchants and civilians filed in and out of the city gates in great swaths, and she followed the line inside, trying not to look suspicious as the guards looked her over.

Once she'd entered, free to explore, she stared at the expanse of city streets before her. Most of the buildings stood three stories tall, their stuccoed white walls framed with dark oak that'd come from the mountain behind the city. Everything slowly sloped upward to the east, where she suspected the massive river Conrad had warned her about would be.

She stared up at the arched bridge that passed over the outer gate of the city.

Where do I even start?

If Conrad had been summoned by the queen, then it made sense he'd be taken to the palace.

Ahria asked a guard for directions, but it still took her most of the day to cross the city and locate the actual palace. Though, if she'd only followed the steady incline of the widest street in the city, she'd have found it naturally.

A twenty-foot high marbled wall ran along the outer edge of the palace. A pair of elaborately carved oak gates stood closed, blocking all view of the courtyard between it and the palace proper. She could only see the tops of the buildings, their grandiose towers adorned with rippling purple and gold flags. Gazing up the wall, she spied the crested helmets of guards on the upper walkway, but she didn't allow herself a lingering look. The guards who stood at the gate only glanced at her before she moved on.

Finding a nearby stable, she boarded Tyn and stashed her pack with him. She'd draw less attention on foot as she made her way back to the palace. Slipping through narrow alleyways, the two and three-story townhouses towering around her made her feel small. But she maneuvered her way back to the front gate, flipping the sides of her cloak over her shoulders to look less threatening.

It'd been over two weeks since she left Treama, and she hoped Conrad might still be here.

"Excuse me." Ahria approached one of the guards. "I'm looking for someone, and I have reason to believe he's staying at the palace. I was wondering if you could help me?"

"Move along. No entry." The guard didn't even look at her, lips pursed into a tight line beneath the visor of her helm.

Gritting her teeth, Ahria glanced between the two guards and opted not to make a scene. Not with the rumblings about the queen's upcoming coronation and discontent regarding the common folk losing access to the palace gardens. With daylight fading, the last thing she needed was to get arrested for disturbing the peace. Conrad had warned her of the tension in Ziona, and that the nascent royal military may escalate matters unnecessarily. She needed to be careful, so she walked away.

A little voice at the back of her mind told her yet again

that her search was in vain. Fruitless. A complete and utter waste of time. She'd never find him, and she'd never find Talon.

But Ahria shook it off. She'd let the desolation set in while in Haven Port, but the captain had come for her. He'd proven that little voice wrong, and she was determined to do the same.

Finding a small tavern, she warmed up inside and filled her belly, eager to banish the hunger pains of rationing food on the road. She didn't bother inquiring after a room, certain she wouldn't be needing it that night. The truth became more and more apparent as she plotted, and she decided that the best way to gain access to the palace would be to sneak in. After all, she'd used similar tactics to board not just Conrad's ship, but Warrin's, too.

They won't catch me.

Ahria waited until dark, packing half her blades and leaving the rest in her pack at the stable. Finding a dark alley, she climbed stacked crates that butted up against a building near the palace wall. Pulling herself onto the roof, she crouched and eyed her surroundings. She'd need to cross the roofs of three buildings to reach the palace wall, and even then, the wall was another story taller.

Gulping, she kept low as she made her way closer, ducking out of sight whenever a sentry passed.

In one of those moments, she closed her eyes and

hesitated. She could practically hear her father's voice in her head telling her to go back. Go home. Be safe.

This is the stupidest thing I've ever done.

Ahria shook off the notion, reminding herself she had little other choice to see if Conrad was within the palace. The need to know where he was felt like another rock in her stomach, beside that of her missing father. She *had* to find him. And if he was inside, he'd protect her, regardless of how she got there.

If he can...

As soon as the sentry passed, Ahria closed the remaining distance to the palace wall. Shoving her fingers into the tight space between bricks, she climbed, her boots barely catching on the thin gaps. Her whole body ached, muscles shaking with the effort, but she stopped just before mounting the top and stilled.

Voices murmured above her, moving at a leisurely pace along the wall's walkway. She couldn't make out the words. But weapons rattled against armor, confirming they were guards.

Sweaty, her fingers slipped. She gripped harder, pain rippling through her limbs. Blood smeared over her fingers and palms, small abrasions stinging with every movement.

Through the glare of pain, she lost track of the guards. But the sound of their weapons came a moment later from further down the wall. She huffed and swung herself onto the walkway, rolling onto her stomach. Shaking her bleeding hands, she cringed, but turned towards a stairwell she spied on the other side.

At least I don't have to climb down, too.

The thought of how she'd get out of the palace again made her pause briefly before she urged her feet forward.

I'll figure that out later.

Descending the stairs with quick, quiet steps, she kept to the shadows of the courtyard. Skulking through the darkness against the wall towards the palace, she passed by an archway, glancing inside to ensure it was empty, and then continued closer.

The half moon glowed along the rough hewn marble courtyard. It was the size of a city block, each corner hosting a square of lush grass and flower beds. At the center stood a barren pedestal, which she imagined might have once hosted a statue of some kind, but now there was nothing but smooth stone. At the far corner of the courtyard were the palace doors. Stairs led to a balcony and another closed gate, though this one was unguarded.

Probably guards inside that big ass door, though.

Soft footsteps sounded behind her, and her heart leapt into her throat. She turned just as something hard struck her head, and the world went black.

Chapter 14

STARING UP AT THE TOWERING cliffs of the Astarian River to the parapets of the New Kingston palace, Conrad's head spun. A pier stuck out from a human-crafted cavern dug into the base of the canyon, stone statues of two Zionan soldiers forever frozen in a salute at either side. They stood at least fifty feet tall, grand and formidable. A pair of real guards stood near the entrance into the cavern, the high ceilings still rugged stone, but the finely polished floors gleamed with artificial light.

"You can close your mouth, now." Talon snuck up behind him, making Conrad twitch.

"Apologies for looking impressed." Conrad hardened his expression, forcing his jaw closed. "Can't say in all my trips to

New Kingston that I've had the opportunity of traveling this far up river."

"It is quite the sight." Talon leaned on the banister, facing him. "But I should prepare you for what's going to happen once we enter the palace."

"And what exactly do you have planned to prepare me for my mother's *coronation?*"

The auer's expression flattened. "I can only brief you on what to expect. Things will move quickly, and much will be expected of you as crown prince."

The title made him nauseous, and he swallowed, trying to recall the lectures Talon had already inflicted upon him about how to dress and behave, what titles to use for whom, and the general runnings of the palace. "But the monarchy has no power. We have a parliament."

"Ziona's citizens wanted the monarchy restored, too. But it is now a power that will work in tandem with parliament. The parliament still holds the majority of governmental control, but the nation has a deep, ingrained loyalty to the crown. The most elegant solution was to create a joint government to rule and hopefully heal a broken country." Talon's smooth voice seemed so practiced for someone who apparently had no experience beyond the last few months with managing royalty.

"So parliament decided to just *unbanish* my family because it suited them."

"Because it suited most of the country's population." Talon crossed his arms. "Probably one of the smarter decisions they've made in the last ten years."

"Why didn't I know? Mum never mentioned any of this to me. And shouldn't my grandma be inheriting the throne if she's the old banished Pendaverin?"

The auer shook his head. "Your mum didn't know, either. And political news often takes a while to reach those at sea." Narrowing his eyes, he paused before continuing with a softer tone. "And your grandmother joined Nymaera a couple years ago."

A slight stab echoed in his stomach, only to be quickly overcome with his anxiety about walking off the ship. "No need for condolences." He pushed the memories of his overbearing grandmother from his mind. "But she's probably rolling over in her grave knowing that I'm about to walk into the palace right now."

Talon's lips pursed into a thin line, and he looked to where a gangplank had been moved into position. "When we disembark, Mister Credish will escort you to your dressing room, where the tailor will be waiting to dress you... properly." His gaze roved over the captain. "From there, he will take you to your mother, where your bloodline will be confirmed before parliament by way of a blood contract. Talia will formally acknowledge you as her first born child, and you will acknowledge her as your mother. You'll sign a document confirming the same, and then you'll have about an hour to breathe before dinner."

"So much formality." Conrad closed his eyes, already fighting off an encroaching headache from it all. "These people really expect to dress up a sea captain and a barmaid from Treama and have us play royals like this?"

"It is not playing anymore, Conrad. This is your country, and you have a responsibility to make sure this goes well." Talon's voice took on a schooling tone. "It is not just your mother you need to worry about disappointing. I will not downplay the importance of your arrival. You are no longer a sea captain."

His heart sank at the words, as if it plummeted to the bottom of the Dul'Idur. His head shook. "I can't do this."

Talon's hard grip took Conrad by the elbow, as if he was still the child the auer had watched in Thorn's Edge. "You can. And you will. For your mother. She needs you right now."

He closed his eyes again, trying to breathe as he tapped his foot, but it was weighed down by Andi's shaggy head, the dog who had refused to be more than two feet from him.

The auer's grip eased. "Your mother was terrified in the beginning, too. You'll be all right. Just remember it's in your blood, whether you knew it or not."

How in Nymaera's name do people wear this stuff all day?

Conrad shifted, trying to find a comfortable position among all the layers of formal attire. He'd always been partial to wearing as few as possible, and while his leather coat had always slightly restricted his movement, he doubted he could lift his hands above his head in the finely stitched doublet they'd trapped him in. At least the color wasn't insulting. A plain stone grey with deep amethyst embroidery.

Even Andi had been forced to endure the attentions of some of the palace staff, having her golden coat washed and brushed out until it shone. A new studded collar encircled her neck, made of finer leather than Conrad would've purchased for her. Though, she seemed to enjoy the experience far more than her owner.

They'd been led down a hall after by Mister Credish, followed by a pair of guards, like he was being escorted to the gallows rather than another part of the palace. The palace that was to be his home, now. He still had to focus on his footing, not used to the lack of sway beneath his boots.

Talon was nowhere to be seen, which sent a flutter of annoyance through the captain. The auer's presence had become a steadying force, but at least Andi pranced down the hall with him. He would occasionally reach out to stroke her soft head for comfort. At least one thing would remain constant for him.

Credish stopped at a towering set of doors and turned to

bow a farewell to Conrad as the guards stepped forward.

He swore one of them gave him a suspicious sidelong look before they opened the doors in unison, as if the moment had been perfectly rehearsed.

"I look forward to the next time we meet, your highness." Credish bowed a little lower, prompting Andi to dance forward, but Conrad caught her collar before she could lick the steward's face.

"Thank you, Mister Credish." Conrad inclined his head in the barest nod.

"Connie!"

Conrad's gaze shot to the newly opened room, where his mother stood in the center.

Talon stood beside her, hands behind his back.

His mum looked beautiful. Wrinkles had formed at the corners of her eyes, but her dark skin still glowed as if she hadn't aged much at all in the eight years he'd been away from her. She was smaller than him, but her fine clothing made her seem far more grand. The perfectly tailored waistcoat was embedded with jewels, a pair of loose satin pants flowing to the elaborate rug of the study.

Talia strode towards him, eyes wide and glassy. "By the gods, I hardly believed it when Talon told me he'd finally brought you here." She stopped a few feet away, a hesitance in her frame that made Conrad's chest ache.

The captain approached her, feeling the ghost sways beneath his feet stronger under his mother's stare. He let go of Andi's collar, and the golden pup bounded to greet Talia before rushing to the auer with a wagging tail.

Gods, let me be as carefree as that animal.

Conrad questioned the rigidity of his back, and realized he hadn't taken a full breath since hearing his mother say his name. He glanced at Talon, not entirely sure why, before stepping entirely into the room.

Talia's brow knitted upward in the middle as she watched him, the doors closing at a gesture from Talon while the auer scratched the dog's chin.

"Connie... I missed you so much. Are you well?" Talia rolled her lips together, waiting.

"A little in shock." Conrad relaxed minutely, comforted by their privacy.

Her shoulders sagged at his words, and she smiled. "I was too, my dear."

Staring at her, he realized the distance still hovering between them, and questioned it. He questioned his own uncertainty about seeing his mum before, and now only felt relieved, especially with everything going on around them. Some child-like instinct took over as he closed the gap, wrapping his arms around his mother's waist to hug her tightly.

Talia let out a soft, relieved sob as she closed her arms

around his shoulders, pulling him down into her with arms he'd forgotten the strength of. She kissed his temple, wetness from her eyes soaking into his skin and hair.

"I'm so glad you're here." Her voice was soft, the comforting tone he remembered from every time he'd returned home with a scrape or a bruise. It made his chest feel like it was caving in.

"I missed you, too, mum. I'm sorry I haven't been in touch. I..."

"That's all right," she murmured, squeezing him. "It's all right. You're here, now, and I'm so happy for that."

Andi yipped, pushing against the back of his knees as if she wanted to be part of the embrace.

Conrad carefully pulled back from his mum, looking at her glassy eyes. "How did this happen?"

Talia gave a short laugh as she gestured to herself. "Your guess is as good as mine. My mother never said a word. Though, I always did get the impression that she was used to a far more noble life before the one I remember as a child. All those lessons about manners like she thought I was going to use them somewhere... Like she forgot we lived in the poorest district of Treama." Talia never fully let go of her son, keeping a hold of his hand. "You remember how she was, don't you?" Grief shone in her eyes, and Conrad knew the loss for her was much greater than it was for him.

"I do... And I never understood it either. But what

happens now? We just abandon our previous lives and live as Zionan royalty?"

"We must. It is our duty." Talia glanced at Talon, who petted the dog again. "We have help. Talon will return home after the coronation, but we hope to bring him back permanently. He has been invaluable to me, and is here to help you adjust, too."

The auer looked up. "And you'll get used to the layers."

Conrad almost made a face in response, but schooled it quickly.

At least I'm practiced in keeping a straight face.

"Is there anything you need?" Talia drew his attention back. "I know you must have been taken rather quickly from your ship, but if there is something that would make you more comfortable here, happier here, do tell. We will do our best to turn this into your home, too."

Conrad considered the reality he now faced. Returning to Dawn Chaser would never happen. The life he had worked so hard for had vanished. Replaced by a life he had earned no other way than by being born. It felt unjust, and caused a new sour note in his stomach. But looking at his mother, he knew it wasn't her fault. And that he'd never leave her to face the unknown of this life without him.

"I need to write some letters. Explain in a little more detail where I've gone and why I'm not going to return to my ship. Leiura, my first mate..." She hadn't truly been his first thought, but it felt more logical than jumping straight to the other. "And I need help finding someone. She and I were supposed to meet back on Dawn Chaser in a few months, but I need to find her and explain what's happened."

"Her?" Talia's eyes sparkled as if she already understood the importance Ahria carried for Conrad. Or hoped, as any mother would.

"Yes, she's on a journey of her own here in Ziona, but with the resources of the palace, we could help her in her search far better than I could as a ship's captain. But I need to find her first."

Talia glanced back at Talon, who had settled into one of the armchairs at the side of the sitting area, Andi's head in his lap. The auer nodded, and Talia smiled. "Of course we can help find her, especially if she's within our borders. What is her name?"

"Ahria."

A flicker of familiarity entered Talia's expression, followed by confusion.

Talon's gaze shot to him. "What did you just say?"

Conrad looked at the auer, who's hand lay frozen on Andi's head, his narrow pupils had all but vanished in the color of his irises. Distrust bubbled in Conrad, but then he assured himself how much his mother trusted Talon. "Ahria. She came to Ziona looking for her father."

"Ahria? Ahria Xylata?" Talon stood, blind to Andi's

requests for more attention.

Conrad narrowed his eyes at the auer, ignoring his mother's surprised look. "Yes..."

Talon's chest rose at a faster pace. "She's here, looking for me?" He muttered what could only be an Aueric curse under his breath, turning as if unsure where to walk. "That's why she never wrote me back..."

"Hold on. What?" Conrad shook his head, turning to his mother's touch.

"Ahria is Talon's daughter, Connie. And you know her?"

"Why isn't she still in Olsa? Did she travel here alone?" Talon stared at him again, concern etched over his now pallid features.

Conrad fought the headache as it doubled in his forehead. "Ahria is... your daughter?" He'd never considered that her father was auer, but her comment about him attracting attention suddenly became clear. If he'd have known... "Son of a bitch."

"She is." Talon's jaw flexed. "And my questions?"

"Ahria's looking for you because she hasn't heard from you. If you sent letters, they must not have made it to her. She..." Conrad considered the news he carried, and that Talon likely hadn't heard. He softened his tone, despite his confusion. "She said her other father passed away, and she needed to find you to tell you. She boarded my ship with a man named Davros, but they parted ways in Treama right before your guards came and snagged me."

"Lorin is dead?" Talon rubbed his hands over his face. "And Davros left her?"

Conrad's jaw twitched, his palms suddenly sweaty with the truth. "She made that decision, not him."

Talon heaved a sigh. "So she was in Treama when I picked you up there? Where was she going to go?" He strode to Talia, face tight. "How do we find her? That was over two weeks ago, and she could be anywhere by now."

"We'd worked out a plan. She was going to leave Treama and make her way east to Dragon's Gate."

Talia looked at Talon. "So she's coming this direction."

The auer straightened. "I need to write a letter. Please excuse me." He waited for Talia's nod before crossing to the doors, opening them and exiting the room.

Conrad didn't ask for his mother's permission before turning on his heels and hurrying after Talon. He couldn't explain the sudden need to apologize to the auer. Like he should have somehow known.

Andi barked as she charged after them.

"Talon!" Conrad shouted down the decorated stone hallway after the auer, who was somehow already halfway to the next hall. "You can find her?"

Talon waited until Conrad had caught up before replying. "No. But I know someone who can." He scowled and stopped, facing the captain. "You speak like she's important to you. Is that why she split from Davros?"

Conrad straightened, forcing himself to look Talon straight in the eye.

How could he know that? Am I that easy to read?

"She is important to me. And she told me that Davros didn't make her happy. That's why they split."

Anger flashed in the auer's gaze. "Maybe not, but at least he helped keep her safe. Now she's alone."

Guilt seethed in Conrad, but then he frowned. "Wouldn't be if those guards hadn't shown up. I was about to go find her before you up and surprised me with the whole *you're a prince* news."

"You should have said something to me right then."

"I didn't know you were her father!" Anger bubbled into his words. "Forgive me, but you don't really have a familial resemblance."

Talon let out a slow breath, features twitching slightly before his face returned to a visage of calm. "No. You didn't. And at least now I know what's going on. Thank you for telling me." His tone, while controlled, still held an undercurrent of genuineness. "As much as I want to find her, we will need to keep this quiet. No posters, no military. This must stay between us."

Conrad's brow furrowed, and he winced as he rubbed the soreness in his forehead. "What? Why?" He'd hoped that the political power would enable them to find her even faster.

"That's not something I can tell you, but Ahria would agree with me, so I expect you to respect that. I can't have her face everywhere."

I wonder how he's gonna feel when a prince wants to court her, then.

Talon started to move ahead again, but Conrad didn't follow. He needed to go back to his mum. "Please tell me if you learn anything?"

The auer glanced back as he walked. "I will."

Chapter 15

AHRIA CHUCKED ANOTHER TINY PEBBLE through the bars, hitting the far wall with a tap. She'd woken in the cell, surrounded by iron bars. No matter how much she called, no one came, and no one answered except the annoyed prisoner next to her.

Though, a gravelly *shut up* was hardly a response.

It'd been all night, at least, with no sign of anyone coming to question her. A tray with a meal had been left, but she'd eaten most of it already.

No windows adorned the walls, leaving her nothing to judge time by. Her head ached where the guard had knocked her out, a lump beneath her hair.

Leaning her head against the wall, feet stretched in front of her, she debated her own stupidity. Breaking into a palace, alone, with no plan. They'd caught her before she'd even touched the building.

She'd gotten caught on Conrad's ship, too.

I'm not cut out to be a criminal.

Frowning, Ahria picked at the bread roll still next to her on the tray. It had staled over the hours, but her stomach grumbled.

Hinges squealed somewhere beyond, but in the dimness of the space, she couldn't tell where. A single candle sat on a shoddy wooden table, providing the minimal light needed for prisoners to use their buckets.

Footsteps echoed through the chamber, and she quickly stood, gripping the bars. "Hey, who's there? Let me out, I can explain."

"Finally," the prisoner next to her murmured, not even looking at her as he moved to his barred door. "You sure took your time."

A man walked past Ahria's cell, hardly glancing at her from beneath his hood, and continued to the other occupied cell. "Took us a minute to realize the guard fancied Karin more than Keigan. And I got a feeling it won't last long. But I'm getting tired of bailing you out. They're going to catch me one of these days." The man's voice had a subtle drawl, and he knelt next to the lock.

"Hey, you mind doing mine, too?" Ahria tilted her head, trying to summon a charming grin. "Please?"

The man glanced at her, flashing a handsome smile. "No can do, princess. You could be an assassin with all the hardware they took off you." He motioned to a far wall, where the guards had stored all the daggers they'd confiscated from her.

The pile of blades in the cubby had tormented her since she'd woken. They'd even found the ones in her boots and at the small of her back.

"I'm not an assassin," Ahria whined. "Please. I'm just looking for someone. I don't hurt people."

The man chuckled, reminding her for a moment of Conrad if not for his lighter skin. "Exactly what an assassin would say." He pulled lock picking tools from his belt, inserting different picks into the cell's lock. "I don't rescue people for free."

The prisoner next to her scoffed. "Except me."

"I'm only freeing you because Evelyn ordered me to. Besides, she promised me I could take your act in the next show."

"She *what*?"

"You'll be swallowing swords this time, while I work the fire. She's getting sick of your side hustles causing problems."

The lock clicked and the door swung open.

"You're what, then? Performers?" Ahria hurried to speak before they could leave her. "A traveling troupe?"

"Not traveling." The rescuer rose to his feet, approaching

her cell. "And we have enough fortune tellers and maids."

"I can be useful." Ahria followed him along the bars as he strode back the way he'd come, his friend in tow. "I can throw blades."

"We got that, already."

"I can sing." Ahria gulped as she said it, nerves bubbling in her gut at the idea of doing it in front of anyone other than her friends and family back home.

The man paused and looked at her.

Silence settled through the dungeon, his eyes narrowing a minute degree with each second that passed. Surprisingly, the rescued friend kept his mouth shut.

The man finally spoke. "You'd have to prove yourself to our leader. And if she finds you're not..."

"I can do that." Ahria nodded, reaching through the bars in an offer. "Let me out. I can prove myself. I'm Ahria."

The man eyed her hand, ignoring his friend's grumble. "Vaeler. This is Ambros." He took her hand and shook it, smiling in a way that looked both charming and sinister.

It took him less time to pick her cell's lock, and she went straight for her blades. Rushing to replace them in their hiding spots, she hoped they wouldn't leave without her.

"For *not an assassin* you sure carry a lot of hardware." Vaeler stood in the hallway entrance, propping the door open with his boot and whispering, "Hurry up." Somewhere beyond, a low conversation buzzed through the walls, filled with laughter.

Ahria stuffed the last blade up her sleeve and jogged after him. "I like daggers," she muttered with a shrug, and followed Ambros through the door.

The door behind her closed with little more than a whisper of sound and Vaeler hopped off the back step of the door they exited into a narrow alley. He spun, inserting his lock picks into the door before the lock snapped shut with a satisfying click.

Ambros stalked down the alley along the dark wall, and Ahria blinked to try to get her eyes to adjust to the shadows of night as quickly as possible. With no true understanding of where in the city she was, she blindly followed Ambros and heard Vaeler creeping behind her.

They escorted her through the city, and she recognized nothing until they passed by a familiar stable with a red barn door.

"Wait, I need to get my things." Ahria hurried into the dark building, quickly locating her horse's stall, which had been padlocked shut. "Shit." She'd only paid for one night. Grabbing her pack from inside, she left a coin on the stall door for the barn master to find the next morning. Slinging the pack over her shoulder, she returned outside.

In the stillness of the night, she wondered if her new friends had moved on without her.

"Psst, over here." Vaeler outstretched a hand from the shadows and motioned for her to follow.

The rest of the journey through the capital turned Ahria around so many times, she had no idea which direction they walked anymore. They went through alleys and low arches, meandering a path that was surely meant to confuse her.

They reached a residential district, rows of townhouses adorning the streets with carefully kept flower boxes on each porch. The clean street suggested some affluence in the area, and Ahria looked around before Ambros led the way into one of the middle residences. He didn't knock as he pushed through the elegant front door with a diamond shaped crystal window.

"This is pretty luxurious living for a troupe," Ahria whispered.

"We're a successful troupe." Vaeler frowned as Ambros disappeared up the stairs directly in front of the door. "Albeit a rather ungrateful one."

A woman appeared in the doorway beside the stairs, her attractive features dappled with freckles, illuminated by the candle she held. "Hey, Vaeler. Glad you're safe."

The man stiffened, but took the candle when she offered. "You should be asleep, Jaqi. Evelyn will be pissed if you're exhausted tomorrow."

The female frowned. "I was supposed to go instead of Karin this time." She crossed her arms, sneering at Ahria. "Who are you?"

"New singer. Evelyn's been wanting to expand on the music side of the performance, hasn't she?" Vaeler shut the front door, latching the lock, which Ahria noted the style of in case she had to make a fast exit.

"Ahria." She stepped forward, offering her hand to Jaqi. "It's nice to meet you."

Jaqi lifted a thin dark eyebrow, but didn't take her hand. "I'd say likewise, but..." She made a face and then looked up at Vaeler. "Night, Vaeler." Without another look at Ahria, she walked away.

Ahria dropped her offered hand, sighing. "I suppose I shouldn't have expected a warm welcome."

"We're a quirky bunch. She'll warm up to you. Come, I'll take you to the spare room and you can meet with Evelyn in the morning." He started up the stairs, and she followed.

"Just like that? You trust me in your home, just like that?" Ahria could hardly believe it, especially since he knew how armed she was.

"Just like that."

"But you know nothing about me. And you found me in a prison cell."

"And what do you know of me?" Vaeler glanced at her. "We were all outcasts once. All nameless, directionless souls.

Not saying you are, but you're far from the sketchiest person to join us." He strode down a narrow hallway lined with doors and paused outside one before opening it. "Here. You can sleep until breakfast."

"I need to find someone." Ahria stopped in the doorway. "Will you help me?"

It seemed insane to even ask. He was a stranger, who already offered her help when she'd hardly been able to offer anything back. But something about the man told her she could trust him. Rely on him. Something deep in her gut, and Talon had always told her to trust her gut.

Vaeler shrugged and handed Ahria the candle. "We're all looking for someone or another. Wish I could say we could be useful, but we just entertain people. Maybe who you're looking for will end up in our audience. Goodnight."

As he walked away, Ahria leaned against the door frame. She'd lucked out, and she knew it, but it didn't soften the ache in her chest. The capital was far larger than she ever expected.

How am I supposed to find Conrad here?

Her dad would know what to do, and the thought lowered her gaze. Stepping inside the room, she shut and locked the door. She set the candle on the small desk, eyeing the windowless bedroom. Placing her pack down in front of the door, she precariously balanced a dagger on the top, hilt leaning on the door.

No one will get in here without waking me.

Ahria crossed to the single cot, moving the candle to the bedside table. Laying down, she watched the flickering flame. "I'll find you," she whispered, wondering what she'd gotten herself into with this troupe. She owed them, and running off wasn't an option.

Not yet.

"I'll find you both. I promise." She blew out the candle.

Chapter 16

TALON'S HEAD SPUN WITH ALL the implications of the conversation he'd had with Conrad. He hadn't considered that Ahria wasn't still safe at home in Gallisville with Lorin.

But Lorin is dead.

Another fact that Talon struggled to grapple. Over the years of raising Ahria and Lorin's older son, he and the man had become close friends. While Lorin preferred a simple life rather than an adventurous one, Talon always found a steady calm within the man that he'd admired. It was a calm that he had hoped Ahria would inherit as well, even if she wasn't his blood.

However, with Ahria traveling to Ziona to find him, Talon saw only her mother in her.

Yet, she's so much more naive than her mother ever was.

And it was his fault. He'd protected her, kept her away from the cruelties of the world, all while making sure she knew how to defend herself. But isolating her in a small village had its downfalls, too. It was unfair to keep her there. He had done it anyway. And Ahria had never protested. She didn't know anything else, and had always seemed content. Only when she'd turned nineteen, as if some latent trip-switch had been triggered, did she wish for adventure.

Talon flung the door open to the palace aviary, causing the poor attendant to nearly topple backward in their chair. "I need to get a letter to Drych, right away."

The mousy haired man scratched his scruffy chin. "Didn't you send one yesterday, sir?"

"I need to send another." Annoyance colored his tone, which he didn't bother to hide. "Parchment and quill, please." He stepped to the desk, pulling up a short stool without waiting for the man to answer.

The attendant pursed his lips but obliged the auer, handing him an inkwell and fresh parchment from within the desk. "I'll see to the bird, sir." He gave Talon another sideways glance as he slipped through the creaky door into the room with the perches, excited screeches erupting before it closed.

Talon stared at the paper, his fingers closing tightly on the quill before he reminded himself not to break it.

Why didn't we establish a more reliable form of communication?

But the truth was that Deylan didn't really care about Talon. Not in a professional context. Sometimes, Talon wondered if Deylan was annoyed by the need for them to remain in touch. He'd pushed too many questions about the mysterious faction on the man, to the point of him learning more than he was ever supposed to. Deylan had sworn him to secrecy, of course, and Talon had no one he would plausibly tell who wouldn't think he was insane to imply a secret faction watched over his daughter.

And in all reality, Deylan might blame Talon for the current situation of Ahria traveling on her own. While the faction itself wouldn't particularly care, as Ahria's uncle, Deylan certainly would.

> *Deylan,*
> *I've heard the news of what has transpired at home. Ahria is somewhere in Ziona. I know what you're thinking already, but please, help me find her. You know all I do is to keep her safe, and I hope you understand how desperate I am to keep her so. I am in New Kingston, temporarily serving as an advisor to the new queen of Ziona. I will use whatever influence I*

have to find her, and hope you will do the
same.
Talon

He hastily folded the paper and pinched a bit of wax off the edge of an unlit candle on the desk. Squeezing it between his fingers, his soul buzzed as he reached for a piece of the Art within him. It answered without hesitation, bubbling onto his skin as heat made the piece malleable before he pushed it down to seal the letter shut. With a twist of his thumb, he urged the wax to take on the shape of the classic wide petal depiction of the araleinya flower, which Deylan would recognize. Above it, he scrawled, *relay message to Deylan Salte*. Even if whatever faction member was running interference for Deylan's letters read the text inside, there was nothing overtly damning. Better to not accidentally expose all he knew to any faction leaders.

He stood, impatience taking him to the aviary door himself. He opened it, stifling his flinch at the sudden cacophony of squawking, and held out the letter to the man who now had a falcon on his arm. A small cylindrical container had been attached with a leather strap to the animal, and Talon carefully rolled his letter into it before latching it shut.

"Should reach Drych in two weeks or so. This is my fastest bird that knows the route." The attendant stroked the tawny bird's chest as it cooed.

"It'll have to do." Talon fought the remaining anxiety in his stomach, urging himself not to take it out on the man who had already shown infinite patience with him. "Thank you, Kreal."

"Pleasure, sir." The man walked towards the end of the aviary, where it opened out over the canyon behind the palace.

Talon didn't stay to see the bird off, making his way back out to the hallway without knowing what to do next.

She's smart. She's trained. She'll stay alive.

Yet Talon felt sick at the idea that she was genuinely on her own, and every inch of him wanted to go back to Conrad and strangle some sense into the young man who had let it happen. The same young man Deylan had accused him of playing father to instead of being with Amarie when she needed him most.

Another guilty pang pushed him against the hallway wall, the cold stone seeping through the delicate material of his tunic. Closing his eyes, his mind tortured him with an image of Amarie and what he imagined she looked like in those months after Ahria's birth. When sorrow and loss had all but consumed her.

He'd never allowed himself to forget the pain he'd caused, which made his current torment all the more fitting.

I deserve to feel this.

"Mister Di'Terian." A cheery voice bounced down the hall, and he looked up to see one of the stewards carrying a tea set.

"Mister Credish." Straightening, Talon walked closer to the steward. "Thank you for your attention to our future prince. He looks the part now."

A rosy color touched Credish's pale cheeks. "Truly didn't take much. He's a quiet one, and real rigid. But I suppose that is to be expected." He bobbed the tray in his hands. "Hoping a bit of tea may do the trick to help calm those nerves of his before dinner."

Talon eyed the tray, a shadow of a thought crossing his mind before he held out his hands. "An apt thought. Do you mind if I take him this myself with your regards?"

I have plenty of questions with him knowing my Ahria.

Credish smiled, passing over the set. "Of course. Shall I return to escort him to dinner, or do you expect you'll still be in his company?"

"I'll make sure he finds his way." Talon gestured down the hall Credish had come from. "Go enjoy your own relaxation for the evening, Mister Credish."

The man's smile widened. "Thank you, sir."

Talon waited as the steward walked down the hall, then reoriented himself to where exactly he stood in the palace. It'd been weeks, but the maze of hallways still proved a challenge to navigate. It took him a moment to remember the hidden stairwell Credish probably intended to take to the upper levels, where the royal chambers were located.

When he arrived at the entry to Conrad's rooms, he paused to stare at the carved oak door and collect his rampant thoughts. Conrad knew Ahria. And by the way his voice hitched when he talked about her, it was more than a common acquaintance. The boy was fortunate the guilt in Talon's chest lightened his distrust.

Balancing the tray on one hand, Talon rapped on the door before he could change his mind.

He imagined Ahria on a ship while he waited at the door and wondered if she had stood at the bow and sang like her mother had so many years ago. Despite the passage of time, Talon could still recall how the wind had brushed through Amarie's hair while she stood on the deck of that trader's ship bound for Rylorn. Could still remember how hard his heart pounded to even consider touching her.

Just like her mother, Ahria had the gift of song. Her voice enchanted him and anyone else who happened to hear it, but the talent wouldn't help her in the tumultuous nation.

The door cracked open, and Conrad peeked through before his eyes widened.

"Talon." His voice piqued, but he cleared his throat before it evened. "What are you—"

"May I come in?" Talon lifted the tea as if it was some kind of peace offering. "Mister Credish thought this might help you relax."

Conrad eyed the porcelain teapot decorated with a painted weave of thistles and briar. "Is it going to kill me?"

Talon frowned, but had to admire the audacity of the accusation. "Depends." He opened the lid of the teapot and let the aroma of the leaves into his senses. "Are you allergic to cardamom or ginger?"

The young man pursed his lips before he stepped back from the door, opening it further. "Come in. I'm willing to bet it's in my best interest not to turn you away. In more ways than one, considering current circumstances."

With the albeit reluctant invitation, Talon entered the formal sitting room of the prince's chambers.

Conrad had opened all of the curtains in, exposing the extensive floor to ceiling panels of fused glass that overlooked the canyon and river below. Despite the vague chill in the early spring air, the multiple sets of doors were also open, causing the gauzy curtains to ripple in the breeze.

Talon considered the table out on the L-shaped balcony before settling the tea tray onto the low slung one in front of the unlit fireplace instead. He looked for Conrad's furry companion, having grown rather fond of her over the past weeks.

"Where's Andi?"

"One of the staff took her out for a walk in the gardens. She's probably rolling around ruining that nice bath she had." After closing the door, Conrad stuck his hands in his pockets, hovering near the exit.

The room to the left of him was still open and mostly unfurnished, while the sitting chairs and tables were positioned near the windows.

"Have they told you that you can ask for anything you'd like to be brought up to you?" Talon settled into the chair at the end of the table rather than give Conrad the option of requesting solitude. "And I mean, beyond just food. If you find the furniture offensive or inadequate, they'd find you some alternatives."

Conrad glanced around, looking lost in his own chambers. Of course, he'd only spent perhaps five minutes in them. "Credish mentioned it. But I don't know what I would possibly ask for."

"Well, what are your hobbies? A painting easel perhaps?" Talon poured a cup of tea before moving onto the second.

"I'm a ship's captain. I don't have time for hobbies."

"Unfortunately, I don't believe we can fit an entire ship inside your chambers, as spacious as they may be."

"No offense, Talon, but I'm sure you're here to talk about Ahria, not my lack of hobbies." Conrad approached, his body remaining rigid.

"She is my daughter." Talon lifted his cup to his lips. "Whom you seem to be rather familiar with."

Conrad somehow grew straighter. "Sure, familiar I guess. She was on my ship for a few weeks. We got to know each other a bit."

"Enough that you seem quite concerned with finding her. Despite the part you played in her adventuring off alone."

"Look, I explained that to you already. I was about to go after her when—"

"Right, before *my* guards came and seized you. I still don't understand why you didn't say something at the time, but..." Talon waved his hand at the couch beside him. "I'm not your enemy, Conrad, never have been."

"You're referencing a past I don't remember." Conrad hesitated, but took a seat. "I was what? Two? Three? Human memory doesn't exactly work great at that age."

And yet, Talon could still envision the toddler in the tavern, slamming his toy boats together while his little voice shouted *boom*. He'd believed he was paying penance in helping to care for Conrad at Thorn's Edge while Talia worked to support them as a young single mother. Until Deylan had arrived and punched him in the jaw.

"And ironically, you had quite the fascination with ships at that age, too." Talon settled his cup on the arm of his chair, absently rubbing the spot Amarie's brother had bruised all those years ago. "We're both interested in finding Ahria, so let's focus on that. As well as how to get you through the next two days."

Conrad groaned as he dropped his head into his hands. "I know, I know. Coronation." He rubbed at his forehead. "I'll feel better when I know she's safe."

"Well, she is looking for me. So, in theory, if you stay near me, you'll see her again when she succeeds in her quest." Talon considered the look on his daughter's face if she arrived to find him beside Conrad. Of course, that really depended on exactly what Ahria thought of the young man. And that Ahria arrived safely.

Conrad shrugged, which Talon noted as a habit he would need to break the prince of.

"What are your intentions towards Ahria?"

Whatever slight relaxation the prince's shoulders had gained vanished. "Excuse me?"

"Your intentions." Talon spoke each syllable slowly. "Towards my daughter."

Conrad narrowed his eyes, as if spying the trap Talon was weaving at his feet. "I have none other than to ensure she is safe. And to be whatever *she* intends me to be."

Talon examined him, wondering if the captain could even fathom what he was getting himself into. If she had told him anything about the tangled web she walked already, though even she didn't know the full extent of it.

The bone chilling thought of the evil that pursued her and her mother made Talon's eyes flick to Conrad's right forearm. But he'd been with the man for weeks already.

I'd have noticed the Art in him.

"You hold an important role now, as the crown prince of Ziona." Talon sipped his tea, watching Conrad cross his arms and lean back on the couch. "The extent of that responsibility has yet to be determined. Parliament has some rather archaic laws to sort through and either reenact or rewrite. But if your mother has her way, she will name you as her successor, rather than it passing to one of your cousins because they're female."

"Cousins?" Conrad blinked.

"That was not the part of that statement you were supposed to cling onto..." Talon rubbed his jaw. "You will be king one day."

The prince shrugged, crossing his arms tighter. The look on his face suggested his distaste for the idea. "I don't really care about one day right now. I just care about today."

"A tactic that will only get you to tomorrow, maybe the next day. You'll need to broaden that horizon."

"I believe I have the right to ask for some time to adjust." Conrad sighed, uncrossing his arms. "What can I do to assist with finding Ahria?"

"Right now? Nothing. You don't have any connections in the city. The most you could do is write that letter to your first mate, like you suggested before. I'll show you to the aviary after dinner. But as far as Ahria goes, I will do what I can, but you won't be able to leave the palace to go looking for her. And for your mother's sake, I hope you don't try to do anything foolish like sneaking out."

Conrad shook his head. "I'm not leaving Mum. But if there's anything..."

"I'll keep you updated. Now, I did promise you a bit of time to rest before dinner, and should probably allow you time to *adjust*, as you suggest." Talon settled his glass back onto the tray and stood.

"What, no more interrogation about my intentions?" Conrad gazed up at him, still with that edge of defiance to his tone, but all he looked now was tired.

"No need." Talon stepped around the couch and started towards the door. "I'll be back to fetch you for dinner in an hour or so."

Conrad peeked back over the back of the couch, but didn't speak before Talon closed the door behind him.

Chapter 17

AHRIA DRUMMED HER FINGERS ON the wooden table, trying her best to ignore the flecks of varnish peeling off the sides. She wanted to pick at them, but surely Evelyn wouldn't appreciate tiny bits of varnish dusted all over her floor.

"Vaeler tells me you're a singer," Evelyn poured a cup of coffee, not looking in Ahria's direction with the comment.

"That's right." Ahria gave Vaeler a tense smile as he set a mug of black coffee in front of her, giving her an encouraging nod. "I haven't performed much... at all, but I'm sure I can pick it up. My dad says my voice is—"

"Beautiful, I'm sure," Evelyn muttered.

Jaqi snickered in the corner behind Ahria, where she'd tucked herself to eavesdrop on the morning conversation.

Ahria bit her tongue to contain her annoyance.

"She gave me a preview on the way back last night, and she's good."

Shooting Vaeler a look, Ahria narrowed her eyes. She'd done no such thing.

"Well what do you sing?" Jaqi's condescending tone already felt like nails on stone. "Isalican ballads? Helgathian war songs?"

"I thought I might write my own songs." Ahria sat straighter. "But usually, I prefer ballads."

Jaqi scoffed. "Of course you do."

"Do you have a purpose behind your presence here, Jaqi? Or just looming to make unnecessary commentary and hope Vaeler's clothes start falling off of him?" Evelyn cast a glare to the corner behind Ahria that made her suddenly never want to invoke the troupe leader's attention like that.

Jaqi gave a little squeak, her cheeks turning rosy as she frowned. "I was just—"

"Leaving? Right answer." Evelyn darted her eyes towards the doorway before furrowing her brow at the woman. "You using that damn bee venom again? Your mouth looks like you ate a pineapple. Throw that shit out."

Ahria looked at Vaeler and mouthed the single-word question. *Pineapple?*

Vaeler's shoulders jerked as he withheld a laugh and whispered, "She's allergic."

"Good to know," Ahria mumbled into her coffee.

Jaqi stomped to the door. "I need to talk to Keigan anyway." The door slammed shut to the dining room, vibrating the table beneath Ahria's palms.

"Don't mind her. She can be a bit of a brat, but there's no arguing with the coin she can bring in in a single night." Evelyn settled into the chair across from Vaeler and Ahria, lifting her black coffee to her lips. "Let's hear this voice of yours, assuming you're able to after all those danishes you ate."

Ahria stiffened, those danishes flopping over in her stomach. "Right now?"

Evelyn gave a single nod, eyes pinned on her. "Right now."

Swallowing, Ahria glanced at Vaeler, who also nodded at her. She rolled her lips together, grateful for their patience while her mind whipped from song to song to choose one. She settled on a lullaby Talon used to sing her, having once heard her mother sing it.

Taking a deep breath, she let the melody flow. The Aueric words danced from her lips in practiced notes. It told a story of a ship sailing off into the horizon, and falling in love with the sea.

Evelyn's coffee mug sat frozen halfway to her mouth as she listened, eyes only leaving Ahria once to glance at Vaeler.

Ahria continued through the verse and into the chorus, damning the slight shake of her voice before regaining control over her nerves.

No one spoke. No one interrupted her. Even when a set of soft footsteps descended the townhouse stairs, they paused, and no one entered the kitchen.

As the song concluded in a long, soft note, Ahria breathed out her tension and swallowed, waiting.

The footsteps from the stairs resumed, and a blond woman entered the kitchen with bright green eyes. "Who are *you*, and where in Pantracia did you come from?"

Vaeler grinned. "Karin, this is Ahria. She's our new—"

"Singer, I guess?" The woman beamed, sitting next to Ahria and looking at Evelyn. "She must join us."

Evelyn hummed, finally taking that sip of her coffee. "I'm inclined to agree. You sing very well, and in Aueric no less." Her impressed tone made Ahria's chest swell with pride. "If you do well in rehearsals, we will put you on stage." She gave Vaeler a deadpan look. "She's *good*? Really?"

Vaeler chuckled. "Maybe she didn't actually give me a preview."

"Go take the trash out." Evelyn stared at him until he straightened and hurried off without another word.

Karin grinned at Ahria, her excitement contagious. "This is going to be so fun."

"What do you do for the troupe?" Ahria debated reaching for another danish, but took another sip of coffee instead.

"I'm a fire dancer." Karin tapped her feet, like she wanted

to twirl on the spot. "I can teach you, if you like?"

Ahria laughed. "Thank you, but I think I'll stick to less dangerous acts."

Evelyn stood, taking her coffee with her. "Rehearsal starts promptly at midday in the basement. It's the most open space we've got." She walked to the side door that led to a little side garden. "Welcome to Mysterium. Don't be late."

One week later...

The Gilded Arm had blocked off a small room beside the stage, thick navy curtains hiding the growing crowd from the secrets the performers maintained for their acts.

Ahria pulled them open just enough to peek out, her heart pounding. All the tables were full, leaving little space for the poor waiters to maneuver. Even more people continued to pile in through the door, no longer chiming because it was just being held open by the soldiers standing at the back.

The room roared with conversation and boisterous laughter as foaming mugs of ale were passed around. An entire tray needed to be conveyed by the customers across the room, handed from one table to the next by the patrons themselves.

Jaqi's high-pitched laugh managed to break through the ruckus, and Ahria spied her at the closest table to the stage, an array of colorful cards spread on the wood in front of her. The men sitting across from her didn't seem to be watching the cards, but rather the cleavage she had carefully displayed as she leaned forward to scoop the cards back towards her. She smiled, looking far friendlier than Ahria had ever seen her. She tapped the bowl at the side of the table, reminding the men where to pay for the fortune she just read.

"You ready?" Vaeler appeared beside Ahria, his guitar in hand.

Ahria closed the gap in the curtains and glared at him. "You said it would be a few people!" Her hushed words came out between clenched teeth. "The tavern is packed!"

Vaeler shrugged. "Seemed an easier way to settle your nerves."

"Well it's not working," she ground out. "Can't someone else open the show?"

"Lenitnes will introduce us, and I'll be right beside you. So will Keigan. Just like rehearsal, you got this." Vaeler patted her shoulder. "The high you'll feel after is like nothing else, I promise."

Ahria groaned, but caught Evelyn's eye from their makeshift dressing room.

The woman raised an eyebrow, though the stern look on her face actually settled Ahria's stomach.

This isn't about me. Or my voice. It's about finding Conrad or Dad.

She'd spoken about it with Evelyn, who had agreed to let her write her own music for the sake of finding them. Though she needed more time to finish the lyrics of a song that might get Conrad's attention, an Aueric ballad would always catch Talon's ear.

Everything passed in a blur as they finished setting up, and before she knew it, Lenitnes was on stage in front of the cheering crowd announcing their act.

The beginning of Lenitnes's speech was only a buzz in her ears, lost in the growing anxiety.

As if sensing it, Vaeler's hand closed on her bicep, squeezing in a way to encourage her to breathe with the rhythm he set.

"For our first illustrious performance this evening, we bring you something you've never seen before. Straight from the wilds of Eralas, where she was raised among the auer despite her human blood... Prepare to be tantalized by an Aueric hymn. So quiet those shouts and settle those mugs so you all may hear the beautiful music... of Mysterium." Lenitnes bowed, patrons still applauding as he exited the stage.

The story rocked Ahria for a moment, and she didn't realize at first Lenitnes was talking about her. But then Vaeler pulled the curtain aside, exposing her to the warm air of the tavern. Taking a deep, rather strained breath, Ahria walked forward with Vaeler and Keigan. Keigan took a tall stool to her left, lifting a flute to his lips. While Vaeler took the one to her right, strumming his guitar.

Ahria stood in the center, having declined a stool. Her floor-length black dress danced around her ankles in translucent layers of lace and satin. The melody started, and she counted. When she was supposed to sing, she faltered, and her heart picked up speed.

Vaeler looked at her, and his gaze grounded her. He discreetly bobbed his head with the rhythm, and even took a breath the moment she needed to.

Following his lead, she inhaled, and the music... flowed. Tearing her eyes from her friend, she focused on a spot on the wall at the back of the tavern. She sang, needing no written words to remember the Aueric lyrics streaming from her mouth. The place quieted to listen, and through the words of the song, Ahria found a steady calm.

Just sing, Talon had once told her, in that calm, loving voice he used with her. *They will adore your voice.*

Of course, that had been when she was performing for her family, not a tavern full of strangers.

But Ahria sang, hitting the notes just as she wanted, and when she concluded the song... When she saw Evelyn's grin at the side of the stage, and heard the eruption of cheers, she bit her lip and grinned right along with them.

And a breath later, Vaeler started the intro for their next piece.

Chapter 18

Two weeks later...

SHUTTING THE DOOR TO HIS room, Talon heaved a sigh and loosened the buttons at his neck. It'd been a long day of meetings, and despite his time in the palace, his interest in politics hadn't increased.

With the queen's coronation complete, he had intended to be back on his way to Gallisville, but he'd delayed in the hope that he might hear from Deylan.

Ahria isn't there, anyway.

Halfway across the chamber to his bed, he froze.

A folded paper laid on his pillow, perfectly centered. But all correspondence went through Credish. This wasn't usual practice. Far from it. Which meant only one thing.

His heart thudded in his ears as he approached the note, lifting it from the bedding and inspecting the scrawled writing on the front depicting his name.

"Sneaky bastards," Talon whispered, wondering who the faction's connection was within the palace.

Breaking the seal on the letter, he unfolded it and read.

> *Talon,*
> *Ahria is safe. We have someone with her in Ziona. I'm prohibited from providing you with her location, especially in writing. If her safety becomes compromised, I will notify you immediately. In the meantime, perhaps you'll find her on your own. She's in good hands.*
> *Deylan*

Scowling, Talon huffed as his hand closed around the note in frustration. A pulse of the Art rushed into his fingertips in a surge, a bruise-purple cloud cutting into the edges. He crossed to the fireplace and tossed the crumpled ball among the logs. He could let it sit until the evening when staff would light the fire, but since someone in the staff was apparently faction, he didn't want to risk Deylan's reputation. With a flick of his fingers, he summoned the Art again with greater control. As the logs sparked and caught fire, Deylan's words murmured through his mind.

Perhaps you'll find her on your own...

Rubbing at his jaw, Talon stared at the white center of the

flames spreading to the parchment, blazing brighter as they rushed to consume Deylan's words.

Does that mean that Ahria is somewhere nearby?

The man usually left subtle clues in his correspondence, hinting at facts he wasn't permitted to outright share. Every word was chosen with meticulous purpose, relying on Talon to read between the lines. It kept Deylan's conscience cleaner while appeasing Talon's need to know.

A ripple of unexpected gratitude flowed through him.

Deylan had no obligation to tell him anything at all, but he always tried. As frustrating as it was at times, even the slivers of information were usually all he needed.

If Ahria was nearby, that could mean the capital itself or the surrounding area. He'd have to make himself known, draw her out, since she sought him. It would take more excursions into the city, more public appearances with Talia. Anything to draw more attention to himself, even if every prior habit had been to keep to the shadows. He would also find time to roam the streets, ears and eyes open.

To find Ahria... Whatever was required of him, he would give, and nothing would stop him.

Chapter 19

AN ENDLESS HEADACHE.

Royalty, defined in the simplest of terms.

Conrad's eyes strained in the dim light of the study. Rubbing his brow, he stared down at the neat, concise handwriting of the judiciary's clerk, but the lines blurred together.

And he thought his ability to read and write was horrid already, but it turned out that the complex language used at court combined with the never-ending stress made it even worse. And people watching him hardly helped.

Wendelin stared, her gaze unfaltering. With his new role came hours spent in her company, reading over documents and reports in nauseating quantities. The source of the dim light, the study's hearth, accentuated the wrinkles at the corners of her eyes and mouth. Her waning patience didn't help his nerves. Her fingers drummed against her bracer, arms crossed in obvious annoyance as he set the latest report on the same pile as all the rest.

"You can not remain undecided on all cases, your highness." Venom coated her tone, and the pair of guards behind her tensed. "With all due respect," she added between clenched teeth.

"It's not enough information." Conrad glowered at the papers. He couldn't say for certain what all of them said in their entirety. But considering the crimes, clearly labeled at the top of each document, a single page to contain all details seemed hardly sufficient.

"You can't expect a city guard to interview each and every criminal they arrest to get *their* side of the story. You have the facts. That is enough to pass judgment." Wendelin leaned back in her chair. "It's your job to read the arrest statement and pass a verdict. That is all."

Conrad shook his head, picking up the sparsely-filled document on the next 'criminal' he was expected to exact judgment on, but stopped when he spied the handwriting of a particular clerk he had determined thought too highly of himself.

Must have an inflated ego to use words that size, no matter how official the document.

He placed the report by Senior Clerk Rigbey in the

undecided pile out of sheer frustration. Picking up the next, he skimmed the first few lines before nodding. "I disagree. See, read this one." He slid the paper across the table, and the woman picked it up. "What's it say?"

Wendelin's eyes darted back and forth as she read. "That a woman punched another woman at the Barclay Inn after a verbal disagreement. So? What's the problem?"

"The problem is that I want to know what the disagreement was about. But it doesn't say, does it?" Conrad crossed his arms.

Skimming down the page, Wendelin shrugged. "No, it doesn't. But it doesn't matter. The crime is the assault, not the argument. Details are irrelevant."

"So you're saying that if the woman punched the other because she stole from her, that wouldn't matter to you?" Conrad challenged.

Wendelin gave him a dramatic exhale. "No. It wouldn't. Because we're not passing judgment on the other woman, just the one with flying fists. You're overcomplicating a very simple task."

"It shouldn't be *simple*," Conrad growled, clenching his jaw. "These are people's lives. Their well beings and their livelihoods. I can't, in good conscience, pass judgment without an entire understanding of what transpired. This task is a lot of things, but the least it should be is *simple*."

Wendelin tossed the notes back onto the desk in front of

him, rising from her chair. "I was sent here to teach you how to perform this role. As crown prince, there are expectations. You will need to accept these duties if you wish for your family to maintain the faith of parliament."

His chair ground along the hardwood floor of the meeting hall. He could already read the thoughts in the old woman's eyes. They reminded him far too much of the way his grandmother had looked down on him.

"With all due *respect*, Chancellor, I believe it will better serve the people our parliament claims to represent if we eradicate this heartless practice of choosing a cell or the blade by reading a piece of paper." His nails dug into the parchment on the table, and he wished he could see the faces of the people they judged.

"Most of these don't even result in the dungeons." Wendelin sighed. "Most are fines. A silver florin or a few. Hardly life-altering decisions."

"For some, that might as well be the blade. And sometimes for more than just them, but their children as well. I find that hardly just when all factors are not considered."

"And you believe *you* are the best person to decide what is just?"

"Hardly, but apparently the system has deemed it so." He thrust his finger down at the stack of fates he was supposed to decide. "But doing so off of this piece of paper rather than by looking at the face of the person accused is ridiculous.

Hearing their story, and not just that of the accuser, is far more fair. As a politician, I would think you would understand that some people *lie*, Chancellor."

Wendelin paused, narrowing her eyes as she leaned on the table. Lowering her voice, she murmured, "You *do* know how to read, don't you? Some of these documents have three sentences, yet you stared at them for ages. If you're trying to cover up your lack of education by asking to hear the stories instead..."

Heat cascaded down the back of Conrad's neck. He turned to the stack of papers, flipping through them with little regard for where they landed as he looked for one he could still recall. The accused was a man who had been caught stealing. It was one of the few written by Clerk Hannigan, who seemed willing to document more than the arresting guard's words and was succinct with her language enough.

Pointing at the document, he read aloud as best as he could. "Mister Yestin stole a bag of grain from Armily Mill. Pleaded for it not to be taken from his family, despite his arrest." He threw the paper back onto the desk. "If you demand that I pass judgment on a man based on those two sentences, I can, but doubt you would like my decision."

Wendelin frowned. "Those who steal are thieves. Thieves deserve to be reprimanded based on our laws."

"Which laws are you referring to? The ones that arrested

this man, or the ones that allowed his family to starve long enough that he saw no other option but to steal?"

A bored look crossed her face. "We have soup kitchens for the poor. Being sick of soup doesn't give him the right to steal from a mill that also needs to sell grain to feed their family."

Conrad slammed his hands down onto the table, every muscle in his body screaming. "Have you eaten at one of those soup kitchens, Chancellor? I doubt it, or you would know they often run out before half of the waiting crowd can be fed. And for those who do receive a meal, it's hardly enough to fill the belly of a toddler." Memories of the few times his mother and he had needed to visit the soup kitchen in Treama made his stomach roil. When work at the tavern had stopped due to an outbreak of Cerquel's Plague, there'd been no other choice.

"Over time, you will see that feeling sympathy for every single person in this country will leave you not just exhausted, but defeated. Best to learn to do your job and let the sad stories go." Turning, the chancellor strode towards the door. "If you want to overhaul the entire judiciary process, you'll have to take it up with the queen. It will be up to her to convince parliament to change, since I doubt they'll listen to a ship's captain. This isn't Isalica. Your blood will only get you so far."

Conrad clenched his jaw as he watched her leave, biting back fury-fueled words for the sake of his mother.

The guards at the door straightened as Wendelin passed, but then assumed the more relaxed stance Conrad had worked hard to assure them was perfectly fine in his presence.

He considered the scattered papers, hating each and every one of them, regardless of how much he understood on the page. He snarled at himself as he reached across the table to gather them up, pulling them into an untidy pile. As he forced the pages together, he considered what the chancellor had suggested. And she was right. Conrad had already noticed how little his title meant to some of the higher up dignitaries he'd been forced to interact with. It was only the staff who showed any kind of respect, though none more than he'd have expected if he was a paying customer at an inn. A very fancy inn, perhaps, but all the same.

It brought an odd sense of relief.

"You can go. I can find my way to my mother without your escort." Conrad looked at the two guards, who nodded their understanding and saluted him before leaving.

Finally alone, he let out a breath, looking out the window at the blossoming trees. For a brief moment, he let himself wonder where Ahria was. If she'd made it through the pass. If she was at Dragon's Gate or if she'd continued on to the capital yet. He wouldn't even know if she'd entered New Kingston, and that thought was the worst of all. That she could be there, right under his nose, and he'd never know it.

But if she stuck to the plan, it'll still be a while before her search leads her to New Kingston.

Conrad found his way to his mother's rooms without too much difficulty, though he needed to backtrack twice when he ended up in the wrong corridors.

Approaching her tall doors, he ignored the guards stationed there and knocked.

The left door creaked as it opened, and the stationed guards saluted without looking at the queen.

Talia's eyes flickered to them, a familiar emotion on her face that Conrad still felt himself. Neither of them were accustomed to so much formality, but she still smiled at her son. "I thought you'd be in meetings all day. Would you like some tea?"

She must have read something on his face because her smile grew more understanding. With her gesture, Conrad entered the room, and she shut the door behind him. "Mum, we need to talk about this judiciary position." When she raised an eyebrow, he sighed and shook his head. "No tea, thank you."

"Did things not go well with Wendelin?" Talia crossed to the sitting area of her main room, where a hearth sat unlit beneath a striking, carved mantle. Dragons and fire swirled around grand columns, with horseback armies of stone along the top.

"She wasn't particularly helpful, no, but my bigger

concern is these reports. They hardly tell the whole story about any of these incidents, and I don't feel it's fair to judge people on biased, one-sided reports." Conrad sat on the sofa across from his mother and put the papers he'd brought on the low table between them. "We need to change the system so there are *hearings*. Let those accused of crimes plead their case. Hear what happened from more than one perspective."

Talia picked up her tea cup, furrowing her brow as she sipped and stared at nothing, thinking. "It would be a drastic change," she murmured, rolling her lips together. "And as much as it makes sense, to overhaul an entire process like that... It would be difficult. Slow. And might not make us many friends in parliament."

"The people of Ziona have already made it clear that they are looking for change. Otherwise, parliament wouldn't even exist and the military wouldn't have been removed from power. Now is as good a time as any to enact more changes, create space for true justice. Even if we do answer to parliament, they'll have to hear us out, and there's enough members who have at least half a soul to consider the morality in this."

Pausing again, Talia leveled her gaze on him. "And this isn't because reading the reports is challenging for you?"

Conrad huffed, throwing himself back into the couch as he crossed his arms. "I won't lie, that's part of it. But even if I can't comprehend half of what I read, I get enough of it to still know it's one sided."

The queen nodded. "If this is something you truly believe in..."

"It is. And I already know it works because Delkest founded the first open court a hundred years ago. Hells, even Helgath does it now."

Talia pursed her lips. "Helgath has evolved with its new ruling family." She took a deep breath and let it out slowly. "All right. But if we're going to approach parliament with this, we need a solid plan and detailed budget required to accomplish it. We can start the process in the morning, but you must understand that if we do this, you need to see it through. It will put a lot of pressure on you to lead the change and there will be no room for hesitation or back-tracking."

Closing his eyes, Conrad tried to urge his body to relax. The couch beneath him was soft, yet he might as well have been sitting on a bench of bricks with how he felt. "I know." He steadied his thundering chest at the implication his mother was making. "I will see it through. If this is to be my life now, my duty, then I'm going to make it mine and this change will help." His eyes still ached as he rubbed at his face, wishing he hadn't been forced to read for so long. "Plus, I'll be able to focus on it instead of my mind wandering whenever there are words in front of me." In many ways,

Conrad's thoughts were always somewhere else, even when he was a youth starting school in Treama. He'd never been able to convert the language on the page into images in his head. And it didn't help when the letters he believed he knew might as well look like they were ancient Aueric on every page.

"All right." Talia's tone held finality. "Then it's settled. But let's relax, you look exhausted. How is the search for Ahria going?"

"Nothing." Conrad's chest tightened at the mention of her name. "There's nothing to be found. I sent a letter to Leiura weeks ago, telling her to write immediately if Ahria happened to return to the ship, but she hasn't responded. Not that I can blame her. I dropped Dawn Chaser on her shoulders rather unexpectedly." He winced, knowing Leiura would have a difficult time establishing herself as the new captain because of how frequently they had changed crew members. But if anyone could do it, it'd be her.

"Well, if Ahria is looking for her father, then she's bound to find us eventually, since Talon is here. And he won't stop looking for his daughter, either. He wrote to her uncle in Olsa, but I don't think he's heard back yet, either." Talia sipped her tea. "She sounds like a capable young woman, even if she lacks experience. What is your next step to find her? I know you can't just sit on your hands and wait."

He shrugged, hating himself for doing it. "I don't know

what I can do. I can't leave the palace and Talon made it pretty clear he didn't want to share her face across the country to have the guards searching for her."

"He must have his reasons for that." His mother fell silent for a moment, tapping her cup with the pad of her thumb.

"The only thing that could be done is to try to follow the route we'd planned together backwards. But that's only if she stuck to the plan. Not that I would fault her if she didn't. She's probably already completely forgotten about me, anyway."

Talia's brow twitched. "Are you and her... together? I know why you might not want to be forthcoming about it with Talon, and I won't tell him either way, but I'd like to understand just how deep your connection is to her."

The question swirled around in Conrad's mind as he tried to find what the answer actually was. "We agreed to find each other again. But that hardly feels like a formal commitment. And that was before..." He gestured at his mother's grand chamber, which was easily twice the size of his own. The high vaulted ceilings were intricately painted with dramatic battle scenes and rimmed with gold. He found a face among the Zionan warriors in the scene that looked ever so slightly like Ahria, and a pang went through his heart. "I can't imagine she'd want to get wrapped up in all this."

"It *is* a lot to handle," Talia whispered, studying her son. "But perhaps she would decide you're worth it."

He smiled, but shook his head. "Let's see if you still think that in a few more weeks, after you've had to put up with me a bit longer." He met his mother's gaze, wondering how he had been apart from her for so long. He'd missed the stability of her presence, and how it always managed to calm him. "But if I haven't heard anything about Ahria in the next few months, I may end up going out and looking myself."

Talia smiled, wrinkles touching the corners of her eyes. "I think that's a good plan."

Five weeks later...

Conrad frowned down at the woman standing at the base of the dais, trying to resist the temptation to tap his fingers on the narrow table in front of him like a disapproving father.

The copper-haired woman avoided eye contact with the crown prince, wringing her scarf between her hands. The woman's accuser stood behind her, along with the city guard who'd been first to arrive at the confrontation.

"Let me get this straight, Lady Sydney. You threw a punch at Lady Dari because she suggested she'd slept with your brother..." He rubbed at his eyebrows, wishing Wendelin hadn't been right about this one.

The bashful woman nodded quickly, hardly looking the type to lash out. "Apologies, your highness. I guess I got a few too many ales in me that night."

Conrad sighed. "You will pay damages to Lady Dari in the amount of a half silver florin. And perhaps lay off the drinks so it won't be a full florin next time." Looking at the guards, he gestured with a finger. "Bring in the next case."

The two women and the guard bowed before leaving, the next accused being brought forward.

"Madam Sureena, caught stealing various food items from the market, including apples, grain, cheese, and flour," the court attendant drawled with a bored tone.

The woman bowed her head, shoulders slumped, but there was a strength in her form that suggested she'd been a warrior at some point in her life. Though Conrad noted the unusual bend in her leg and old clothes. Before he could ask her for her recount of the events, she spoke. "Your highness, it is true. I stole the food."

"Then you do not challenge the report filed by the officer who arrested you." Conrad tapped on the paper as the court attendant slid it onto his desk. He hadn't been able to fully escape all the paperwork, but now he could prompt people to explain what was on it for him.

"I do not." She lifted her chin but didn't meet his eyes. "I am guilty of the crime listed."

Conrad watched her face carefully before looking at the report. He slid his gaze down the list of regular pantry items.

"And why did you steal the food, Madam Sureena? It says here this isn't your first offense."

Her jaw flexed. "Why does one ever steal food? To eat, of course. To feed my children. Finding work has been difficult since my discharge from the military. My injury makes it..." Bowing her head again, she squared her shoulders. "I deserve whatever punishment is due."

"Perhaps, but I'm the one privileged with that decision." He considered the paper again, allowing the silence to prevail through the hall, which had once been the foyer for one of the ballrooms. With the people seeing a member of the royal family, it needed to look official, even if Conrad had tried to convince Wendelin that a standard meeting room would suffice. So now he towered over every soul who came through for judgment. He tried to convince himself it was no different from when he stood at the helm of Dawn Chaser.

"How many children, Madam Sureena?" He didn't look up, focusing on the vague words of the report that hadn't even mentioned a family.

"I have two boys and a girl, your highness."

"And your partner?"

"He works at the river docks, but he got laid off last week and is struggling to find work again." Sureena kept her voice even.

Conrad had heard about the mass layoffs at the river in light of the season change. With the passes clearing of their snow, the current made it difficult for ships to reach New Kingston and land caravans were more prevalent. No work for someone more familiar with docks unless he took to a ship full time.

"How did you sustain your injury?" Conrad ignored the confused look from Wendelin, who still hovered near the back of the room. He almost expected her to question him aloud, but her jaw only twitched.

The woman didn't answer him right away, brow furrowed. "An accident during a training exercise. The healers weren't able to restore full function to my leg. But without them, I wouldn't even be walking."

"So it happened while you were in service to Ziona, then?" Conrad pushed the report towards the edge of the desk as options mulled around his mind.

Sureena nodded. "Two years ago."

The general punishment for a repeat theft would warrant not just time in prison, but also a hefty fee due to the merchants, even though they received their goods back, according to the report. Neither punishment would solve the problem. Her children would still be hungry, her partner still unemployed, and she'd suffer for being a good mother.

It's all so unfair.

Conrad looked at the guard at the side of the room, one of the few men among those stationed in the judiciary. "Hardeep, see that Madam Sureena receives an escort home, as well as five silver florins from the coffers to compensate her for the injury sustained while in service to our country. As is our policy for all those who serve now, regardless of when that service was completed and for how long. Charges are dismissed."

Sureena's gaze shot up, her mouth agape. "Five... Your highness, this is..."

"There is still dock work to be had at the coast. I know moving a family is no small feat, and if I may be so bold, I would recommend the use of your military compensation to aid in relocation so your partner may find work that will not take him from home longer than the day." He could tell by how Sureena's leg already quaked that she only remained standing out of sheer stubbornness. She'd need her partner at home with three children.

The woman's breath came faster, and she smiled. "Thank you, your highness. Thank you so much. I'll not forget your kindness."

As the guard escorted her out of the hall, Wendelin exited without a word.

"That concludes the cases, today, your highness." The court attendant bowed before following the others out.

A servant by the side door, having been hovering during the last hearing, finally approached him. He held out a silver platter, boasting a small scroll with his name on it, written in Leiura's hand.

Controlling his eagerness for the letter, Conrad stood and calmly took it. "Thank you." He considered waiting to read it, but after the servant's departure, he stood alone in the echoing foyer. He stared at the letter. The potential it held.

The seal's snap echoed throughout the hall as he broke it, unraveling the document while he stepped down the stairs of the dais.

Conrad,

I am writing this at my earliest opportunity. I pray it finds you safe. The day after you left, Ahria returned to Dawn Chaser. I told her what happened, and she set off for New Kingston to find you. While I don't know if this information will be of any use to you, perhaps she's found you already, I felt it my duty to tell you. Your ship and crew are well.

Leiura

He read the letter again, finding himself repeating the third sentence over and over to make sure he was understanding it properly. "She came back..." he muttered, a stone weighing in his chest. Looking up at the double doors that led to the courtyard of the palace, he imagined the city beyond. And wondered how close she'd been this entire time.

His feet moved, and he pushed through the double doors into the crisp evening air.

Night jasmine caught on the breeze, whipping back the capes of the two guards standing at the door. The vibrant purple looked black in the dying daylight. He gazed towards the open front gates of the palace, welcoming the people to the courtyard of the palace once more. Though there were far more guards present near the main entrance of the palace itself, as well as at each doorway like the one where he now stood.

"Your highness." One of the guards faced him, a concerned look on her face. "Are you scheduled to go into the city today? We've not received a request for escort but we can assemble a troop if need be."

"No need." Conrad descended the stairs to the courtyard. "I can manage on my own."

Both guards trailed after him. "We can't allow you to leave alone." They muttered to each other under their breath. "Would you please wait for an escort?"

Conrad turned, trying to control his glare. "Look, I've lived my whole life without needing to be shepherded around like a lost lamb. I'm fairly certain I can find my way around a city without any help."

"While we do not doubt your competence..." The guards exchanged a look. "If you don't at least allow us to accompany you, we'll lose our posts."

Groaning, Conrad shook his head at the guard he'd had several interactions with before. But her name eluded him. "Fine." He gritted his jaw at his own frustration.

As he passed through the gates into the city, the two guards fell into step behind him. It drew some curious glances, but he'd stayed out of the public eye as much as possible, save for the judiciary hearings. Few, if any, would recognize his face.

Small things to be grateful for.

"Might I ask where you wish to go?" One of the guards behind him strode closer, but kept an arm's distance from him.

"Just a walk." Conrad didn't look back at the guard, keeping his eyes on the crowd of the city. The outdoor street lamps had been lit already, casting eerie shadows on everyone's faces. Even if he saw Ahria, he questioned if he'd recognize her right away in the dusk. Yet, he couldn't wait for the next morning. If what Leiura said was true, she was here and looking for him. With how much he avoided the public eye, it was now a disadvantage. She wouldn't have seen him and wouldn't even know where to start looking. And with a city the size of New Kingston, it could take months to find a particular shop without detailed directions.

He strode into the entertainment district, where taverns lined the streets. Cart merchants sold hot pastries and beverages, music and chatter emitting from every open door and window. The city had awakened with spring, outdoor patios stuffed as full as the taverns themselves with thirsty patrons.

"Your highness, this isn't an appropriate street for an evening walk. Perhaps we can choose another?" The guard walked closer to him, now, her partner flanking him.

He could sense more eyes gravitating towards them, attracted by the mere presence of two fully armored royal guards walking beside a finely-dressed gentleman. People paused to whisper to each other while watching, and it made his stomach curdle. "You two do make it difficult to blend in."

The other guard spoke this time. "I must insist we return to the palace."

Maybe she's right.

Conrad paused his step, looking down the long street as a sense of hopelessness overcame him. But then a song lyric reached his ears, making his heart skip a beat as he faced the guard. "Did you hear that?"

Her eyes darted around him. "Hear what, your highness?" She whispered his title, hand on her sword's hilt.

Centering his hearing on the music coming from a particular tavern, he listened to the singer's voice. It struck a chord within him, but he couldn't place why. "That song. I could have sworn she said Dawn Chaser in the last verse."

The first guard stepped in front of him as he moved to get

closer to the tavern door. "I didn't hear it clearly, but we must return to the palace."

The singer continued inside, her voice flowing over the night air like a warm embrace.

Conrad glowered at the guard's armored throat, contemplating how angry his mother and Talon would be if he gave his escort the slip to indulge in a night at a tavern. It was odd to miss the sticky floors and chaotic noise. Yet he wished desperately for all of it.

And for someone to share a bottle of fire wine with.

As he looked over the guard's shoulder, the light of the tavern flicked over the porch as the door opened briefly, letting a longer, more solemn note on a wood flute free into the night. He wanted more of the voice that'd harmonized with the instrument only moments before, but it was drowned out by the applause and cheers of the tavern patrons.

The second guard touched his arm. "We can return another day."

Conrad hesitated, but a little voice at the back of his mind told him he'd never find Ahria. Not so easily. "Fine."

Chapter 20

One month later...

AHRIA LAUGHED AS SHE FOLLOWED Vaeler out the back door of the tavern. "You said you played the lute!"

"I said I *liked* the lute. Never been better than below average with my playing ability." He bumped her shoulder with his, beaming. "You, though. Wow. You were incredible. The crowd loves you. I've never seen this place so packed, and can't fathom everyone was drawn in to watch me pluck the same four chords over and over."

Heat rose to her cheeks, and she shook her head. "I just hope one day they'll hear it and know it's me."

Vaeler hefted a bag of their equipment into the cart hitched to their pack horse. It lacked their usual stacks of props and crates of costumes, since their morning performance had been focused only on music. "They will.

You keep this up, and everyone in Pantracia will know your voice and your songs."

Unease stirred in her gut at the idea. With who she was, her father had always taught her to keep a low profile. Sure, the events that would forever change her life may never come to pass, but she always needed to be ready in case they did.

The door opened behind them, and Jaqi stepped out, knocking Ahria into the horse before moving towards the back of the cart. "Oops, sorry."

Ahria rolled her eyes, patting the animal. Dark horse hair and dust marred her white outfit, but she brushed it off. "Perhaps one of these days, you'll look where you're going."

Only days ago, Jaqi had 'accidentally' walked into Ahria outside in the rain, making her slip and land on her backside on a muddy stretch of road. She tried to ignore the woman's attempts to make her the fool, but they grew more infuriating by the day.

All because she wanted Vaeler, and in her contorted mind, Ahria was to blame for her not getting him.

"Don't be such a child, Jaqi. You both performed well tonight, so take it as a win." Vaeler hefted another bag.

Jaqi scowled, gripping her own breasts and squishing them together with a challenging look at Ahria. "When you have assets like these, you don't need to *sing*." Her low-cut tunic left little to the imagination, and it worked. The woman never failed to attract men, selling tickets to shows and palm readings. "You want to know your future?"

"No, thank you," Ahria murmured, helping Vaeler with the packs. "Doom, death, and betrayal, I'm sure."

"Not far off. Though it's more like... betrayal, death, then celebrations." Jaqi grinned, leaning against the cart and twirling a lock of her dark hair around her finger. "Many celebrations. Preferably without clothing, wouldn't you agree, Vae?"

Vaeler eyed her, then drawled, "Didn't happen before Ahria joined us, and wouldn't happen that way, either. Bark up a different tree, Jaqi." His tone had lost most of its patience, but he covered the annoyance with a dryness that made Ahria chuckle.

They were still just friends, but he'd become the closest person in her life after she'd failed to find her father or Conrad. It'd been months, and she had no idea where either of them were, or if they were even in New Kingston anymore. Or Ziona. But she sang every night, hoping one of them would hear.

"Did you just laugh at me?" Jaqi stepped around Vaeler, but he dropped the pack he was loading and put himself between them.

"Calm down, there's no need to get catty." He didn't touch either of them, keeping his hands up. "What's gotten into you?"

"Nothing. Just tired of this bitch thinking she's the star of the show. We're a team and we ain't got room for entitled ones like her." Jaqi sneered, curling her upper lip. "You better watch your back."

Ahria squared off towards the woman, gritting her jaw. "Watch it for what? What the hells is your problem with me? I haven't done anything to you."

Jaqi's face flushed, and the vague look of surprise shifted into fury. She evidently hadn't expected Ahria to snap back. "Everything about you is my problem. Vaeler just up and breaks you, a criminal, out of jail, then you come here and decide you deserve center stage. I don't know who you're fooling, but this isn't your troupe. You aren't one of us, and no matter how hard you try, you *never* will be."

Vaeler lifted his hands. "Why don't we go home, cool off, and—"

"How is any of that your call to make?" Ahria threw her hands up, ignoring Vaeler. "Everyone else has welcomed me with open arms, and Vaeler—"

"Vaeler is never going to be yours," Jaqi snarled. "Mysterium is mine, and you're not going to replace me."

"Pretty sure I can speak for myself," Vaeler grumbled, but neither of them acknowledged him.

"I don't *want* Vaeler!" Ahria cringed, throwing her friend a half-hearted shrug. "You know what I mean." He waved her off, and she continued, "I don't have any desire to replace you in Mysterium, Jaq, I'm just trying to keep my shit together long enough that my life doesn't fall apart. Why can't you just leave me alone?"

Jaqi huffed, shaking her head. "Because you're still here, stringing everyone along, like you're part of this family. But you're just using us, and one day, you'll leave." She approached until her face hovered half a foot from Ahria's. "And if it's in my power, I will make that day as soon as possible. I will *burn* your life with whatever I have. Lies, truths, you name it. I hope you never find your father. I bet he doesn't even care—"

Without thinking, Ahria reacted. Her fist flew from her side, colliding with Jaqi's face. The woman's head jolted sideways, and blood spewed from her nose.

"All right, I think that's quite enough!" Vaeler stepped between them, a hand on each of Ahria's shoulders. "You can't just hit people," he whispered through clenched teeth, a conspiratorial glint in his eye. "It's against the rules."

"You bitch!" Jaqi cupped her face, touching her nose. "If you broke my nose!"

"I would say you asked for it," Vaeler cut in. With a sigh, he gave it a quick inspection. "It doesn't look broken, but—"

"What the hells is going on out here?" Keigan laughed until he saw Jaqi's face, quickly stifling the rest. "Oh, darling, you're going to ruin your dress." He gave Ahria a pointed, almost impressed look, before wrapping an arm around Jaqi's shoulders. "Let's get you back inside. Get some ice on that."

Jaqi whimpered something under her breath to their troupe-mate, letting him guide her back inside.

Ahria stared after her, knuckles aching and heart thundering. "Gods, she makes me so..."

"Pissed off? I know." Vaeler threw the last pack onto the wagon and shut the back gate. "You want to turn this around and go see the queen's speech? Or you need to punch more things?"

Throughout the entire city, celebrations roared with the midsummer festival. It'd been going all morning, the scents of fruit tarts and lemon drinks prevalent in the air, and would continue through the afternoon and well into the night. The queen would speak, addressing the people in a long lost tradition for Ziona. It wasn't the first time she'd made public announcements, but they were usually too preoccupied with shows to attend.

Ahria nodded, exhaling the rest of her tension. "I don't think my hand can take more punching. Let's go see it. Maybe we can get some tarts on the way to the palace?"

"Do you ever stop eating?" Vaeler laughed, then shrugged in a way that reminded her of Conrad. "I don't see why not. No one is expecting us back any time soon. Though we're probably already missing the start of it. We've definitely missed the prince's introduction. Perhaps you'll have another opportunity to swoon over how handsome he is with the rest of the kingdom."

Rolling her eyes, Ahria climbed into the front of the wagon with Vaeler. "I don't need to swoon over the prince. I'm sure he's handsome, but..."

"Your heart belongs to someone, I know." Vaeler gave her a sideways hug with one arm around her shoulders. He shrugged again, whispering, "But perhaps ogling a prince will distract you."

Ahria chuckled. "Next time he's speaking, we can go. But are you sure it's for me?" Looking up at him, she wiggled her eyebrows.

Vaeler huffed. "I doubt he's my type. And just because I don't want to be with Jaqi, doesn't mean I don't like women. Just... not *that* type of woman."

"And here I was, thinking *rich* was your type." Ahria smirked, poking him in the ribs.

Choking on an abrupt laugh, her friend cleared his throat and grinned. "Well, maybe you're not too far off."

After returning the horse and cart to their home, they wandered through the streets towards the palace. Ahria bought a fruit tart, a sausage roll, and a mug of sweet lemon water before they reached the entrance to the palace courtyard. She'd climbed a wall to enter it last time, but since then, they'd opened the gates to the public. The people of the city had filed in, though it seemed plenty were perfectly fine witnessing the queen's address from the gates. Citizens stood shoulder to shoulder, with others already exiting the courtyard through the single wide gate, forcing Vaeler and Ahria to squeeze between them to get a better look.

In the distance, the queen stood at the top of the steps. The crowd cheered, and she waved.

"Did we miss the whole thing?" Ahria pouted, but moved through the crowds to get a closer look at the queen's face. The woman stood with two others, all of whom wore the colors of Ziona. Her dark skin shone against the pale lilac of her bodice, the long skirts falling from it woven with depictions of Ziona's thistles. She glanced quickly at the others beside her, a paler man who stood behind and to the queen's right, holding a thick clipboard and quill. Some politician, she guessed.

And...

Her heart stopped as her eyes settled on the other man next to the queen.

The *auer* next to her.

"Dad," Ahria whispered, dropping her mug. It clattered to the stone ground, and her heart jumped into a faster rhythm. "Dad!" Her shout barely made it any distance at all, and she lunged forward.

Vaeler grabbed her, hauling her back. "What are you doing? Do you see your father?"

Ahria nodded furiously. "He's standing next to her. Next to the queen. He's right there!" She pointed, but those on the stairs were returning inside. As the grip on her arm vanished, she plowed ahead, shouting as loud as she could over the crowds. Losing track of Vaeler, she pushed through people, but only made it fifty feet before the doors to the palace shut.

He's in the palace.

Disbelief rippled through her.

I need to get inside.

Ahria ceased her shouts, maneuvering through the throngs of people

Something seized her arm, tearing her back from her approach to the palace steps where guards moved to close the gate that'd been opened for the address. Her wrist screamed as Vaeler's grip tightened, and he pulled her towards the still-empty column at the center of the courtyard.

"Don't do anything crazy." He lowered his voice, drawing close to her. "You sure it was your dad?"

Ahria nodded, glancing at the palace windows, looking for side doors. "It was him. I need to get inside."

"We could send a message tomorrow, or ask—"

"No. I tried to talk to the guards before. I need to see what I can do now. Everyone's distracted with the festival, I can sneak in." Ahria looked up at Vaeler. "Tell Evelyn I might be late for the show tonight, will you?"

"Ahria, I can't let you do this." Vaeler scowled at her, shaking his head.

"I have to. Break me out again if I get caught, all right?" She flashed him a coy smile.

He groaned. "If one of the guards recognizes you from before..."

"It's been months. Don't worry. I'll do better this time." Without waiting for his response, she rushed off through the crowds along the side of the palace, looking for anything that could grant her access inside. An open window, an ajar door, even a cellar.

A cracked window on a quieter side of the palace gave her hope. She scanned her surroundings for anyone watching before sliding the window the rest of the way open. Lifting herself to the sill, she rolled inside and landed within an unoccupied study. The walls were lined with bookshelves, and a desk piled with books and papers dominated a space near the center of the room. A tea setting perched on a side table, the only tidy thing in the room. A single cup sat upside down beside the teapot, unused.

As she looked around the space, she shut the window, then crossed to the interior door.

Voices murmured on the other side, growing louder.

"Shit," she whispered, taking a step towards the window before deciding she didn't have time. She spun, hiding behind the door just as it opened.

"Her majesty will be looking for a fresh pot of tea, Rumond." One of the men walked into the room, towards the unused tea set. He considered the setting before picking up only the teapot and turning back the way he'd come. His eyes remained on the floor, but not long enough.

Ahria held her breath as his eyes met hers. She subtly shook her head, silently pleading, but he opened his mouth.

"Guards!" he bellowed, dropping the teapot. "Guards!"

Ahria rushed for the window, but footsteps charged into the room seconds later. She fumbled with the window, then pressed her back against it to face the threat. "I'm not here to cause trouble, I just..." Her voice trailed off as one guard paused, grabbing the other.

Everything stilled in the room for a breath before the guard who'd stopped looked at her, face contorted with shock. "She's got the Art, seize her!" The guard lunged as the other drew her blade.

Ahria stared at the guards, wide-eyed. "What? I don't..." She leapt to the side, pulling the dagger from her belt.

Why do they think I have power?

Her back hit the wall, and as one guard closed in on her, she dropped to a crouch and rolled out of the way. Looking at the window, she sucked in a deep breath. More running footsteps pounded outside the doorway beside her, eliminating her other option of escape.

I need to get out of here.

But the cold metal of a blade touched the back of her neck, and she froze, dropping her dagger. "Please, I need to see the auer working with the queen. I need to see Talon."

"The only person you'll be seeing here is the warden. Let's go." The guard hauled her to her feet, and as she opened her mouth, the woman scowled. "Don't make me gag you."

Ahria clamped her mouth shut, gritting her teeth.

"Don't even think about using the Art, either. I felt what you did, so there's no point in denying it. But it'll be easier if you behave rather than cuffing you."

But I didn't do anything.

Ahria cringed as her arms bent into an uncomfortable position, giving up her struggle as they led her out of the room.

Chapter 21

AMARIE, WAKE UP!

Her eyes shot open, and she gasped in a breath of musty air. Vivid streaks of violet washed through her sight before fading to a pale green. Motes of light buzzed above, following the curves of roots extruding from the dirt ceiling.

She blinked, urging her senses to focus on the room. The rich scent of the loamy earth filled her nostrils with a hint of something else. Lavender, but smoky. Like the haze in the air hovered from some unseen incense. As she tilted her head, the tiny green orbs absorbed the haze, trickling up the roots above her. Like water defying gravity. Bubbles of power that made her skin buzz.

The low hum of the room shifted, as if something had interrupted the pitch and forced it to another key. Someone beside her gasped and coughed, breaking the steady tone.

On another stone bed like hers, a man struggled upright, still rasping for air. A lock of dark brown hair fell over his brow as he hunched at the edge of the carved slab.

Amarie touched the surface she laid on, finding similar grooves as she sat up. "Who are you?" Her voice echoed with a foreign timbre, not matching the one that had woken her.

The man rubbed his face, a short beard over his jaw. In the dim light, his steel-blue eyes shone. "I..." His voice bounced like hers through the chamber. "I don't know." He reached towards the twist of roots that dangled over the stone bed he'd been laying on, his fingers hovering curiously beneath them.

A flash of the green light surged through the space, and he recoiled as she blinked the specks from her vision. The pitch in the air heightened again before finally dissipating into nothing.

Furrowing her brow, Amarie slid off the stone to her feet, her boots quiet on the dirt floor.

The man stood slowly, thick black fabric swaying around his ankles as his cloak settled into place. "Where are we?"

"I don't know." Amarie shook her head, staring at her hands.

Why can't I remember anything?

Circling the rectangular stone platform, she paused near the head and trailed a fingertip over an inscription in the stone, written in Aueric.

Amarie Xylata
2612 R.T.
Wake if necessary.

Amarie frowned.

Necessary?

The man flinched as he touched his forehead, a low hiss escaping his mouth. "Gods, it feels like a dire wolf is digging into my head." His cloak drifted to the side as he rubbed, exposing the hilt of a dagger in his belt. Its black, glass-like surface reflected the green motes and caused a stir of unease in her gut.

She glanced down at herself for a weapon but found none. Her veins heated, calming her nerves with a reassuring rise of power.

I have the Art.

"You don't have a headache?" He squinted at her, scratching his right forearm through his tunic.

Amarie shook her head. Her eyes wandered to the inscribed stone at the head of his altar. "Mine says my name. What does yours say?"

He hissed again, shuffling to the end of his stone bed. Blinking, he touched the plaque akin to hers. "I guess it's a name. Kinronsilis? Gods, who would name their kid that?" He crouched to get a closer look. "I don't think this is a language I can read."

Gritting her teeth, Amarie approached and waited for him to step aside so she could read it. "Kinronsilis Parnell. 2611 R.T. Wake upon direction from Damien Lanoret."

He glanced from the text to her, a sideways smile on his handsome face. "Any idea what that means?" He shifted back onto his heels, looking up at the dirt ceiling where roots wove in patterns to support the odd light.

"No." Amarie shivered. "But I want to get out of here. This place doesn't feel right."

Kinronsilis grunted in agreement, looking behind her towards the open doorway. "Maybe we'll find answers to why you can read that language and I remember things like dire wolves but we can't remember our own names." Walking forward, he brushed past her, but paused and turned back, holding out a hand to her. "Shall we go together?"

Amarie looked at his hand, her heart quickening. She swallowed, ignoring the swell of pressure in her chest as she took his warm hand. "What if we're enemies?" Her gaze lifted to meet his.

His fingers slid comfortably between hers, and he shrugged. "Maybe we're strangers." That oddly charming crooked smirk crossed his lips again. "What's your name?"

Stepping with him, she studied the scar on his temple. "Amarie. My name is Amarie Xylata."

"Well, Amarie Xylata, do you have any opinions about how to get out of here, or where here even is?" He moved towards the exit, the worn hem of his cloak wisping along the floor. He paused at the open archway, which led to more dirt-ceilinged tunnels. Everything coated in that green light.

"Wait, I think..." She let her voice trail off as she breathed deeper, sinking into her Art in a way that felt too practiced to be her first time. She surrounded herself with the power and noted the barrier that contained it all. Kept it from leaking into the air and into the awareness of others.

I have some kind of hiding aura. Probably better not to mess with that, yet.

Letting out the breath, she abandoned her exploration and followed Kinronsilis. "Sorry. Let's go. Maybe we'll get a better idea of where we are once we see outside."

"If we can find the outside..." Kinronsilis looked up and down the wide hallway devoid of any other living beings. Like the tunnels had been created by enormous beetles and then abandoned.

As they paused, Amarie let go of his hand and moved to rest her grip on something at her side, only to have her fingers pass through air.

I must usually wear a blade.

Listening to her inner voice, she picked a direction and started walking. "Gotta be a way out somewhere."

They passed by an arched doorway, and Kinronsilis paused to lean into it. "This place looks like a crypt," he whispered, as if afraid to raise his voice. "There's more bodies in here, but they all look auer."

Bodies.

Amarie shuddered and kept walking. "This doesn't feel like a friendly place."

His footsteps resumed behind her, and he hummed in agreement. "Makes me wonder what we're doing down here."

"And perhaps if we came willingly?" Amarie glanced back at him as she rounded another corner, followed quickly by another.

At the end of the hallway, stairs led up.

"Who would be willingly put in a crypt?" He stepped up beside her, looking up the stairs which felt promising. "Feels more like we're prisoners and someone forgot to shut the door."

Amarie stared at the steps, unable to see the top from her position further back. Her heart raced, her body screaming with nerves she knew better than to ignore. "Whoever put us here won't be happy if we leave, then." With slow strides, she approached the base of the stairs and gazed up. Brightness blurred the top, making her squint.

The sound of a blade rasping from its sheath echoed from behind her, making her jump, but he only partially withdrew it.

Amarie motioned to it. "How come you have that, but I have nothing?"

"Maybe you're not a fighter? Which probably means I should go first."

She frowned and ascended first, keeping her gait smooth and silent. As they approached the top, she had the distinct sensation that they were no longer alone. She slowed as the sun glinted off a bit of armor, a hot spot radiating down into the stairwell.

Pausing, she held up one finger, craning her neck to check the other direction. Another armored guard flanked the opening, but faced away. She lifted two fingers behind her, then gestured with them to the right, claiming the left should the guards cause trouble.

"I don't know. Dara left in a hurry and gave me no answers." A male voice.

"Either way, we can't leave until our relief comes." A woman, her tone annoyed. "We're stuck here guarding those who hardly need it. No one cares about anyone down below."

The man huffed. "Maybe you don't, but I take pride in guarding this place. This is important."

"Do you suppose the council is assembling to discuss whatever that surge was? I thought the island was about to explode with the flurry it caused."

"Without a doubt. They'll have answers for us soon."

Amarie understood the language, but one glance at Kinronsilis's face confirmed he didn't. She took the last stairs, lifting her hands as she stepped into the daylight.

The guards both sprang back, drawing their chakrams. "Halt! What are you doing here?" The man towered over Amarie, his ebony skin matching his stark black hair.

"We don't want any trouble," Amarie said in Aueric.

"Get back inside," the woman hissed, holding her weapon ready. "You shouldn't be out here. How are you awake?"

"I can't do that," Amarie murmured, shaking her head. "Don't try to force me." She spoke the second sentence in Common for the benefit of her new ally.

The female auer leapt at her, blade aimed to maim rather than kill, but Amarie's hands shot up.

A transparent power locked around the attacking guard, freezing her in place.

A leaf that had been falling from the tree above stilled in the air behind the guard, frozen mid twirl.

Looking at her own hands, Amarie furrowed her brow. But as soon as she relaxed, the power over the guard failed.

The chakram barely missed as she dodged sideways. Bringing her hands up again, she refocused her power and pushed on the invisible fabric of the Art with all her might.

The guard's face contorted with surprise as she was flung backward, and steel clashed behind Amarie.

She spun, throwing out a palm to send the male guard sprawling away. Breathing hard, she grabbed Kinronsilis's hand and tugged. "We need to run." Letting go, she sprinted away, adrenaline coursing through her blood.

How did I do that?

Racing for the trees, she didn't look back, cutting through the dense woods. Her ally plowed after her. The monstrous forest overtook the sky, hiding the blue behind a dense canopy of beech and banyan trees. Birds protested their arrival into the dense flora, scattering in panic.

After several minutes of nothing but wild, she skidded to a stop and faced him. "We're on an island, so I'm assuming this is Eralas. We need to find a way to the mainland." She panted, but mostly out of shock rather than exhaustion. "We need a boat or something."

Think. Think.

Amarie looked at her hands, but quickly dismissed the notion of her Art helping them escape. Even if she once knew how to use it, now wasn't the time to experiment.

He breathed heavily behind her, leaning against one of the massive trunks nearby.

She focused on a single deep breath, then looked back the direction they'd come. "We were close to the beach, but we can't go back that way. We should go west, find a boat to borrow."

"Lead the way." Kinronsilis gestured, though not in any clear direction.

She'd spotted the sun in the sky as they fled whatever chambers they'd been kept in, but couldn't tell if it was mid morning or mid afternoon. They could have been on any side of Eralas.

Amarie shook her head. "I can't tell which way to go until some time passes and the sun's position changes."

He nodded, his shaggy hair falling over his forehead as he leaned heavier against the tree. "I won't say no to a little break." He looked back the way they'd come before plopping among the roots. A hiss escaped him as he shifted, gingerly touching the hilt of the dagger poking him in the thigh.

Serves him right for not keeping it in a sheath.

He withdrew the dagger, tilting the smooth obsidian edge in a stream of light in front of him. The onyx stone boasted intricate carvings and runes she'd never seen before, its edges far smoother than seemed possible.

Narrowing her eyes, Amarie tried and failed to ignore the chill down her spine. "What is that?"

Kinronsilis glanced up at her as he turned the blade again to look at more runes on the other side. "A dagger? That's all I know. But I feel like I'd break it before it would do any damage." He shrugged as he tucked it back into his belt, closer to his back. "Looks ceremonial or something. Maybe someone will pay for it. I'd trade it for a loaf of bread at this point." He rubbed at his gut. "I feel like I haven't eaten in months."

"You probably haven't," Amarie muttered, studying the sun's position. Looking down, she spotted a bush a few feet away, branches heavy with dark berries. Huffing, she gestured towards it. "You can eat those."

Glancing at the bush, Kinronsilis rocked forward to get back to his feet. "You sure?" He plucked one of the berries from the bush and took it to his nose first before popping it in his mouth. His face contorted as he sucked on his tongue. "Little sour." He picked another before eating it.

Amarie gave him a droll look. "The darker ones are sweeter."

"Aren't you hungry?"

She shrugged. "Not really."

He furrowed his brow, but turned back to the bush to gather more berries into his palm, putting every other one directly into his mouth. Stepping away, he held out his hand to her. "Even if you're not, you should probably eat because we don't know when we'll be able to again."

Eyeing the offering, Amarie nodded and let him tilt them into her palm. "We need to borrow a boat once the sun's down. Make it across the strait."

"Unless we intend to come back, or leave the dagger in

exchange, I'm pretty sure you mean steal a boat." He chewed thoughtfully on another berry. "And I think I'm all right with that."

With a flat expression, she raised an eyebrow. "So am I."

He chuckled. "Might explain why both of us seemed to be imprisoned. Maybe we're thieves. Think we used to work together?"

Amarie studied him as she ate a berry, finding no familiarity in his ruggedly handsome face. "Maybe. Does that mean I'm supposed to trust you?"

"The way I see it, neither of us have a reason not to trust the other. Considering neither of us remember anything." He poured more berries into her hand. "Clean slates, right? Think that's the purpose of whatever the auer did to us?"

"For us, perhaps. But everyone else remembers. So I think it's more like being the only blind person... people." Amarie frowned. "What if we have families? Lovers? Children?" She rolled her lips together, wondering if anyone was missing her.

His face grew more serious, his jaw flexing. "Trying not to think about that." He popped the rest of the berries in his hand into his mouth, cringing again at the flavor. "I just want to focus on the next hour. And how to get away so we're not put back in that pit." Brushing his hands together in front of him, he looked back the direction they'd run from. "I get the impression I'm used to running like this."

Amarie took a deeper breath, nodding. "Do you?" She

smirked. "By the way you panted after such a short run, I figured you were a noble."

His face scrunched, but then he laughed. "Maybe a little out of shape? I'm going to blame that I've been laying in a tomb for gods know how long."

She smiled. "A year longer than me, which makes me doubt the partners in crime theory. Wish I knew what year it was now."

Kinronsilis motioned with his head towards the beach. "Could go back and ask them, if they're not too upset about whatever you did to them." He returned to the same tree, leaning against it as he crossed his ankles. "You have the Art?"

Amarie popped her last berry into her mouth, which seemed to wake up her stomach enough to ask for more. "Apparently."

He looked at his own hand. "Pretty sure that makes one of us." He scratched at his right forearm again.

"One of us," she murmured. "Kinronsilis and Amarie... Your name is too long. I'm going to call you Kin, instead. Or Ron. Or... perhaps Silis." She chuckled. "Have a preference?"

He frowned. "Let's just stick with Kin." He scratched more intently, pulling back his sleeve to expose a tangled looking scar. It marred his skin like a strange spiderweb, as if it stretched to hide something beneath.

"Kin it is." Amarie met his gaze. "And tonight, we steal a boat."

Chapter 22

CONRAD BEGGED HIS EYES TO focus as he poured what had to be his fifth cup of coffee for the morning. Too many trials had been postponed over the past two days for him to allow another day to go without. His morning report had already referenced concerns about overflow in the local prison cells with the lack of judgment. And innocents could be locked away from their families.

"I'd still advise taking another day or two, just to be sure. We still don't know what that disturbance to the Art was." Talon stood near the door, arms crossed. "Putting you back in the public eye is a risk. Threats may still loom."

"It can't wait any longer, and you already know why." Conrad schooled the annoyance from his tone. "We agreed if I sat through those damn planning sessions for the palace socials, you'd support the reopening of the judiciary hearings." He tipped cream into his coffee, glancing up at Talon. "I sat, so now I get to do my job."

The auer's expression remained unreadable. "That you did." He sighed. "Very well. I'll have the cases brought to the hall."

"And please tell Chancellor Wendelin that we will be addressing these in the *true* order they were arrested. I don't want her trying to sneak some noble's drunk son ahead of the rest again." The bitter coffee instantly awoke more of his senses as it touched his tongue.

Talon pursed his lips, but the corner of his mouth twitched. "I will see to that, but I won't be attending the hearings today, so you'll have to debrief me on her behavior this evening."

He lifted an eyebrow as he lowered his drink. "Does that mean you are actually going to look for Ahria?"

A frown took over the auer's face. "I look for my daughter every day. And today, I will be following a lead in the city. I will let you know if anything comes of it."

"Sorry." Conrad lowered his mug. "I don't mean to sound impatient. It's just..."

Talon nodded, reaching for the door handle. "Difficult to wait? Yes. Yes, it is. I didn't think it would be this long, either. But we mustn't give up. The hall should be ready for you within the hour. Good luck today."

Conrad nodded his thanks as Ahria's father closed the door behind him, leaving the prince alone.

After finishing his coffee, he returned to his chambers to change into his formal judiciary attire. It felt almost foreign after not wearing it for two days, but he welcomed the weight it placed on his shoulders. He was finally doing some good for the people, and pride eked through him as he strode down the hallway towards the hearing atrium, which had replaced the foyer for the proceedings.

With the recent celebration of midsummer, he braced himself for a plethora of drunken crimes that would likely result in a monotonous day. And the pile of papers already on his desk at the front of the atrium confirmed it.

The clerk, court attendant, and chancellor rose at his entrance, remaining standing until he sat at his desk on the dais. Tapping the carved mahogany armrest, he nodded to the attendant. "Bring in the first case."

The doors opened before the attendant could reach them, a pair of guards clearly having been listening.

With a glance, Conrad caught the line of people already waiting for the trials to begin. The guards bringing them from the nearby prison had learned quickly that Conrad kept the trials as brief as possible, and came prepared.

I wish I'd brought my coffee.

The cases were as he expected.

Drunken brawls. Minor assaults. Disorderly conduct.

Indecent behavior.

All providing simple sentences with fees to help further fund the system and pay for any damage done. He'd finally gained Wendelin's trust upon the confirmation that he would only reward compensation to the falsely imprisoned from the same coffer the fees paid to. Self sustainment, just like his ship had always operated.

"Your highness," the court attendant paused before opening the doors for the next case. "The next accused is under strict guard, for she possesses the Art. Would you prefer to read her case, as it would be the safer option?"

His back straightened. There was the occasional Art user to pass through the system, but rarely with more than the most basic of abilities. He had limited experience with practitioners, too. The Art was one of the mysteries of Pantracia that Conrad had never had a deep interest in exploring. With no natural talent of his own, or among any of his closest friends, a deep seated distrust had always lingered, despite how he battled his own prejudices. The stories of atrocities the war artisans of Helgath used to inflict in battle had been popular among the children of his home town.

But there's no way I can comprehend anything about the Art on a piece of paper right now.

Wendelin looked about to speak when Conrad lifted his hand to stop her. "Bring her in. I trust the guards to do their job in keeping us safe."

The attendant bowed and started towards the door again as Wendelin shot to her feet and hurriedly walked to the base of the dais. With a quick nod from Conrad, she ascended, stepping in front of his desk and blocking his view of the doorway.

"Your highness, this is not wise." She kept her voice low, a marked improvement to her outright questioning of him in the past. But over the months, he'd gained the respect of the now familiar faces of the room, and Wendelin knew it. "I recall reading the reports on this particular criminal. She was apprehended within the palace itself, which already suggests she may have nefarious intentions towards your family."

Conrad's throat tightened as he looked down at the report he hadn't even bothered to glance at. His eyes blurred, but caught the location and time of the arrest, which had been the queen's study.

But that was also when all our artisans felt that ripple in the fabric. The guards could have mistaken that as the intruder.

Regardless of the prisoner's potential power, the nerves in his gut hardened as he considered this person could have had ill intent towards his mother. He shook his head, focusing on Wendelin as the artisan entered outside of his vision. "Thank you for the warning."

Wendelin remained, her knuckles white where she gripped the edge of his desk. "Your highness."

"I trust the precautions the guards have taken to bring her from the prison. You should, too." Conrad gestured to Wendelin again, who sighed as she stepped down the dais, revealing the prisoner to the prince.

Two guards dropped the woman onto her knees, her head hanging forward. A mess of dark brown hair hid her features, and shackles held her bloodied hands together where she barely caught herself on the floor. She coughed, lowering her forehead to the cold stone.

The court attendant cleared her throat. "This woman stands accused of forcefully entering the royal residence without permission, resisting arrest, using the Art against two guards, and several escape attempts."

"I need to speak to Talon," the prisoner rasped, her voice barely audible in the spacious room.

"Be silent," the guard hissed.

Conrad paused, leaning forward in his chair to get a better look at the woman. There was something familiar in the way her hair trailed down to the marble floor and the wisps of the strands at the end. A remembered curl. And the desire to run his fingers through it.

The woman sat partially up, hands on the floor. "Please. I need to speak to Talon."

"You do not speak unless the prince addresses you directly." The guard took a step closer to the woman, hovering over her.

Conrad's heart stopped as he followed the line of the woman's hunched body, the curve of her shoulder. Her request.

Nymaera's breath.

He started to move, but remembered himself at the brief groan of his chair on the floor.

The prisoner's breath came in shaky inhales, but she hit the floor with the bottom of her fist. "Talon Di'Terian," she whispered, her voice near cracking. "He's my father. Please."

The guard on her left raised her hand to strike, and Conrad stood, slamming his palms onto his desk.

"Stop!" Everything grew hazy as he hurried to step off the dais. Everyone in the room had stood with him, their eyes all on him as he looked only at the female prisoner.

She looked up at him, face still hidden behind her hair, before lifting her cuffed wrists to brush it aside. He was already at the bottom of the stairs, rushing forward without a second thought, even as guards reached for their weapons.

"Conrad?" Ahria's glassy eyes struggled to focus on him, disbelief radiating through her tone. Scrapes marred her skin. Over her jaw, her hands, her knees. Dark bags beneath her eyes suggested the guards hadn't let her sleep. "What..."

He dropped to his knees before her, regardless of who watched. His chest felt as if it had cracked open, his very being raw and exposed at the sight of her and how she appeared. The guards looked back and forth at each other in confusion as Conrad lifted his hand to her cheek, touching his palm to an undamaged patch of skin. "It's me. Ahria, I'm so sorry."

If I hadn't allowed the trials to be delayed for two days...

She leaned into his touch. "I'm so... tired," she whispered, collapsing forward into him.

He caught her, lifting his hand in a silent gesture to the guard who looked ready to pull her away. Wrapping his arm firmly around her waist, he shifted closer to fully encompass her with his arms. "You're safe now." A kiss formed as he pushed his lips to the top of her head without another thought. "But let's get you somewhere you can sleep."

Ahria's eyes slid closed, her breathing even as she slumped, limp.

"Your highness?" The court attendant stepped forward, the first brave enough to speak to him.

The guards all stood like statues, their hands still on their weapons, despite having been returned to their sheaths.

"There has been a grave mistake." Conrad looked up at the guard who'd almost struck Ahria, and the woman took a step back with an apologetic salute. "This is Ahria Xylata, Advisor Di'Terian's daughter. Her imprisonment and arrest should not have happened."

He knew by the look in Wendelin's eyes that she had far more questions, but that the current time was inappropriate. Yet Conrad didn't move from Ahria.

"That's enough for today. Send fresh clothes, linens, and hot water to my chambers." Conrad rose, lifting Ahria from the cold floor. "Remove the cuffs from her wrists."

A guard leapt forward to obey, releasing the metal off her skin.

Carrying her in front of him, Conrad strode for the side door. "Advisor Di'Terian is in the city. Get word to him as soon as possible. Tell him that Ahria is with me."

Chapter 23

A COOL SUMMER BREEZE DANCED over Ahria's cheek, gently rousing her from whatever hellish purgatory she'd been stuck in for days. Her body ached, and she groaned, turning her face to the side. Something soft cradled the back of her head. Something warm.

Blinking her eyes slowly open, she took in the dark room. Only faint orange light emanated from behind the curtains, hinting at dawn.

Or dusk. Where am I?

The last thing she remembered was being dragged to the judiciary for her hearing. No one would listen to her. To her claims of knowing her father, to her pleas to see him. That cell. It had been so cold. So damp and cold. But then...

A subtle snore broke through the silence of the room. The sound came from a shadow beside the bed, hunched over in a chair.

Her heart picked up speed, feeling around herself for any of her blades. But there were none. Taken in her arrest.

Ahria's eyes narrowed at the sleeping figure, and she realized he was no soldier. Sitting up, she winced at the ache in her body as she peered closer at her keeper.

Conrad?

His arms crossed, and head hanging in sleep, Conrad looked very different from the captain she'd grown accustomed to. His clothes were far finer, tailored to fit his broad chest and shoulders. Gold filigree shone in the dim light penetrating through the distant windows, shrouded by dense curtains.

Breathing faster, she blinked again, trying to clear her eyes. It all rushed back. The hearing, and how he'd been there. How he'd stopped the guard from hitting her.

But why was he there?

Furrowing her brow, she touched her forehead and murmured, "I'm dreaming." She looked down at herself, but her clothing was still the same she'd worn to the show at the midsummer festival. But now it was dirty, torn, and hardly suitable for the soft, clean bed she lay in. But her skin was clear of the muck, and her mouth felt fresh, cleaned of the blood from her split lip.

Someone healed me.

Conrad stirred, sleepily lifting his head from where it rested against his palm. As he rubbed his jaw, his eyes struggled open. But when they met hers, he straightened in his high-backed chair, rubbing sleep from his eyes. "You're awake."

Ahria swallowed, nodding. "Where am I? Why are you..." A headache splintered between her temples, and she cringed again.

"Here." He stood from his chair, moving to another vague shape in the dim room, and the sound of pouring water tickled her ears.

The dryness in her throat suddenly doubled as he pushed a cool glass into her hands.

Lifting it to her lips, she drank. Too quickly. Coughing, she paused for only a breath before downing the rest. It chilled her insides, waking her hunger pains. But she ignored the rumble and waited for him to explain.

"You had us pretty worried." He settled back into the chair beside the bed, as if he'd played the part of watchful guardian for some time. "You've been asleep for nearly two days."

"Us?" Ahria set her cup on the bedside table.

Conrad jolted as if he'd forgotten something, getting back to his feet. "I need to tell Talon you're awake. He asked me to..." He hesitated, but she couldn't tell why.

Her stomach flipped over. "He's here?" Heat burned her eyes as she reached for his hand. "You know my father?"

"Apparently I have for a long time, but that's a different story." He encompassed her hand with both of his, the warmth of his skin encouraging her heart to speed. "But you're safe here in the palace. And Talon was here at your bedside just last night. He'd be here right now if duty hadn't necessitated otherwise."

Ahria slid from the bed to her feet, studying his face. How it had changed. How it hadn't. "I can hardly believe you're here. You've been here this whole time? I've been in the capital for months..."

"I..." He lowered his gaze, his jaw twitching. "It's complicated, but yes. I wanted to look for you, but with everything." His arms twitched as he took a step closer. "I should have searched harder, Ahria. I'm so sorry."

Confusion muddled her thoughts, and a sinking feeling made her take a step back. Bumping into the bed, she sidestepped. "Why didn't you? Did you not want..."

"No, no, it wasn't that. But my responsibilities here made it hard for me to look myself. And your father made it pretty clear he didn't want to share pictures of you with the guards."

Wincing, she shut her eyes, running her hands through her hair. "I don't understand. Your responsibilities? In the palace?" Meeting his gaze again, she wrapped her arms around herself. "Why are you here and not on your ship?"

"I'm still the same man, but I won't be able to go back to Dawn Chaser, no matter how much I wish I could. Turns out my family had a bit of a secret, one that isn't much of a secret anymore with my mum being crowned queen and all."

Her stomach dropped out. "Q-queen?" She ached to touch him, reach for him, but didn't dare.

He's royalty?

Dipping her chin, she stared at the floor, jaw clenched.

"Still the same man." He held his hands out to his sides, but didn't close the distance between them. "One who is damn glad to finally find you."

Taking him in again, she realized now his appearance made sense. Her chest cracked, relief eking through her. "I missed you so much."

His shoulders dropped as if he finally let the tension go. "I missed you, too." He moved his hands towards her, beckoning her closer by opening himself.

Ahria hesitated for only a few seconds before closing the gap between them. She wrapped her arms around his waist, pressing her chest to his. As he embraced her, she breathed his scent, burying her face in his neck. "This better not be a dream."

His chest vibrated with a soft laugh as he pressed his cheek to the top of her head. "Not a dream." His hug tightened for a brief moment before relaxing to simply hold her. "Though it certainly has the makings of one. It's really me, and this is really you."

She smiled, absently kissing his skin before she could think it through. Turning her face the other way, she took in the room without letting go of him. "Is this your bedroom?"

He hummed softly in affirmation, his fingers tangling with the ends of her hair and tracing circles along her spine. Goosebumps formed on the exposed flesh of his arms where his sleeves were rolled to his elbows, and Conrad sucked in a slow breath. "I brought you here from the judgment hall. Your father had suggested moving you, but I..." He pulled back from her just enough to meet her eyes. His thumb traced her jaw, some unspoken question in his eyes as he looked at her lips. "I didn't want to let you out of my sight."

The sun broke over the horizon, sending orange and pink light over the ceiling. It radiated off his skin, his eyes, and suddenly she was back on Dawn Chaser after drinking a bottle of fire wine.

"I'm glad," she murmured. "With you... with you is where I want to be."

His fingernail trailed along her skin as a gentle smile formed on his lips. "That's all I've thought about for the last several months." His arm wrapped firmly around her waist as he stepped into her, the hardness of his body sending fire through hers. "You found a way to get under my skin, Mouse." His breath tickled her lips. "I was about to walk off that ship and come find you before all the politics got in the way."

Something within her melted, and she huffed a quiet laugh. "I came back to your ship the next morning. I'd decided I could look while aboard," she whispered. "But we're here, now. The stuff in between doesn't matter anymore."

Her words must have triggered something within him, because Conrad closed the space between their mouths in an eager kiss. His lips moved against hers as his fingers found their way back into the tangles of her hair.

Ahria breathed in through her nose, her eyes sliding shut as the world spun. Her veins scorched as an inferno, smothered by time and distance, awoke.

As Conrad renewed the kiss, a knock echoed from the adjoining room before loud hinges creaked with a door's swing.

Despite another wall and door standing between them and the arrival of another, Ahria drew away and smiled. "Can I still call you captain? Or must I call you prince now?" Her stomach turned over again at the word. The title.

And everything that came with it.

How can he be a prince?

"Oh, please don't call me that." Conrad hovered close, as if another kiss still lingered on his lips. But a subtle knock at the bedroom door pulled him away from her, and he tucked his hands into his pockets. "Come in, she just woke up."

A pause. Then the door eased open.

Ahria's knees wobbled when she saw Talon's face. His bright emerald eyes shone, and she tried and failed to contain a quiet sob. "Dad."

The auer strode across the space, his expression far softer than the one he generally kept in public settings, and swept her into a hard embrace. His firm grip brought an instant sense of safety that settled deep in her bones.

Clutching her father, Ahria gritted her teeth to keep her tears at bay, but they found their way out, anyway. "I'm sorry I didn't stay put," she blurted, voice raw. "Lorin died, and you weren't back. And I didn't hear from you, and I just, I just—"

"Shhh." Talon stroked a hand through her hair, tightening his hug. "You don't have to explain, Ree. I'm sorry *I* wasn't there. For you and for Lorin..." His voice softened as he loosened his hold, stepping back to put a hand on her shoulder and stroke the side of her head. "Are you all right?"

Comfort washed over her. A contentment she hadn't known in months creeping into her muscles and easing their tension. She wiped tears from her cheeks, laughing through her sobs. "I'm really hungry."

"I'll have some food sent up." Conrad's footsteps sounded gently on the wooden floor as he moved towards the bedroom door. "And give you two some time."

He and Talon exchanged a look, and Ahria wished she could read more of what was in it.

Talon gave a short nod. "Thank you."

"Thanks." Ahria yearned to remain close to Conrad, but emotions warred within her, and she let him go. When the door shut again, she looked at Talon and tears built on her lower lids. "I saw you at the midsummer festival. At the queen's address. I called, but I was so far away. The guards didn't listen when I said I was your daughter." She leaned against his chest again, listening to his heartbeat. "I've been so homesick."

"And we are far from home." Talon rubbed her back, like he had when she'd woken from nightmares as a child. "I'm sorry my messages never made it to you. I should have tried to check in more. I thought you'd be safe in Gallisville. With your uncle."

"Uncle Deylan wasn't there, either," she murmured, closing her eyes. "It doesn't matter. None of it matters, now. I have you. And I have Conrad and my friends. I don't need anything else."

Talon's grip shifted as he pulled back from her, briefly pinching her chin before he moved towards the bedside table where her empty water glass sat. He tipped the pitcher to refill it, then offered the full cup back to her. "You made friends here in the city?"

Ahria took the water and sipped. "I did. I've been living

with a troupe for the last few months." She paused. "They're probably wondering where I am. I should go see them as soon as possible. I've probably missed a few performances." She shook her head. "They've been kind to me."

"Performances?" Talon's gaze turned serious, and she could already sense his wariness at the idea..

She shrugged. "I've been singing."

He frowned. "While I know full well you deserve to be compensated for sharing your voice, we've discussed the risks of bringing attention to yourself. You shouldn't be drawing extra eyes, Ree."

Ahria lifted her chin. "I was trying to draw *your* eyes, Dad. It may not have worked, but it kept me paid and safe over the last few months. And no one cares about a tavern singer, anyway."

"Still, you should be cautious. This world is far more dangerous than I could ever possibly prepare you for." Talon touched her hair briefly. "I worry."

"I've learned some things since I left home." Ahria straightened.

He lifted his brow. "Oh?"

"I stowed away on two ships. Stole a hat. Tried Xaxos fire wine... I usually have more blades on me, but maybe you can get those back for me. I've been all right, Dad. I've made a couple questionable choices, but at least I'm learning from them."

"Like the choice that got you arrested and brought before the head judiciary of the country?" He crossed his arms in his usual disapproving look.

"You mean brought before Conrad, which finally led me back to you? How can I regret that?" Ahria crossed her arms, tilting her head as she mimicked him.

"You were lucky." Talon shook his head and relaxed his arms. "And none of that changes that you still need to be careful. You carry too great a secret to allow the wrong people too close."

Ahria let out a breath. "I know. Unfathomable power runs in my veins, should I ever inherit it, and it is important that the wrong people don't find me." She rattled off the sentence like she had a hundred times. "I know. But I have to live, too. I have to do things I want to do. And I want to be here, and I want to sing."

"I'm not telling you not to live. But I am telling you that you have to consider all the ramifications of the decisions you make." Talon sighed, brushing a hand back through his thick raven hair. "I... can tell you care for Conrad, but Ahria..."

"Dad," she warned. "That's not something you need to worry about."

"It's not?"

"No."

"So you don't intend to carry on a relationship with him?"

Ahria quieted, chewing her lower lip.

Talon sighed again as he stepped into her, lifting her hands in between his. "My daughter, you are the Scion of the Berylian Key. Conrad is the crown prince of Ziona. Consider, for a moment, if you and he were to remain together. And consider what that would mean if something did happen to your mother and you inherited that power I have tried to prepare you for."

She swallowed the lump in her throat. "So you'd have me brush him off because of his title? Have me live without him over some circumstance that may or may not ever come to pass? That's not fair."

Talon hesitated, rubbing his thumb over hers. "Those with power like that which runs in your blood hold great responsibility. You'll be putting yourself, and Conrad, in a very tenuous situation. In a public position, you're opening yourself unnecessarily for *him* to find you."

"*He* can't find me if he doesn't know who to look for, or that there's even someone to find. If I just explain to Con—"

"No." Talon's tone took a hard edge. "The less who know, the better. Your mother fought to keep the secret of the Berylian Key from as many as possible, and you must do the same."

"Which is why you know, right? Because she kept it a secret?" Ahria's face heated. "And from my birth father, too, I assume."

Talon huffed. "That's different. Circumstances—"

"Why?" She threw her hands up in the air and then let them drop. "Why is it different? She loved you. She told you."

"You've hardly known Conrad a month in total, and you're willing to—"

"And how long did you know her?"

He stiffened, and shook his head. "I did not come here to argue with you, Ahria."

Ahria softened her voice. "How long, Dad?"

He shook his head more vigorously. "Not long enough. But it's a good thing she let me in, so I would be prepared to raise you. To write down all the knowledge I gained through training her." He glanced around the room, suddenly, as if searching for something. "Where are your belongings?"

Ahria waved him off. "At the townhouse with my friends. I'll fetch them later today."

He scowled. "Even the Art shrouding a loq'nali phén isn't unbreakable. You shouldn't let that journal out of your sight."

"No one I live with has enough Art to break that enchantment. It's safe. And I didn't have much of a choice when I got arrested, now did I?" Ahria's shoulders slumped with the familiar weight of not meeting Talon's expectations. "I'm doing my best, you know. But apparently I'm not allowed to fall in love, not allowed to have a life, and gods forbid I make my own choices."

"Is that what this is with Conrad, then? Love?"

Ahria swallowed. "We haven't said those words to each other."

"But you *loved* Davros, didn't you? But you never once suggested telling him the truth about your lineage."

Her lips twitched in a sheepish smile as she lowered her gaze. "Davros was kind. Easy to be with. I thought I loved him, but then I met Conrad, and..." She looked up, eyes hot. "I didn't know what it was supposed to feel like, but he just... he sets my soul on fire and I want to be near him. All the time." She sighed, bowing her head again. "I was going to stay on his ship. Give up everything else to be with him. And now that I'm here and he's here..."

The thought of leaving him now tore a hole in her chest, and she turned away. Breathing harder, she tried to stifle the tears burning her eyes.

Silence filled the room as Talon stood perfectly still before the subtle rustle of his tunic gave away his approach.

"How am I supposed to leave him?" she whispered. "Now that I finally found him again?"

Her father's hand closed on her shoulder, encouraging her to turn before pulling her into a firm embrace. "I'm sorry." He held her gently. "I know what I suggest is unfair, and ultimately, Ahria, the choice will be up to you. I cannot tell you who you are allowed to love. I only ask that you consider all the possible ramifications. Especially with Conrad's position here in Ziona."

Ahria let out a breath and rested her head on his chest. "I'll think about it for a while before I say anything, all right? And take it slow. You're right. It hasn't been that long, and maybe he feels differently than I do." Even just saying the words aloud made her chest ache. "I don't want you to be disappointed in me. You're all I have left."

Talon squeezed her before pulling back and placing a hand beneath her chin. "I could never be disappointed in you." He pinched her chin lightly and smiled. "You'll always be my daughter, and I will always love you."

A smile tugged at her lips. "I love you too, Dad. But I suppose I shouldn't need to say it after traveling halfway across Pantracia to find you." Lifting to her toes, she kissed his cheek. "Did I mention how glad I am to see you're safe, too?"

"Not yet, but I suppose it was implied." Talon kissed the top of her head. "I missed you, Ree."

Chapter 24

AFTER LEAVING AHRIA AND TALON, Conrad wandered the halls of the palace. Despite the several months he'd already been there, he found new rooms and areas that he hadn't visited before. Though it attracted the interested glances of some of the staff when he accidentally walked into the kitchens.

If I live here, I should know where everything is.

The mental mapping of the palace proved a worthy distraction for the first hour away from his chambers and Ahria, but then all he could think about was her. How desperate and helpless she had looked on her knees in the judiciary hall. It'd been entirely unfitting for the independent, enthusiastic woman he'd come to know. It'd broken a piece of him to see her like that, and he'd struggled to put it back together while watching over her.

Kissing her hadn't been part of his plan for when she woke, but the inclination had come on too strong for him to deny it. Something about her touch and skin was addictive, and he'd desperately missed it after being apart. She filled a hole he hadn't realized was there at all, and he craved more.

Ahria would need time with her father, but staying away took constant concentration as his feet often started back towards his chambers without his intention. With all that had happened, Talon deserved the reunion as well. The more he walked, the tighter Conrad's entire body felt and the more claustrophobic the stone and wood of the palace became. He craved the sky and the wind. The scent of salt water and the cry of gulls. And maybe a furry companion to distract him.

Walking past his chambers, Conrad forced himself to continue towards the short extravagant stairs at the end leading to his mother's rooms. He nodded a greeting to the guards at the door, who shifted subtly to salute before resuming their rigid stance.

Knocking lightly, he was greeted by Andi's enthusiastic yips before Talia called from within, muted by the thick oak door, but he took it to be a welcome.

Andi wriggled through the door before he could fully open it, her tail beating against the wood as she pressed into his legs and licked at his fingers.

"Whoa, girl." Conrad forced the door open the rest of the way, dodging the animal as he walked into the grand front room.

"She's been pretty insistent about how much she misses you." Talia sat straighter where she'd wedged herself into a corner of a couch. A pile of books sat on the low table in front of her, along with untidy stacks of parchment. "Been hard to get work done with her constantly whining for attention."

"You love it," Conrad scratched behind Andi's ear, and she plopped happily into a sit and leaned against him. "Thank you for taking care of her."

"Of course. How's Ahria? She must be awake if you're here."

"She is. Talon is with her right now. I felt it appropriate to give them some time." Conrad avoided his mother's curious glance as she set a book on top of a pile.

Talia smoothed the edges of her long tunic and stood. "I'm sure Talon is relieved to see her recovering, as are the guards he gave a stern reprimand to in the city prison. He was rather livid about it being misinterpreted that she had the Art."

"Oh, they're going to get an ear full from me, too," he grumbled. He hadn't had a chance to impart his displeasure on those who'd failed to listen to her pleas, instead torturing her with no sleep or food to keep her 'Art' at bay. He'd hardly left her side, taking meals in his chambers and postponing all judiciary hearings. Now, away from her for the first time in a day and a half, he could only guess what rumors were flying around the palace. Especially with the added excitement of the mysterious flux of power that'd washed over the world.

Conrad hadn't felt when it'd happened, though the palace had instantly become abuzz with panic. He couldn't walk two feet without an armored escort amid the fear it was a cataclysmic attack like that which had befallen Isalica's capital nearly fifteen years ago. The stories and rumors of attacks by great shadow beasts and Corrupted left the entire world on edge.

Nothing like it had occurred since, allowing most of the population to fall into blissful ignorance regarding an unknown force strong enough to level a city. But when every Art user in Pantracia had felt a pressure against their senses in the same instant, security at the palace had tripled, and the streets were still far too empty for Zionan summer.

And there was still no explanation.

"Everyone has enough on their plates right now, Connie. The important thing is that Ahria is safe and reunited with her father. And with *you*." Talia crossed to him, placing a warm hand on his bicep. "Though you still haven't elaborated on what, exactly, that means."

Conrad shook his head. "I'll tell you when I figure it out." He lifted his chin towards the stacks of papers and books.

"Has parliament decided what to tell the people about that anomaly yet?"

She sighed. "They're stalling for time. No one understands it. But reports have confirmed it was felt from End in the north all the way to Derryton in the south. Not an inch of Pantracia was excluded. Not even Lungaz."

He patted her hand. "I just hope they choose to be honest and don't play politics pretending they know."

Talia gave him a shallow smile. "I won't let them hide the truth." She stood on her tiptoes and placed a kiss on his cheek before returning to her couch. "Will I see you for breakfast?"

Conrad rubbed a hand over his short hair. "Probably not breakfast, but I'll see what I can do about dinner."

"Good enough for me." Talia sat down as Conrad started for the door, Andi rushing ahead of him.

His dog ran through the palace halls, stopping at every corner to verify he was following before charging ahead. The guards stationed at the major archways throughout didn't even look twice at her anymore. She barreled past the familiar doorway he remembered from his initial journey and something tugged him that direction.

Andi yipped from further down the hall as she saw him turn, racing after him and down the long stairwell that led to the chasms beneath the palace. His boots clicked on the marble floors, echoing against the natural stone ceiling of the entry chamber to the palace dock. A warm summer breeze came through the open archway ahead, flanked by the massive statues of Zionan soldiers, a living pair at their feet.

Both guards turned at the sound of his approach and rushed into a surprised salute before he could wave them off.

"Your highness, there are no scheduled departures of ships today."

"I know, I just came to get some fresh air and give myself the illusion of being at sea." He looked to the three-masted ship tied to the end of the dock, her sails secured, and Andi waited beside him. "Am I allowed to board? I promise I have no intention of stealing her."

The guards exchanged a quick look, but then the first nodded. "Of course, your highness. She's technically yours, anyway."

Conrad looked back to the elegantly crafted galleon, considering the fine paint and carvings of her hull. She'd have given Dawn Chaser a run for her money, most certainly, and was in far better condition.

Hardly any work at all, and already have a new ship.

One of the many reasons he was so insistent on continuing his work in the judiciary hall. It was the only place he felt he could accomplish something that would make him even somewhat deserving of all the gifts royalty offered.

Conrad resisted comparing other aspects of the royal ship with Dawn Chaser as he walked past the repositioned guards. He climbed the decorative gangplank, eager to step onto the deck and feel the gentle movement of the river below.

His dog's nails tapped over the wood as she trotted to the stairs that led to the helm.

The wind rushed through the canyon, bringing with it the warm scent of creosote. He looked farther up the Astarian River, admiring the weathered stone walls. Here, he could hear the commotion of the city somewhere up above the lip of the canyon, and the distant rumble of a waterfall further north, hidden behind the terrain.

The boat swayed gently beneath him, ebbing with the current of the river while forced to remain in place by the ropes securing it to the dock.

Conrad followed his dog to the helm, where he caressed the smooth handles of the wheel. Closing his eyes, he imagined the wind through the canyon as the familiar sea breeze that still filled Dawn Chaser's sails.

But that isn't my life anymore.

Opening his eyes, Conrad focused on the golden crest mounted at the center of the helm, the thistle bloom that represented his family line. The royal line of Ziona for the last five hundred years, save for the military coup. And if parliament got its way, the royal line for the next five hundred, but only under their careful guidance.

His stomach soured at the pressure he'd already been saddled with. As his mother's only child. She'd already begun the process of revising law so he would inherit the crown rather than cousins he didn't know. As much as he didn't want the crown, it would be vital for such a law to maintain equality between genders in the country. He was sure his grandmother was rolling over in her grave.

Movement near the guards drew his gaze.

Ahria stood before them, holding a pack over her shoulder and dressed in different clothing. She seemed to be arguing, albeit politely, with them and gesturing to the ship.

Sitting beside him, Andi perked her ears and whined. Cocking her head to one side, she looked in the direction of the gangplank, and Conrad smiled as he scratched the back of her golden head.

"Go get her, girl." He nudged the back of her head, but Andi hardly needed the encouragement. She bounded down the stairs in a single leap, running across the deck at an all-out sprint.

The guards turned in surprise, one nearly drawing their sword before they realized the thunder down the gangplank was aimed at Ahria. Andi barreled into her, throwing her weight against Ahria's legs and spinning in happy circles as she yipped.

"Andi!" Ahria's voice finally grew loud enough to carry over the air. She faced the guards, speaking quietly again.

One looked in his direction, and he nodded from where he leaned against the stairway banister.

Finally standing down, they allowed her to pass.

Her gaze found his as she approached the ship, pausing at the gangplank with the dog. "Permission to board, Captain?" She smiled, but something else lingered in her eyes.

"Granted. Though I'm a little worried that you're not even *trying* to stowaway this time." He wanted nothing but to step towards her and wrap his arms around her. But he tucked his hands in his pockets, maintaining what he hoped looked like a nonchalant lean.

Ahria strode onto the deck, idly petting Andi. She looked like the woman he'd met before, not the prisoner thrown at his feet. Her clean leather breeches fit her well, ending at her knees to compensate for the heat. Her tunic rippled around her collar, held in place by a fitted violet vest. "Hardly able to stowaway. Your guards didn't even want me to board properly." She rolled her lips together. "I figured I might find you here."

"Am I that predictable?" He looked down to the deck where the guards had resumed their station, their backs to the ship. Not quite complete privacy, but at least they were trying to mind their own business.

"Perhaps." Ahria climbed the stairs to the helm, sunlight catching in her icy blue eyes. "You must miss it terribly."

"Some days more than others." He ran his hand over the polished wood he leaned against, finding none of the small nicks and flaws that coated Dawn Chaser. The scars of all she'd endured with him. But this ship held none of those memories, and he frowned. "Mostly miss the simplicity of it. Make enough to keep the ship floating and pay the crew so they don't mutiny. This prince business, while perhaps somewhat applicable metaphorically, is a bit more complicated."

Ahria nodded, crossing her arms and leaning on the banister across from him as she set her pack down. "I feel like my showing up only added to those complications."

"Not as much as you might think. Makes it a little harder to want to go about my duties... but you could never be a burden." He studied her face, checking for any remnants of the scrapes and bruises the healers had seen to while she slept. He found his gaze wandering down her, as he had when they first met, admiring every inch before he could school himself to stop. "I imagine it feels good to stretch your legs. You look..." He had so many different words he could have chosen from, but each sounded cliche in his mind. "Good."

One of her eyebrows quirked up. "Thank you?" She smirked. "I just got back here from the townhouse. My father doesn't want me staying there, anymore, so I suppose he'll find me a room here." She paused. "If that's all right with you and your mother, of course."

"Of course you're welcome to stay here." Conrad cursed himself silently for not having considered arranging accommodations for her yet. Though, he'd been rather distracted not leaving his chambers. "I can ask Mister Credish to ready a room for you right now, if you'd like." He stood, but hesitated as Ahria lifted her hand.

"There's no rush." She motioned to her bag and sunlight glinted off the hilt hidden in her bracer. "It's not like I have much unpacking to do."

I'm surprised she got past any of the guards with that.

But Conrad knew she likely had several more stashed in various places on her person too, and it made him smile. "I suppose not. But I hope I can assist with remedying that as well."

"You want to help me unpack?" She smiled again, and this time, it reached her eyes.

"Not exactly what I meant, but I'm not opposed." Conrad kept talking before he could analyze the words. Ahria just spurred it out of him. "I meant more in getting you more things to *have to pack.* Perhaps it will encourage you to stay in one place for a while. Or have you become accustomed to adventure?"

"I know I've only just arrived at the palace..." She made a face. "But, I've been in *one place* for months now. And while it may seem I have a desire for adventure, I think I'd prefer to just stay put, things or no things to pack."

The thought made his heart thud as he suddenly imagined her staying nearby. He pursed his lips at the implication of the rest, however, and took a step closer. "I'm sorry that I didn't look harder. I should have found you since you were so close for so long."

Ahria shook her head. "It hardly matters anymore. I wasn't under duress or living in horrid conditions. I made friends. I found my way. As much as I am grateful for finally finding you and my father, I'm still grateful for the time in between." She reached between them, offering her hand for his.

Conrad didn't allow himself to second guess, slipping his hand into hers. Their fingers entwined comfortably as he leaned on the banister beside her. "I'm glad, then. That the time between still brought you happiness. Or at least as much as possible considering your predicament of a missing father and absconded sea captain." He looked briefly at their hands. "Where did you live the last few months?"

"In the residential district on Cape Street. We have a townhouse there. Or, they do, I suppose. Vaeler broke me out of the palace dungeon the first time I was arrested and took me under his wing, so to speak. They let me join their troupe. Mysterium." Ahria smiled, biting her lip.

"There's a few different elements of that statement I have questions about." He smirked, his control slipping the longer he spent with her. "Arrested? The first time?"

Ahria chuckled under her breath. "I tried to break into the palace the first day I arrived in New Kingston. The guards wouldn't even let me into the courtyard, so I scaled a wall, but I didn't even make it to the building proper before someone knocked me out. I thought you might have been here because of what Leiura had told me. Vaeler came to rescue his friend shortly after, and I convinced him to let me out, too."

He flexed his hand in hers, needing the reminder they still touched with how comfortable the position had grown. "Sounds like you were fortunate to convince this Vaeler. I didn't imagine you as the type to join a troupe, or were you wowing the crowds with dagger play?" He teasingly pushed their hands against the hidden blade she kept at her hip.

Rolling her lips together, she smirked at his prod. "They already had a dagger thrower. So I sang for them. Taverns, mostly, but I had this crazy notion that if I wrote music, you or Dad might hear it. So I sang about Dawn Chaser and Olsa and the araleinya flower. Anything only one of you might recognize."

The memory of one of his early searches for her made Conrad's eyes widen. His dispute with his escort about wanting to investigate a tavern where he heard singing and the name Dawn Chaser on the night air. His stomach flipped as he realized if he'd pushed a little harder to go into that tavern, he might have found her sooner. Might have stopped all the neglect performed during her second arrest.

"I heard you," he whispered. "A month or so ago in the gambling district. My guard wouldn't allow me to investigate.

I didn't know that was you."

A relaxed look of content washed over her face. "It *was* me. Somehow, I'm glad you heard it, even if you couldn't come inside. I have a few more shows I need to perform while Evelyn looks for a replacement for me. You should come to one." She bumped him with her shoulder. "You know, if you're allowed."

He bumped her back. "I'll make it happen. What good is being a prince if I can't make some demands from time to time?" He cupped her cheek, tracing her jawline. "I can't wait. You just tell me the day and I'll be there. Even if I have to drag a whole battalion with me."

Ahria grinned. "I'd love that."

He ran the pad of his thumb down her neck as he looked at the familiar necklace resting at her throat. He reached to touch it, using the excuse to caress the curve of her collarbone. "Talon uses the image of this flower to seal all of his correspondence, but any time I ask him about it, he avoids the topic." Conrad looked up, meeting her eyes. "This was your mother's, wasn't it?" A number of different possibilities had begun running through his mind after Conrad discovered Talon was Ahria's father. They clearly weren't blood related, but Conrad hadn't dared ask the auer for details. But the flower... "And your father, Talon, he loved your mother."

Ahria offered him a soft smile. "It is the araleinya flower, a rare bloom in Eralas. My father nicknamed my mother for it, when they were in love. Though, I know he still loves her, even if she..." She huffed, shrugging. "He uses it to honor her, I think. Sometimes I worry I must remind him of her constantly."

"And would that be so bad if it were true?"

"Well, reminders of something long lost can be bittersweet, can't they?"

"Perhaps, but they can also be the basis for all that we do. And a reminder of fond memories.

Ahria paused before nodding. "I suppose you're probably right. My mother's last request was for Talon to find me. To be a part of my life. I'm sure you realize we have no blood relation, but he's been my dad for as long as I can remember."

Conrad nodded. "I guessed as much." He touched her chin. "Does that mean Lorin was your birth father?"

To his surprise, she shook her head again. "No. My mother gave me to Lorin and his wife before she left the town I was born in. Talon found us months later, after Lorin's wife had passed, and he ended up raising me with my adoptive father and brother."

"How old were you when she left?" He felt terrible asking the questions and didn't fully know why. It felt invasive, yet with how close they stood, the intimacy urged him to learn all he could.

Ahria ran her thumb over his skin, looking up at him. "A

baby. I have no memory of her."

He brought her hand to his chest, turning into her more. "I'm sorry."

"Don't be." She smiled. "I've led a nice life, with a loving family. My mother did what she needed to do, and although I used to hold onto a lot of anger about it, now I understand a bit better why she had to."

Lifting her hand, he kissed the back of it as he looked at her. "You're remarkable. To not let the anger drag you down."

Her eyes flickered to the guards, stationed too far away to hear them, before returning to him. "Conrad, there's something about me that I wish I could explain. I wish I could tell you the reason my mother left, and the reason Talon refused to put my face on posters."

Meeting her eyes, he watched them for a moment as her pupils flicked between which of his they focused on. "Do you think it was a good reason?"

Ahria nodded. "It was. And it still is."

"Then that's good enough for me." His fingers brushed over her cheek, encouraging her face towards his. "You don't need to explain anything. I'm just grateful that we have this second chance."

She tilted her head, letting the tip of her nose graze his. "As am I. But... but what do you see coming of this second chance? You're... a prince, and I..."

His stomach twisted. He'd thought about it, of course, but the realities felt more tangible when she spoke them. His loathing of the title only deepened. It was too much pressure, inflicted with a single word, and Ahria deserved better.

He squeezed her hand tighter against his chest. "I see this." His other hand followed a lock of her hair down, twirling the strands between his fingers. "I'd think by now you'd know I don't have much care for political games or rules. My title doesn't matter."

"But it does, Captain," she whispered. "Because if your face is known by a country... how can mine remain anonymous?"

His heart dropped into his flipped stomach as he realized what she was saying. His grip tightened again, but he shifted back from her ever so slightly. The space he added somehow felt more empty than the rest of the air. "So this is not a temporary need to remain unknown."

Her throat bobbed. "It's not."

Conrad swallowed. "And my need to remain in the public eye is not, either."

Ahria's gaze drifted down his face to where he held her hand. "If the depth of your attachment is shallow, then I might suggest it best we don't take things any further. But... if it's otherwise..." Her eyes shone, growing glassy as she refused to meet his gaze.

The instinct to insist his attraction ran deeper than the crevices at the bottom of the Dul'Idur roared to his lips, but Conrad bit the edge of his tongue. He'd made plenty of mistakes in his life by not giving himself the time to consider all implications, and their lives were not a trivial matter. Yet, everything in him screamed at the hesitation. At the questioning of what he already knew beyond doubt.

He reached beneath her chin, urging her gaze up to meet his. He studied the smooth well of a tear on the lower lid of her right eye, wanting to wash it away. "I care for you, Ahria." His voice remained low, as he fought his brain's war with his heart. "I more than care for you. And I don't want this to be the end." Letting go of her hand, he cupped both of her cheeks. "We'll find a way to make this work for both of us. But I cannot deny my desire to take this leap with you into the deepest ocean, as long as you are willing to jump with me."

Gliding closer to him, she pressed her body to his. "I will always jump with you," she murmured. "But for now, no one else should know. Until we figure it out."

He couldn't help a little smile, wrapping his arm around her waist. His eyes flickered to the guards, ensuring both still had their backs to them with her suggestion. "Like back on the ship, then." He brushed a strand of her dark hair behind her ear. "I'm remarkably good at secrets. And arguably, that task is even easier in a giant palace with lots of various rooms to sneak off to."

She suggested they needed to figure things out, but Conrad was convinced he already knew the outcome. In the months apart, his mind had constantly wandered to her, only furthering his absolute craving for her.

The hardest part about the secret is going to be not touching her every moment.

Conrad brushed the tear from her cheek with his thumb. "No one needs to know. I assume this includes our parents?"

Ahria smiled. "After my last conversation with my father, I doubt he'd believe me if I told him we were no longer involved. If you trust your mother to keep it to herself, I don't see the harm in being honest with her."

"She suspects already, anyway." He shrugged, but then guided her hips close to his. The feel of her body against his own set every inch of him alight. "If she asks, I won't lie. But now I'm awfully curious about this conversation with your father."

Her smile broadened, a mischievous expression overtaking her face. "I'm sure you are."

"More secrets?"

Laughing, Ahria slid her hand up his neck and around the base of his hairline. "I think I used words like... soul, and... fire."

The very words she spoke seemed to ignite the things inside him. "I see." He leaned closer to her until he felt her breath on his lips. "Then you won't mind if I kiss you while the guards still aren't paying attention?"

Tightening her grip on him, Ahria lifted her chin and caught his mouth with hers, her eyes sliding closed.

He eagerly responded, tilting his head to grant better access to her lips. Their tongues met, and the entire canyon around them blurred into nothing but a hazy mix of tan and grey. His body screamed for more as the kiss deepened, and something within him finally broke free. His shoulders loosened as he pulled her against him, wishing desperately they weren't so exposed. He doubted he'd have noticed if a full size dragon thundered through the canyon.

But this needs to be a secret.

The overwhelming desire to protect Ahria's secret overtook his senses, and he broke the kiss, pulling back as he sucked in a steadying breath.

"Should we go somewhere more private?" Desire scorched through his body, and he wanted nothing more than to feel her skin against his.

Ahria hovered close, undeterred by the guards' presence in the distance. "I'd like that." Her eyes finally left his mouth to meet his. "But I'd also like to take this slow. Not that you should question my desire, but perhaps, just my level of experience." Color touched her cheeks, and she rolled her lips together.

He blinked before he could control the automatic response. Not only at her confession, but her willingness to speak it aloud. To him. It made the heat in him double, a new excitement rising to the surface. "And here I was, worried about admitting the same thing." He couldn't believe at first that he was telling the truth of it. He'd never have allowed his crew to know, but with becoming a young captain, Conrad had never felt ready to let his guard down, regardless of his body's desires. And there was never the right companion. Until now.

Her eyes widened, but her smile did, too. "You've never...?"

He shook his head before he leaned in and gently kissed her lower lip. "Almost, a few times, but no."

"Me, neither." Ahria kissed him slower, and didn't draw away after.

"Then only when we're both ready." He pressed his forehead to hers. A pressure he hadn't realized had begun to build, faded abruptly. The undercurrent of control he always fought to maintain snapped the final bonds of tension in him. And suddenly, he knew he didn't want to wait anymore. He yearned to lay himself completely bare to Ahria.

The need pressed into another kiss as he claimed her mouth, desperate to taste more of her. To somehow tell her that he would be ready as soon as she was. That he wished it to be her.

Ahria kissed him back, drowning his thoughts deep beneath the ship somewhere at the bottom of the Astarian River.

Chapter 25

KIN'S BOOTS SANK INTO THE sand as he stepped from the surf, watching the boat drift back into the strait. Salt water soaked the bottom of his cloak, weighing down his shoulders and gathering up more sand.

Amarie stood behind him, silent as the boat surged faster into the ocean water, propelled by some unseen force.

He turned, striding up the bank to her. "At least they won't know where we went."

The woman nodded, moonlight shimmering on her skin in the dead of night. "I'm exhausted," she murmured.

They'd taken shifts rowing across the open water over the past eight hours. Night had descended some time ago, leaving them to navigate in the dark. But the sun's warmth failed to fade through the night, making the season they'd awoken to more evident.

His companion rubbed her palms but didn't complain about the angry red blisters marring her skin. He certainly had matching ones.

He nodded in agreement, stifling the yawn that began with the suggestion. "We should find an inn. I have enough coin in my cloak pockets for at least one room." As inconvenient as the cloak now felt, weighed down with water, he'd searched it thoroughly while on the boat and discovered a multitude of hidden pockets.

Amarie shook her head. "We don't need to spend it for half a night's sleep in a bed. I'm sure we can find a spot to rest in the wild. Can't be worse than a stone bed, right?"

While a real bed sounded far more promising, he nodded again. "Fair enough." He felt the inclination to reach for her without knowing where it came from.

Her azure gaze met his. "What is it?"

His heart pounded, but he shook his head. "Trying to make sense out of instincts." He rubbed at his jaw, fingers prickling on his scruff. "They feel like the only clue to who I was before."

Amarie's brow twitched, and she ran a hand through her hair. "And what are they telling you?"

"That I know you and care about you."

Her shoulders relaxed, her expression softening. "Better

than you wanting to strangle me."

He frowned. "I hope that wasn't what my face just suggested."

She laughed, biting her lower lip briefly. "It's not. You just looked so intent."

The fire within him surged, encouraged by the tiredness. He reached for her, slipping his hand into hers. His fingertips brushed gingerly over the sores on her palm before he laced them with hers. "I know that this..." He lifted their hands between them. "Feels right."

Looking at their hands, Amarie rolled her lips together. "But would we know if it didn't?" She sagged, her grip on his hand tightening as she swayed. "Let's go find some grass, otherwise I might just curl up and sleep on these rocks."

"That hardly sounds comfortable." Kin wrapped his heavy cloak up around his free arm as he walked towards the grove of trees nestled against a stone city wall. What city they'd landed beside, he didn't know, but they needed to avoid the docks with a stolen boat. Despite the desire for an inn, entering a gated Helgathian city late at night without supplies or goods would raise suspicions.

Best to sleep in the woods like she suggested and enter the city in the morning.

He looked to where he still held Amarie's hand as they traversed into the darkened trees together.

Kin argued against the knot in his stomach as he passed the obsidian dagger to the starry-eyed merchant who'd been the only one to show any interest. Fortunately, it seemed to be enough interest to earn three silver florins for it.

Hopefully that's what it's worth, and I'm not being ripped off.

He and Amarie had separated that morning, going on their own quests to sell whatever valuables they had on them. The first thing he did away with was the unwieldy cloak, which proved far too thick for the heat that rose with the day. A clothier accepted it in trade for a satchel he could sling over his shoulder. It had plenty of room for all the odd supplies he'd found in the cloak and made far more sense. He had another fruitful trade of the long-sleeved black tunic for a pair of leather vests and undershirts.

The dagger was the last to exchange, and oddly the one thing Kin struggled to part with, despite not knowing its purpose or origin. Something about it told him he'd had it for a very particular reason.

But it won't do me any good if I can't remember it.

Kin nodded his thanks to the merchant, tucking the coins deep into his new satchel. The man's spectacled eyes remained on the blade as he waved a dismissive farewell before striding into the back room of his shop.

Kin had known this would be the perfect buyer for the dagger the moment he walked through the door. The glass displays throughout the shop housed a variety of trinkets. Some of which looked too simple to match the price listed beside it. He couldn't fathom who would spend so much on something that looked like nothing more than a shard of crystal. And the merchant's blatant showcase practically begged a thief to try their luck.

Returning to the open air, where summer already heated the cobblestone beneath his feet, Kin oriented himself north. He and Amarie planned to meet at the north side of town where the stable was, intent on traveling inland after purchasing mounts.

Almost halfway there, he tensed at fast footsteps behind him.

Amarie's chuckle reached his ears right before she slapped him in the back and stopped next to him.

"You seem cheerful." Kin couldn't help the smile she brought to his face.

"I am. We did well, I think." She wiggled her eyebrows.

He scanned over her, seeing nothing different other than a missing cloak. "What did you sell?"

"A few things. I started with my dagger."

Kin looked at the Aueric dagger still strapped to her thigh. "That one?"

Amarie patted it. "That's the one."

"Does the merchant know that you still have it on you?" Kin crossed his arms, trying to hide his amusement with a feigned look of disapproval.

A mischievous grin spread over her lips. "Probably not." She pulled a dark object from the back of her belt and presented him with the obsidian dagger he'd only just sold. "Want it back? Or should I try selling it to him again?"

Kin's eyes widened, and he shook his head as he reached for it. "How did you get it back? I couldn't see any security, but that shop had to have something." He pushed the dagger carefully into his satchel, hoping it wouldn't tear any holes in his new vest.

"Oh, I got most of your stuff back." Amarie pulled other objects from a new pack slung over her shoulder, offering him a few precious gems, a gold ring, and a vial of coarse salt. All items he never thought he'd see again. "Though I didn't catch up to you until after you sold your cloak and tunic."

"You've been following me?" Kin held out his hand, and she dumped the items into his palm.

"Only a little." Amarie beamed.

"I'm unsure whether to feel flattered or afraid." He looked down the sidewalk as he quickly put away the stolen goods. "You sure no one saw you? We can't really afford more trouble right now."

She shook her head. "No one saw me. Did you get enough coin for a horse? Can't steal those as easily. I got three and a half florins and some iron."

Kin lifted his brow. "Someone gave you that much for that dagger?"

Amarie shrugged. "Well, no. I got a half florin for my cloak, and one florin for the dagger. I just sold it to three merchants."

He snorted a laugh, and shook his head. "You sure are something, Amarie." He brushed his thumb against the underside of her jaw. "But we should probably go get horses before one of those three merchants notices they're short an Aueric dagger.

"Probably a good idea." She bit her lower lip, making his blood rush unexpectedly. "I want a black one."

"How about we go to a stable on the opposite side of the city from the market and see what they have before you start setting your heart on a particular horse?" Kin's hand comfortably slipped to her waist as he guided her to start walking again, moving them further from the streets where someone might recognize them.

She didn't protest, drifting a little closer to allow him to easily walk while still touching her. They hardly spoke, but it was a comfortable silence. He didn't feel the need to fill the void, content to merely revel in her presence and the pressure against his arm.

Once they'd found the stable and purchased two horses, they rode northwest. There hadn't been a black horse for

Amarie, but she settled on a dark bay gelding, while he rode a buckskin.

Riding at a walk, Kin struggled to figure out what to do with his hands and reins. "I don't think I've done this much before."

Looking the picture of perfection, Amarie laughed as she urged her horse into a trot, circling Kin. "Maybe we should have stuck with one horse?" She made a thoughtful expression. "Do you think I'm a coffee or a tea person?"

As if it would somehow help, Kin squinted at her. "Tea, I think." He shifted, his legs already sore from the saddle, and fumbled the reins again. The horse lurched with a whinny. His heart jolted into his throat as he gripped the horn in panic, convinced he'd almost fallen.

Amarie guided her horse next to his, laying a hand on his forearm. "Whoa," she murmured, and the horses stopped. "Hold the reins like this." She showed him her hands, with the reins weaving beneath her pinky finger. "Toes up in the stirrups, and ride with your seat. Open your thighs to go faster and—"

"Slow down, what? All I got in that was thighs."

She sighed, infinite patience in her expression as she dismounted. Looping her horse's reins over her saddle, she left him to stand by Kin. She touched his boot, angling his heel down and pulling his foot out of the stirrup until only the ball of his foot remained on the metal. "Toes up." She guided him through the rest of a short lesson, showing him where to squeeze to go faster and how to guide the horse to a halt.

"That will have to do for now." She patted his knee and returned to her own horse. "We'll keep to a trot, at most, while you learn."

He tried to focus on the exact position of his feet, daring a lean to look at his toes. "How do you remember how to do this so well, while I'm just lucky to not be falling off?"

"You must not have been a rider." Amarie settled into her saddle, urging her horse forward again.

"Maybe I wasn't much of a traveler. Makes me wonder where home is."

She shrugged. "Maybe not. Maybe you lived a life of luxury. Or you were destitute... Or, or! Maybe you're a prince!"

"Destitute to prince in one sentence." Kin chuckled. "Though I doubt either one of those. My tunic was far too nice for someone with no money."

"I doubt it, too. All the princes I know are fabulous riders." Amarie grinned.

"Ouch. Just wait, I'll be a prince and you'll feel bad for the insult." Like the comfortable silence, the banter felt natural. And he greedily wanted more of it. "In all seriousness, though, where do we go from here? How do we find out who we are?"

Amarie quieted, looking ahead with a somber expression. "I don't know. I guess we have to hope that somehow, somewhere, the past will find us." She pulled her hair to the back of her head, looping a strap of leather around it to hold it in place.

What if I'm not sure I want it to find me?

As his forearm itched, something in Kin told him he might be better off not knowing.

They rode for the rest of the morning, with Amarie giving him brief lessons on trotting along the way. Short breaks only served in providing him time to appreciate the soreness of his muscles.

They neared the distant thick tree line as the afternoon progressed, and dark shapes appeared against the cottonwoods that lined a river. But there had been no village on the map Amarie had purchased in town, and as they grew closer, he realized the roughly hewn sheds housed mounds of stone rather than residents. Something that resembled a gallows felt ominous until Kin spied the large platform rising up from the depths of the earth.

He lifted his hand to shield his eyes from the sun, squinting at the operation as a pair of horses with harnesses struggled against the weight of the stone piled on the rising platform.

"Didn't think there'd be a mine this far from a town." Kin looked at Amarie, gesturing with his head in the direction he looked. "I suppose that explains those piles of gravel we kept passing." Old pits, filled once they'd yielded whatever precious resource Helgath was gathering.

Shouts echoed from the distant mine, accompanied by the whinny of the horses.

"Sounds like they're having a grand time," Amarie murmured, walking her mount next to his.

The deep grooves in the road, from continued cart travel, made more sense suddenly.

"As much fun as you can have while performing back-breaking labor, probably." Kin dared himself to relax in the saddle as they continued towards the curve of the road, leading them around the edge of the mine and towards the forest beyond. He wished Amarie would quit side-eyeing him like she expected him to fall off the horse at any second. "Ever seen a mine before?"

Amarie's eyes narrowed at the sight as they approached, and she shrugged. "I have no idea."

A shudder rippled through the air, vibrating the ground beneath them, and their horses balked. The air around the mine pit plumed with sudden debris rushing from the shaft. The pulley structure cracked, and it all happened a moment before the thunder reached them.

Kin's horse stomped, snorting before shaking its head and backing up.

Amarie leaned sideways, grabbing one of his reins. Kin

could only look at the mine as the rope secured to one side of the platform snapped. The platform tilted, its stone toppling back down into the pit below, taking splintered wood with it.

"Nymaera's breath."

Having stilled the antsy horse, Amarie followed his gaze while her own mount pawed the ground. "Shit. Did that just...?"

Another rumble shook through the ground beneath them, as the plume of dust from the collapsing shaft expanded, and the shouts of the miners at the top of the shaft grew frantic.

Kin's chest tightened, and every instinct in him went to war.

What do we do?

"I can help them." Amarie circled her spooked horse, patting its neck. "Dismount before that horse throws you off." Without waiting to see if he'd obey, she nudged her horse towards the mine at a pace Kin didn't dare try to keep up with.

"Dammit." Kin's horse balked again the moment Amarie loosed his reins, and he adjusted his weight as she had instructed. If he didn't at least try to make some of the distance on the horse, it'd take him far too long to get there on foot. "Dammit. Dammit. Dammit."

He squeezed his calves against the horse's flank, urging it forward. He forgot how to breathe as the horse sprang into something much faster than a trot. He clutched the reins and the saddle horn together, gritting his teeth as he fought to keep his ass in the saddle.

Another rumble through the ground set the horse turning away, but he yanked on the reins the way Amarie had shown him as an emergency stop, forcing the horse to pace in tight circles while he slid off the saddle on the outside. His boots slipped in the dirt as he tried to regain control over the animal, guiding it to a nearby post to loop the reins over. Tying a fast knot, he raced after Amarie.

She stood near the opening, exchanging heated words with a man while another plume of dust erupted from within the mine. "How many?"

The man growled and threw his hat. "Stop asking me! I don't know. Five or six, maybe."

Amarie glanced at Kin as he approached. "Several men are trapped inside. The shaft is collapsing. I can hold it up long enough for them to get out."

Kin panted, shaking his head. "You don't know your limits. It's a bad idea."

"I don't have a choice. I can't do nothing."

"I beg you would," the miner grumbled. "I don't need to add your name to the list of casualties. The ground is unstable. We all need to evacuate." Ignoring her attempt to reply, he hurried off, grabbing the reins of a disgruntled donkey still attached to a cart.

Amarie stared at Kin, her eyes bright and flickering with strange violet hues. "They're going to leave them down there. I can't do nothing."

Kin looked at the pit, where the cracked pulley system lay diagonally across the opening. He couldn't fathom how far it dropped, but he nodded to her anyway. "Then I'm here. Let's do something."

Her lips twitched in a faint smile before she spun, rushing towards the rope. "Don't let me die!" Running towards the gaping hole, she dropped to her hip to slide into the opening. She grabbed the rope mid air and plummeted out of sight.

For a breath, he could only gape.

The pulley squealed, thrust into motion with Amarie's rapid descent, and rope whipped through it from a haphazard pile where it'd been unclipped from the horses.

Kin rushed to the diminishing rope, picking up one of the massive clips. Before he could second guess the inclination, he looped it around his own waist, making sure to include his satchel at the small of his back. He didn't have time to question whether the logs supporting a nearby half-shattered post could take the strain, wrapping himself around it as quickly as he could. The rope doubled on itself, and he glanced up just as the rope went taut.

Letting out a yell, he braced a foot on the post and prayed Amarie wouldn't lose her grip on the rope with the sudden stop.

A few men lingered, unsure whether to follow their orders to evacuate.

Kin gritted his teeth as the rope burned his palms. "Get over here and help!"

They needed no further encouragement, dropping their packs. One ran to Kin, grabbing the rope, while two others returned to the mouth of the mine, supporting the partially ruined pulley.

"Lower her slowly," Kin ground out, easing the tension on the rope only a few inches at a time. After a few feet, the rope slackened.

He held his breath and gave the rope a single tug.

Don't be dead.

Kin waited, focusing on the rope for any movement.

And then Amarie tugged back.

Chapter 26

AMARIE HANDED THE END OF the rope to a miner after feeling a strong tug from Kin high above.

The man sputtered his thanks, wrapping the rope around his leg before giving it a couple jerks. Grime marred his face and exposed skin, making him resemble a wraith in the night. The cluster of miners huddled in the beam of light from the shaft above looked the same, watching as their companion lifted off the ground. But it wasn't their stained faces that made Amarie's heart race. Nor the crumbling mineshaft shaking the ground.

It was the walls.

The dirt floor and suffocatingly low ceiling in the tunnels.

The murky splotches of dampness through the dirt.

And most of all...

The shadows.

Her heart thundered in her chest, as loud as a stampede of horses. Her vision blurred as she momentarily forgot her purpose, wheezing in a breath through her panic.

I need to keep this shaft from collapsing.

Amarie breathed out her nerves, but nothing rid her of the fear deep in her belly. A sickening feeling that made her grateful not to remember the root cause. Sweat beaded on her brow and her hands shook, but she dove into her Art. She let it surround her, but kept the oceans of it at bay. The subconscious aura keeping her energy hidden faltered, but she let it wane in the hopes of focusing on more pressing matters.

With another shuddering rumble, debris fell from above, and she lifted her hands, angling her palms up. Mimicking how she'd felt when she threw the auer guards back, she pushed at the invisible threads of the world's power, thickening the fabric to turn it into a solid force.

The rocks paused mid-fall, and the weight of them pushed against her Art. Gritting her teeth, she shoved them harder, remembering to support the sidewalls of the shaft to prevent a complete cave in. "Hurry up!"

The rope lowered again, and the next miner grappled to secure himself to it before it started to rise.

As the stone ceiling continued to crumble, more weight plummeted against her energy, but the Art held fast.

Amarie sucked in a breath through her clenched jaw, the shell of her hiding aura cracking further. Keeping it intact only drew more of her focus and energy, so she let it drop. She didn't have time to notice any ramifications, her eyes widening as a fissure ruptured through the side of the open shaft, splitting all the way down to the ground where she stood. "Faster!"

The last miner leapt forward as the rope dropped again, looking at her. "Thank you so much, I—"

"Just go, dammit!" Amarie's arms shook with the weight, but she focused on the blurry image of the last miner rising out of the depths.

It left her alone in the blackness, and an imaginary boulder crushed her chest. Searing pain radiated up her legs, invisible snakes burning trails over her skin. She coughed, dirt falling around her as she concentrated only on the small circle of sky above her and keeping it open. Keeping it visible. The bright spot of sky flickered, shifting to a sconce flame.

Focus. Don't let go.

Amarie's vision darkened, eerie laughter echoing in her ears that caused tears to spring from her eyes. Something heavy crashed down next to her, slicing her arm on the way. She cried out, dropping to a knee as her power whirled above her, as if it no longer needed guidance to form a vertical cyclone within the mineshaft, keeping it intact.

The shadows closed in around her, hazy and distorted in her struggle.

Mildew and cave moss filled her nose before a gasp for breath replaced it with dirt. At the collapsed eastern wall of the mine, the crevices between stones formed a short shape, a thick black hood shrouding a pale feminine face.

She blinked, but the woman vanished, pain lashing over Amarie's sides.

"Kin," she whispered, reaching but finding no rope in the abhorrent darkness. "There's something evil down here."

Stumbling into the sconce light where the sun should have been, her knees hit the ground with a squelch, and the rich iron taste of blood filled her mouth. Lifting her hands from the soaked ground, they were coated in red.

"So much blood," she murmured, staring at her hands and wondering why the failing shaft hadn't buried her and ended the horror.

The rumble of the world around her turned into a high-pitched drone, as the pool of blood around her swelled. But a familiar voice broke through the din.

"Amarie, get up."

She spun towards the voice, blinking past the haze surrounding her. "Who's there?"

Something grabbed her, firm but gentle. Her shoulders bunched within the grip as someone crouched beside her. The impulse to break away came, but faltered as one of the hands loosened and brushed soft fingers over her jaw.

"We have to go."

"Kin?" Amarie sucked in a deeper breath, her mind returning to the collapsing mine. "Shit." The weight of her effort returned to her muscles, and she fought to maintain control as she reached for him.

The tornado of her power whipped up around the outer edge of the shaft, the once-invisible force taking on motes of beryl pink and azure. It still poured from her, arcing from a source she couldn't sense the bottom of and melding with the natural energies of Pantracia.

Kin's pale eyes reflected the prism of color as he seized her around the waist and pulled her to her feet. Slinging the rope tied around his waist to include hers, too, he pulled her close before frantically tugging.

Amarie buried her face in his tunic, not needing her eyes to control the Art pulsating around her. Her feet left the dirt, and as they rose back into the light, her mind cleared. Sunshine hit her face, and hands grappled for them both.

Miners yanked them to solid ground, hauling them farther away from the hole as Amarie let go of her power.

Chunks of land plummeted into the shaft, spreading outward as they rushed to safety. Kin half carried her, keeping her mostly on her feet before they dropped to solid ground twenty yards from the rubble.

Breathing hard, she rolled onto her back and stared at the sky.

Kin lay beside her, his bare arms shaking as he heaved in a breath. He remained close to her, his leg still pushed against hers as if the contact grounded him. Or that he somehow sensed she needed it.

A cough shook her chest, tears falling sideways down her temples.

What happened in there?

Flashes of the hallucinations returned to her, and she squeezed her eyes closed. "Did everyone make it out?"

The last miner to leave the tunnels below stepped forward, his face grim beneath the grime. "Everyone not killed in the initial collapse." He surveyed his companions behind him, three slumped on the ground. Only one had visible wounds, already being treated by the men who must have helped Kin.

"Are you all right?" Kin's hand moved to her knee, resting there as he sought her eyes. His were reddened by the clouds of dust still rolling through the air.

Amarie sat up, eyeing her legs. Her unscathed legs. "I am." She nodded, furrowing her brow before looking at him. "You came for me at the bottom of a collapsing mine. Why did you do that? Why not just send the rope?"

"I did. But I pulled it back up when you didn't grab it." He looked behind him to where the ground now lay still, cracked and sunken. Turning back to her, he shifted to block her vision of the miners, and so they couldn't see her. He whispered, "What happened? What did you see?"

"I don't know," she murmured. "I saw things in the shadows. I felt... so much pain. There was a woman, but she was not a friend. Perhaps not even human."

His hand passed down her leg, following the trail of his eyes as he surveyed her body. "But you're all right? It didn't hurt you?"

Amarie shook her head. "Not in reality, anyway. I just... my arm..." Looking over her shoulder, she cringed at the slash down her tricep. "Something cut me."

Kin hissed as he shifted closer, removing the strap of his satchel still over his shoulder. He pulled out his spare shirt, wrapping it around the wound while pressing hard to staunch the bleeding. He turned his head over his shoulder to the cluster of men gathered around the one injured miner, who already had color returning to his cheeks. One of the men who hadn't been in the mine knelt beside him, his hands placed in a way that suggested a purpose beyond comfort.

Kin must have noticed, too. "Looks like they at least have a healer. They should be able to patch you up. Least they can do after all you just did." Kin's familiar half smirk graced his face.

"I'm fine."

"I'm not a healer, at least I'm fairly certain I'm not, but I can tell this is bad enough you'd need someone to sew you up at the very least." While still holding his shirt on her arm, he placed a firm hand on her thigh to hold her down. "Stay put until I can get the healer over here. You have to be exhausted after expending all that energy."

Amarie didn't bother fighting him, holding up a hand in defeat. "Not as exhausted as I feel like I should be." She touched his wrist, waiting until he looked at her. "Thank you. You didn't have to do what you did, but I'll be forever grateful."

He almost looked surprised as he shook his head. "You didn't have to either." He paused, as if he was about to say something else. But then turned over his shoulder to focus on the miners, waiting until the apparent healer looked in their direction. He gestured at her with his chin, not removing his hands. "Can you come take a look over here?"

The healer, a white-haired man who looked too frail to be this far from town, stood up from where he crouched beside the injured miner. He shuffled over to Kin and Amarie, motioning briskly for Kin to get out of the way as he knelt beside her injury.

The old man took her arm, peeling back Kin's blood-soaked shirt to look at the cut that felt worse with every passing moment. Gingerly pinching her skin together, the healer's energy poured into hers. She felt it briefly, like the tickle of a feather against her own power. But then hers absorbed it, not allowing the healer's Art to alter her body.

The old man scowled, lifting his hand from her briefly before pinching her wound again.

"What's wrong?" Amarie fought the growing butterflies in her gut.

"I can't... seem to heal you, miss. My energy only dissipates." The healer kept his hands in place this time, eyeing her. "I can feel your power. Perhaps you could heal yourself?"

"I don't know how," she muttered, cringing as he tightened his hold on the wound.

Pulling a strip of linen from his satchel, he wrapped her arm and tied it. "We will have to stitch you. Stay here."

Amarie sighed, watching him go. "Why can't he heal me?" She focused on the aura that had fallen. A strange panic entered her at the realization it'd been down so long. With a rapid thought, she reinstated it.

The healer returned quickly, needle in hand. "This will hurt." He said nothing else as he got to work, piercing her flesh with the first stitch.

She winced, swallowing. "Could be worse."

"Need something to bite down on? Or squeeze?" Kin held out his hand to her uninjured arm.

Eyeing the offering, she tried to smile and took his hand.

Three stitches later, Amarie felt a tremble in the ground and looked at the mine, but nothing shifted. As she faced

Kin, tension rippled back into her at the sight of a rider approaching at a gallop from the northwest. "Someone's coming."

"Probably heard the collapse, too, and is coming to see what's going on." Kin didn't look behind him at the rider, his focus on Amarie as the healer worked.

"Kin," Amarie warned. She couldn't make out the fine details of the man's face, but the sun shone in his blond hair, a beard making his expression hard to read. And his eyes were very clearly on her.

"The rider is coming straight towards *us*, not the mine." She looked over her shoulder at the healer's unhurried hands. "Almost done?"

"A few more stitches," he mulled. "Won't take long."

Kin met her eyes before tilting his head towards the approaching stranger. The man, who had dismounted his horse near where their own still stood, faltered with Kin's glance. He didn't secure his horse's reins before he started towards them. He was finely dressed, but had relaxed the formal collar of his tunic. It exposed the navy edge of a tattoo on the side of his neck, the other end of the ink just visible beneath his rolled up sleeves.

"Think he knows one of us?"

"By the look in his eyes, I'd say so." Amarie fought the instinct to run as the healer finished with her arm and walked away. She rose to her feet with Kin's help.

Kin faced her to keep the approaching stranger from seeing his moving lips, his satchel again over his shoulder. "Do we want to find out? He looks rather pissed off, so I'm not sure I'm eager to meet him."

"We can't make it to the horses." She looked behind them, at the tree line they could run to. "We'd never get away..."

"My lord, is that you?" A miner rose, approaching the stranger with a dazzled gaze. "By the gods, it's such a pleasure..."

The voice trailed out of Amarie's awareness as she stiffened, watching the stranger pause with the distraction. "Now's our chance. Get to the trees and find a place to hide. Ready?"

Kin nodded once. "After you."

Chapter 27

AHRIA WOULD HAVE THOUGHT the presence of a prince in the tavern would have tamed the usually raucous behavior. But, as she sang, it seemed to further encourage it. Conrad's appearance, with several guards in tow, had excited the crowd beyond reason. Not to mention the auer advisor who'd insisted on being there to witness his daughter's performance. Murmurs hadn't ceased since their arrival, though they'd simmered whenever she began a song.

She chose the set based on what they'd appreciate, filled with all the songs she'd written for them over the months they'd been apart.

The cheers exploded at the end, and Ahria watched Jaqi try again to speak to Conrad. It made her insides bristle, but the woman had no idea why the prince was there, and Evelyn had made it clear to capitalize on the royal attention as much as possible. Which meant making connections, gaining favor, and ensuring the royal family knew how to contact them should they require entertainment for an event.

Yet, Conrad brushed Jaqi off again, eyes never leaving Ahria, even in the presence of the fortune teller's provocative attire.

With the performance ended, Mysterium stepped down from the meager stage, packing up their equipment and retrieving their ales.

The tavern, in the reputable part of the craft district, was packed with fancily dressed merchants. The large dining hall easily fit over one hundred patrons in a day, but it looked as if they'd squeezed in twice as many. It was one of the largest crowds Mysterium had performed for.

She glanced to the left of the stage, where a raised seating area with a large bay window had been sectioned off for the royal visitors. A guard stood at the base of the narrow stairwell, with several more protectively behind Conrad and Talon. Conrad had stood, starting down the stairs before Jaqi, once again, slipped in to cut him off before he could make his way past the guard.

Ahria frowned.

Does she ever give it a rest?

Vaeler appeared at her side, grinning with a mischievous look. "I see he showed up. They both did."

"I told you they would." Ahria gave him a cocky smirk. "Not my fault you didn't believe me."

"You spent days in their prison, then told me the crown prince was coming to watch us perform. Can you really blame me?" Vaeler laughed. "You said you were looking for a ship captain, not a prince. This mystery would have been solved much sooner if we'd gone to more of the royal speeches."

She laughed. "That definitely would have helped. And to be fair, when I met him, he *was* a captain."

"Who's a captain?" Conrad emerged from the crowd beside them, glancing between Vaeler and Ahria.

Butterflies erupted in her gut as she motioned to her friend. "Conrad, I'd like you to meet Vaeler. Vaeler, this is Conrad."

Conrad held out his hand with the introduction.

To his credit, Vaeler didn't even balk, taking the prince's hand. "A pleasure, your highness."

"Mine, more so, considering what you did for Ahria." Conrad gave an annoyed glance over his shoulder at the guard who moved closer as the crowd began to shift. "Thank you for that. Especially considering my failure to know she was in the city." Conrad's tone took on a curious formality as he spoke, unlike when they were alone together.

Ahria scanned the crowd, looking for Talon, and caught Jaqi's furious glare in her direction. Even in the midst of a palm reading, the woman sneered, before finally returning her attention to her patron.

Something about the man she read for sent a wave of unease down Ahria's back. Maybe it was the black cloak, or his...

In that moment, the man turned and looked straight at her, an ominous smirk on his face she could only stare at. Something in the wrinkled features of his face didn't match the gleam of youth in his dark eyes.

Someone stepped between them, and Ahria gasped a short inhale of relief at the broken eye contact.

"Ahria has been a welcome addition to our group. We're sad to see her go." Vaeler looked at her with a warm gaze, eyes narrowing only slightly as she regained her composure. "But I suppose I understand."

Conrad's stern visage broke in the hint of a smile. "I appreciate that. But I suspect you'll have a hard time finding a replacement." He looked at her, his eyes softening with the glance even though he didn't reach for her. She could imagine his arms wrapping around her with the look, the touch of his lips on her neck. A warm shiver passed down her spine, and heat blossomed in her core.

"That we will. Evelyn's still searching, but for now we will return to the way we were before her arrival." The musician put a hand on her shoulder. "But we'll always be here if you need anything or just want to visit."

Ahria grinned. "And I'll visit often, I promise."

"Oh, joy." The sarcastic remark drawled from behind her, where Jaqi had approached. The woman's eyes landed on the prince a breath later, and she straightened, wiping the anger from her face. "Your highness. I apologize." She bowed while Vaeler crossed his arms. As she righted herself, she opened her mouth to speak, but Talon joined them the same instant, and instead she merely bowed again and hurried off.

"Apologies for interrupting." Talon also donned the regal attitude deceptively well. He stepped close to her, lovingly placing a kiss on the side of her head while still somehow seeming refined. "You were amazing, Ree."

Heat rushed to her cheeks, but she leaned briefly on her father. "Thanks, Dad." She motioned to Vaeler, making the introductions.

"You raised one hell of a daughter," Vaeler said as he shook the auer's hand.

Talon smiled and nodded as he returned the greeting. "There's no changing the nature of the ocean." He gave a loving glance at Ahria. "She is very much her mother's daughter."

"Sometimes I'm not convinced that's a compliment." Ahria looked at Conrad, her chest cracking with happiness.

"In this case, I'm fairly certain it is." Conrad looked at Talon, something in his gaze suggesting the two had recently exchanged some words. During the performance, she'd seen

Talon talking with Conrad, and it warmed her heart to see them smiling together.

"When will we see you next?" Vaeler laughed. "Let me rephrase. When will *I* see you next? I don't expect you to visit *all* of us." By his tone, she understood who he meant.

"I'll come to your show next week, and we can grab a drink after, if that works for you." Ahria tilted her head.

Vaeler nodded, pulling her into a hug. "If we still don't have a singer, just hop on up here with us, all right?"

Ahria laughed and let him go. "Sounds good."

The carriage ride back to the palace would have typically given Ahria and Conrad some much needed privacy, but Talon's presence made it more awkward. Despite his knowledge of Ahria and Conrad's attraction, it felt wrong to be so blatant in front of her father. She just hoped the auer wouldn't read too deeply into the pointed glances and subtle touch of their feet as they sat opposite each other.

The guards dispersed as they entered the palace proper, leaving the trio almost alone in the grand entry hall. The chandelier above still blazed with life, even in the late hour of the evening, and several guards were posted at each of the main hallways that led deeper into the palace.

Talon kissed Ahria again on the temple before bidding her and Conrad goodnight. The auer disappeared down the west hallway past Mister Credish. The squirrelly older man gave her a curious glance before he bowed respectfully to Conrad, who frowned in distaste.

"Please, Mister Credish, I've told you before that is unnecessary."

"Your highness, apologies. But I wish to speak to you about some important business."

"It's almost midnight, can't it wait until morning?"

"All due respect, sir, but no. Invitations and acceptance must be handled this evening." He cast another glance at Ahria.

"I'll leave you," she murmured, shoulders drooping that they hadn't even managed a minute alone. "Goodnight, your highness." It felt so impersonal to address him formally, but anything else would have been suspect. And there were too many eyes still in the room. She walked away with soft steps over the lush rug, rounding a corner and pausing. She shouldn't have stayed to listen, but they often performed similar maneuvers to dodge prying eyes.

"We must know your decision for who will accompany you to the queen's birthday celebration ball. Invitations will be sent first thing tomorrow morning, and from my understanding, you've yet to choose between the ladies presented." Credish spoke quietly but firmly. "If any of them are to arrive in time, we mustn't delay the invitation."

Ahria's gut twisted. He hadn't mentioned anything about the need for him to escort a woman to the celebration, but she understood why.

And it was my choice to keep us a secret.

Conrad sighed. "I don't see the importance of a partner for my mother's birthday. Can't I just attend alone?"

"I know you have been putting this decision off, your highness, but you can't any longer. It is expected that you begin to express dedication to finding a future partner. The queen has told me that parliament is rather insistent that you be married soon."

Conrad grumbled, "I also do not like parliament continuously sticking their nose in my private business. Perhaps I don't wish to marry?"

"Your position is a tenuous one, sir. To maintain the faith of parliament and the people, it is necessary for them to know our future queen soon. Even if parliament chooses to formally recognize you as the ruling *king*, you will need a woman at your side to aid in the transition of power." Credish lowered his voice. "Be mindful with your associations. Indulging in the company of commoners at taverns hardly inspires the confidence of the government."

Ahria held her breath until her lungs burned, but couldn't bring herself to stay to hear Conrad's response. She turned, quietly hurrying down the hallways. The joy that had occupied her chest plummeted into her stomach, creating a bundle of knots that made her eyes heat.

She found her way to her room, located conveniently

across the hall from the prince's chambers. Hesitating, she nodded to the guards stationed outside Conrad's door and entered her own living space.

Commoners in taverns. Gods.

What right do I have to be with him?

Crossing the room to her bed, she sat, staring out the window. She'd chased a sea captain, but found a prince. And a prince had obligations beyond what potential she could offer. He should wed a princess, form an alliance, or a political gain. Being with her would give him nothing but complications. Her heart ached, and she imagined Conrad dancing at the ball with a beautiful stranger.

A knock sounded on her door, making her jump out of the rampant thoughts.

She stood, but couldn't bring her feet to move. The knock meant Conrad had distracted his guards. Her opportunity to sneak into his rooms. But her feet wouldn't budge. Minutes passed, nothing changed.

After a time, the knock came again, this time in a different pattern.

"Ahria?" Conrad's voice echoed mutely through the thick door. "Can I come in?"

She clamped her mouth shut, breathing evenly through her nose. Her insides screamed to answer him, but Credish's voice circled in her mind.

Commoners in taverns.

She didn't belong here. Not with him.

"I'm coming in." The door opened soundlessly a moment later, and she cursed herself for not thinking to lock it.

Conrad paused in the doorway, his two guards repositioned at his doorway. One held a tray with a silver tea set atop it. He met her eyes and then turned back to his guard, motioning. The guard passed the tray to the prince before Conrad entered her room with it.

"The door, please, Grettin."

The guard nodded and leaned into the room, pulling the door shut behind Conrad.

The prince walked to the low table in front of Ahria's empty fireplace, setting the tea down.

Ahria stood stiffly, eyes wide. "What are you doing?"

"We've always rendezvoused in my chambers. I don't mind a change of scenery." He arranged the ceramic cups before he poured the tea.

"But the guards were right there. What if they tell someone?"

"Let them." He lifted the first cup, holding it out to her. "I'd be willing to bet they already know, and I'd love for word to get back to Credish at this point." When she didn't move towards his offer, he set it back down before he stood and approached her. "I know we said we'd keep this secret, but..." He reached for her hand slowly, pausing a few inches away in an offer. "I don't want to anymore."

Ahria eyed his hand. "I don't want to, either, but it's not safe. And Credish had a point."

"Credish doesn't know what he's talking about." He bobbed his hand, but didn't drop it. "And I trust you, Ahria. With whatever secret you have. You can keep it for eternity, and no one will ever need to know. Especially not those old women in parliament who keep trying to tell me how to live my life."

"But someone could know. Someone could find out, and I have no way of preventing that." Ahria took his hand, dropping her gaze.

"Then we'll protect it together." He stepped closer to her as he tightened his grip on her hand. "Whatever it is, I'm not afraid of it. And I know that you and I will be able to handle anything together."

Looking up at him, she swallowed. "Even if, one day... One random, unexpected day, I..." She took a deep breath. "I inherit unfathomable power that I cannot refuse, and it makes me the biggest target of a very, very dangerous being that will never stop hunting me?" Her hands shook, her eyes hot.

Conrad narrowed his eyes, but only moved closer. He lifted her unsteady hands to his chest, and stroked her cheek. "This really scares you, doesn't it?"

Ahria nodded. "If my mother ever dies... This is my fate."

"I don't believe in fate." Conrad shook his head. "We choose our paths."

"It doesn't matter," she whispered. "I don't have a choice in this. It is in my blood."

"But you have a choice in whether or not to be afraid of it."

"You don't understand." Ahria pushed against his chest, but not to shove him away. His unmoving presence eased her breath, but she still shook her head. "You don't understand. My mother's power... if it ever becomes mine..."

"You're right, I don't understand what this power really is. I doubt I can without the full picture." He stroked her jaw again. "And that's not me asking for the rest of it. But this I do know, Ahria. There is no one in this world that I would trust more with infinite power. As far as I'm concerned, you already have it over me. I trust you with every fiber of my being."

"Why?" Ahria blinked through the heat gathering on her lower lids. "What have I done to earn such trust?"

"Some things aren't meant to be understood. And I can't fully explain why. But I know I do. It's part of *who* you are. I know you would never allow harm to fall on those who don't deserve it. And I know you'll always do what you believe is just and right. That's all I could ever ask of you. That's all anyone could ever ask of a queen."

Ahria stepped back, stiffening. "A queen?"

He pursed his lips. "You deserve to be one. I know you don't see it, and gods know Credish doesn't either... and it wouldn't be for a long time. I trust my mother to stubbornly live forever."

She stared at him, breathing faster as she wondered if he'd forgotten the necessary commitment required to make her a queen at all. Not that she wanted marriage, not yet. Or perhaps ever. It wasn't something she dared consider, not when her father had made it so clear that no country could own the Berylian Key.

Conrad hesitated in her silence, but his shoulders relaxed as he stepped towards her again. "Come with me to the ball in a few weeks? Be my partner for the evening?" He gingerly touched her waist, looking at her face as if it would give him some answer to whether he could move closer. "I know it's a risk, but I need everyone to see my love for you. And I know they will love you, too."

Ahria forced herself to keep breathing. "You love me?"

His eyes met hers, sucking her deep into the hazel pools. "Ardently." He gave the barest smile, but it warmed as he moved closer. "And that was before I heard your siren-like voice tonight." His mouth neared hers, but he kept the teasing distance he always did to encourage her to close it. To give her the power. The choice. Hot breath tickled her lips as he whispered, "I love you, Mouse. And I want the world to know it."

Her chin tilted up, and she tried to focus on his face to keep the room from spinning. "I love you, too, Captain." She grazed his lips with hers, her control slipping.

As he pressed into her, Conrad's mouth danced against hers, his hands roaming down her body in the way that made her skin ache for more.

Ahria let out a breathy whimper, opening for him as his tongue caressed hers. She stepped into him, not breaking the kiss as she guided him backwards to the wide armchair near the vacant hearth. Giving him a little shove, she grinned when he dropped into the seat.

He stared at her with dilated pupils, gaze flowing down her body before returning to her face. "You were amazing tonight."

With confidence she didn't know she had, she lowered one knee to the seat beside him, placing a hand on his chest. A low growl rumbled in his chest as she settled herself on his lap, straddling him. "I'm just grateful you came."

The prince's eyes bored into her with an intensity that made her shiver. His chin tilted up, lips parting. "What are you doing?" His voice came as barely a whisper, but the need in his tone only encouraged her.

"I want to be close to you," she breathed, dipping her chin so their lips could touch again. "Is that all right?"

He hummed his agreement, the stiffness of his arousal beneath her making her toes curl. And then his mouth was on hers again, fiery kisses speeding their breath as her body rocked against him. His touch tightened at her hips before rising over her waist, ribs, and palming her breast.

Ahria moaned into his mouth, her nipples hardening beneath her clothing.

Conrad kissed her fiercer, hips moving beneath her as she ran her hands over his hair. He broke away a breath later, lips damp and swollen. "If you want to wait to tell everyone, we can." His words came out breathless, and it took all her concentration to hold still as he spoke. "I trust you with more than just whatever monumental power you might end up with. I trust you with the decision of what is best. I don't want to pressure you into anything. Ever."

Ahria smiled and buried her face in his neck, kissing his skin and trying to ignore the heat between her thighs. "Let's keep it quiet a few more days and give me a chance to warn my father that we're going public with our relationship. But I will attend the ball with you." She bit his neck. "As long as I can still carry my daggers."

He chuckled, leaning into the bite as the laugh turned into a groan. "As if I could tell you no." He ran his hands around her middle, pulling her closer.

"You could try," she murmured.

"Already testing that, now, aren't you?" His breath hitched as she placed another kiss on his neck, skimming her teeth on his skin towards his ear with a slight tilt of her hips.

"Did you expect otherwise?"

He groaned again, pressing his body harder against hers. "No, but if you want to wait a few more days, I really should return to my own chambers before those guards start talking." He pressed lightly on her hips, but made no real effort to lift her off him.

She withdrew her face and looked down at him. "A few more days, then," she whispered, brushing a kiss over his chin. "And then I'd like to see *all* of you. Touch all of you." She ran her hands down the sides of his neck, over his chest. As they roamed lower, she imagined the ridges of muscle at his abdomen.

He hummed, pressing a wet kiss to the underside of her jaw. "I would like that." Rocking his hips into her slightly, he ran a hand over her thigh. "Just a few more days."

Chapter 28

·DAMIEN LANORET HARDLY BELIEVED IT when he felt it. The moment the unleashed Berylian Key's power hit him in a disoriented haze, he'd pulled his horse out of a gallop so hard the gelding reared. But as he'd approached the collapsed mine shaft, and his eyes fell on the two beings covered in dirt...

Even with the Berylian Key's power once again hidden, he'd never have forgotten the sensation of it from over two decades ago.

And there they both were, together, and definitely not in Slumber.

With the prison's completion, their plan was ready to move forward. Amarie and Kin—the Berylian Key and Shade redeemed, needed to wake. Needed to be ready to seal Uriel away.

This is either amazingly ironic timing, or...

His last-minute solo journey to Eralas had only taken a day to prepare for, since he had no reason to involve a political entourage. His role as King Jarrod Martox's personal advisor wouldn't come into play here. This day, he could only focus on his duty as the Rahn'ka.

Rae had wanted to join him, but with Sarra's approaching seventeenth birthday, their daughter would never have forgiven them if both her parents were away, world-altering cataclysm or not. And waking Kin and Amarie to bring them back to Veralian hardly required both of them.

Yet, as Damien stared at Kin, he wished more than anything that his wife was with him.

This just got a whole lot more complicated.

"My lord, I saw your speech at the refounding of Hoult. It was inspirational." The miner had somehow recognized him, despite Damien's attempts to look more ungroomed than he typically did around the royal palace. The plain clothes obviously hadn't achieved the anonymity he'd hoped for.

Before he could call to Kin and Amarie, before he could even shout their names, they were on their feet.

Running.

And of course, they ran in the opposite direction.

Son of a bitch.

"I apologize, you must have me confused with someone else. I'm just passing through." He didn't wait for the stammered words of confusion before he dodged through the men to pursue.

His horse nickered and moved forward in tandem with Damien, knowing what the Rahn'ka asked of him without any verbal command. The gelding wove around the outbuildings of the mine, galloping past Damien as he rushed through the dry meadow encircling the collapsed mine.

Neither he, nor his mount, were going to make it to the trees before Amarie and Kin disappeared among them.

Thinning his barrier, he allowed the voices of the forest ahead into his mind. The chorus hummed against the threads of his soul, welcoming the Rahn'ka and feeding him with offerings of energy to empower his muscles. His gait shifted to the beat of nature's heart, his steps dodging the most delicate of sprouts. With a stride to the right, he wove into the dense pines, swinging back to angle after Kin's fleeing form.

The moment he entered the thicket, warnings erupted from the foliage surrounding him.

Amarie reappeared, hand thrust out and eyes vibrant with pinks and purples.

Damien's heart leapt, and he dove to the forest floor as a burst of energy pulsed where his head had been. The power crackled through the air above him, raw and potent. And somehow it left the fabric above him drained of all capability to carry the Art before it began to ebb back into the empty space.

He rolled towards the raised roots of one of the dark-barked trees, pulling strings of ká from the ferns into his being. He pressed the power through the tension of his muscles as he rocked back to his feet. Reaching to Amarie's own ká, he used it as his focal point for where to funnel the weaves of his Art. But... it all felt a blur. Like aiming into the dark. As if the space around the woman wasn't fully there. As the bubble of ká formed into an orb around her, it popped without explanation.

What the hells...

She advanced, fingers twitching, and threw a wave of power at him.

The force slammed into his chest, pushing him back against the tree that he'd used to regain his footing. The breath left his lungs in a huff, his back screaming in unison with the ká of the foliage crushed by his body.

Amarie lifted her chin as she approached, studying his face while she held him with what looked like minimal effort. "Who are you?"

Chapter 29

KIN JOGGED BACK TO AMARIE, determined to at least appear to be of some assistance. His hand slipped under the flap of his satchel, grazing the smooth hilt of the obsidian dagger.

When Amarie peeled away from him in their mad dash, he thought she had completely lost her mind. She disappeared behind, and he determined his purpose was to keep the stranger's attention on him so she could catch him by surprise. It'd almost worked, but the stranger had avoided her first blow.

Panic had coated his throat when a flicker of pale blue light formed in a dome over Amarie's head after the man had thrown his hands out. Something in Kin's subconscious told him the action was that of an Art user, yet nothing happened.

Then the man cried out as his spine collided with the hard trunk of a pine tree. The thump echoed through the forest, the wood vibrating and sending squirrels and birds chittering away from the top branches.

"I'm a friend." The man wheezed his answer. His hand formed a fist, despite the pressure of Amarie's power against him. Flickers of color ran over him like ropes lashing him to the tree.

"Then tell me who we are," Amarie demanded, unrelenting on her hold of him.

"Amarie." The man jutted his chin in Kin's direction. "And Kin. I'm no threat to you."

"You haven't given me your name." She stepped closer to the stranger, hands shaking.

A strange glow erupted from the barely visible tattoo at the man's collar, pulsing down his arm. Whatever Art he funneled into his own flesh seemed to grow, the runes becoming sharper in the radiant blue light. It bled through the fabric of his shirt, revealing the tattoo covering his entire arm in unfamiliar runes. But just as the light reached its brightest, it fizzled like a dying ember, the markings returning to a dark navy color. He gritted his jaw. "Damien. I'm Damien Lanoret."

Kin's stomach flipped as he recalled the words Amarie had read from the stone plaque on his prison bed.

Amarie looked over her shoulder at Kin before back at

Damien. "Why don't we remember anything?"

"Let me go. I swear I'm not a threat to you. I'll explain once you have."

She hesitated, an odd calm on her face as she glanced at Kin again. "What do you think?"

Kin's jaw twitched as he considered the man pinned by invisible force and tried to size him up. He easily had a few inches of height on the man, and saw no weapons at his side. Yet, whatever flicker he'd seen on the man's arm and in the air above Amarie was not hers. If he was an Art user, then he was still a threat without a weapon.

"One more question before she lets you down." Kin stepped beside Amarie. "Why was I in that chamber below Eralas?"

Damien met his eyes, his own steady with determination. "You asked me to take you there."

Amarie's shoulders eased. "I can feel your Art within you. I can tell how much energy it can withstand. And I can overfill it in a heartbeat. I'd rather not take a life, so keep that in mind before you try anything." Without waiting for his answer, she exhaled, and Damien's boots hit the ground.

Gasping, Damien straightened, brushing his hand down his left arm as if feeling for whatever power had started to emerge. He shook his head and looked at Kin with narrowed eyes. "When I give you your memories back, it'll be good to know *why* you left that particular detail out about Amarie's power."

Kin's back straightened at the accusation, and he exchanged a glance with Amarie. "So we did know each other before."

Damien's face hardened beneath his blond beard as he looked between them. "I don't understand how you both aren't in Eralas. What happened?"

"We woke up," Amarie muttered. "A few days ago."

Damien scratched the back of his head, running his hand up into his hair. "Can you be more specific? How many days ago?"

Kin crossed his arms. "Three. I'd still like to know what that place was, too."

"Early afternoon?" Damien paced away a few steps, his body tensing. The rough clothing did little to hide clues to who he was. Callused hands, corded muscles, and a sharp gaze. The man was a soldier. Yet, that miner had called him a lord.

"Yes. Now where were we, and why did I ask you to put me there?"

"It must have been the prison's completion," he muttered. "You were both in Slumber. Both by choice from what I understood of the circumstances for you, Amarie. Though, I admit I don't know the full reasoning behind your decision to ask it of the auer." He looked at Kin. "It was to help you get through some... difficult side effects you were dealing with. I said I would wake you after a year." A slight flinch in Damien's expression made Kin's chest tighten.

"Why do I get the feeling it's been more than a year?" Kin moved closer to Amarie, fighting the temptation to touch her.

"I'll explain, but it will be easier after I've returned your memories." Damien crossed his arms as he focused on Amarie. "Though... we might have another complication now that I see exactly how that power of yours works."

"What do you mean?" She rolled her shoulders, glancing at her hands.

"I can't use the Art on you. The moment I try, your power nullifies mine. Which means I can't manipulate your ká to restore your memories." Damien rubbed his temple, staring up at the canopy in thought.

Amarie blinked. "The healer couldn't heal my arm. Must be a similar issue. But how do we work around that? We *can* work around that, can't we?" Her even tone finally shifted to show her worry.

Kin touched her arm, stepping closer to her. He tried to think of something reassuring to say, but couldn't find any answers in what he could remember of the world. "There has to be a way to freeze your Art, right? Like a back door?" He looked at Damien, who had closed his eyes and tilted his head as if listening to something unheard.

"Not a way, but there is a place." Damien crossed his arms. "I think it'd work. In theory."

Amarie shifted her weight between her feet. "How far?"

"Three days on horseback, give or take." Damien moved, his steps uneven on the forest floor as he walked briskly past them towards the forest edge. "We should go before we lose the day."

"What about Kin's memories?"

Damien stopped abruptly, glancing back as he shook his head. "I think it's best to wait. Knowing what I know, It'd be better if the two of you came to remember at the same time. Or as close to it as possible."

Kin's stomach churned.

I don't like the implications of that.

"But we do know each other?" Amarie whispered, an undercurrent of suspicion in her voice.

"Yes, but I only know one side of your stories. Thus, it's better to wait."

"And how do we know that we can trust you in all this?" Kin refused to follow even as Damien started to walk away again.

"You don't." Damien called over his shoulder. "But I'm the only chance you have at getting your memories back. And trust me, you're going to want them with what's coming."

Amarie looked up at Kin, standing so close to him he could see the darker rim of blue around her azure irises. "Do you think we should go?" She spoke in barely a whisper, her hand finding his.

Entwining their fingers, Kin studied the soft features of her face. "If he's lying, then we travel three more days without having a single clue of where we should be going anyway. But if he's telling the truth, then he really is our only chance."

She paused before nodding, gripping his hand tighter. "Then we go. But until he's proven himself, we only trust each other."

The journey northeast was awkwardly quiet. Damien didn't seem interested in conversation, and neither Kin nor Amarie felt inclined to speak in front of him. They rode through every day, stopping only in the darkest part of the summer night to sleep a few hours before moving on.

Kin had enough sense of direction to know they were moving towards the coast, which meant closer to Eralas. The suspicion that Damien could be a hired auer mercenary was something he would have discussed with Amarie if it hadn't sounded so ludicrous. Auer didn't hire humans. He remembered enough to know that much.

The one comfort lay in the certainty that Amarie could overpower whatever Art Damien held.

Cresting over the top of one of Helgath's rocky hills, the sun glittered on the crystalline waves of the strait. The shadow of a massive tree dominated the distant horizon beyond, reminding Kin once more how close they were to where he'd been imprisoned. Damien claimed he'd chosen to enter Slumber, but that knowledge didn't ease the growing knot in his stomach.

Waves crashed against the cliffside of Helgath's coast, the land dipping sharply towards rocky beaches below. The natural curve of the ocean cracked inland near the base of the hill, like a giant had slammed a massive fist down into the land. The ground appeared as if it'd been carved to look like the landscape that'd once been there, now encased in smooth ashen stone. It dropped to where the ocean swirled in a miniature maelstrom at the center, forced into existence by the constant ebb of water moving in and out of a narrow opening to the sea.

The curve of grey land rimmed the crater in a uniform band, suggesting whatever might have caused the destruction had begun at the perfect center of the maelstrom. In the strange lumps of the frozen land, the outline of building foundations were apparent from this distance, all that remained of the village Damien had claimed once stood there.

Kin could just make out where a road might have been, its end vanishing into the gnashing waters. Just outside of the ashen circle, grass and wildflowers bloomed, defying whatever catastrophe had happened. But they didn't dare reach across that deathly border.

Amarie paused her horse at the cliff edge, looking over the crater and sunken village. They were near their destination, which now suspiciously seemed to be the crater. And Amarie's eagerness had evidently faded.

While Damien drank from his waterskin twenty feet away, Kin stopped his horse next to Amarie's. The days of riding had helped improve his skill on horseback, but his legs screamed every time he forced them to continue. "What is it?"

"I feel like I've been here before," she breathed. "And there's this little voice in my head that says I don't want to remember it. Any of it." A haunted expression dominated her face, eyes still pinned on the strange landscape.

"You have been here before." Damien drank again before reaching into a pouch in his saddle, pulling out bits of dried fruit he'd been snacking on all day. "There's a few things that we should probably talk about before we start. And we're walking from here. Horses don't react well to the crater."

"What caused it?" Amarie dismounted, looping her reins loosely over Damien's saddle. His horse never wandered, so they'd taken to using it as a hitch post.

Damien lifted a hand, wobbling it back and forth as a way of answer before slinging a pack over his shoulder. "It was a joint effort between two beings of immense power." He looked at Amarie in a way that made Kin narrow his eyes. The man's demeanor had been shifting gradually, and he kept a wary eye on Amarie. As if he expected her to do something destructive.

He probably distrusts her Art if it can stop his. And this is one hell of a trap if this is his way of nullifying her as a threat.

"What do we need to talk about?" Kin copied what Amarie had done with his own reins. Flinging his satchel over his shoulder, he wanted to keep the obsidian dagger close with the shifty looks from their guide.

"Just some precursory knowledge that may stop one of you from overreacting."

Amarie lifted an eyebrow. "Which one of us?"

Damien averted his gaze from her, looking back to the barren terrain ahead.

She made a face and muttered to Kin, "Definitely *me*, then."

Kin shrugged but gave her a crooked smile. "Maybe you'd have a good reason?"

They started down the hill after Damien, who appeared anxious to reach the ashen break in the land. As they neared, the world fell eerily quiet. Only the wind and the lash of the sea beyond touched the pale stones as the usual buzz of summer bugs faded to silence.

"Which of us should remember first, you think?" Kin moved in close to Amarie, his hand brushing hers, though he stopped himself from entwining their fingers again. He didn't want to be far from her, especially the closer they moved to the strange, twisted land. Damien seemed oblivious to their discomfort as he paused at the warped edge, facing away from them.

Amarie looked hard at Damien before she met Kin's gaze. "I'll be powerless while I'm in that void, so it might be beneficial to return your memories first. I can guard us while you recall everything you know about our new friend," she murmured under her breath.

He nodded, sucking in a breath. "Makes sense. But what if he's not able to return your memories at all? It would feel odd for me to have them without you."

She paused, considering his words, before speaking. "But we knew each other, so even if only you remember, you can tell me all the stories until he's able to return mine, too." She looked up at him as they walked. "You'll tell me the truth."

As he met her eyes, he knew she was right. "I hope this feeling is still here when our memories are back." He swallowed back the temptation to tell her of the latent emotions that had been boiling in him since they'd escaped Eralas.

"What feeling?" Her steps stilled, and she faced him.

He looked down as he tentatively reached for her hand, grazing his fingers against hers. "The feeling that I'm supposed to be with you. That I would do *anything* for you."

Her throat bobbed. "If you feel it now, I don't see why you wouldn't after. But in case anything changes..." Rising to her toes, she kissed his cheek and smiled. "Not long, now. Good luck."

Warmth flooded his chest, and he wished he could sweep her up in his arms and know that they were meant to be together forever.

"You ready, Kin?" Damien didn't even glance at them.

He wasn't sure if the man had been listening to their conversation or came to his own conclusion. Hesitation caused him to squeeze Amarie's hand before lifting it to his lips and placing a soft kiss on her fingertips. "Gods, I hope we're not related," he whispered, smirking. But before she could enthrall him again, he turned towards the crater.

Damien had removed his shoes at some point while they'd been distracted. They sat neatly together at the grey edge of the frozen landscape, but he moved away from them, stepping into the short grass. "We don't need the void for you." He lowered himself to the ground in a smooth movement, crossing his legs beneath him.

Kin approached, his gut tangled as he patted the satchel on his hip for comfort. He looked back to where Amarie waited before he forced himself to sit in front of Damien. "Do I need to take my boots off too?"

Damien shook his head, and Kin noticed the slight pulse of blue light penetrating from the man's collar. Whatever power he had radiated with the steady movement of his breath. "I need free access to your ká, and the easiest way is through your head. Best if you lay down. This shouldn't take long, as I'm already familiar with your ká."

None of what he said helped the anxiety still raging in him. Even if Damien's suggestion meant Kin was the one he was closer to. He considered asking again what Damien wanted to talk about before, but could see in the man's eyes that the conversation didn't need to happen with him.

Pulling his satchel into his lap, Kin sat with his back to Damien and allowed himself another look at Amarie, before his feelings could be changed by the past. He soaked in all he could of the woman he somehow knew he was meant to be with. He could feel every fiber of his being pulled to her. Belonging to her. He kept eye contact with her as long as he could while he laid down, the position uncomfortable. Perhaps because his body had been stuck in the straight position for so long on that stone slab.

Damien never told him how long he'd been in Slumber, seeming unwilling to say it. Kin hadn't really wanted to know. It might have changed what he wanted to remember if it'd been so long that everyone he knew was gone. But he knew Damien, somehow... and he didn't look any older than thirty.

"Try to relax." Damien pressed his palms to either side of Kin's skull. "It is normal to feel some pain."

Chapter 30

AMARIE TRIED NOT TO PACE, but her feet wouldn't hold still while Damien worked on Kin. It'd only been minutes, but her insides were restless. Her Art unwilling to remain quiet. It surged through her veins, speeding her heart, but she kept her hiding aura firmly intact. Damien had revealed that was how he'd found them, when she'd let the barrier slip during the mine collapse. She wouldn't make that mistake again. She opened her mouth to ask something, but with the stranger's face set in concentration, and Kin laying by his feet, she gritted her jaw and kept silent.

Touching the dagger at her thigh, she thumbed the pommel and paced in the other direction, careful to keep her boots from making noise.

Damien's power hummed in the air, making hers react. A spiderweb of pale blue danced around his hands, penetrating Kin's temples.

Kin's face contorted in a flinch, but his eyes remained closed. Another convulsion passed through his entire body, but Damien's grip held firm even as Kin's back arched. He made little sound, but Kin's muscles spoke of the pain Damien had warned about.

She dared not speak, voice her concerns, for fear of causing irreparable damage if Damien became distracted.

So she paced some more, further away. Leaving her back to the men, she focused on her breathing.

This is for the best.

When Kin let out a shout of pain, she looked back at them, but quickly averted her gaze. Whatever he endured, a rock in the pit of her gut told her her memories would be no kinder than his. The way her body had reacted to the mineshaft only confirmed the notion.

Pain is better than ignorance.

Amarie exhaled as the sounds behind her quieted, but she couldn't bring herself to look.

One of them took a sharp inhale, and something thunked against the ground as movement shuddered behind her.

"Easy." Damien kept his voice low.

Reluctantly, Amarie turned, peeking over her shoulder at the two.

Kin sat on the ground, his face buried in his hands as his curved back shuddered in an echo of pain. He rubbed his left hand hard against the webbed scar on his right forearm before he became oddly still.

Gulping, she took a step closer to them before stopping again, nerves roiling in her stomach. "Did it work?" Her voice barely carried over the breeze.

His head jerked up, as if he'd forgotten she was there. His steel blue eyes were rimmed with red, and they grew wider at seeing her. His lips parted, but then he stopped, bracing his hands on either side of him. "Amarie."

Suspicion glided through her at his tone, and she retreated the one step she'd taken. "You remember me."

He nodded, gaze locked on her. "I remember. And I owe you so many explanations."

Damien put a hand on Kin's shoulder, bracing himself before he stood. "After. They'll mean more when she remembers, too."

Kin looked up at Damien, the respect and appreciation for the man evident in his eyes. He looked at the scarred over tattoo on his arm again before he stood and held her gaze. "There are a few things though, that you need to know before that happens. The first and most important is that you are safe with Damien. And with me."

Amarie swallowed, his words far from the reassurance he meant them to be. "And the others?" She kept her distance from him, unable to approach with the disparity of information between them.

"Kin is not a threat to you." Damien moved towards the crater rather than her. "He is no longer what he used to be."

"Amarie, please." Kin held out his hands. "What you said before Damien restored me is still true. I will not lie to you. I never will. Which is why you need to get your memories back, too. So we can work together on what to do next."

She hesitated, but stared at his face until it calmed her. Nodding, she approached the edge of the desolation and eyed Damien. "All right. Do you need time to rest, or shall we do this?"

Damien rolled his shoulders. "I should be fine, assuming this works at all." He looked back at Kin before gesturing for Amarie to step into the grey. "I suspect the feeling is unpleasant to lose touch with the fabric. I'll need at least one part of you still on this side of the void so that I can use it as a channel to pull your ká away from your body."

"That sounds perfectly safe," she muttered, stepping over the threshold into the void.

It yanked her breath away, doubling her over her knees with a wheeze. Shutting her eyes, she focused on the air passing in and out of her mouth, rather than the nausea rising in her throat. Voices murmured from the men, but she couldn't make out their words amid the pounding of her heart.

A gaping hole had suddenly appeared within her soul. The ocean gone in a wave of darkness, hidden from all sensation. It felt as if a part of the world had fallen away entirely as all awareness of her Art was drawn behind an impenetrable veil.

But as minutes passed, the sensation calmed. Her stomach settled... slightly.

As she slowly righted herself, she blinked and found Damien. "Unpleasant." She swallowed. "Is not accurate. So you know, for next time this happens. Use a word like horrible or sickening. Or both." Running a hand over her hair, she tried to ignore Kin's worried gaze as she settled on the smooth stoney ground. With direction from Damien, she laid down, reaching her hand outside the line of nothingness.

Her heart wouldn't slow, her breath uneven. "Will this work?"

Damien took her hand, sandwiching it between his palms. "Not ideal, but it'll work all the same." He poked his index finger into different parts of her palm as if trying to find a specific muscle. He found the most tender spot and jammed his thumb down, making her flinch and bite her lip.

"Please, Amarie... remember when you wake up." Kin moved to where she could see him. "I'm not a Shade anymore. I gave it all up. And I only want to protect you."

A Shade?

Her mind whirled as Damien's Art stirred against hers.

"What's a Shade?" But before anyone could answer her, a vice tore her from her body. She gasped, closing her eyes as the world tilted on a foreign axis. Colors blurred, the air swimming around her face. She took short, shallow breaths, cringing at the bodiless sensation.

Is this how it's supposed to feel?

Amarie opened her mouth to ask, but something jerked her sideways and the world fell away.

It reemerged in a wave of heat, blasting from an inferno nearby. The acrid smoke stung her lungs, burdened further by her screams. The scene shifted to sword fighting, but with a man who cared for her. Then to another escape as she ran out the back door of a home and into the wilderness alone. Her feet smarted with each step, carrying her deep into the woods.

Then up stairs. Many, many stairs, where a breath later she stared at Kin's face. The library. The beach. The Delphi Estate and the desperate ride to Lungaz. It flooded her, cracking her back and forth like a whip between joy and agony.

Kin. Alana. Talon. Her heart fractured, stilling to a deathly pause when Trist's face emerged.

Amarie tried to scream, to yell, to shout at Damien to stop. Stop everything. She didn't want to remember. Not everything. Not this.

Anything but this.

The shadow tendrils lashed at her legs, tearing her flesh and spilling her blood. She kicked at the dirt floor as her strength waned. It waned and waned until she begged for it to stop.

Kill me, please.

Death came in a peaceful embrace, taking her to her mother for a moment of ease. Before it all began again, showing her the life she'd lived after death. The loss of Kin and then her father.

Joy blossomed with Talon, with her pregnancy, only to be shattered. Darkness fell over her in a suffocating blanket. No light penetrated the shadows as she last glimpsed her daughter playing with her new family, then she fled on Viento, her Art wildly free around her. The darkness engulfed her further, hovering over her as she raced over ice on horseback. It snarled and growled behind her, smothering her senses until the rest faded away and Slumber took hold.

But Slumber wasn't the end.

The auer woke her, and Kalstacia was there. Her memories raced through her training. Her years of training in Eralas, and all the knowledge they bestowed on her. Then, Slumber, again.

The world tilted again as she felt her body thrown, as if striking the stone of Hoult's broken remains. Amarie gasped, jerking upright in a start, and scrambled away from Damien. Away from the desolate grey until her hands and knees hit grass again. She gaped at the man, tears streaking her cheeks as she fought to catch her breath. "Where is he?" Her voice was raspy, and she realized she must have been screaming while her memories returned.

Damien rushed to his feet, glancing around before giving a short relieved sigh. "We agreed he shouldn't be here when you came to. In case..." His shoulders sagged, a bead of sweat on his brow beneath the line of his golden hair. "Remember what we told you before?"

Amarie snarled, rising to her feet with unsteady knees. She tried to recall the words, but they were lost behind curtains of pain. "That he's not a Shade anymore?"

"He's not. Kin came to me and asked me to sever the connection between him and Uriel. He hasn't been a Shade for a while now." Damien watched her, taking a wary step back.

"How long has it been since I went into Slumber?" Amarie pushed the thoughts of Kin aside, seeing only her daughter's icy blue eyes. "How long?"

"Twenty years and a few months."

A knife jabbed between her ribs, and she let out a sob, turning from him. She covered her mouth with her palm, closing her eyes. The emotions raked through her. Grief and hope. And all the questions. Ahria. Talon. Where were they? Did they live?

"I'm sorry." Genuine remorse touched Damien's tone.

"I... I didn't know. About... your daughter."

She whirled to face him. "No." Shaking her head, she pointed at him. "You know nothing. And you will *say* nothing about it. About her."

He lifted his hands into the air. "Nothing. I know I can't possibly understand. But I'm sorry." He looked over his shoulder back up the hill towards the horses, where Kin must have gone. "But you should talk to Kin."

Amarie set her jaw. "I have nothing to say to him, about this or otherwise."

"Maybe not, but this is a whole lot more complicated than whatever happened between you two. This is about Uriel and a whole mess of things you missed while you were in Slumber."

Her power sparked at her fingertips, but she kept it at bay. It was easier now—to control. Now that she knew how to use her power thanks to the years of auer training. A lack of memories had made her an excellent student.

I know how to wield it. They taught me.

"And what does Uriel's mess have to do with me?" Amarie battled to keep her emotions in check, hardly able to hold her hands steady with the knowledge Kin was so close. So close. They'd been traveling together for nearly a week, now, unknowingly.

Her stomach wrenched.

"Plenty, the least of which being that you nearly killed my

wife twenty years ago when you ran across this strait together." Damien gestured at the ocean before taking a calming breath.

"Mira is your wife?" Amarie recalled the spirited woman who'd saved her in more ways than one. "Where is she?"

"Home, for now. With our children. But you'll see her again soon if you're willing to keep hearing me out."

She shook her head, tilting her chin down. "I can't. I mean... I will. I will hear you out, but... I can't breathe." Her next inhale lodged in her throat and she choked, lungs too tight to let air in.

Damien fell silent as she closed her burning eyes.

She focused on her fingers first, touching one to her thumb and then digging her nail into the pad. The small amount of pain helped center her. "I don't understand how this has to do with Uriel if Kin is no longer a Shade."

"There's a way to imprison him. It was done before. And we need the Berylian Key to do it. Divided, but that's something we can figure out later." He waved his hand, his eyes distractedly flicking up the hill again. "Uriel is a far larger threat to this world than to you or Kin. I'd think you'd realize that considering the interaction you had with him. You, of all people, should know the power he's capable of."

Giving him a deadpan look, she huffed. "And my power only strengthened him, so forgive me for not understanding my role in all this." The words were sharper than she intended.

"You might have strengthened him, but you can also strengthen others. You can pour that unfathomable energy into other wielders of the Art. Like me... like Rae. Like Matthias."

"Rae? Matthias?" She scrunched her brow, failing to recall the names within her returned memories.

"Other pieces of the puzzle. Mira is Rae, she wasn't traveling by her real name with you. She's a little too well known, here in Helgath."

"Gods," she murmured, sinking to her knees again. "This is too much."

"We can take it slow with the rest, but you need to know that whether or not you like it... this involves you. And Kin. You're the only chance we have at imprisoning him." Damien let out a slow breath.

"I'm not promising you anything. Not yet." Amarie looked at him. "I have a choice."

"You do have a choice, and I won't force you." Damien rotated his shoulders, his body sagging more with lethargy he'd been hiding. "I need you to understand what is at stake. But it can wait, for now. As long as you promise not to run away."

The tension in her shoulders eased, and she sat on her feet while giving him a sardonic look. "You're not getting any promises from me, remember?" She eyed the weariness in him and took a deep breath. "In the meantime, as a token of my appreciation... may I restore you?" Holding out a hand, she didn't move from her spot in the grass.

He looked at her hand for a moment before he accepted, and she poured energy into him.

Chapter 31

STOMACH GRUMBLING, CONRAD RESTRAINED THE temptation to jump from behind his desk and dash back to his chambers, where lunch and Ahria would be waiting for him. Already looking forward to an afternoon with few trials, he tried to avoid the pointed look Wendelin gave him as he started towards the door.

She must have sensed his attempt to avoid her, and stepped directly into his path. "May I have a word, your highness?"

"I doubt you'll give me much choice in the matter, Chancellor." Conrad pushed his sleeves up before unbuttoning the formal tunic tight at his neck.

"I apologize for the timing," she murmured, glancing behind her to ensure the rest of the staff had departed for lunch. "With your late arrival this morning, I had no chance to tell you first thing. But an unsettling rumor has reached my ears, and it is in your best interest to deal with it immediately."

"Rumors will happen. Ziona hasn't had a royal family for a long time. We're bound to be a focus of curiosity and stories. We can't quash all of them."

Wendelin flattened her lips into a line. "Perhaps not, but ones that jeopardize the trust our nation has in the crown concern us all."

He crossed his arms, but a flicker of worry boiled behind the stoic expression he hardened. "What is it?"

"I've heard a few whispers about a commoner with a lust for power courting you with the intention of stealing the queen's crown." She kept her voice low. "The rumor could affect your mother's life, should the woman succeed." When he opened his mouth to respond, she held up a hand and continued. "I know it's ridiculous, and you'd never be so daft. But the point is the people will never trust a queen who infiltrated a palace, and if you don't *squash* this rumor, any potential bride may be subject to the consequences."

His frown deepened. "That rumor *is* ridiculous. You do seem to forget, however, that my mother and I came from a common life before this, Chancellor. Not all who come from less fortunate situations are desperate for power and a kingdom." He wanted to tell Wendelin straight out how insane it sounded that Ahria would be attempting such things. They hadn't yet made their relationship public, but the plans were set. It was soon to no longer be rumor, but known. And this suggestion that she was somehow also a threat to his mother? He wanted to laugh in the chancellor's face.

Wendelin rolled her eyes. "Did you want me to keep it to myself next time there's a rumored threat on your mother's life, then?" She shook her head, huffing as she turned away. "You're welcome."

As she pushed through the doors of the judiciary chamber, Conrad grumbled and rubbed his brow. He considered if the rumor was purposely directed at Ahria, and regardless of how secretive they thought they were, someone knew something romantic was brewing between them. It felt deliberate, and encouraged a rise of anger in his chest. It couldn't be farther from the truth, considering Ahria's own hesitance for the position.

His mind ran with possibilities of who might have had motivation to turn people against Ahria with their coming announcement. He had no desire to change their plans. They'd waited long enough.

As he nodded to his guards, they gave him a subtle acknowledgement back. They both already knew, though he'd requested they keep the amount of time he spent with Ahria in his chambers to themselves. Grettin wouldn't speak, and her authority over Jelzo would ensure her loyalty as well. Yet, he still found himself wondering if it might have been them to help kindle the rumor.

Ahria placed a covered platter from the food cart onto the table in the windowed corner of the room. Open doors to the balcony beyond let in the warm breeze of the river canyon, swaying the gauzy curtains behind her like an Art-laden aura.

She looked up at his entrance and smiled. "How was your morning?"

Andi lay curled on the bed, muzzle on her paws. Her ears twitched at his arrival, but she lazily opened one eye before rolling onto her side with a groan.

He couldn't help but smile back at Ahria, closing the door behind him. "Mostly uneventful. Petty thefts and some upset farmers." He eyed Andi before crossing to the table. "Looks like you managed to tire out Andi quite efficiently this morning."

"We went for a forest run." She smoothed a hand over her hair, which still held a wet heaviness to it from her bath.

"Wish I could have joined." He wrapped a hand around her waist, kissing the dampness of her hair near her temple before his growling stomach urged him towards his chair, already positioned close to hers.

She lifted the cover off the platter, revealing a stack of sandwiches. Not just simple meat and cheese like he was used to, but fancy compilations of cured meats, pickled and fresh vegetables, spreads, and artisan breads.

He raised an eyebrow as he sat. "You trying to civilize me or something?" He reached for the water pitcher, filling each of their crystal glasses.

"On the contrary, I asked for the usual. I think Jelzo put in a word to the cook to make us something less boring." She sat, taking a sandwich off the top.

"I'm going to just pick it all off, anyway."

"Don't do that." She scowled at him. "At least try it before you dismantle all the hard work." She bit her food, pausing as she chewed to focus on the taste.

Picking up one of the densely packed sandwiches, he studied the various vegetables and the vibrant color they brought to it. He'd tried all of the additions before, having known it was inappropriate to pick and choose what parts of an already assembled meal to discard with an audience. But in his own room, he'd grown accustomed to enjoying what he already knew he liked best.

A little variety won't kill me.

"It's actually really good." Ahria reached for another sandwich half, and he furrowed his brow at her.

"Where do you put it all?" He smirked as he plucked the tomato out of his sandwich and deposited it on the plate.

She blinked at him, shrugging. "I'm hungry. I haven't eaten since they served coffee and biscuits."

"That was an hour ago."

"Well, see. I went a whole hour without eating." Ahria grinned.

Conrad picked up the rejected tomato slice and deposited it on her plate. "There, more for you."

She made a face. "I don't want your scraps." Picking up the red slice, she tossed it back to his plate. "Maybe you can convince Andi to eat it later."

"There isn't anything that dog won't eat." He considered pulling out more from his sandwich with a glance at it, but took a bite instead. She'd been right that it did taste quite good as it was. "Did you want to go for a walk to the harbor this afternoon? I only have a few trials left for the day."

Ahria tilted her head, swallowing her bite. "You think that's wise, when we're waiting until tonight to announce our..." She motioned between them. "Involvement?"

He pursed his lips, recalling the rumor that he'd forgotten amid his hunger and happiness to see her again. "I have no second thoughts about us, but you're right that we should be cautious. I heard a new rumor today that's a little troubling." He took the last bite of his meal, reaching for another as she chose a third piece off the still impressive stack.

"What is it?"

"Someone has decided that I am currently involved with a power hungry commoner that is using me to get to the throne." Conrad added the tomato from the new sandwich on top of the other.

Ahria coughed, sipped from her water, and set her sandwich down. "And *I'm* that power hungry commoner?" She frowned. "No one even knows about us."

"No names were said, obviously, but it's not great timing with our announcement tonight. It's probably some prospect of mine that's jealous that I won't follow through with any social calls. But Wendelin made it sound like people were thinking this commoner plans to murder the queen to quicken her ascent to the throne after ensnaring me."

Ahria's gaze grew distant as it lowered to an invisible spot on the table. She didn't speak, chewing her lower lip.

"Don't worry." He reached across the short distance between them and put a hand on her arm. "The rumor is just that. And it doesn't change anything."

"It's not just a rumor." She lifted her gaze to his and let out a breath. "It's Jaqi. She's trying to get to me, which is stupid, since if I'm with you, I'm obviously not with Vaeler."

"How do you know it's her?"

"That night you came to the tavern, she accused me of that exact scenario. Even with killing the queen, she said I'd use one of my many daggers." Ahria looked away again, thinking. "She said that after convincing Vaeler to be with me, I got bored and needed something more exciting. So I threw him away for a prince. It's also not the first time she's threatened to burn my life to the ground."

"What is with that woman?" Conrad frowned. "I don't understand people who would knowingly want to spread lies. Lies are what led our country down such a dark path when the monarchy was first unseated."

Ahria's chair groaned as she stood without reaching for her food again. "I have to go talk to her and Evelyn."

"Right now?" Conrad scooted his own chair back, abandoning the last bites of his sandwich on his plate.

She looked at him, shoulders slouching. "I'm sorry. I know we were supposed to relax and have lunch, but if she's out there trying to sabotage my life, I can't do nothing. I'll be back before dinner, I promise."

"Hold up, we need to think more about this." Conrad stood, stepping to her. "I agree, she needs to be confronted, but it needs to be done in a way that makes sure she doesn't just do this again later. And so it doesn't jeopardize what we have." He slipped his hand into hers, bringing her knuckles to his lips. "She needs to see how damaging her rumors are to more than just you."

Ahria leaned into him, her lips twitching with a smile. "Is my prince wanting to come with?"

"I do." He kissed her hand again. "People are already talking, so I think it's important we face this rumor head on and out loud. Make it clear exactly how ridiculous it is, and who started it. It's time for Jaqi to get a taste of her own medicine, don't you think?"

Nodding, Ahria set her face in determination and checked her wrists, shoulder blades, and waist for her hilts. They were subtle movements, a finger tap, a shrug, and a slight shift of her vest. He'd learned her tells for where she kept her blades over the weeks .

"I can fight my own battles, but I won't refuse the extra muscle for show." She stepped back, eyeing him from head to toe with a playful expression. "Will the palace let you leave unescorted?"

"Absolutely not." Conrad smirked, but shrugged. "So you'll have plenty of muscle. And it'll make it especially clear to Jaqi that we mean business with the visit." He moved back to the table, plucking up his plate before setting it onto the floor.

Andi leapt off the bed in a flurry as the ceramic clunked onto the rug.

"Didn't you have something with your father this afternoon?" Conrad crossed the room to where his sword leaned against the bedside table. He still hadn't gotten used to the gold-encrusted hilt, but he'd been told it was his great-great grandfather's.

Ahria paused in her stride towards the door. "I do. I'll have Jelzo get a message to him that I might be late and where I'm going in case he needs me."

"And I'll have Grettin tell Wendelin that we will be having

an extended lunch. I'll return to finish up the last cases before dinner tonight." He buckled the sword to his waist as he crossed to her. Kissing her forehead, he paused to play with a strand of her hair. "We will still have our evening."

She eyed his mouth with deliberate intensity before teasing him with the hint of a kiss. "Yes, we will."

Armor clanked behind them, in rhythm with the gait of the horses. Conrad rode in front with Ahria, five royal guards as their escort to the residential district. People stopped and watched as they passed, sometimes waving at the prince or shouting their greetings.

Halfway down Cape Street, Ahria motioned with her chin. "Number eighty-six, there." Her eyes narrowed. "The cart isn't here, so a few of them must be working a show or something. But Jaqi doesn't usually work during the matinees."

Conrad nodded before he dismounted, giving a subtle gesture to the commander of the squad, who turned her horse around to address the back of the group.

Ahria's boots hit the cobblestone a breath later. "Let me go first. Otherwise Evelyn might think we're being raided." She pulled a key from her cloak.

"Does the troupe often get raided?" Conrad gave her an amused smirk.

Color touched her cheeks. "Not often?" She gave him a sheepish smile in return. "They don't get involved in illegal activity, and if they ever did, I'm sure they had good reason. But there are a few sticky fingers among them."

"Thus, Vaeler being so practiced at breaking people out of prison." Conrad smoothed his formal tunic, buttoned to the top now that he was in public.

Ahria shrugged. "Vaeler is talented at many things. Not the lute, though."

"Don't worry, I'm willing to give the man a full pardon for any crimes after all he's done for you." Conrad stepped beside her, looking up at the front door of the townhouse she'd stayed in for the months he'd been looking for her. He'd never looked in the more wealthy residential area, and chided himself for not even considering Ahria may have found a way to be more comfortable in her stay. "I'll be here, acting as the scary, powerful royal who could make Jaqi's life a living hell. I'll only step in if you need me."

She grinned. "Thank you." Facing the townhouse, she sucked in a breath. "Here goes." Leaving his side, she jogged through the front gate and climbed the short stack of stairs to the front door.

He watched as she passed the rows of flower pots on either side of the stairs, his eyes lingering behind on the sun-withered plants. Townhouse eighty-six didn't look horribly different from the rest on the row, though something seemed dreary about it.

Movement at the townhouse next door caught his eye, and he considered one of the neighbors may have seen the royal escort and grown curious. But the man bustled down his stairs, paying no heed to the royal guards. He stopped in front of his home, gaping back at it. He reached to touch the withered bush, cursing quietly with a look of confusion in his eyes.

Conrad looked back to Ahria as she reached the top of the stairs, and noted that the troupe's home also suffered from dead fauna at their front. The flower boxes, which he'd imagined should have matched the homes across the street with vibrant pink and white blooms, were dry and grey.

Lifting her key to the lock, Ahria froze. She stared at the knob for so long that Conrad nearly said something, but then she pocketed the key.

Her hand lifted again, gently touching the door and pushing it open. "Conrad." She stepped back, the heel of her boot hanging off the top step.

He tensed, his hand slipping to the hilt of his sword.

Something's wrong.

She glanced at him, drew the dagger from her lower back, and charged inside, shouting, "Vaeler?"

"Shit." Conrad lunged, withdrawing his sword as he charged up the stairs after her. His heart pounded, mind replaying the tone of Ahria's voice saying his name. The armor of the guards clanked as they moved with him, the commander shouting something, but Conrad couldn't understand it over the repetition of Ahria's voice in his mind.

When he reached the door, he realized what must have caught her attention. The broken lock, busted inward.

The door stood ajar from her entrance, but had bounced back off the wall to nearly close again. The smell wafted from the halls within. It struck him like a physical blow, all iron and sulfur. He almost gagged, but threw the door open with his shoulder before one of his guards even made it halfway up the stairs.

Blood coated the floors, splattered on the walls. The gruesome scene was nothing like anything he'd ever seen before, but there were no bodies. No sign of anyone, living or dead. Just blood. So much that he'd almost thought the walls were painted red except for the rare splotches of white plaster.

Ahria's boot prints in the muck led up the stairs, and his stomach knotted. "Ahria!"

Footsteps sounded from above, and she rushed down the stairs to meet him. Blood marred her hands, but not her blade. "It's everywhere, in all the beds. Like someone came in when they were all sleeping..." Her voice cracked, and she sniffed, holding the back of her arm to her face. "But where are they?" As if answering her own question, her gaze drifted to the stairs leading to the basement. She shuddered, tears gathering on her lower lids. She started to move towards them, but Conrad reached to stop her.

Someone grabbed Conrad's arm before he could catch Ahria, and his heart pounded as he instinctively twisted free of his guard's grip.

"Your highness." The Commander's eyes widened as she looked past him to the grisly scene of the hall. She drew a sword from her waist as she pushed past Conrad, placing herself between him and the rest of the house, including Ahria. "You, upstairs." She addressed the next guard who entered, then the next two. "And you both go downstairs. Rell, get word to the palace that we have a murder and need immediate assistance. Prince, Miss Xylata, I must ask you both return outside while we check for any remaining threats."

The two guards rushed past Conrad, their faces grim beneath their helmets. One stood back while the other opened the door to the basement, both disappearing through the doorway in a matter of moments without hesitation.

Rell rushed back down the stairs outside.

The commander looked at Ahria. "How many people live here?"

"Uhh," Ahria stammered. "Seven. No. Eight." She looked down, and Conrad followed her gaze to a pair of ruddy boots. "Those are Vaeler's boots," she whispered, then raised her voice again. "Vaeler!"

Conrad, still gripping his sword, held out a hand to her in desperation. "Ahria, come outside with me. Commander Vorekai will handle this." Standing in the front doorway, with the rot and blood stuck in his nose, he felt trapped.

Ahria nodded, her shoulders shaking as tears streamed down her face. She seemed rooted in place near the basement doorway. "Where are they?"

A shout echoed from behind her, followed by a crash in the basement, and the commander reeled around. "Get out, now!" she shouted at Conrad, pointing to the front door behind them. The sunlight of midday felt so far away, the cloud of tragedy hanging like a heavy noose.

Conrad lunged towards the basement stairs, snatching Ahria's wrist. His back squelched against the hallway wall as he pulled Ahria to his chest, instinctively recoiling as something flickered in the corner of his eye on the hallway wall. Another shout rose from the basement, followed by a sickening crunch that silenced it.

The commander lifted her sword to a ready stance and barreled down the basement stairs as the guard who'd gone to the second floor rushed past him and Ahria to join whatever was happening below.

The house shuddered with a crack as black vines exploded from the basement doorway, writhing like tentacles of some wicked sea creature latching onto a ship. But instead of a hull, they encircled the final guard, and Conrad heard her bones snap beneath the pressure.

We need to get out of here.

Conrad grabbed Ahria, pulling her towards the door, and she provided no resistance. His foot slipped along the soaked carpet, but he kept himself upright as his shoulder crashed into the wall beside the door.

Ahria grabbed his upper arm. "Go, go."

He could almost reach the door, almost feel the sun hit his skin again.

One more step, but...

Strands of darkness coursed like snakes over the walls, and the front door slammed shut.

Chapter 32

AMARIE WATCHED THE BRIGHTNESS RETURN to Damien's eyes and his chest rose at a faster pace. "Feel better?" She withdrew her hand as he nodded. Her eyes drifted down to the thin lines of the runic tattoo beneath the collar of his shirt. She wondered how it was possible Kin had fallen under Damien's care at the same time she'd been helping Mira make it to Eralas.

Helping Mira...

The truth knocked the air from her lungs.

Mira claimed a Shade was after her, and Amarie had told her to go to Eralas.

Did I take her there? Or did she trick me into going there myself?

Amarie glared at him. "You planned this from the

beginning, didn't you? Your wife finding me wasn't a coincidence, not when you had Kin with you."

As pieces fell together, the illusion of what Mira had been shattered. Her comments about having enough rebels in her life and how she'd been uninterested in the soldiers. All those rings she wore.

She was married. Married to the man who'd been caring for Kin.

Amarie's head buzzed with growing anger. "That's what it was, wasn't it? Kin told you who I was and you sent your wife to lead me to Eralas." The words poured out of her in a rush, and she struggled to catch up with her own realizations. "Tell me. Was Kin already there, in Slumber, when I chose it, too? When we raced across the strait..."

Kin told Damien my secret.

He frowned, but didn't speak. He seemed to be waiting as his breathing evened. Like he knew she was still putting things together.

"You were there. When we reached Eralas after fighting Uriel. You were at the docks...You and... another." Cringing, she closed her eyes, her memory of those events blurred and unstable. "Gods, did she even have a Shade after her? Or did I..."

"We didn't feel like we had another choice. After we sensed you without a hiding aura in Olsa, you were running towards suicide in Helgath. The country wasn't exactly in the most stable political situation at the time. And in Kin's defense, he tried desperately not to tell me. But it's difficult to keep secrets from someone who can sense your thoughts and emotions."

Amarie turned her back to him, her conversations with Mira... With Rae, replaying over in her mind.

"Rae cared a great deal for you, Amarie. That friendship wasn't fake."

"I never even knew her name," she whispered, facing him again. "Rae Lanoret. Damien... You *were* that rebel on the posters, weren't you? The deserter who was rallying forces for a new proxiet."

Damien scratched the back of his head. "Guess that was like yesterday for you. Yes, that's me. But things were infinitely more complicated than simply being a deserter." He gestured at his arm, which she recalled seeing glow. "But if anyone can relate to ancient powers being bestowed on you without your choice, it'd be you."

She narrowed her eyes, tilting her head. "I don't expect a history lesson in this moment, but tell me, did you succeed in your cause? Is Helgath under a new king?"

He smiled as he nodded. "We did. And King Jarrod Martox has led Helgath to a path of being not only prosperous, but also one of the more benevolent countries in Pantracia. People now *want* to live here, rather than how it used to be."

Amarie sighed, a heaviness touching her heart. Helgath had never been her favorite place, but it had given her her horse, if nothing else.

Viento would be long gone, and the hole her bond with him left behind suddenly gaped in a great chasm.

I hope Ahria grew up with him.

Pushing the emotion into a box to examine more closely later, Amarie rolled her shoulders. As she lifted her chin, her whole body stiffened at the man standing out of earshot on a distant hill.

He faced them, probably wondering if his return would be welcome.

It made her heart race.

"I suppose I need to hear him out," Amarie muttered, eyes trained on Kin. The former Shade. Her former lover. Kin. She'd traveled for days with him unknowingly, and something in her chest ached for that bond to return. The bond that could only be borne out of the unknowing.

But there's no forgetting now.

"I'd appreciate it if you gave him a chance." Damien glanced over his shoulder before looking back at Amarie. "I know you have every reason to be angry with him, but I promise you, when he came to me and asked me to help sever him from Uriel's power... you were his reason for all the suffering he endured. It was a painful process. And we'll need both of you for what is coming."

"Will you give us a little space?" Amarie shook her head. "Maybe a lot of space. Voices carry over these hills, as does the Art." Giving him a pointed look, she steeled herself against looking at Kin again as the man began a slow approach.

"Should I try to erect a shield around Hoult? They just rebuilt it about a mile north..." He gave her a wry smile.

Amarie shot him an incredulous look, forcing her lips not to twitch into a smile. "Seriously?"

"Take all the time you need." Damien started to back up the hill. "I'll come check in after a few hours. But you and I will definitely need to speak further about this Uriel business." His expression hardened. "I'd appreciate it if you didn't make it hard for me to find you again."

She quirked an eyebrow at him. "Now I kind of want to, just to see if you can."

"There are many benefits to being a Rahn'ka."

"And you'll tell me them all later, I'm sure."

He put a hand on his chest, over his heart. "I'll keep no secrets if you agree to the same." A high stakes request. He looked behind as Kin reached earshot, giving him a quick nod of greeting. "I'll give you that time now." He turned, and Kin barely acknowledged the man as he jogged past up the hill.

Kin's steel eyes focused on her. Bored into her. Seeing each part of her the way he always had, and it unnerved her. Forced her to assemble an invisible wall around herself. Her emotions. It required no Art, but felt like it should.

She clenched her jaw, refusing to be the first to speak.

Silence hovered between them as Kin stopped five feet away from her, as if a barrier had formed in front of him. He watched her, a fear in his eyes she didn't recognize. "I'm... so sorry, Amarie. For everything, I need you to know that I wish I could take all of it back. Change how all of it happened."

His apology only lit fire in her gut, but he didn't know the truth. He couldn't know. And she'd be damned if she told him.

"Berating you for sleeping with me and then leaving me alone in the wilderness hardly feels like a good use of my breath. Not when there are bigger things at stake. Not when I've suffered worse losses since then." Amarie looked away, the intensity of his gaze too much under her veiled words.

"Yes, you have." Kin's voice quieted. "Your father... he loved you so much."

Her heart cracked. "My father is dead."

"I know. But he asked me to tell you. It was the last thing he said before..." His gaze dropped to the ground at her feet. His hand slipped into one of the outer pockets of his satchel. He drew something out, then extended his hand to her.

Amarie stepped back, spine straightening as she eyed the gold ring in his palm. The ring he'd sold and she'd stolen back. Given back. But it was never his.

"How did you get that?" She couldn't bring herself to take it. To touch it.

"Deylan and I buried your father after getting him out of Rylorn."

Heat built behind her eyes. "I don't understand. You weren't there. I found his body, but..."

"I was there. I had tried to warn Deylan and Kalpheus before the soldiers arrived, but I didn't make it in time. Your father told me to get Deylan out, and I did. But I didn't make it in time, *again*, before the torturer had already done too much damage." Emotion coated his tone.

As much as she didn't want to believe it, he had no other way to know the things he did. And at his visible display of regret...

Amarie shook her head, looking at the ring through blurred eyes before finally taking it without touching Kin's skin. He'd buried her father. Buried him. The very thing she'd tried to go back and do. Struggled against Talon for, hoping to find peace for her dead father.

Gratitude lingered on her tongue, but she couldn't voice it. "Deylan never told me."

"I'm glad he didn't. And that Talon didn't mention seeing me in that room, either. I'd already done enough damage at that point." Kin's jaw tensed as he lowered his hand to his side. "I'd hoped Talon would take care of you. Where was he when you were in Olsa? I thought you were in Eralas. But most of that time is a haze in my memory." He twisted his hand in the air near the side of his head. "Damien's... treatment left it all jumbled."

The mentions of Talon made Amarie's head spin. The auer had seen Kin and not told her. Not even hinted that the Shade had been there.

"I don't know," she breathed. "He promised he'd meet me in Olsa but never showed up." She kept her voice flat. Even. If Kin didn't know about their romantic relationship, there was no point in telling him now.

Kin's shoulders sagged as he pushed his satchel behind his back, his hands playing along the strap diagonal across his chest. "I thought you'd be safe from *him,* from Uriel, in Eralas. I hated asking it of Talon. Did he never take you there?"

Amarie let out a breath, hesitating in telling Kin the details. "He did," she murmured, and told him the rest. The training. How they'd been found. How she'd bargained with the auer to spare him. But she said nothing of the following events.

Kin isn't Ahria's father.

Even as she thought it, she knew it wasn't true. It'd always been true, but not in the sense that mattered. Had Talon returned to Olsa for Ahria? A question she couldn't ask.

"I'm glad he was able to help you learn how to control it." He chewed his lower lip for a moment before nodding again. "It seemed like you had complete control over it in that mine.

Nothing like how I remember it before." He met her eyes, still so full of hope and something else. "You always deserved to have a better understanding of it."

"Well, now I do." Amarie crossed her arms, and just like that, they were standing in the gazebo by the lake at the Delphi Estate. But too much had changed since then. "I know Damien says we must work together, and while I believe his cause is just, it doesn't mean we need to be friends."

"I understand, even if I wish I didn't." Kin tugged on the satchel strap, still adjusting to it as if he hadn't done so the entire week before the restoration of their memories.

She looked at him, so different in the lighter colored clothes and inexpensive leathers. His chin had the familiar shadow of his stubble, not quite a beard.

"Let me see your arm." Amarie had glimpsed it while they'd been strangers, but that wasn't enough. "The mark. Let me see." She couldn't feel any inkling of the Art from him. Not even a wisp.

Kin stretched out his right arm, where the sleeve was folded near his elbow. He pushed it up further, even though the scar was already exposed. It was thick, hiding any sign of the black ink that'd been beneath it. It spiderwebbed over his skin like a wicked burn, but denser. As if it covered what was beneath, rather than replaced it.

Amarie almost reached for it, her crossed arms relaxing.

She gestured for him to stop and fell silent as he lowered his arm. Turning sideways, she kept him in her peripheral vision. There were so many more questions, but her voice refused to make a sound. Her mouth refused to open. It felt like a ripple in time to be standing with him, especially with the tug of her insides to stand closer. Remnants left over from before regaining herself.

"What did Damien tell you?" Kin whispered, as if tentative to break the silence. "I assume he must have said something in my favor since you're still here."

"He wants me to give you a chance." Amarie stared at the horizon. "But he doesn't have the whole story, regardless of what he saw of my memories."

"I'm pretty sure that's the problem with the whole of Pantracia. No one has the whole story... ever." He shifted, crossing his arms then almost immediately uncrossing them. "I still have a lot of questions, too. But that's the way it's always been with us." He started to give a half smile, but it faded as quickly as it'd come. "I don't want it to be like that, Amarie. But I also understand that I will have to work my ass off to gain any trust back. I know we're not friends, but I hope we won't be enemies."

Amarie let out a mirthless laugh. "Isn't that what you said, though? That we *should* be enemies. You may not be a Shade, for now, but I can't see how I could ever trust you." She touched her stomach before lowering her hand to her side. "How I could ever trust..."

Anyone.

The word hovered in the air, but she couldn't say it. So she let her voice trail off, looking at the ground. The stark line between life and desolation. The line she'd created. Something still remained of that shattered, heartbroken woman within her, but her rage had dimmed post-Slumber. All she felt was tired of it all.

"Ask me anything." Kin extended his hands. "I kept too many secrets from you for too long. But I never *lied*. Even if keeping silent was just as bad."

Her eyes slid to him with calm restraint. "What happened to the Shade..." She swallowed. "To Trist?"

"I tracked her to Rylorn after I... left." He swallowed and took a deep breath. "Your father and brother had beaten me to catching her, which is how I first found them. I put my sword through her chest. For what she did to you. She's dead."

Even if she'd wanted to deny the relief the news brought her, she couldn't have. It lightened her chest. Finally, she allowed the words to touch her lips, even if her voice sounded stiff. "Thank you." She pushed her father's ring into her pocket.

"I definitely don't deserve any thanks. I should have done more to protect you. I just..." He bowed his head, body trembling before he seemed to regain control. "I didn't know.

I didn't know or understand the threat."

An unexpected surge of fury swirled in her gut. "I don't need protectors," she ground out. "I need people to protect me as much as I need a saddle on a horse. It's unnecessary, especially now."

He flinched, somehow seeming smaller even though he towered over her. "Then I should have told you more. Armed you better. I've always known you were capable of protecting yourself, ever since the first day we met. But I sure as hells didn't make it any easier on you with all the secrets. I should have—"

"Stop." Cool indifference took over her tone, so cold it made her hate herself a little more. She softened her voice. "It doesn't matter, Kin." Saying his name made her roll her shoulders. "It's all over and done with now. We just need to imprison Uriel and then we never need to see each other again." Forcing her feet to move as his eyes widened, she strode past him in the direction Damien had gone and instantly regretted it. Turning her head away, she tried to ignore his warm scent and the way it beckoned to her.

Kin turned after her. "Wait." His hand grazed her wrist, but he pulled back quickly, keeping his hands exposed near his chest. "Say that again."

Pausing her gait, she looked up at him. At the proximity, his icy eyes engulfed her. Ahria's eyes. For a moment, she lost herself.

What does she look like now?

Amarie wondered where she was, if she'd had a happy childhood. If she'd lived a full life thus far, and what she knew about her mother. Her bloodline. If she knew of the faction. That she was adopted. Did Talon go back to her? The thoughts plagued her. The not knowing.

"Amarie." Kin's cool voice pulled her back. "What did you just say about Uriel?"

She blinked, refocusing on him. "We're going to imprison him for the rest of eternity and Damien needs us to accomplish it. Us and others."

Kin's eyes jerked over her shoulder up the hill, but then returned abruptly to her. "What?" His chest heaved as if in sudden panic. "How?"

Amarie shrugged, narrowing her eyes at his reaction. "I don't know the details, but I'd bet I'm destined to serve as some kind of power source. His wife manipulated me into going to Eralas again, which is how I ended up in Slumber."

"His wife?" Kin shot another look up the hill, this one more dangerous than the last. His frown grew deeper, his jaw tightening just as it had that night they'd argued in the woods before Ormon's attack.

"I'd like to be angry, but she did save my life," Amarie muttered. "Turns out our Rahn'ka and his other half have big plans."

The leather strap of Kin's satchel creaked under his tightening grip. "Son of a bitch." He turned, pacing a few steps away before he turned back. "This is the first I'm hearing about any of this."

"Gee, I wonder why." Amarie raised one eyebrow at him.

He gave her a confused look, but none of the anger faded from his eyes. "What?"

She rolled her eyes. "You're a Shade, remember? Why would he tell you, of all people, his plans?"

"Oh, I don't know, perhaps because I risked everything when I asked him to sever me from the power. Because I could have told Uriel exactly where he was after tracking him down, but I didn't. Besides, not a Shade anymore." He jutted his scarred arm out at her. "And that was one hell of a process. The man basically ripped into every facet of me, pretty sure he knew he could trust me. He *chose* not to."

"Still. Why risk the fate of Pantracia just to keep you in the loop?" Amarie ignored his arm, fixated on his eyes. "If it makes you feel better, I only learned this just now, too."

"Then we were both manipulated into giving up the last twenty years of our lives." He grimaced. "He lied."

Twenty years of Ahria's life.

Amarie shrugged again. "We've all lied." Turning away, she walked away again, needing to put distance between them before she told him every last detail of what had happened.

Heat remained in his tone. "I never lied to you." He called

after her. "And I know there's some small part of you, somewhere, that understands why I did what I did. Why I had to do it. But when Uriel gave me the task to bring him the Berylian Key..."

"Stop it!" Amarie whirled around. "Fuck that, Kin. You didn't *need* to do any of that. You didn't *need* to find me to save me from Trist. We all know how that went. And you certainly didn't need to—"

"No, Amarie. I did *need* to," he shouted as he advanced a step towards her, but stopped. "You clearly don't understand how I've always felt about you. How I still feel about you. Everything I did, every choice, every moment of pain and torture, was because I *love* you."

Her breath came faster, teeth so tightly clenched that her jaw ached. She could not fall into that trap again. Succumb to her desires and be near him. Touch him. It all seared through her like an inferno that'd never died.

"I moved on," she whispered. "And don't bother claiming you still love me. You don't even know me."

The visage of anger cracked, his shoulders dropping ever so slightly. "I will *always* love you. Even if you love someone else." His eyes met hers, a glassiness unfitting of him coating the steel blue. "Nothing can, or ever will, change that."

Fire burned behind her gaze, images of her dream from when she'd been pregnant flitting back into her mind. The dream of him touching her belly. The dream that had inadvertently almost killed Talon.

"You told me that once. In a dream." Her voice softened to a pained whisper. "But I do not love someone else, Kin. Not anymore. And never again." She hated how her voice shook, how it'd been twenty years and still Talon wasn't there. The irrational part of her wanted to damn him forever for it, but he'd likely have no way of knowing she again walked Pantracia.

Perhaps never wasn't fair. Twenty years had passed, sure, but not to them. Not to her. It all felt fresh, still. And the way he stared at her...

Her feet took an unwitting step towards him before she stopped herself. "I would have given... *anything*... for you to be there. But you weren't, and I don't care if that mark on your arm is all scarred over. You left me. I was the most vulnerable I'd *ever* been. And you left me." Tears streaked down her cheeks before she could try to stop them, but she didn't care. "You left me when I needed you most."

He closed his eyes in a pained blink before he looked at her face again, his eyes on her cheeks like he was forcing himself to feel the torment of her tears. "And I'll never forgive myself for that, either. I did leave you." His chest heaved. "I don't deserve another chance for what I did to you."

Amarie looked at the ground, running her tongue along the back of her teeth.

"I made so many mistakes." Kin sagged more, his head bowing as his dark hair shaded his expression.

Her arms wrapped around herself, but she stepped closer to him again. "Look," she breathed, her insides aching. "I'm not saying that this is another chance, but I think we're stuck together for the foreseeable future. I guess we'll see if you stick around."

Kin rolled his shoulders, forcing his head back up. His eyes were red, but had hardened to hide any tears that might have been there before. "You think Damien is telling the truth about this then, that there's a way to imprison Uriel?"

Amarie nodded. "Will you be our ally?"

"I'll enjoy seeing that monster's face when we slam the door on him."

A smile tugged at the corner of her mouth. "Good, because I think I'd like the chance to..." Her voice trailed off as her gaze wandered from Kin's face to the hills behind him. The direction opposite of where Damien had gone.

But there, on the crest of the hill, stood a broad-shouldered figure. Still as a statue.

And it sent a current of ice down her spine.

Chapter 33

AHRIA YANKED ON THE KNOB, but the townhome's front door wouldn't budge.

Shadow ensnared the hinges like brambles, locking them in place.

Conrad slid in beside her, jerking the iron handle. His sleeves strained over his muscles, and he groaned with a foot against the door frame.

A chuckle echoed from the basement.

A low, sinister laugh that made each and every hair over Ahria's body rise.

"Ahria..." A male voice called in the same throaty tone, sing-songing her name. "I'd like a word, if you'd be so kind."

Ahria met Conrad's gaze and whispered, "This is because of me?" She almost choked on the words, mind reeling with how she could have caused such bloodshed. Her gaze fell to the ground, to the pools of crimson that coated the wooden floors and smears along the walls. Vaeler's blood. Evelyn's. She even dreaded the thought of it being Jaqi's blood.

None of them deserved this.

Conrad's hand closed on her forearm, drawing her attention back to him as he shook his head. "Focus on getting out of here."

But her mind reeled as Conrad tried the door again. With no windows in the hallway near the front entrance, the closed study door to the left was their only salvation. As she reached for the handle, tar sprung over it like a snake strike and she recoiled with a yelp. The sulfurous scent of the dead plants stung her nose.

Talon always warned her how destruction could follow the Berylian Key. Destruction and violence and death.

But I'm not the Key. Not yet.

Tapping resounded from below, metal on metal, and she shuddered.

"I just want to talk... There is no need for more death." The man's voice sounded far too calm for someone who'd just murdered an entire household along with almost half a dozen guards.

The evidence rippled through her, settling within Talon's teachings. The shadow. The smell of rot. The dead garden.

"By the gods," Ahria whispered, meeting Conrad's wide

gaze. "It's a Shade." The word came out as little more than a breath. Talon had schooled her hard about the servants of Uriel who were a looming threat. They sought the Berylian Key, but that wasn't the only thing. Their master was hungry for power in any form. She couldn't risk the dark practitioner stumbling into the knowledge she held about the Key. She needed to play ignorant.

"Need some motivation?" The man purred the question from the darkness of the basement's depths, and her brow furrowed.

In a flash, onyx tendrils darted over the blood-stained rug at their feet and Conrad hit the floor with a grunt of pain. The shadow wrapped up his legs as he rolled, lashing with his sword at the darkness. The steel passed through as if whatever held him was a ghost. His weapon thunked into the baseboards of the stairs, and he didn't have time to grab the banister before the Shade pulled, whipping the prince towards the basement stairs.

"No!" she shrieked, and drew two daggers before charging after him. Flying down the stairs, she leapt over Conrad's fallen sword on the landing. As she rounded the corner, gripping the railing, she flung herself down faster. "Conrad!"

Darkness swallowed her as she entered the basement cellar, eyes struggling to adjust. All she could hear was her own breathing, and her heart pounding in her ears.

The sinister laughter echoed from the shadows

surrounding her as the Shade stepped into the beam of light streaming from the stairwell. The bottom of his dark cloak dragged wetly along the floor, and his boots squelched in more gore. "Looks like I have your attention now. Good girl."

"Where is he?" Ahria scanned the unfinished floor for the prince, but found nothing.

The Shade's hand twisted in a claw at his side, tugging at the air before Conrad's body slid limply towards him, twisting vines of black clinging to every inch of his body. "Be good and I won't add him to the pile." The Shade jerked his head towards the back corner of the basement, where she could only make out a vague mound of what she assumed to be her friends' bodies. Unceremoniously thrown on top of each other with limbs twisted in the wrong directions.

Her heart wrenched, legs shaking. "You killed them all," she whispered, fighting the urge to drop to her knees. "Why?"

"For you," he purred, the dim light making the age lines on his face sink further. He looked almost like a corpse himself, and memory struck her.

The man from the tavern. He'd received a palm reading from Jaqi. Nausea rolled in her gut.

What did she tell him?

"To help you see what true power can do. And what you need it for." He looked down at Conrad's still form. "You want to protect your prince, don't you? You want the kingdom?"

"What are you saying?" Ahria's palms grew slick with sweat against the hilts of her daggers.

"I've come to offer you a gift." The words felt twisted coming from the man's lips, and she remembered her father's warning about how Shades came to be.

Ahria let her gaze fall to the prince's peaceful face, tears burning her vision. "You want me to... be like you?" She didn't understand. She had no value, no use to the order of Shades. No Art to speak of, and no position... Her eyes flickered from Conrad to the Shade. "I am no one. I don't want power."

A smile curled his lips. "Want it or not, you're still in the position to have it. And my order could use a woman of conviction on the throne."

"You're mistaken. I won't be taking any throne. I have no interest in wedding a prince and he..." She mustered as much guile as she could. "He means nothing to me. Killing him is pointless."

"No?" The Shade frowned as he looked back down at Conrad's unconscious form. Pale fingers curled and the writhing tendrils tightened on Conrad's body. "I guess we don't need him then. I'm glad I enjoy pointless killing."

Ahria sucked in a breath through clenched teeth and stepped closer. "Wait." Dropping her daggers, she held her hands up.

The shadows paused, but remained cinched against the prince. "You're a terrible bluff."

"You're right. But you can have me." She advanced, keeping her hands visible as she left the two blades behind. "If you leave him here, alive, I'll take the power you're offering me."

"This offer is only valid if you take back all those declarations. We want a queen."

"I will be queen." Ahria rolled her lips together. "Assuming he still wishes to marry me after this." She summoned annoyance into her tone before crossing her arms.

"He'll only remember you saving you both. It will only further enamor him to you." The shadow around Conrad slackened, slipping back onto the ground. "You have made a wise decision, Ahria."

Ahria didn't dare look at her unconscious captain, swallowing as she neared arm's reach of the Shade. "You haven't," she breathed. And lunged, pulling blades from her bracers. She swiped the first down the front of him, and he shouted in pain.

Blackness blasted her backward, and she collided with the basement wall with a crash as all the air left her lungs. The vibration of the strike echoed through the entire house, thundering from somewhere upstairs.

Blood dripped from the Shade's arm and hand as he pulled back the sleeve of his cloak from his right forearm. Dark geometric shapes were etched on to his skin, just as Talon had told her they would be on any Shade. The tattoo of power granted to them by the master, by Uriel. She couldn't count them fast enough before the Shade's skin changed, hardening into a black carapace that spread from his wrist up his arm.

Panic scorched through her, and she started to her feet before a strike hit the wall above her head. Dropping to her knees, she scrambled along the floor away from the pile of bodies. Her friends. Her dead friends.

Whimpering, Ahria held her arm over her face as tendrils shot at her.

Crackling filled her ears as the ground split.

Chapter 34

"KIN," AMARIE WHISPERED, STARING BEHIND HIM.

The fear in her eyes made Kin's stomach tighten into a thousand knots. He felt as if he could sense whatever she looked at on the hill behind him, even without turning. Even without the Art, his tattoo burned. Not an intense pain as it used to, but a dull throb of a reminder. He turned his head north, just enough to catch the silhouette of the person watching them in his peripheral vision. The phantom pain doubled.

She approached him, not taking her eyes from the man on the hill. "That's not our friend."

Kin resisted touching his arm and stepped into Amarie, grabbing her wrist. "We need to run." Panic flooded his veins, his head buzzing.

"Who is that?" Her voice shook. Like she already knew.

He scanned the hillside Damien had disappeared over towards the horses, wishing desperately he could see the Rahn'ka. But the wind blew through the summer grass, unaware of what danger lurked.

It's better if he doesn't see the Rahn'ka.

"I think we both know who it is." His grip hardened on Amarie. "And there's no time to wonder how he found us."

The wind shifted, a gust rushing towards the ocean and bringing with it the acidic smell of dead wildflowers and meadows. The smell Kin had grown used to before now made him choke. Frantically, he looked at the open plains around them, and the barren grey of the destruction of Hoult.

There's nowhere to go.

Amarie finally looked up at him. "He wants me. You should go warn our friend."

He frowned. "And leave you? No. I won't make that mistake again."

Her gaze slid back to Uriel. "Now isn't the time to be chivalrous. You have no power to defend yourself with. I do." Twisting her wrist free, she strode around him. "I'll give you as much time as I can."

Growling, Kin turned after her, only allowing himself the barest glimpse of his old master. He stood perfectly still at the peak of the hill, looking far different than the last time Kin had seen him. Long white hair danced on the breeze, loose behind an angular face. Something about the form seemed vaguely auer, but at the distance Kin couldn't see his master's eyes. Despite the change of body, he still knew him. It was no simple Shade who had come to Hoult for Amarie.

An amused smile graced Uriel's lips, but he still didn't move.

"He's taunting us by just standing there." Kin's hand slid back to his satchel, slipping beneath the flap to reach for the meager dagger he'd acquired during their travels. He longed for his old sword at his hip. But his fingers closed on something far colder than the leather wrapped hilt. The chill of the obsidian coursed up his spine.

"And you're wasting the time you could be using to run," Amarie hissed. Her hands lowered to her sides. "He can't know who we're with."

"Not going to run, then?" Uriel's raspy, tenor voice broke over the wind. A different voice, but... him, without a doubt. "I was hoping for a chase."

"He won't find out," Kin whispered. His hand closed on the handle of the obsidian blade, but held it behind him still in the satchel. "And he won't get what he came for."

"Kinronsilis!" Uriel's tone sounded more amused than scolding, but it still made Kin flinch to hear his name. "I knew you'd show yourself again some day. Though I admit, you're looking far better than I expected for someone without my gift for so long. You will need to tell me how you managed that." He took his first step, and even though it was only one, he seemed to travel ten feet down the hill. The shadows at his feet flickered, and grass withered.

"Don't come any closer." Amarie stepped away from Kin, putting herself between him and Uriel. "I'm warning you. I'm not as naive as I was before."

Uriel clicked his tongue. "Nor am I." Pushing his hands parallel to the ground, shadow erupted around them. A wall constructed of thorny blackness shot to the sky, trapping them in a circle of grass. He stood at the far end of the forty foot clearing, his eyes nothing but black pools. "No escape this time, Amarie."

Amarie ducked her head as the barrier, like inky flames, blocked their view of even the terrain. She panted, eyes vibrant amethyst as she glanced at Kin. "How do I put him down?"

Before he could answer that he didn't know, shadow shot towards them.

Amarie threw her hands up, summoning a transparent barrier of the Art that the darkness collided with, jolting her muscles. As she made a fist, her power encircled Uriel's, trapping it in a sphere before hurling it back at him.

Kin gaped. "When did you learn...?"

"You were supposed to run!" Amarie snarled at him, and Uriel began to laugh.

Spears of shadow lanced up out of the ground, skewering the orb before the darkness within coalesced back into the staffs of shadow,

"Life is his source of power..." Kin breathed next to her, forcing his hand to release the knife. If she had really gained control of her power, perhaps there was a chance against him. "If it's dead, he can't draw energy from it." He remained carefully behind Amarie, even though it felt opposite of the instinct in him screaming to protect her. She was the one with the power in the fight, and the best he could do was remain a smaller target behind her.

Amarie inhaled, then blew the breath out. As she did, blue fire burst from beneath her boots and spread over the land with furious speed. While it didn't scorch his feet, it burned the grass, decimating all the vegetation in its wake. It soared outward, killing everything within the walls of dark and creating a giant plume of smoke.

The blue flickered off the black shell Uriel drew around himself, the flame licking up its sides but failing to penetrate as Amarie's fire guttered. The walls imprisoning them bowed, curving slightly for the smoke to escape quicker before Uriel's shell fell to the ground. A small patch of grass at his feet withered as the shield vanished.

Amarie didn't wait for him to strike again, lunging forward a few steps to send her energy across the field. Power rippled together, slamming into the master of Shades. It rammed him back into his own wall, the black caving just enough to cushion his impact before they wrapped around him. The shadow turned to armor on his limbs, chitinous plates that linked together and perfectly shaped to the auer's frame. As he gained his feet, no mark of her blow remained, and the wall that had caught him faded, opening a doorway to the green field behind him before the grass disintegrated.

"Not that shit again," Amarie ground out, shaking her head as she lowered her voice so only Kin would hear. "I don't know how to stop him without feeding him. This wasn't exactly part of my training."

"Thus my original suggestion to run that you also ignored."

"Running would have led him to someone else," she whispered. "You should have left me here."

Panic returned, and Kin's hand instinctively returned to his satchel again. "I'm not leaving you again."

"Then we'll both die."

"But you'll come back from death and he'll still have you." Kin looked at Uriel as he just stood there watching them again, allowing them to have their conversation. He already knew he'd won.

The master's head tilted curiously as he twisted his hand. A globe of shadow bubbled up from the ground, twisting up towards his palm.

"I don't see another option, do you?" Amarie kept her back to him, eyes on the threat. "I won't be his slave."

"No, you won't," Kin agreed quietly, his grip tightening as he recalled the true purpose of the blade Damien had given him. The Rahn'ka had to still be nearby. He would follow through on his promise. If she was free of the power, then she could still live without being Uriel's prisoner. He'd have no use for her. He'd take what he'd come for and go.

He touched her left shoulder, his eyes burning as he considered what would happen next. The obsidian blade drew quietly from the satchel. "I hope you'll forgive me."

Before he could second guess, Kin thrust the dagger hard into Amarie's side, angled up to strike her heart. He blinked through tears that suddenly filled his eyes at her gasp of pain and surprise. "I'm sorry."

Amarie wheezed, trying to speak, but blood flowed over her tongue instead of words. She grabbed his forearm, nails digging into his skin as she sputtered for breath. Crimson spewed from her lips as she tried to look at him. Tried to tell him something. Her body trembled in his arms, collapsing against him as her blood ran down his hand. Her power snuffed from the air, followed by Uriel's raging bellow.

Her life.

Gone.

Not for the first time, but for the second, and it sliced through Kin's heart.

The world shook as the black walls around him dissipated, but Kin could only see Amarie's face as he gingerly lowered her to the charred ground. He wanted to close her eyes, give her some kind of semblance of peace. Temporary peace, but...

Agony erupted.

He hadn't even seen the blow coming, but it hurtled him through the air to land on the hard, burnt ground. Black rimmed the edge of his vision as he heard his arm snap and the obsidian blade thunk to the ground. Then all Kin saw was the sky as he fell, head snapping back against a stone. He curled over his broken arm, clawing at the ground with his uninjured arm to get further from Uriel.

Red trails covered his legs where shadow had torn through his breeches and flesh, blood flowing freely from his shins and thigh. Looking at the gushing wound for only a moment, Kin hissed as he forced his broken arm to assist in pulling him along the ground. The ground that no longer boasted grass, but hard ashen stone beneath him.

He seized hold of a pale stone, pulling himself further from Uriel, but braced for another strike.

The master stopped at the edge of the grass, the thin strip between the burnt area and the desolation of Hoult. "You have minutes, Kinronsilis, before you bleed out." He stooped, retrieving the fallen obsidian dagger. "And even in your last moments, you failed to stop me."

"But you won't have her." Kin's own voice sounded far

away. He looked at Amarie's body, blood pooling beneath her too similar to when he'd found her murdered by Trist.

But now I'm her murderer.

"Won't I?" Uriel chuckled, turning the bloody blade over in his hands. "You see... I don't need her. You think I don't know what this weapon is? Those silly Rahn'ka tried using something like this on me centuries ago. Either it will have absorbed her power or not. If not... well, then that'll be very interesting..." He smiled, teeth gleaming in the afternoon light. "You'll die for nothing after murdering the only person who ever loved you."

Kin coughed, tasting blood. "But she's safe from you."

She has no daughter, and Damien will bring her back.

His chest felt heavy, and he grabbed his thigh where the blood welled, gritting through the pain to push against the wound to slow the bleeding. He needed to stay conscious, needed to make sure it had worked and Amarie didn't come back as the Berylian Key. Nothing had changed on the dagger. It looked the same as Uriel toyed with it in one hand.

Uriel took another step, the toes of his boots almost touching the smooth pale stone. "Maybe safe in death, but..." He ran a finger through Amarie's blood, holding it up to inspect it in the light. "Perhaps this will hold more secrets to her power."

Kin shook the haze from his vision, staring at Uriel's boots and how they didn't dare cross into the Artless void.

"Why don't you just finish me? I know you'd enjoy it with everything I did to defy you. To screw you out of your hopes for Feyor." He lifted his chin.

A mirthless chuckle ruptured from Uriel's throat. "You are not unique, Kinronsilis. I have no need for you, not with my Shade king running Feyor. I clearly chose the wrong twin all those years ago."

Images of Jarac, holding a knife to his own twin's throat, flashed in Kin's memory. If Uriel spoke the truth... It only made Kin want to destroy his brother more. But he wouldn't get the chance. Not with the blood pouring from his punctured artery at a pace that left him dizzy. This would be it. He'd never know if Amarie would survive. If she would forgive him. If she would understand at all. If she would hate him all over again. If Damien didn't make it to her in time... she'd be gone from this world. A light extinguished far too early. And it would be his fault.

"Enjoy your slow death." Uriel turned, walking away with the dagger. As he passed Amarie's body, he crouched, stroking her face. "Such a shame."

"Don't touch her," Kin rasped, shifting to push Uriel away from her, but he couldn't move. Blood rushed past his fingers as his grip slipped, and he hurriedly put it back in place despite the pain and foreboding darkness at the edge of his vision. His shoulder hit the hard stone of Hoult as he collapsed again, pushing all the breath from him. He almost wished Uriel would just end it as agony rippled through his body.

"Give my regards to your lover in the afterlife. If she'll even look at you." Uriel gestured through the air. Shadow slithered up his legs, encompassing him before dropping back to the ground and vanishing. Leaving Kin, alone and dying, to stare at Amarie's lifeless face.

Chapter 35

TALON SNARLED AT THE SHADOWED doorway of the townhouse, his heart pounding as he yanked at his power. The Art responded willingly, twisting with the panic racing through his veins. The air snapped with cold, and ice coated every piece of foliage around the townhouse and its immediate neighbors. He had to destroy every source of possible power for the Shade and pray he didn't have a substantial enough reserve to keep the front door sealed.

It was lucky the shade hadn't checked the house for Talon's ward. That the use of their power had activated it just as the auer had begun to debate going to check on his daughter after receiving the message that she'd miss their afternoon plans. With what Ahria was, could be, Talon had no interest in trusting things to chance. And on learning about her home in the city, he'd taken precautions.

Yet, despite all the care, he still hadn't made it in time before his daughter was sealed within, facing a Shade alone.

The petals on one of the few remaining sunflowers beside the doorway crackled, shattering on the ground in a clatter of ice. The shadow wriggled, but held firm along the door jamb.

I don't have time for this.

With a deep breath, Talon did the opposite of what he had always encouraged in Amarie and welcomed every ounce of emotion into his gut as he seized a handful of his power.

Purple flames lanced into the door, sizzling against the creeping shadow, and surging outward to encompass the frame and wall several feet wider than the door. Clenching his fists, he thrust them forward with a second wave, and the structure of the townhouse gave way. It collapsed inward in a thunderous cacophony, wood splintering as flame flung the doorway down the entrance hall, spraying bits of plaster and coating the blood-soaked floor in a thin film of debris.

The smell struck him next. Unmistakable death and the iron of gore.

Not allowing himself to take in the grisly entry way, he hurdled for the basement stairs, where the sounds of conflict emanated from. Rounding the landing halfway down, Ahria's whimper hit his ears and lit an inferno within him.

She's alive.

Leaping down the last few stairs, the sight struck him like

a blow to the gut. The Shade, advancing on a crouched Ahria. A mound of bodies off to the side, and an unconscious Conrad sprawled on the opposite side of the room from his daughter.

Tendrils lashed for her like whips, striking through the air with deadly force.

A shout caught in his throat as he seized the latent energy along the floor in front of his daughter, and breathed hard as the ground itself cracked open. Spears of stone collided with the Shade's attack. The tendrils struck and parted, trying to wriggle around the stone. But with a gesture, new shards exploded at each point they tried to pass until the shadow faded. A dog called back from the hunt.

Ahria looked up at him with wide eyes that quickly darted to the Shade. She drew a blade and threw it, and Talon watched with pride as it hit its mark at the enemy's throat, even if it bounced off. Ricocheting like it'd struck metal.

The Shade tutted, turning only slightly as his mouth opened to speak.

Talon didn't give him the opportunity.

Flame shot up from the Shade's feet, the updraft throwing his cloak back and revealing the extent of the strange armor. It covered every inch of the man except for his head, giving him an odd insect-like appearance as he stumbled back from the flames. His cloak turned to ash, and Talon tore with invisible hands at the ceiling beams above the

Shade. They snapped, and a new rain of plaster and wood fell into the basement. The Shade lifted his armored hand above his head, but he disappeared under the cloud of dust from the building as it shuddered.

Ahria rushed around the edge of the room, dodging the falling debris as she dove to the prince's limp form.

Talon had forgotten he was there, realizing now how close he'd come to burying Conrad along with the Shade. He hesitated, weaving the falling boards into a wall as he felt the first dregs of his power seeping away and the familiar lethargy from using too much begin to take hold.

The world tipped upside down as pain lanced through his legs, the caved-in ceiling filling his vision as his back struck the bloodied ground. His shins burned as he looked down to tendrils snaking up his flesh like vipers.

"Dad!" Ahria's shriek cut through the air.

Gritting his teeth, Talon urged the Art through his body to his legs, vibrating it to the surface in familiar flames. With an inhuman screech, as if alive themselves, the shadows recoiled back into the ground, bubbling as the Shade's body coalesced again.

Ahria charged the Shade, empty handed, and everything blurred into slow motion.

Talon focused on Uriel's pawn, ignoring the blows coming at him. They didn't matter. *He* didn't matter. All he needed was to protect her. His daughter. The only soul in Pantracia who depended on him.

His purpose.

Once, he'd thought he'd been meant to be with Amarie. Be her trainer, her guardian, her lover. But it'd only been the spark that'd led him to the truth.

Surging to his feet, Talon moved into Ahria's path just as the Shade held out his hands, blackness leaping forward like a tidal wave. Funneling everything he had, Talon pulled at the stone beneath, new columns erupting upward in a roar. As he spread his hands, the stone curved like the sides of a bottle, engulfing him and Ahria as darkness barreled around.

"This isn't the time to fight. You need to run." Talon looked over his shoulder at his daughter, straining as his power sought to shield every renewed attack. He only had to last until the Shade's reserve ran out. Or until Ahria got away.

"I'm not leaving you," Ahria panted, tears glistening in her eyes. She glanced back at Conrad, who still hadn't moved. Another blow hit the wall, and she whimpered. "Please don't make me."

Talon spun, pressing his back against the stone as it jolted with another blow, but he seized Ahria's face in his hands and tilted her eyes to look at him. "You... are my greatest pride. My greatest achievement. Please, you need to live."

The stone shuddered, particles raining down from the sky. And looking in Ahria's pale blue eyes, he knew that he would remain to destroy the Shade that'd come for her. No matter the cost. The thoughts of holding the Shade off until they could escape faded as he realized it wasn't enough. The darkness in his own heart swelled, demanding death. Because only death would save her. He wouldn't allow this Shade to come for her again.

"Ahria, I love you," Talon whispered. "Now run."

Chapter 36

AHRIA SOBBED, STARING AT HER father's vibrant green eyes. "I love you, too." Tearing her gaze from him, she ran to Conrad and fell to her knees at his side. Gently slapping his cheek, she tugged on his arm. "Wake up!"

Chaos ensued behind her, but she didn't dare look. The expression on Talon's face, the resignation in his eyes, it ripped into her heart with merciless certainty.

Hot tears poured down her cheeks as she shook Conrad. Losing time, she huffed a breath and slapped him harder, whipping his head to the side.

His eyes shot open, and he coughed. Hand darting up to his cheek, and then head, Conrad groaned and rubbed at his face, smearing crumbled bits of plaster and grime on his dark skin.

"Get up," Ahria cried. "Get up."

A crash echoed behind her, and she rose, spinning to face the battle.

Conrad scrambled behind her as more of the building above collapsed into the basement, flames of Talon's Art slithering up the walls.

The sun now poured in from a large hole that exposed the destroyed back garden of the townhouse. All of the luscious green had turned brown or black, frost clinging to some of it while a web of shadow stretched out in search of more to consume.

A gash ran down the side of the Shade's exposed cheek, blood dripping onto his armored neck and shoulder as the tendrils quivered in front of him, snapping up to catch the debris Talon's Art hurled at him.

Blood and gnarled flesh marred her father's body. The once pale blue tunic stained dark maroon at his collar and down his back, where streaks of exposed flesh continued to morph as she watched. Continued to bubble with necrotic shadow birthed by their enemy. Yet Talon still stood, letting out a scream as he hurled a couch that'd fallen from the floor above at the Shade, twisting it with wreaths of flame.

The Shade's tendrils rushed to catch it, tearing it in half as the armored monster stepped closer to Talon, whose shoulders sagged in exhaustion. But even as he wove his right hand to take up more debris, his left twitched as it crafted a different spell that Ahria couldn't see.

The prince tugged at her arm. "Get to the stairs."

Ahria stumbled backward with him, vision hot and blurred. She looked down at her hands, wishing for the first time in her life that she had access to her mother's power.

I can't even help him.

Her eyes locked again on her father's left hand, her heart leaping into her throat.

He's setting a trap.

Ahria shook her head and whispered, "Wait." She gritted her teeth, planting her feet. "Hey! Asshole!"

"What are you doing?" Conrad hissed.

Ahria picked up a stone and chucked it at the side of the Shade's head. It pinged off an upraised plate of the shadow armor, thudding to the ground. "I'm talking to you!"

Tendrils quivered as if in anger as the Shade's eyes twitched to Ahria, a scowl on his pale features. He turned just enough, and Talon's right hand joined his left in the weave. They rolled together in an intricate dance and Ahria gaped as the ground beneath the Shade began to ripple. The stained floor liquified, shimmering like molten lava. Strange circular etchings surrounded the Shade's feet, and a section of the emulsified ground dropped away just as the Shade stepped back from it. Like a hole had been dug straight into the ground, the rim crackling with power.

The Shade spun to face Talon, the air sparking as he struck the invisible wall that rose from the sigils on the ground. His wide eyes darted around, breaths suddenly panicked in recognition.

A flicker of movement materialized in the gaping hole. Ahria couldn't avert her gaze as several dark shapes blocked out the fiery cracks deep within. A deformed claw, something from her wildest nightmares, tore at the ground of the crevice, hauling itself upward into the air.

She pressed her back against Conrad, fear squeezing her insides as the little monsters, only known to her by way of stories, emerged from within. Small blackened bodies, charred husks of creatures no bigger than a house cat. Their beady eyes flashed about the room, bodies hunched as wings tested the unfamiliar world's air. One darted directly towards the crumbled walls of the basement, to the freedom of outside, but smashed into the same invisible wall that'd stopped the Shade. It hissed, spinning with needle-like teeth towards Talon, but then its bulging eyes slid to the man trapped with them.

"No, not this." The Shade collapsed to the ground, a terrified position that Ahria had never imagined she'd see from someone like him. He lifted his hands as he turned back to Talon, begging. "Not this."

Talon's face hardened, his green eyes reflecting the flickers of pale orange as another ingvald scurried from the hole, a pack of seven now sitting perfectly still and staring at their enemy. They didn't move, other than the occasional flex of their dagger-like claws on the ground, and a flick of a black tongue. A light chitter filled the air as they spoke quietly to each other.

But as the Shade turned completely from them, pounding his fists on the barrier with a cry of desperation, they moved in unison. One small, dangerous step at a time. Their chatter grew louder, like a million of their tiny teeth gnashing.

"What are those?" Conrad whispered in her ear, fear in his tone.

Ahria pressed harder against him, gripping his forearm. "Corrupted. Ingvalds. My father..."

Conrad froze, his breath stopping as he pulled Ahria closer.

Like rats after a single scrap of bread, the ingvalds swarmed. They lashed forward, crawling on top of the Shade as he howled. Their tiny hands tore, teeth snapping on the Shade's armor. They tugged, wings beating in the air as they hauled the howling man back to where they'd come from. His shadows flickered, but they only passed through the ingvalds as they shoved him into the hell from which they'd been summoned. He fought, nails breaking on the ground as he tried to stop himself. His wail echoed as his dark form disappeared over the lip of the hole.

Behind the Shade, the opening snapped shut, and the chatter and screams silenced.

The sigils faded, any sign of what Talon had done vanishing. As their light diminished, the auer let out a slow sigh. Then collapsed.

Ahria lurched from Conrad's grip. "Dad!" All fear of the Corrupted forgotten, she launched across the basement's ruptured floor to where her father lay. Skidding to her knees beside him, she touched his face, his arms, looking for the injuries that must be there. "Dad. Where are you hurt? We can fetch a healer."

Talon wheezed, something in his chest rattling. "It's too late for that, Ree." His voice sounded hollow, but not in pain.

Her heart constricted, tears burning her eyes again. "Don't say that," she whispered, only vaguely aware of Conrad moving around behind her as she unfastened the buttons of her father's tunic.

His hand lifted, catching her wrist. "Some things are better not seen, sweetheart."

Ahria sobbed and shook her head. "Would you say that if our places were reversed?" Her chin quivered as she somehow succeeded in forming coherent words. His grip slackened, and she continued her investigation.

Above the neck of his tunic, his skin bore black streaks of necrotic damage from the Shade. As he tilted his head in resignation, his breath became shallow and rough. The damage had to be far worse beneath the material.

But with each button she unfastened, the dread in her gut doubled over, ricocheting between grief and denial.

The black, charred skin extended down his entire upper body, but the necrotic devastation hadn't stopped at his skin. It went deep. So deep that she could see his ribs. The bones, crusted with ash, did nothing to protect his chest cavity, where a thin layer of darkened flesh covered his heart like a gossamer curtain. The organ beneath still thudded, but barely.

Ahria gaped at it, fighting the bile in her throat from rising. She pulled his tunic back over the exposed internals, hands shaking. "I don't want to lose you. I'm not ready," she choked, voice cracking. "How do I save you? Please tell me what to do. I'll do anything."

"Just be here," Talon rasped, turning his hand to hold hers. His eyes had lost their brightness, glassy and withdrawn. They flickered somewhere behind her, then returned to her face. He lifted a hand feebly to her cheek, touching the wetness. "I'm sorry I have to go. And that you had to see these things." His hand fell as a rattling breath shook his entire body. "But you can do this without me now."

"No, I can't," she whined, fresh tears dripping from her chin. "I still need you." Picking up his hand, she held it to her chest, squeezing it.

"You never needed me, Ree. I needed you." His fingers gripped for only a moment. "Just... be you, and you will accomplish everything."

Ahria sobbed and crumpled over him, careful not to touch his gravely wounded chest. She kissed his face, pressing her cheek to his. "If that's true," she whispered. "It's only because I have you for a dad."

A smile twitched on his lips, eyes closing in a slow blink. When they opened again, the color of his irises had faded behind half-open eyelashes. He exhaled, but then nothing more came. It was oddly peaceful, despite the carnage beneath his tunic. And his lungs did not fill again.

Drawing in a shaky inhale, Ahria sniffed and whimpered with her exhale. She could hardly see beyond her tears, withdrawing her face from his. "I love you so much, Dad." Squeezing her eyes shut, she gasped for air, clutching his hand to her face.

Distantly, there was shouting, but Ahria didn't care. Thumps along what remained of the upper floor. The sound of Conrad's boots along the wet floor. The scent of frozen and decayed summer. Horses. Birds. The world beyond the townhouse carrying on.

Heat gathered in her chest, anger, but... Not anger. She opened her eyes and looked down, seeing nothing wrong with her body before a strange spark of fire danced from her fingers. Blinking quicker, she struggled to focus on it. "Oh, no."

The embers along her skin grew brighter, in a pure azure blue. One bounced from her palm to the floor, where it lit into a flame.

"Oh, no, no, no..." Ahria gulped, shuffling back in the dirt. "Not now."

Footsteps sounded on the half destroyed stairs. "Ahria?" Conrad, returning from wherever he had gone.

She turned to him, agony ripping through her. "Get out. Get everyone out. Now!" Her body retched, and she dropped Talon's hand as she buckled forward. Her palms hit the grimy ground

And exploded.

Fire lanced across the floor, sweeping up the walls and over the debris. No smoke billowed, as it failed to burn, but the danger remained regardless.

Conrad shouted, but she couldn't make out the words. She couldn't make out his shape in the wild torrent of flame blurring every inch of her vision. Only Talon remained close enough for her to see, the raging fire cascading over him like a blanket.

Her skin felt as if it had been laced with lightning, every hair and cell raging with unfathomable power. A suffocating ocean that she'd never be able to fully grasp soaking into her very soul.

Grief tore through her as she stared at her fallen father. The flames only meant one thing, and it took every ounce of her strength not to collapse under the weight of her mother's death, too.

Wherever she'd been, it no longer mattered.

The Berylian Key's power had found her.

Chapter 37

URIEL HAD FOUND THEM.

Damien recognized the shadow on the horizon, despite the new shell the creature inhabited. He could sense the decay and filth a mile away, encouraging him to keep his distance. There was nothing he could do. Other than make sure Uriel remained ignorant of who he was. What he was.

So he waited. The ká of the grass screamed in agony as Amarie burned it, then Uriel took everything that was left.

Damien crouched among the tall grass, matching his energies with what stood around him to remain invisible.

They're already dead.

He didn't dare extend his power to confirm. Uriel knew he'd been present in Nema's Throne fourteen years ago, but he'd made sure the creature still didn't know his identity.

After the encounter to free Matthias, Uriel was probably looking for Rae.

The stench of Uriel's Art faded from the air, and still he waited before he dared get closer.

If they were dead, it would mean a multitude of things. He hated himself for the pragmatic thought that their deaths didn't necessarily mean the end of the plot to seal Uriel away. But his stomach soured at the prospect.

Especially with what he knew after restoring Amarie's memories.

His heart thundered as he debated his options and the risks of crossing the crest of the hill towards the crater.

"Damien!" Kin's gruff, desperate shout barely carried over the breeze.

He jolted at the sound, breaking through the buzz of voices he'd buried himself within. "Shit." There was no point in remaining hidden if Kin was going to begin screaming his name. He rushed to the hilltop, slowing for only a moment to take in the destruction.

The meadow beyond the pale stone of the crater was charred black, great gashes through the topsoil. It spanned one hundred yards in patches, outside the crater, funneling to its narrowest point as it grew close to where Kin and Amarie lay. Red streaked across the pale stones of the crater, pooling to the edge where Amarie lay in a circle of burned grass.

A thin thread of her ká barely clung to her body, but Kin's faded at a startling rate, too.

He ran, taking only small bits of energy from the terrain as he did. He'd need everything he had. Everything Amarie had given him.

"Gods." The coppery scent stuck to Damien's tongue, and Kin groaned as he moved to sit up. "Stop. Just stop moving."

Judging by the streaks in his blood on the stone, Kin had tried to crawl to the edge, towards Amarie. He couldn't tell at first where the wound was, until he saw Kin's blood-soaked hand pressed to the inside of his thigh, the other arm tucked awkwardly against his body. His ká screamed in more than physical pain as Kin beheld Amarie, and the Rahn'ka hardened his barrier against the turmoil.

Kin groaned as he collapsed onto his side, crying out as he landed on his broken arm. His eyes hung heavy as unconsciousness threatened him. "Bring her back first." He jerked his chin to Amarie, panting.

"You'll bleed out in the time it takes me." Damien forced himself to look beyond Amarie's body, ignore the rising guilt at what he knew would happen to her power now. Where it would go. But he didn't know what had killed Amarie. And he didn't know which option was the worse. If Kin had used the dagger, and it had done what it was intended...

Damien spared a moment to look at the ground around Amarie, coated in more blood. But the obsidian blade was nowhere to be seen.

Kin grimaced, but didn't seem to have the strength to argue with Damien as he stepped towards him onto the pale stone.

Sudden silence permeated Damien's mind, and he felt dizzy as the power he'd grown so accustomed to vanished. Desperate to get it back, he seized Kin roughly beneath his armpits and heaved.

Kin didn't remain conscious long enough to give any further protest as Damien pulled him onto the charred earth. The power of the Rahn'ka surged back into every limb, and he used the inertia to plow into the energies necessary. Healing felt as natural as breathing now, considering how much he'd done it over the years. A scratch on his son's knee, a broken leg from when Corin had grown overzealous with training. But bones were intense to heal, and he didn't have the time, so he focused on the flesh wound draining Kin's life.

The blood slowed as Damien watched the flesh, then the skin, knit together. But Kin remained still on the ground. Bringing him back to consciousness wouldn't have taken much, but the lingering pressure of Amarie's weakening bond to her ká made it impossible to justify. Damien had never known Amarie, yet he'd never forgive himself if he didn't bring her back.

She's going to need to be around to teach her daughter, now.

As Kin's breathing stabilized, Damien crawled to Amarie, pulling her limp form towards him. Her ká had fled, leaving behind a narrow trail of where it'd traveled. It'd remain in the Inbetween, where he could still reach her, for a time. But only if she truly needed that time to process her death. He had to hope it wasn't already too late.

Chapter 38

COLD SURROUNDED AMARIE.

A distant, directionless, and painfully familiar cold.

At first, breath caught in her throat and couldn't fill her lungs, but she focused on her body and opened her eyes. Something like air entered her a moment later, the memory of breath, and her vision focused on a ceiling shaped of wood and root.

A beam of sunlight poured through the long window above the head of the bed, but the patter of rain danced down the branches and vines of the banyan.

Amarie sat up, grabbing at the back of her ribs. A spark of pain cut through her, where Kin's ominous black dagger had stabbed. Had killed her.

Dammit, Kin.

Had Uriel killed him for that? For killing her?

"I'm back in the Inbetween," she whispered, studying her old home she'd once shared with Talon in Eralas. The spot on her ribs ached despite no visual injury. "Why'd he kill me?"

To save me from Uriel?

She rose, walking around the bed that looked exactly as she remembered. Crossing through the kitchen, she ignored the bowl of ripe berries on the table and made her way outside.

Shielding her eyes from the afternoon sun, she squinted at the big black form that nickered at her. "Viento?" She almost laughed, even though the horse wasn't real. His velvet nose pushed into her palm, and she stroked it.

Vague shapes of foals flickered in and out behind the stallion, but Viento's shape remained steady despite the restructuring of time behind him. A white mare nuzzled the foals, the trees behind them morphing from the banyans of Eralas to another familiar tree line of pine and cottonwood, then back again. As if the horse's corral existed in two places. Both Eralas and Olsa, where she'd abandoned her child.

If I'm dead, then Ahria...

Her heart sank.

Lynthenai's image solidified as the horse lifted her head to look at Amarie, her tail flicking.

The sound of rain grew harder, but drops didn't seem to fall immediately around her. Instead, the curtain of water surrounded the homestead, feeding the growing pools on the forest floor.

Amarie glanced back at the banyan home, still petting her horse. "Years ago and yet... yesterday," she whispered absently, leaning against the stallion's neck. All the tumultuous emotions from her pregnancy, birth, and subsequent departure now seemed frivolous. What had her leaving accomplished? Besides leaving Ahria without a mother, nothing. Her daughter had become the Berylian Key anyway. She could only hope her childhood had been peaceful. Loving.

Movement in the clearing where she'd used to train caught her eye, and her hand paused on Viento's coat. A man sat in the grass, and her shoulders stiffened.

The first time she'd died, she'd reunited with her mother. But those broad shoulders and raven black hair made her freeze.

He can't be real.

Amarie blinked a few times, seeing if he'd vanish, but nothing happened. "Is that you?" she called, taking a few steps closer to the clearing.

The man's shoulders tensed, his head shifting as if to turn before he stopped and settled back into the relaxed sitting position with his back to her. As if he was afraid to face her.

The clearing dipped into the shape of the crater she'd created when her power had nearly killed him, but grass and tiny wild flowers had reclaimed the soil.

Talon sat perfectly in the raised middle, the ring of rain curved to match that of the crater. Small streams danced down the slopes near where he sat, filling the edges with crystalline water.

"You're not really here." His voice was a whisper that sent a shiver down her spine. It felt like centuries since she'd heard it. "Just another memory." His shoulder rose with a steep inhale before sagging slowly.

"No..." she murmured, still approaching from behind him. "I believe *you're* the memory." Taking slow, long steps, she circled the crater until she stood in front of him. Her heart picked up speed as her eyes fell on his face.

His spring green eyes fluttered open, pin-point pupils taking a moment before they focused on her. As his lips pursed, his breath hesitated, growing uneven and making her heart pound. He shook his head as his eyes grew glassy. "No..." He pressed against the ground, standing in a smooth motion. "No, you can't be here. Not here." He reached out to her, but recoiled. A tear flowed down his cheek. "Amarie?"

A rock sank to the bottom of Amarie's gut. "You're really here, too." She approached, taking the hand he'd extended. "What happened?" Heat built behind her eyes. Grief for the man who now joined her in death. "Tell me what happened."

"So much." Talon's grip closed around hers, the other moving to the side of her face as she stepped into him.

Slipping it back into her hair, he embraced her, taking her against his strong chest where his heart no longer beat. But there was still a warmth there, like she remembered from what felt like so long ago. "But we don't have much time."

"I know," Amarie breathed into his chest, resting her head on him. The biggest question in her mind weighed like a guillotine. "Did you go to Ahria, all those years ago?"

His hold on her tightened. "Yes."

A burden lifted from her shoulders, and a surprising sob shook her shoulders before she smiled. "Good. I'm glad she had you."

"You would be so proud of the woman she has become, Amarie." Talon ran his hands through her hair. "She's so much like you. Brave, giving, and kind. Perhaps a little reckless at times."

Pulling her face back, she looked up at the man she once loved. "Where is she? Is she safe?"

He met her gaze. "New Kingston. With the crown prince of Ziona." His lips curled in a half-hearted smile. "I wish you could see the way that boy looks at her. She'll be safe with him and through her own ability."

Amarie smirked. "Crown prince, huh? She aims high." She tried to ignore the parallel of Kin's lineage, and focused on the shadow in his gaze. "And the rest of that thought?"

"There was a Shade, but I destroyed him. Just not before he got some good hits in on me."

Her shoulders drooped, a tear falling down her cheek. "I knew you'd be a wonderful father, but I'm sorry I wasn't there to help."

"Stop." Talon lifted her chin gently. "You have nothing to apologize for. I'm the one who put you in that situation. I'm the one who is sorry. And I wouldn't take back a day of raising Ahria. I wish I could have done more. But I did all I could to prepare her for..." He looked down for a moment, as if taking her in. "I hope she's ready. You shouldn't be here. You were safe in Eralas."

"I was, but... Something happened. Something woke my Art from Slumber, and it woke Kin, too." A darkness entered her tone. "Apparently he was next to me."

Talon frowned. "Kin?" But the expression softened. "I knew Uriel was searching for him, but I never bothered to try to find him." He took her face between his hands, stroking his thumb along her skin. "But why are you here?"

Amarie shuddered. "Uriel found us." Her eyes wandered to the trees, where she imagined the charred grass arena she'd stood in with Kin and Uriel only breaths before. "We were going to lose, so Kin... He didn't know. I didn't tell him. About Ahria. He killed me."

The auer tensed, anger flooding into his still glassy eyes. It lingered for a moment, but he didn't speak, as if searching for more in studying her face. "You're not angry?"

She shrugged. "I am, in a way. I didn't want the Key to fall on Ahria's shoulders, but... Uriel would have taken me. One way or another, he'd have gotten my power. My death is a gentler price than that fate. So I suppose I'm not angry because I understand why he did it."

Talon nodded, a small smile returning to banish the remaining fury. "Death... is not so simple when it comes to the Berylian Key." He brushed her hair back from her face, tucking it behind her ear. "I know Kin. And I know the pain I saw in him when we found you in that cave in Aidensar. While he can be callous, and brutal, if he did this to you—"

Amarie touched a finger to Talon's lips. "I know. But I don't want to talk about Kin. I want to hear about Ahria and your time with her. Will you tell me? Does she wear the necklace left for her? The flower?"

"She never takes it off, my araleinya." He kissed the edge of her fingers. "I told her all I could about you. About the power. I kept no secrets from Ahria about the Key. I knew that you'd want it that way. But I never told her about Kin. She knows I'm not her real father, there was no hiding that as she grew older, but she doesn't know about him. Nor about the faction. Deylan still watches her, too, and I know he'll keep her safe from faction politics."

Huffing, Amarie leaned into Talon again, basking in the safety it pulsed through her body. "I was so angry with you for not meeting me." She continued before he could interrupt. "But I understand now. And I'm so... so grateful you loved her. Raised her. I wish I could have met her, but the Key's power won't bring me back this time." She looked up at him, taking in each detail of his face. Touching his cheek, she let out a shaky breath. "And while it breaks my heart that your life is already over, way sooner than it should be, these moments with you bring me so much peace." She smiled through her tears, her chest warm.

"I don't deserve such forgiveness, my araleinya." Talon leaned forward, placing a soft kiss on her forehead. "And loving her was the very least I could do."

Water lapped around them, flowing through the trees and gently filling the crater, but she ignored it. "What will happen, when we leave the Inbetween?" She hadn't dreaded the silence of death before, and while regret tainted her heart, the dread still wasn't there.

"A mystery." Talon took her into another hug, resting his chin on her head. "And while I have made peace with this for me, I still wish it wasn't so for you. You deserve more of a life than the one you've had. You deserve happiness, too."

Someone cleared their throat, and Talon jolted in unison with her.

"Apologies. I didn't want to interrupt. But I don't think we can wait much longer."

Amarie faced Damien without moving from Talon. "Are you dead, too?" She narrowed her eyes, but it made no sense that the Rahn'ka would experience this location for his Inbetween.

Damien lifted his brow. "What? No." A ripple of light blue power radiated down his left arm. "I've come to take you back."

"Take me back?" Amarie shook her head then looked at the auer. "What about Talon? Can you..."

Damien pursed his lips and looked at Talon.

The auer's grip around Amarie loosened. "Go." Talon encouraged her away from him.

Amarie resisted the push. "But... But then I'll be... there... and you'll be..." The thought of walking Pantracia when Talon couldn't made her insides burn.

"You deserve some happiness, too." Talon pinched her chin. "You deserve to meet your daughter. New Kingston. Crown prince." He leaned into her and kissed her forehead, letting it linger. "If this man can really take you back, you need to go."

Tears slipped from her eyes again, warm as they rolled down her cheeks. "I will never, ever forget you. I promise. And I will always have love for you." She swallowed hard, but the lump in her throat didn't budge.

"And I am grateful for that." Talon's calm expression reminded her of all those hours they'd trained together. The bliss they'd had for a time in that house in Eralas. "I have never stopped loving you. But I also want you to be happy,

Amarie. Whatever that looks like. Whoever that means you love."

Amarie tried to smile. "I will find her. And I will never leave her again. The rest doesn't matter." She touched his chest while Damien approached her side, and she offered the Rahn'ka her other hand. "May Nymaera grant you the rest you deserve, Talon, until we meet again." Her chin quivered, and she made no effort to stop it as Damien gripped her hand.

"Be smart. Be safe," Talon whispered as he dropped away from her, back into the deeper pools of water at the edges of the crater. "She will love you and understand. Trust me."

Damien tugged, pulling Amarie up the shallow slope back to the even terrain in front of their house. "This is very important, don't take in any of the water. No matter the pain, hold your breath."

Amarie tried to hear his words, nodding, but couldn't look away from the auer. "Hold my breath," she whispered, then rolled her lips together and took a deeper breath as she stared at Talon and mouthed the word, "Goodbye."

Chapter 39

PUSHING HIS BACK AGAINST THE wall of the stairs, Conrad gaped at the rush of blue flames coating the basement floor. The inferno licked up the walls, over the debris, and into the sky, but no smoke rose. His head ached, still hazy from unconsciousness and the blur of events after it. From the images of Corrupted pulling the Shade into a pit. From the vision of Talon's mortal injuries.

He stared at Ahria, at the center of those flames, tears wetting her cheeks and creating paths through the grime. She had her eyes closed, one hand on Talon's, while her shoulders shook.

Anticipating the heat in his lungs, Conrad took a careful breath, unwilling to go up to the first floor where a squad of guards had arrived. The captain now organized more than the royal soldiers as peace officers and local fire guard responded to the destruction in a city district. But as he breathed, the air was oddly cool. Even as the fire wafted off the walls towards him, no heat touched his face.

His chest felt empty, yet shattered for the woman who wept. Who grieved the loss of her father while struggling against whatever power now held her in its grasp. But what could he do for her? As a captain, as a crown prince, he'd never before felt so useless.

She'd lost her second father, now, and if he recalled correctly, she'd only come into this power if her mother perished.

An orphan, in one, tragic, fell swoop.

The need to comfort her drove him towards the fire, preparing for the pain as he tried to gauge the safest path towards her. But as his boot touched the basement floor, he felt nothing. And he didn't bother to question it as he hurried to Ahria.

At the sound of his steps, her chin lifted and she looked at him. Not with the ice blue eyes he'd always admired, but with intense irises that swirled with pinks and violets. "I can't stop it," she whispered, tears still flowing.

Conrad crouched, ignoring every instinct in him screaming to get away from the fire. He reached for her, taking her shoulders firmly in his hands and drawing her to look directly at him. "Yes, you can." He urged his voice to remain steady, a practiced skill from his years as a sea captain. "You can control this. He taught you how."

She inhaled a shaky breath, the fire flickering with it, but shook her head. "He's gone," she choked. "He's gone. I can't do this without him."

"Yes, you can," he repeated, scooting closer to her. He tightened his grip on her shoulders. He slid a hand to her sternum, pressing over her heart lightly. "And he's here. Remember what he taught you, and breathe." He hardened every emotion, hoping his calm would somehow pass into her. "Look at me and *breathe*."

Ahria tried again, closing her eyes for only a moment before focusing on his. She breathed, jaw flexing with each inhale. Her hand found his forearm, and she squeezed.

Minutes passed without a word between them, only her focus as she slowly calmed. Sorrow still leaked from her gaze, but the inferno dimmed. Flames lowered until eventually they snuffed out. The only evidence remained in her eyes, in the color that hadn't been before.

"I need to leave the city," she whispered. "Right now."

Conrad nodded. "There's an estate owned by the crown in the mountains north of here. We can go there." He looked back and forth between her wild eyes, wishing there was a way for him to understand everything that had just happened. But the chaos, the Art that had been present in the room, left his head spinning and him feeling grossly incompetent.

How am I supposed to protect her when I have nothing?

Ahria's sad eyes drifted to her father's body, and her throat bobbed. "He would want to return to Eralas... He has family there." She rolled her lips together, jaw tight. "Can you...?"

"Of course." Conrad squeezed her. "You don't need to ask anything. I will take care of all of it." He moved into her, wishing he could somehow kiss away all of the tears and pain in her. Bringing her into his chest, he held her tightly for a moment before he started to stand, encouraging her to do so with him. "They're bringing a carriage. We'll go straight to the estate, and I'll have our things brought to us."

Her hazy eyes focused on him. "Don't you need to stay here? In the palace?" Her hands shook where she touched him, and she wavered on her feet.

"You're more important." He closed his hands over hers, wishing it could steady her. "The palace can find a way to cope without me for a little while. I need to be with you."

Ahria nodded, but he wasn't sure she heard his words as she knelt again. Taking up her father's hand, she slid the braided leather bracelet off his wrist and pressed her lips to his forehead. Whispering something Conrad couldn't hear, she kissed him again before rising.

She said nothing as he led her from the townhouse, away from the carnage of her friends. Away from the father she'd never see again, and into a carriage that did little to shelter her from the world.

The only steps he took away from her were to utter rapid directions to the captain of the guard. Instructions for what to do with the bodies inside, and to send word ahead to the estate house he only vaguely knew about. The time it took felt like eons apart from Ahria, and every word felt more and more desperate until he was finally able to join her in the carriage.

Her eyes didn't even flicker to him, as if she was hardly aware of any of it as they lurched into motion. She stared at nothing with a blank expression, cheeks renewed with wetness after each slow blink.

He held her hand, resting them together in her lap as he positioned himself close to her, their shoulders touching. He glanced out the open windows of the carriage, debating drawing the thin curtains, though they'd have done little. He could see the occasional curious eyes on them, some far more intense than standard looks any royal transport received. While he couldn't feel it, the strange color in Ahria's eyes suggested something invisible hovered around her. The aura he'd heard many Art practitioners carried. And with the pressure of the secret Ahria held, he understood how dangerous it would be to remain where people may recognize it.

Leaning forward, Conrad beat a quick rhythm on the front wall of the carriage to the driver, who responded by quickening the pace of the horses. The prince settled back into the seat with Ahria, squeezing her hand again. "You'll get through this. I'm here. If there's anything…"

But he already knew there wasn't anything.

She leaned sideways, resting her head on his shoulder. Tears dripped onto his tunic, and she sniffed. "How am I supposed to keep going?" Her voice was barely more than air, and she lifted her hand before them, Talon's bracelet on her wrist. Sparks still danced around her skin, like she struggled to keep the fire contained, even then.

He took her hand, interlacing their fingers despite the danger the sparks should have posed. Holding their hands up in front of them, he kissed the side of her head. "I can't answer the how for you, exactly. But we'll find it. Together."

"You put yourself at risk, staying with me." Ahria's voice held steady, but sounded hollow. "It's safer for you at home with your mother."

"I'm not going anywhere." He lowered their hands back into her lap. "Not going to make that mistake again. I might not understand what is happening, but I know you won't hurt me. And I'm going to do anything I can to help you figure this out. I don't have the Art, but I have connections now, and a kingdom. We can send for the best Artisans to come help you sort through this."

Ahria finally shifted to look up at him, her eyes bloodshot. "No. I don't want any Artisans near me. It would only take a nightmare for me to kill them by accident. Are you sure *you* don't...?"

"Oh, they checked that the second I came into the palace. I am blissfully ungifted." Conrad lifted her hand, kissing the back of it. "You tell me what you need then. If we need to clear out every Artisan within a five-mile radius of the estate, we'll do it. Whatever it takes to keep you safe."

"Five miles should do it," she murmured, nodding. Her expression flattened again into thought before she let out a shaky sigh. "I need to find out what happened to her. Does Ziona have alliances with Eralas? Will they tell us?"

"Shaky ones, but I'll find out what I can. Is that where your mother was?" His chest tightened as he considered the loss that Ahria suffered in knowing that her mother was dead. Even if she'd never really known her, it had to weigh on her far more than just the face she'd acquired this strange power from. "I'll send missives as soon as we arrive."

Ahria nodded, resting her head on his shoulder again. "She was in Slumber there..." Unspoken thoughts followed the information. Had she woken? Had she tried to find her daughter?

He nodded, the motion brushing against the side of Ahria's head as he did. "I'll find out all that I can. We'll discover what happened." He didn't care what it took. He'd do whatever was necessary to get Ahria the answers she needed. Every fiber of his being insisted he not let her out of his sight after everything that had happened. After whatever that person had been that'd come for her at the townhouse. She'd called him a Shade, but he didn't understand. He had so many questions, yet none of them really mattered in comparison to what she had endured.

A shiver passed down Conrad's spine before he pressed another kiss into Ahria's hair. Something told him he would see more danger in the future if he remained with her, but he would willingly face it even without the Art to be the one to hold her.

Ahria pulled her legs up onto the bench seat, turning her knees so they rested on his thighs. Tears in the fabric showed cuts on her skin, abrasions on her hands from the fight. "I almost lost you, too," she whispered. "Dad saved us both."

He nodded, running a careful finger over her exposed leg. "You sure I couldn't send for a healer? I know they're minor, but..."

She shook her head, not lifting it. "I can't be healed. Not anymore."

Chapter 40

WHITE LIGHT FLOODED KIN'S VISION as he blinked, and it gradually turned into blue sky. He groaned, pain rushing back to banish the disorientation. For a horrible moment, he curled against himself, his stomach threatening to revolt in response to the agony and sulfurous smells around him.

"About time." Exhaustion tainted Damien's tone. "We need to get out of here, and I wasn't about to carry you."

Kin rolled onto all fours, his hand slipping in the crimson mud. He sucked in another breath, gagging before he managed to swallow back the bile in his throat. Memory ransacked his mind and he almost collapsed again as he looked to where Amarie's body had lain.

She'd vanished.

The blood remained, soaked into the charred ground like

a pool of tar. It sent a shiver through him at the thought of Uriel and how it looked so like the power Kin once hid within. But his eyes found Damien as he heaved another desperate breath and looked to the sealed wound on his leg. His right arm collapsed beneath the weight, screaming in pain as he hit the ground.

"I couldn't heal the break entirely. So... take it easy." Damien sat at the edge of the charred grass, his hands behind him as if seeking comfort from what was still alive there. He looked pale, his eyes half closed, fighting sleep.

"Where is she?" Kin ignored the pain as he pushed back onto his knees. "Amarie."

Damien rolled his eyes before he jutted his head back up the hill. "Getting the horses. She's alive, Kin. You're welcome."

Kin's chest still ached, and he desperately looked up the hill to where he could just make out Amarie past the horses. She'd yet to collect them, staring unmoving eastward over the strait. With her back to them, she hardly moved, hair whipping sideways in the breeze.

Letting out a slow breath, he settled back on to his heels. Then the memory of Uriel's taunts made him flinch. "He took the dagger. If *you* brought Amarie back, it means it worked, and now Uriel has the Berylian Key. I bet that's going to screw up the plan you didn't tell me about."

Damien sucked in a slow breath, pursing his lips. "Less so than you might think." He groaned as he rocked onto his feet, slowly standing. His body sagged, but the Rahn'ka's bare feet spread to support him regardless. "We still have time."

Furrowing his brow, Kin hesitated. "You're far too calm, considering everything that just happened."

"There's no point in panicking. It won't change anything. You're alive. Amarie is alive. I fulfilled my promise to you. Now you should talk to her before I break the one I made her."

His stomach clenched. "What promise?"

Damien shook his head and waved a hand as he turned to walk up the hill, one slow step at a time. He spoke without looking back at Kin. "I'm still going to need your help to imprison him. It's not all about you and Amarie anymore."

"You think you really can, then... imprison Uriel?" Kin tried to get to his feet and failed, forced to push himself up with his hands despite the screaming pain.

"It's been done before. Four-thousand year old texts hopefully aren't wrong, though perhaps a little vague about the details. But the prison is ready. And now only one piece is missing."

"Piece?"

Damien paused, looking back. "There's a lot to catch you and Amarie up on. But you should talk first. Because we need to find the Berylian Key. So we're going to New Kingston."

Kin fought the nausea as he steadied himself. "Uriel is in New Kingston?"

Damien waved a hand again, turning away. "No, her..." He heaved a sigh. "Just talk to Amarie."

He continued up the hill, leaving Kin alone near Hoult's crater. The lingering dizziness of unconsciousness seemed to have doubled in the twisted conversation with Damien. He focused on Amarie, as her hair drifted in the wind and his breath caught.

Does she understand why I did what I did?

He fought to take the first step, afraid of each subsequent one as he approached her.

Damien stopped with the horses, going directly to his and running his hands over its nose. The horse nickered, pushing hard into him as if some unspoken conversation took place between them.

Kin turned to Amarie, who stood with her back to them, a hand on her chest as she stared out at the distant shadow of Ny'Thalus.

The massive beech's leaves quivered with the sea winds, sheltering the slow movement of Eralasian ships sailing along the coast.

Even as he approached her, she didn't turn. Her clothes were bloodied, a hole in her vest from the dagger. A thin white scar remained on her perfect skin, a permanent reminder now of what he'd done.

He swallowed, voice catching as he stared at her. What could he say that wouldn't sound trite? Wouldn't sound ridiculous? He'd killed her. Stabbed her in the back while she shielded him from Uriel. Yet, he'd do it again.

Mustering his courage, he stepped beside her, daring to glance at her face. To his surprise, tears streaked her cheeks rather than the determined, angry glare he expected.

Apologies stuck on his tongue. He felt as if he should fall to his knees and beg for forgiveness. Beg for her to even look at him again.

But her eyes turned to him, bright with emotion. For the first time, he noticed the differences in her face. Subtle, and barely recognizable, but she'd aged. Perhaps only a few years, as her skin remained smooth, but a maturity resided in place of her previous youth. It made her all the more beautiful, constricting his throat. "I have two truths I must tell you." Her voice quivered, halting his unnecessary thoughts. "And neither, I suspect, will be easy for you to hear."

His chest tightened, the nausea returning, but he nodded. "If you think I need to hear them, then I will. Even if they hurt."

She took a deeper breath, her eyebrows upturning in the center as her voice caught on a quiet sob. "Talon is dead." Bowing her head, she shuddered. "I saw him in the Inbetween."

A crack ruptured through Kin, a wave of grief crushing him. Even if he and Talon had had their differences, the auer had always been there for him. And more importantly, he'd been there for Amarie when times were desperate.

He looked to the ground. The man he'd thought would outlive them all was gone. The thought hadn't even crossed his mind as a possibility. He looked back to Amarie's face, wishing desperately that he could comfort her. Could comfort himself for the loss of a brother. Heat rose in his face, and he choked back a surprised sob. "How? Do you know?"

Amarie wrapped her arms around herself, nodding. "That's the second truth." She sucked in a slow breath, composing herself. "He died today... protecting my daughter from a Shade."

The crack split open like a volcanic eruption. The words she spoke ricochetting across all of his senses. At first, the words didn't make sense. Any part of it. Talon never involved himself in protecting others. But then the word daughter. The implications that came with that word.

The nausea doubled as Kin fought not to buckle over right there. He struggled to breathe, unable to keep his eyes on Amarie as he looked down to steady his footing.

Daughter.

And suddenly he understood why Damien hadn't seemed concerned about the dagger being taken by Uriel. A flicker of anger at Damien for not telling Kin came, then left, buried by the overwhelming guilt. For what he had done to that daughter. What he had inflicted on her by killing her mother.

"Oh, gods," Kin whispered, running his hands back through his hair, wishing it made him less dizzy. "Amarie, I had... no idea... or I wouldn't have..." He swallowed, holding his breath to control every instinct of his body.

Amarie looked at him. "Yes, you would have," she murmured, her tone lacking the rage he expected. "Damien told me the plan, about the dagger. And even if you'd known, it would have been your only choice to keep me from him." Her lips twitched, and she shook her head. "I hurt for what she is enduring, but I am grateful you did what you did, for the Key in Uriel's hands would have been a much worse fate for all of us."

He wanted desperately to believe her, and somewhere deep in his soul, he knew it was true. But it'd never been about keeping the Key from Uriel. It'd always been about keeping Amarie from him.

Kin shook his head. "I wish you knew... how much I wish things were different. I still wish I'd known. And Talon..." His voice caught as he considered it. Talon had been with Amarie's daughter, had protected her. He'd done what any father would, yet the loss still held strong. His own grief couldn't compare to what he was certain she felt. "I'm so sorry, Amarie." Tears welled in his eyes, heat rushing down his cheeks. "I'm so sorry." The sobs could no longer be contained as he pushed a hand to his face, his body convulsing despite his desire to comfort her. He wished he could feel numb.

Amarie stepped into Kin, and her arms wrapped around his middle in an embrace that knocked the air from his lungs, regardless of how gentle. But his arms naturally took her into him, pulling her close to seek comfort in the warmth. Her body trembled, hands gripping his back. "She's in New Kingston," she murmured. "And we're going to find her."

Chapter 41

CONRAD THREW BACK THE CLOTH neatly laid over the goods he'd lugged from outside. The collection of vegetables and packets of grains looked so precise that whoever had packed them probably had a specific plan of what they were going to make with them, leaving Conrad to guess the intention. Though he'd begun to make it a game for himself whenever it came to meal preparation. He'd refused to tell Ahria where the kitchens were so he could continue to take care of her.

They'd been at the estate for two days, and Ahria had barely slept or eaten. Not that he could blame her for either. She spent the majority of the day on the sprawling balconies outside the mansion's ballroom, where she claimed it felt less suffocating. And he just tried to give her whatever space she needed, then held her through the night.

She'd speak in her sleep, eyelids moving with nightmares. All he could do was stroke her hair and kiss her forehead, hoping it would calm her enough.

"What's for dinner?"

Glass clanked together as Conrad started, turning to see Ahria in the doorway behind him. He chuckled as his heart slowed.

"I should have known you'd follow me one of these times."

She slowly stepped inside, reaching into the crate on the large center prep table and pulled out a head of lettuce, shaking it at him in mock discipline before adding it to the piles he'd been sorting. "It's in my nature. I can help, you know."

"I like taking care of you."

She smiled, but it didn't reach her eyes.

The pale blue of her irises had returned, and he wasn't entirely sure what that meant, but during her nightmares, they'd occasionally revert to a purple hue. He'd tried not to ask too many questions about the Berylian Key, the name she'd told him for the power, knowing she didn't need to be questioned on top of the pressures she already felt.

"You're sweet. But I'm not broken, even if it sometimes feels that way." Ahria paused. "Did my letter to my aunt get sent to Eralas? She should know about... what happened." Her voice caught.

"It went out this morning." He took her hand, entangling their fingers before lifting her knuckles to his mouth. "And, no, you're not broken." He kissed her skin, which still smelled of lavender from the morning bath he'd drawn for her. "But this is something I can do for you. I have some cases to review this afternoon that Wendelin brought, so I'm going to do what I can for now."

Ahria squeezed his hand, her shoulders drooping. "I'm sorry I'm keeping you from your duties."

"Don't apologize. You don't need to." But he frowned at the brief conversation Wendelin had forced on him by arriving with the food delivery. She'd obviously planned it so he couldn't avoid it.

Wendelin had thrust a bundle of papers out to him, a familiar disappointment on her face. "You're needed back at the palace. But if you truly insist on shirking all responsibility, the least you can do is review these."

Conrad fought the anger in his chest as he tucked the papers into the food crate he'd be carrying back to the house from the estate gate. "I have other responsibilities, too. I'll take a look."

Wendelin's frown deepened. "This is not helping the rumors that are already rampant throughout the city. The complete destruction of that townhouse... the murders... Advisor Di'Terian's death."

"None of that was Ahria's fault." Heat rose in his tone. "I don't appreciate you implying it, either. I have my mother's support to be here."

"Support or not, you have to worry about public *perception.*"

"I don't really give a shit about public perception right now." Conrad sucked in a breath as Wendelin's eyes widened. "With all due respect, Chancellor, my focus right now is on my girlfriend, and rightfully so as you'll remember that Talon Di'Terian was her father. And those murders you speak of were all her friends. So, find the heart buried in that chest of yours, and give me time to be here for *her.* I'll look at the cases and respond with what I can. And in the meantime, I appreciate your *understanding* in continuing to assist back at the palace."

Wendelin's lips formed a thin line. "There is one more thing."

He sighed. "What?"

"After clearing out your lover's townhouse, we discovered... a discrepancy." She stared at him, jaw tight.

He narrowed his eyes at the silence that followed. "Explain."

Wendelin glanced behind him, ensuring their privacy. "With Ahria's statement and the documents we have for residency, it would seem someone is missing. The number of deceased is short one."

"One of her friends? Who is missing?"

The chancellor nodded. "We can't be certain, as the state of the remains didn't allow for accurate identification. But we can conclude that the missing person is male. We also found adequate amounts of blood leading out the back door. One of her friends may have escaped."

He sighed, nodding. "It's something at least. Thank you. Please have the guards search for him. And alert me the moment he's located. I'll pray whatever injuries he sustained were survivable." Running a hand back over his hair, he wondered if it would hurt or help to tell Ahria that one of her friends had possibly survived. There was no telling if he'd bled out in an alley somewhere else even if he escaped the Shade.

He considered Ahria's hand in front of him, bringing it back to his lips while debating what to tell her. He'd sheltered her from as much as possible with the aftermath of what had happened. She was showing the first signs of starting to heal, and bringing up the death of all of her friends felt unwise. He pressed the thought from his head.

"You hungry? I could make lunch?"

Ahria met his gaze, looking straight through him in that way she'd always done. "Did your chef pack any sweets in there?" She asked the question with a stoney expression, and he wondered if her new abilities let her hear his thoughts.

"We can hope." For good measure, he began to sing the lyrics of a rowdy bar song in his mind as he sorted through what remained in the box, finding a small bundle in a white napkin. Undoing the knot, he lifted the cookies in his palm towards her. "I'll check the stores here to see if we have the supplies for more. I know these won't last long." He offered her all six before picking up the empty crate and dropping it to the ground to slide beneath the table. "Cookies seem a better use of the butter and milk than whatever elaborate cream sauce the cook probably had planned for the fish."

Ahria took a bite of a cookie, setting the rest on the counter. Her usually voracious appetite had dimmed since her father's death. So much so that she rarely finished her meals. "I never thought cream went with fish, anyway." She sighed, chewing her lip. "I think I'd like to go outside today. For a walk."

"Of course." He piled the chilled goods into his arms, moving across the kitchen to the cold store box. "I'll come if you don't mind company?"

Ahria nodded, her throat bobbing. "I miss Andi."

Conrad reached for her hand again. The instinct to touch her as often as possible after everything that had happened only continued to grow. "I could send for her if you want?" They'd come straight to the estate from the destroyed townhouse. The palace staff had put together their things from their rooms for them, delivering them the day before, but Andi hadn't been part of the conversation. And besides a change of clothes, both of them had barely sorted through the piles still shoved into the corner of their bedroom. The only item of significance that Ahria had searched for was her leather-bound journal, which she took with her whenever she went out onto the lower balconies.

She nodded again, taking a deep breath. "If they recovered my daggers, they'd be nice to have back, too. Even if..." Her voice trailed off as her gaze grew distant, and she rolled her lips together.

"Don't think about it. I'll ask." He swallowed. "They've been processing the scene, so I'm sure they've found them." He grimaced, the thoughts of what Wendelin had told him re-emerging.

Ahria looked up with a forced smile, her eyes shining with wetness. "I'll get my boots."

"Ahria." Conrad held onto her, encouraging her back to him. She deserved to know. "They... think one of your friends may have escaped. But... there was still a lot of blood. I wasn't sure if I should say anything."

Her gaze snapped back to him. "What? Who?"

"They don't know. It was too difficult to determine with..." He shook his head. "But he slipped out the back door, whoever it was."

"He?" Ahria's brow furrowed.

"They're looking for him." He took both of her hands.

"But why would he be hiding?" She shook her head.

"Lots of reasons. That kind of attack could have really messed with his mind. He might not know that it's safe enough to come out. Or..." He didn't want to say he could have still died somewhere, alone, and they just hadn't found the body yet. "The guards will find him."

Ahria's expression faded. "Or he's dead." She exhaled slowly, squeezing his hand before letting it go. "Thank you for telling me."

He nodded, wishing he could help her smile return. Wished he could somehow make everything better with a wave of his hand. But at least he was there with her.

Never been so grateful to not have the Art before.

"How about that walk?"

Chapter 42

FOR THE FIRST TIME SHE could remember, Amarie felt hollow. Where her power used to be held only a void. It made her feel weak, empty. It negated the point of the spell she'd woven into Ahria's necklace. With no Art, she couldn't track it. But Talon had provided her daughter's location.

Damien had shut down her desire to go straight to New Kingston. As personal advisor to the king of Ziona's once-rival nation, he needed permission. Not just permission, but treaties and documents to make the trip a formal one. They had to do it right, and even Amarie saw the logic. Especially since Talon had pointed her towards Ziona's crown prince.

Amarie rode behind Damien in silence, the late afternoon sun warming her face as they traveled southwest.

Kin lingered at the back of their small travel party, his comfort on the horse transformed by him getting his memories back. He cradled his still fractured arm at his chest, a crude sling crafted of one of his shirts holding it still, though he'd grimace when his horse jostled over rough patches of road. The pain she'd seen in his eyes after telling him the two truths hadn't faded. Talon's death still held a dark cloud over both of them.

She resisted the urge to glance at him. After telling him about Ahria, though without using her name, she'd let Kin assume Talon had given her the child. Conflicting thoughts warred in her mind of whether he needed to know right away. It wasn't a ruse she'd be able to maintain. Not with Ahria's name and eye color. She wondered if his guilt would be greater if he knew he'd inflicted such a burden onto his own blood. But she doubted it, not with how much it already weighed on him.

He cares about her because she's mine.

The truth of it warmed her chest and stung her eyes. For all she knew, he'd hate her for not telling him sooner. For not finding him and presenting him with their baby girl.

But why should I care if he hates me?

Still, the idea left a sour taste in her mouth.

They'd arrive at Helgath's capital in another day or two, and chaos would undoubtedly ensue once again. Politics, reunions... She'd meet Mira again. Rae. Damien's wife and the only friend she'd had in ages. The name didn't matter, not anymore.

Amarie lifted her palm, focusing on it as she'd done time and time again since losing her Art.

Nothing.

A part of her hoped she'd be able to will it back to herself. Knock on the Berylian Key's metaphorical door and say, 'I'm alive, come back.'

But it never worked. It never returned.

She stared at her palm, trying harder, but lowered it a moment later.

"We'll stop here for the night." Damien turned his horse off the road, towards a dense thicket. "There's a clearing on the other side of this that will shelter us from any other travelers."

She'd stopped wondering how he always knew the best spots to stop, assuming it had something to do with his own Art. Knowing that he could use it so easily made her stomach churn with envy, even if Damien didn't flaunt it.

Amarie followed without responding, defeat rippling through her muscles.

They made camp with ease, eating a light meal, except for Damien who seemed to put away three times what either her or Kin did in fruit, bread, and root vegetables. As the sun vanished, the Rahn'ka sprawled out on his bedroll. Only a few moments passed before his snores filled the air.

She saw to the dishes, rinsing them with a waterskin before she rose from her bedroll. "I'll be back in a bit," she murmured to Kin. In a new habit, she'd taken to nightly walks alone. Giving herself space to think and process all that had happened. Grief still weighed in her heart with Talon's death. Not just for her loss, but for Ahria's.

"You... mind if I join you tonight?" Kin carefully dropped another log onto the fire as he asked, rubbing his hand on his breeches afterward. "It sounds nice."

Amarie hesitated, looking at him. Her eyes flitted to Damien before she nodded. "All right."

He nodded, gratitude in the motion even if he didn't say it. He slipped his satchel from over his head, depositing it onto his bedroll before shifting the tie of his sling behind his neck and moving to the edge of the camp with her. "After you."

As they walked from camp, Amarie's thoughts wandered to how different things were now between them. Not just on a personal level, but in the Art. Neither of them had power anymore, and suddenly his choice to abandon the Art meant so much more.

"The auer woke me, you know." She kept her voice low on the night air, slowing to walk beside him. "When I came to them, I was badly injured. I'd made a mistake and fought Uriel in Helgath. I fled to Eralas and requested Slumber. But they woke me shortly after carrying it out, rehabilitated my body and trained me in the Art."

She didn't elaborate. Now wasn't the time, and she wasn't even sure if she'd tell him about it all. At the time, she hadn't known who she was, but that hadn't stopped the auer. For that, she felt surprisingly grateful.

He remained quiet as they walked, but his face told her he was processing. He chewed his lower lip slightly as they wove through the distanced trees. "I knew you were serious about facing Uriel that day at the river. After... Trist. And I'd hoped that would change, but I should have known better." He looked over at her, shaking his head slightly. "But I'm relieved you survived and that Eralas was able to help in the end. That... Talon was there when I couldn't be."

Amarie's heart twisted. "Talon had left me by then," she whispered. "I was pregnant, and he was supposed to meet me in Olsa, but..." She swallowed, remembering how dark her thoughts had been during those days. "I gave birth in my brother's house, stayed there for a time. It was on my second journey to Eralas that it all happened."

A familiar flash of anger washed over Kin's face, but it faded back into grief. "I'd hoped Talon would be a better man than me and not make the same choice. The same mistake." He slowed, forcing her to do so to stay beside him. "You should not have been alone, Amarie."

Amarie looked at him, halting their pace. "I wasn't alone, but I couldn't see it. It's ironic that I spent my entire life running from this power, and then when I finally know how to use it…" She huffed.

"It's taken." Kin nodded. "I chose to give up mine, so it's different. And I wanted to give you a choice, to talk to you about it." He faced her entirely, but kept a distance away as if afraid to be too close. "When I saw you use your power against Uriel, I hoped for a moment that it would be enough. Then I hoped that you would forgive me for taking it from you. But…" His voice caught and he ran a hand up through his hair, pushing the locks on his forehead back. "I wish there'd been another way. Especially now, knowing about your daughter."

"I do forgive you." She surprised herself by how easily the words came. "Not just for that, but… for all of it."

"I don't deserve it." Kin started to wrap his arms around himself, but flinched as he shrugged the shoulder of his broken arm. "And now with what I've thrust upon your and Talon's daughter…" He looked down at the ground, hiding any chance she had at trying to read his thoughts. A dry chuckle came as he looked back up, the steel of his eyes sparkling with wetness. "Things just got so complicated. And to think, I thought having the Art would simplify my life. Shows what a stupid kid I was."

Amarie tried to smile, but it faltered. "You need to know that I loved him. Talon. We made a life, a home, even if it didn't last. Even if he made a mistake. He made up for it by raising her, being there for her, when he didn't have to."

His brow furrowed for only a moment, but he nodded. "I'm glad that you and Talon could have that, at least for a time. You deserve a life like that, where maybe things can be a little simpler." He hesitated, meeting her eyes. "But I don't understand. Of course Talon needed to be there for her. A father should—"

"Ahria," Amarie breathed, swallowing. She touched the side of Kin's face, drawing a shaky inhale as his eyes widened. "Her name is Ahria."

He remained still, as if he couldn't even breathe at what she admitted. His lips parted, but nothing came out as his eyes searched hers, flicking back and forth. "Ahria?" It came as a raspy whisper.

Her hands shook, heat building behind her vision. "She has your eyes."

"My..." Kin sucked in a shaky breath, but it froze in him again as his face contorted in a number of different emotions, each as brief as the last. Excitement. Confusion. Guilt. Joy. Sadness.

His hand brushed into Amarie's hair, a shallow breath sucked through his parted lips. "We... I... have a daughter?"

Amarie nodded, sliding her hand from his face. "Talon never had to look after her because she isn't his blood. He knew from the beginning that she was yours. And he loved her all the same. And he is... he was her father. But so are you."

"I never deserved the friendship Talon showed me, despite all the mistakes I made. And he just continues to prove that to be true." He ran his hand back through her hair again, and she stepped closer. Tears welled in the bottom of his eyes. "I understand why I couldn't know. Why you never told me." He winced as he moved his broken arm, but it slid to her side, holding her. "And you still didn't need to."

"Yes, I did." Amarie smirked. "Believe me, you would have noticed when you met her."

His lips quirked with a crooked smile. "Maybe." He brushed a thumb over her cheek as they leaned closer. She hadn't realized how close they'd grown until she felt the heat of his breath on her lips. "I'm willing to bet she also looks remarkably like her mother. Beautiful and stubborn."

Amarie bit her lower lip, giving him a playful cringe. "Hopefully not *too* stubborn."

"Are you kidding, with our traits together, Talon probably had a hell of a time." Kin's grip grew tighter. "*Our* daughter."

"Our daughter."

"I never stopped loving you, Amarie. I can't." Kin's eyes bored into her with mere inches between them, and her heart thundered in her ears. "I never will. No matter how insane or dangerous it becomes. And I'm not making the same mistakes again." His gaze flickered to her mouth, and it sent a spark through every limb. "I want to make every moment up to our daughter. Our Ahria. And to you."

Her world tilted, and she lifted her chin. Before she could form words, Kin's mouth claimed hers.

The story will continue with...

FATE OF THE
DAE'FUIREI

www.Pantracia.com

THE PRISON WAITS WHILE SHADOWS HUNT.

After learning of their daughter's location in Ziona, Amarie and Kin struggle to abide by the political rules of court. Danger looms around every corner, but without the Art they once had, they are left powerless against the monsters hunting their child.

Deep in the throes of grief, Ahria wreaks havoc with her newfound abilities. With only each other to trust, she and Conrad make a desperate plan to flee Ziona—unaware that those coming for her are her only hope of understanding the power now lurking in her veins.

As the leaders of three major nations come together, the future of Pantracia hangs on a precipice. With old allies returning to the quest to save their world, the stakes soar higher than ever as time runs out in a deadly game of secrets and lies.

Fate of the Dae'Fuirei is Part 2 of *The Vanguard Legacy* and Book 12 in the *Pantracia Chronicles*.